# INSTINCT

# INSTINCT

A NOVEL

# JASON M. HOUGH

SKYBOUND BOOKS / GALLERY BOOKS

NEW YORK   LONDON   TORONTO   SYDNEY   NEW DELHI

Skybound Books / Gallery Books
An Imprint of Simon & Schuster, Inc.
1230 Avenue of the Americas
New York, NY 10020

First Skybound Books/Gallery Books hardcover edition April 2021

SKYBOUND BOOKS/GALLERY BOOKS and colophon
are registered trademarks of Simon & Schuster, Inc.

For information about special discounts for bulk purchases,
please contact Simon & Schuster Special Sales at 1-866-506-1949
or business@simonandschuster.com.

The Simon & Schuster Speakers Bureau can bring authors to your live event. For more information or to book an event, contact the Simon & Schuster Speakers Bureau at 1-866-248-3049 or visit our website at www.simonspeakers.com.

Interior design by Michelle Marchese

Manufactured in the United States of America

10  9  8  7  6  5  4  3  2  1

Library of Congress Cataloging-in-Publication Data is available.

ISBN 978-1-5011-8139-9
ISBN 978-1-5011-8140-5 (ebook)

The very essence of instinct is that it's followed independently of reason.

—Charles Darwin

"Hey, Doc. What can I getcha?"

"The usual, please, Kyle."

"Usual? You never come in here, Doc. What usual?"

"Consider this a mental exercise. A little experiment. Imagine I come here every day and always order the same thing. I'm curious what you think that would be. What it says about how you perceive me."

"Uh. Okay."

"There's a catch, though."

"Is there now."

"You must bring the same for yourself, and we'll toast my newly minted usual together."

"Huh. Well, fuck it, all right. As long as you're paying for both—"

"Of course."

"—then sure. I'm game. Lessee. Okay. Some of this . . . bit of this—"

"Keeping your back turned, eh? Nice touch. That's the spirit. No pun intended."

"—and boom. Here we go."

"Hmm. Clear. No ice. Any clues as to what it is?"

"Sure. It's your usual."

*"Fair enough. Bottoms up?"*

*"Definitely. Cheers."*

*"Cheers. Mmm. Hmm. Um, Kyle, is this water?"*

*"Yep."*

*"That's what you imagine my usual would be?"*

*"Yep."*

*"Now, you see, that is interesting. Care to elaborate on your thought process?"*

*"Absolutely not."*

# CHAPTER ONE

Only after the funeral ends do I have the courage to mention the owl.

"Please tell me you saw it," I say to Greg as he pushes the last of the road cones into the trunk of his cruiser.

"Saw what?"

"The bird. The owl."

He grunts. "Yeah, so?"

"Aren't owls nocturnal?"

Greg's wiping dirt from his fingers onto a pristine white handkerchief. He stops to look at me, those wizened and kind eyes just barely peeking out from under bushy gray eyebrows. "I don't really know. I guess so?"

"That was just . . . weird, wasn't it? Not just an owl in daylight, but the timing."

It had happened in the middle of the service. The whole town had been crowded around the grave as the casket was lowered. The pastor reciting a verse in his somber, even voice. The mother quietly weeping. Not the father, though. He'd remained stoic throughout his son's burial.

But then, right as Pastor Osman said something about the wings of angels, an owl flew over the whole gathering, just ten feet above everyone's heads. Most eyes were downcast in that moment, in prayer or in respect of others. I'd been a bit lost in thought myself, and happened to be looking up for signs of rain. The animal had glided right over us, silent and serene, in a path that took it in a perfectly straight line over the casket, leaving not even a shadow to mark its passage.

I sorta wish I could say it was albino, or even black as night. Something ominous or significant, but the bird was the typical speckled brown and gray. Just like any other owl in the Cascades, I suppose.

"A *little* weird, sure, but I've lived my whole life here, Mary. You get used to it. A little weird isn't the problem."

"What is the problem?"

"Embellishment. Just watch, by midweek the story being told in town will have that owl recast as a raven. One with a seven-foot wingspan and glowing red eyes. Something along those lines. In my experience, weird always starts with something pretty mundane. My advice? Don't mention it to anyone else, lest the story grow."

I absorb the words in scholarly silence and fall in beside my chief. We walk back up the hill toward the place where Johnny Rogers was buried. The cemetery is old and small, with a gravel parking lot made to hold perhaps twenty cars. Today there were dozens, though, filling the lot and overflowing all up and down both sides of the narrow lane leading up from the mountain road. That many cars meant Greg and I had to step away at the very end of the service in order to direct traffic and, finally, gather up all the cones we'd placed earlier this morning.

I'd thought we would be done once the cones were packed up but now find myself instead standing with Chief Greg Gorman at the graveside of the dead boy.

"Such a tragedy," Greg says, more to himself than to me.

"He seemed like a good kid," I say, lamely. I'm still the new arrival in this place, a place where everyone knows everyone, but no one really *knows* anyone. That's another nugget of Greg Gorman wisdom, imparted to me at the job interview many months ago.

I consider asking Greg about the boy's case. It's been officially ruled an accident. A tragic, bizarre accident, but an accident all the same. Only, I noticed this morning that the file was still on Greg's desk. Active, in other words. Chief isn't in the habit of leaving something out unless he's still working it, so there must be a reason. But now seems like the wrong time to ask, so I let it go.

"What's next on the agenda?" I ask casually. "Should be a quiet day. We could—"

"*I* am headed home," Greg says pointedly. "You should go home, too. I mean that. Take the rest of the day off. Don't worry, I'll keep my radio on."

"Suppose we get a drink, then? A funeral should be followed by a toast, shouldn't it?" The idea of going home, of being alone, couldn't be further from my mind.

"Maybe tomorrow," he says. "After that service, I think an evening of quiet contemplation is in order."

I nod, but internally I'm already considering other options. A drive down the mountain to Granston, maybe? Plenty of friendly, talkative strangers there who aren't grieving.

"Listen, Mary," Greg says, "there's something I've been meaning to talk to you about. Shouldn't have waited this long, really, and I'm sorry for that."

"Okay?" I don't know what else to say. My stomach tightens as I think of all the things he might say next, none of which are good. Am I already out of a job? Has someone complained about me?

He shoves his hands into his suit pockets. We're both dressed in civilian clothes for the funeral. Greg still pinned his badge to his lapel, though. Mine's in my purse, along with my phone and my service pistol.

He sighs. "Thing is, with everything going on . . . what the hell's that sound?"

The change of subject trips me up, and for a few seconds I have no idea what he's talking about. But then I hear it, too. My first thought is the engine of the tiny bulldozer the cemetery uses to dig and fill graves. It's an old rusty thing kept in a shed behind some trees on the other side of the parking lot, and at a distance it makes the same sort of low hum I now hear.

But the earthmover finished its work twenty minutes ago. I remember watching it lumber over there as I was waving cars out onto the main road. Still, I say it, because it's all I can think of. "Bulldozer?"

We both know it doesn't fit. The sound is too even, yet also somehow not. It has a kind of wavering quality to it. Almost like someone humming. A chill runs up my spine. It's not what I'd call a good sound. It seems to come from everywhere, though as it grows in volume I get the sense that's wrong, too. The source is somewhere nearby. I start to look around.

"I know that sound," Greg says in the same instant that I spot the phone lying in the grass, just a few feet from the fresh grave.

It's an old model iPhone with a cracked screen, tucked inside one of those rugged cases people up here love. Adds a bit of outdoorsy charm to a dreaded piece of fashionable technology. An alarm icon dances on the screen, with a label just below:

ANOTHER DAY ANOTHER DOLLAR

The chosen tone to go with this is that of an Aboriginal didgeridoo, a wind instrument that sounds a bit like someone chanting in a very low voice.

"I've heard that before," Greg says, studying the screen over my shoulder. "Can't remember where, though."

"Somewhere in town?" I suggest.

"That's some fine detective work," Greg says, grinning under his thick mustache. "Here, let me take it. Someone must have dropped it during the service. Once they realize, they'll call it and I'll sort it out."

"You were about to say something, before the phone went off . . ." I prompt.

Greg gives a little shrug. "Know what? Never mind. That can wait until morning. Right now I think some 'quiet contemplation' is what the doctor ordered. I'll see you tomorrow, Mary."

# CHAPTER TWO

I've lived here only a few months, but it seems to me that on any given issue, Silvertown is a place that always manages to divide itself evenly.

Examples:

Tourism. Brings in heaps of money, but ruins the secluded quiet so many residents cherish. You'll see small-town neighborly friendliness at one house, and an overly large NO TRESPASSING sign in front of the next. Count them up and I bet it's nearly fifty-fifty.

Technology is another hot-button topic. Half the town is up in arms over the new cell phone tower on the mountainside, claiming it gives them brain cancer or screws with their chakras or whatever. The other half is overjoyed that we finally have fast, reliable service so they can check their grandkids' Facebook posts.

I could go on. The biggest wedge, though, relates indirectly to my job. Or rather, to my boss, Greg.

See, up until about ten years ago, Silvertown was a company town. The original silver mine that started it all was built by the Conaty family, who turned the lucrative business into a global corporation. They branched out, aggressively. From minerals to lumber, chemicals, even pharmaceuticals. Through it all they kept their business headquarters right here, and were by far the largest employer in the region as a result.

All that changed about ten years ago.

I'm still learning the gory details. Suffice to say, it was Greg's efforts that forced the Conaty Corporation to leave town, mired in scandal and disgrace. For every person here who praises him for that, there's one who would point to the abandoned buildings and shuttered houses and say the price was too high.

My point is, people up here rarely agree on anything. Always split down the middle, like this road that splits the town in two, or the way Keller's Gorge divides us from the rest of civilization.

A divided place. Today, though, was an exception.

Seeing everyone come together for the funeral of Johnny Rogers has really impressed me. I've never experienced anything like it, much less been a part of it. Not during my childhood growing up in a rural part of California, or more recently in Oakland, where my status as a rookie cop had me more often than not at arms' length with the people there.

Despite the circumstances, today made me feel like part of a family. Corny, I know, but there it is. I loved it.

I rode that strange high of shared grief all afternoon, but it's twilight now and things have already turned to Silvertown's special weird brand of "normal." Just as Greg predicted, most everyone sought out the solace of their own homes after the service ended, looking for the comfort of silence after a day of mourning and remembrances. Greg included.

Me? I may have mentioned already, but solitude isn't my thing. It makes me itch.

I'm parked on the edge of town. Sitting in the patrol car alone with the engine running, pondering a patrol down the mountain that would just happen to take me over Keller's Gorge and all the way to Granston, the nearest proper city. Silvertown only has one bar, but there are no cars in front of it, and I haven't seen anyone go in or out since I parked.

Granston, on the other hand, has a dozen bars at least. Each one full of strangers who won't know I'm a cop, and thus won't want to gossip about the unfortunate death of a teenager. Normally this would be a no-brainer.

Yet I've been telling myself "in a minute" for the last ten, fighting this deep urge for companionship. I'm not really sure why.

Whatever the reason, instead of driving I'm just staring blankly at a twilight sky speared by countless Douglas firs lining the two-lane road. Like a TV's picture-in-picture, the rearview mirror offers a contrasting portrait: the dark buildings of Silvertown. Other than the red neon glow of the bar's OPEN sign, everything is shadow and gloom.

I look at all of it, without really looking at any of it. Part of my brain knows I'm in this weird, almost trancelike state, and yet I can't seem to break out of it.

Then the streetlights come on, and do the job for me. They flicker to life one at a time, creating pools of warm yellow along the length of Main Street. Each one revealing just a little more of Silvertown.

Over the next few minutes, moths find their way to the fuzzy golden cones and begin tracing lazy figure eights in the glow. Is that me? I wonder. A moth drawn to the flame of companionship, no matter how feeble?

Yeah. Yeah it is me, I think, and this pathetic realization finally tips the scales against my true nature. With a supreme force of will I opt for the solitude of home over companionship in the brew-pubs of Granston.

The car rumbles as I start it up, pull out of the lot, and make a U-turn, heading back toward town.


I roll slowly down Main Street. Except for the red glow from the pub, the shops that line the road are all dark.

Half of them are always dark, of course, abandoned years ago and never leased to new tenants. But still, there's something deeply oppressive about the place when it's entirely deserted. Narrow dark alleys run between brick facades. Old gaslights hang over the sidewalks, dew glistening dimly on the spiderwebs that cling to the black iron fixtures.

Robbed of sunlight and the colorful townspeople, it's like I'm in a completely different place. I shiver.

Ahead, a figure emerges from one of the shops. A man, I think. He has long black hair and wears a long black coat to match.

I pull up closer to the curb, slowing to match his brisk walking pace. The store he emerged from is one of several souvenir shops along the row, catering to the tourists who flock here every summer looking for Big Foot merch.

"Evening," I say.

He glances at me and nods, pinching the brim of an imaginary hat between two fingers as he does so. "Officer."

"Didn't think you'd be open today."

"I wasn't," the man replies. "Just had to put something in the . . . fridge. Good evening."

And then he's gone. Not vanished, but about as close as one can get. He's turned down one of those dark alleys, his long coat snapping with the speed of his change in course. The shadows swallow him up after only two long strides.

I'm a little tempted to switch on the red-and-blues and follow him. Back in Oakland his behavior would be probable cause. But here? I'm not so sure.

"Nice meeting you!" I call out.

The only reply is the receding sound of his boots.

"Go home, Mary," I remind myself, and drive on.

My first port of call is not home, however.

Halfway down Main, I'm doing another U-turn, parking my cruiser right in front of the police station.

I flip the power off on the bulky data terminal beside the shotgun and kill the engine. There was an instant when the headlights lit up the tavern, which is right across the street, and movement stirred inside. Not entirely empty after all, then.

It's tempting.

But no, I tell myself. I made a choice, I'm going to stick to it.

I step inside the darkened police station long enough to hang the cruiser's key on its hook and grab my uniform coat. The place is dark and whisper quiet. In the back are four holding cells, all of which are currently empty, as per usual. Between me and them is the office part of the building. It consists of two desks that were probably picked up for pennies at the Conaty Corporation surplus sale. My desk is pristine and tidy. Beside it, Greg's is a cluttered mess of forms, pens, and empty coffee cups. I spy Johnny Rogers's file on top of the mess and let out another sigh. *A damn tragedy.*

Back out on the cracked, uneven sidewalk I'm surprised to find the number of parked cruisers has doubled from one to two. Greg heaves himself out of the driver's side of the new arrival with an audible grunt.

"Heya, Chief. Just locking up," I say. "Did we get a call? Something up?"

"No, no, nothing like that."

"Thought you'd headed home?"

"I did head home. But then that iPhone rang and . . . hang on a sec, I thought you were going home, too. You know you can park the car in your driveway, right?"

"I know. But the walk helps me acclimate." I flap my arms, clad in the bulky fleece-lined coat. None of the locals need such a heavy jacket at this time of year.

"Fair enough," he replies. Then he squints at me. "You okay, Mary?"

"Oh. Yeah, fine." I gesture down the street. "Just saw this guy in an overcoat. Weirded me out a bit."

"Black hair, pale skin?"

I nod.

"That's Damian Blackwood. He's harmless enough." Greg seems about to add something, but thinks better of it. "Well, good night, Mary."

"Whose is it? The phone, I mean. You said it rang."

He jerks his chin toward the bar. "Kyle. The bartender at O'Doh's. He was actually going to close up shop just so he could come get it, so I offered to drop it by." Greg steps off the curb toward the bar.

"Well, maybe we should both go?" I suggest, without a moment's hesitation. All that time convincing myself to go home and be alone for once, gone just like that. "Come on, Chief. Let's raise a glass to the kid."

"Hmmm" is Greg's reply. He might have missed my disappointment at the graveyard when he'd declined the drink, but he's a sharp cookie and spots it this time. "One can't hurt, I guess. All right."

Silvertown's lone watering hole is called O'Doherty's, a half-assed attempt at an Irish pub situated directly across the street from the police station. From appearance alone it's obvious the place has been there forever, and it is about as basic and cliché as you can get. In fact, the only real selling point it offers is its liquor license.

We cross the empty street together. The pub, on the bottom floor of a four-story brick building that has to be a century old, is quiet tonight. That's not usually the case.

The door creaks as Greg pushes through.

It's a small place. "Maximum Occupancy 40" is what the sign would read if they had one, I think.

The decor is all hardwood and brass. Everything within has an air of . . . not neglect, that wouldn't be fair to the guy who runs the place. He keeps it clean and well maintained, but I doubt anything in the room was purchased new or professionally installed.

The bar's on the left. Stalls and a few tables line the wall on the right side, except the back corner, where a very small stage struggles to live up to the massive sound system resting atop it.

Pink Floyd spills softly from the huge karaoke machine. The device is a beast, nearly as tall as me, and sports two speakers with cones the size of serving trays. Luckily the volume is turned way down, the music not much more than ambient background noise. A pair of microphones rests atop the black cabinet, gathering dust.

Two locals—the only other customers—are playing pool. The worn old table sits under a single lamp in the center of the room, its green felt surface stained and even sporting a six-inch length of duct tape covering a tear near the center. Hardly regulation.

On the far wall is a faded mural that depicts Silvertown's surroundings. It's cheesy and amateurish, yet to me it captures the region with near total perfection: on the right is the old mine, boarded up with a CONDEMNED sign in front of it. On the left is Fort Curtis, the old abandoned army base. Front and center we have the hairy form of Big Foot, striding confidently, posed in homage to that classic faked footage. Behind the notorious monster is Lake Forgotten, and beyond even that, a decent rendition of two rocky peaks officially called Two Sisters, but known to the locals here as Two-Shits, as in "I couldn't give . . ."

There's a banner above the mural, taped to the wall:

OCTOBERFEST BEGINS IN 8 DAYS

The eight is handwritten on a piece of plain paper, thumbtacked in place. Some joker has rotated it ninety degrees, though, implying an infinite wait for the big day.

There's a sharp crack, loud enough to make me jump.

The pool balls, being broken. A few clunk as they drop into pockets.

"I'm stripes," the woman says to her companion as she begins to prowl around the edge of the table.

The man leans against the wall, chalking his stick as if it were the most important task ever undertaken. With each grinding twist of the blue chalk cube he whispers, "*Stripes. Types. Cripes . . .*" The rhyming words go on like some kind of chant.

I hang my coat on the rack by the door and we take stools at the bar. As we're sitting down the bartender, Kyle, pushes through from the kitchen area. He has keen brown eyes and a trendy lumberjack beard. Shaggy golden hair pokes out from under a Ford baseball cap. A greasy white apron covers his tartan-patterned shirt.

"Evening, Chief," he says. Then to me, "Officer." His eyes flick downward for the briefest of instants, an appraisal of my figure that I can't quite find fault with, seeing as I'm usually rocking a Kevlar vest under a stiff blue uniform, which is not what you'd call flattering. At least the man is subtle about it. "Hell of a day," he says to Greg.

"Hell of a day," the chief agrees. "Here's your phone." Greg slides the device across the bar.

Kyle picks it up, studies the screen for a second, then nods to the chief. "Cheers. Thanks for finding it."

"It was Mary who found it," Greg says. "You two have met?"

"Once or twice," Kyle replies. He eyes me. "You're always in uniform, though."

"My boss never gives me time off."

"Not true," Greg mumbles. He almost laughs, but then the weight of the kid's funeral seems to settle back on his shoulders. "Hell of a day," he says again, sighing this time.

I smile, sadly, at the memory of it. For a moment we all just stare at the bar, not talking.

High up on the wall, a flat-screen TV is tuned to the local public access channel. A goofy, awkward commercial is playing, wherein our town's only doctor, technically a psychiatrist, kindly asks for residents to come see him if they need someone to talk to. It'd be sweet if it weren't so stilted and poorly made.

Kyle picks up the remote control. With a tap of his finger the TV goes mute.

"Dude," I say, "I was watching that."

"Oh shit, sorry."

As he twists to turn it back on, my sarcastic tone finally registers. With a sheepish grin he puts the remote away. "Good one. Got me."

I beam. "No one wants to watch that. Do they?"

"It's the only channel I get. And Doc's the only one who pays for airtime."

"You could just turn it off," I suggest.

Kyle scratches behind his left ear. "Yeah, well, some people like it. Don't ask me why, I genuinely couldn't tell you." His eyes swivel pointedly to the couple at the pool table, just for an instant.

I nod, and we share a conspiratorial smile.

He sucks in a breath, his attention shifting to Greg. "Thought we'd be crowded tonight. The whole town needs a drink, if you ask me."

"Naw," Greg says. "It's more of a go-home-and-hug-your-loved-ones kind of evening."

There's a pause as the subtext—that neither Greg nor I have loved ones to go home to—is absorbed by Kyle. He lifts his chin. "Well . . . what can I get for Silvertown's finest?"

"Just a Bud for me, and whatever the lady is having."

"Same," I say. "And yeah, put it on his tab so we get the senior discount."

This time Greg does laugh. A dry chuckle, but a chuckle all the same.

"Pretzels? Peanuts?" Kyle asks.

"Sure," Greg replies. "Pretzels. Why not."

Nodding, Kyle starts to root around beneath the lacquered hardwood bar.

I nudge Greg with my elbow. "See? This was a good idea. Beats sitting at home, staring at the wall, doesn't it?"

"I guess it does."

He can't quite shake the somber tone entirely from his voice, but I'll take what I can get. Feels good to have some usual banter. Some camaraderie. It's something I've worked hard to foster since the day he interviewed me for the job, despite our differences in gender and age. I suspect my ability to verbally spar with him is a large part of why he hired me. That and our checkered policing pasts.

"Be right back," the bartender says, evidently unable to find any more pretzels under the bar. As he walks away I do an appraisal of my own. Fair's fair. Tight jeans, nice butt. The beard isn't to my taste, but for the umpteenth time since moving to a six-hundred-person town I have to remind myself of two things: beggars can't be choosers, and if I do end up with a local the whole town will know about it within twelve hours. Maybe less.

"Owls become ravens," I mutter.

"Huh?" Greg asks.

"Nothing," I reply, thinking Granston is the safer place to look for a date if only to keep the rumor mill quiet.

A dish clangs in the kitchen, followed by a frustrated curse from Kyle.

"Okay back there?" Greg calls out.

"Yeah, yeah."

"Good." Then he hikes a thumb toward the big karaoke machine in the corner. "Hey Kyle, thanks for letting Pastor Osman use your speaker thing today."

Kyle pokes his head out from the kitchen. "Comes in handy, doesn't it? Craigslist find of the century. Goes through batteries like a bastard, though."

"Well, it was nice having some music out at the graveyard."

"My pleasure, Chief." He returns to the kitchen.

An awkward silence begins to stretch. At the pool table, the woman is still sinking shots, one after another, while the man continues to mumble words vaguely rhyming with "stripes." A game within a game, I suppose.

"Listen, Mary," Greg says, suddenly serious. "What I started to say earlier: I'm going to take some time off."

A tiny siren goes off in my head. This is out of the blue. It's a struggle to keep the worry from my voice. "Why? When?"

He sighs the long and tired kind of sigh. "Day after tomorrow. For a week, I think. Maybe two. My mother's ill. Don't fret, it's nothing new and hasn't gotten suddenly worse. It's just, after what happened with Johnny, I thought maybe I should . . . you know . . ."

I did know. *A hug-your-loved-ones kind of evening.* I nod and try to smile, but inside I'm already wrapping my head around being the only cop here, even for a few days.

"Look," he adds, "I just need to know if you can handle things. Everything I've seen says 'hell yes' you can, but after the whole Oakland thing, I'll understand if—"

"What happened in Oakland?" Kyle asks, setting our beers and a bowl of pretzels down in front of us.

"Nothing," I say, keeping my tone light. "Long story."

"Give us a minute, will you, Kyle?" Greg asks.

The bartender understands at once, and moves off.

Greg leans in a little, lowering his voice. "I'll understand if you have concerns."

"No concerns," I reply. Even if I did have some, there's no way I'm going to deny him some leave to visit an ailing mother, even if that was my choice to make. He is the boss, after all.

"Want me to walk you through the daily routine?" he asks.

"I can handle it," I say.

Chief Greg studies me, surprised. "Well, well. You sound confident. Maybe too confident."

I set down my glass. "Give me a scenario. I'll prove it."

A twinkle of amusement flashes under those bushy gray eyebrows.

"All right then. Uh, let's see. Say there's a downed power line across the road."

"Which road?"

He shrugs at this.

"The state route?" Kyle suggests. "Sorry, quiet night so I can't help but listen in. A wire fell across the SR last year. Remember, Chief?"

"Sure," Greg agrees. "The state route, Officer Whittaker. Downed power line."

"Easy. First I'd radio State Patrol to manage traffic on the Granston side of the gorge. Teresa Carver is usually on dispatch there, and she'll know which roads to close and who's in position to get to them quickly. Then I'd call the utility district—on our direct line, not the public one—to report the location of the incident. All this while heading to the scene myself. I'll use cones and flares to keep traffic away until a technician can confirm the wire's no longer hot. Clara could be enlisted to cover our phones while I'm down there, and maybe I'd get the electrician, Mr. Ferguson, to join me as a . . . consultant, I suppose. I'm no expert on power lines, that's for sure."

Greg says nothing. I glance at him, and find he's staring at me, a little bemused but mostly sort of shocked.

"Wrong?" I ask.

He squints a little. "How the hell do you know Teresa Carver?"

"I don't."

"But—"

"I've had to contact State four times since coming here, and she's answered every time. Big Seahawks fan if I remember right."

Greg just stares at me.

"Gotta admit, Chief, that was pretty impressive," Kyle says. He grins at me, then shoots a glance at Greg. "When it happened last year, Chief was out there with a stick trying to push the cable off the road. Didn't call anyone, I don't think."

"Wood is nonconductive," the chief says defensively. "Clearing the wire was my first priority."

Kyle's expression turns skeptical. "Sure thing, Chief. Her version works, too."

"Just . . . different approaches," I say. I turn to Greg. "Point is, I won't be alone. I don't do 'alone.' It's how my brain works, I guess."

He nods at this. Slowly at first, and then more vigorously. "Okay. Okay. You put my mind at ease a little. Just . . . you know, think about our budget before you call in an airstrike on a B and E."

"Copy that."

We clink our mugs together, and sip cold beer in contemplative silence.

Another loud crack signals the start of a new round of pool.

"Solids," the man announces.

"Every frickin' time," the woman hisses, chalking her cue. She sighs, annoyed, and thinks for a moment. As the man lines up his second shot, another rhyming chant begins, barely audible. "*Solids. Olives. Motives.*"

My thoughts drift back to the funeral.

The teenager, Johnny Rogers, died unexpectedly while his parents were away. The poor couple had gone off on vacation while halfway through an argument "to-be-resolved-when-we-get-back-young-man." They'd never dreamed such a thing might happen while they were gone. They'd been robbed not only of their son but also of the opportunity to say goodbye, to tell him they loved him. Tragic. More pain than I can imagine.

The sound of the mother's wailing comes unbidden into my

mind. I'll never forget it, yet desperately want to. No one should have to feel grief like that.

"'Course," Greg says suddenly, "there's another benefit to you handling things for a while. Maybe everyone will stop asking for me every time you answer the phone." He's misinterpreted my silence, but that doesn't mean he's wrong.

In hiring me Greg ended nearly a decade of running Silvertown's department solo. Sure, there were some who still held a grudge against him for chasing the Conatys out of town, but from what I've seen in my short time here, he's established himself as a fair, even-tempered, sensible cop. I've no doubt it will be years before we'd be seen as equals by the townspeople. Guess we've got to start somewhere.

There's another part of me that can see his taking leave serving another purpose, though: a trial run. Someday Greg will retire. It's not something he and I have discussed, but maybe him taking some leave will open that door.

Greg chuckles again. "It's the worst cliché ever. The aging career cop handing over the reins to the rookie—"

"Whoa. Hold on. Are you calling me a rookie?" I snap, though I'm grinning. "Four years with Oakland PD does not a rookie make, dude."

Greg knows my résumé, of course. "You know what I mean. A rookie in the eyes of this town. This place couldn't be more different from Oakland, and is its own special brand of weird. You need to learn its quirks, earn its trust." He brings his beer to his mouth, and into the glass says, "Maybe start by not calling everyone 'dude.' They can smell the California on you."

He's got me there. I sip my drink, and we stare at the bottles behind the bar for a moment. "You'll miss Octoberfest," I say, pointing out the banner with my thumb.

"Damn. That's true. Didn't think about that." He sighs. "That's the one thing up here worth attending. Lift a stein for me?"

"If you insist."

Kyle comes by with a tray of shot glasses. He sets one in front of each of us, then takes two to the couple at the pool table. The last is for himself.

"To Johnny Rogers," Kyle says to all, lifting his glass of amber liquid. "A great kid and—"

The man at the pool table turns and points at the drink with his pool cue. "What the hell's that, Kyle? I didn't order it."

His companion *tsks* him, loudly. "The town's in mourning, idiot," she says in an almost serpentine whisper. "The Rogers' kid is dead."

He stares at her with a vague recollection before exhaling pointedly. "Welp. We all gotta die, at some point. When I go, I hope it's with my rifle in my hand and a grin on my face!"

She rolls her eyes. "Get over yourself and drink to the boy, already."

The man shrugs and reaches for the shot glass. In a matter-of-fact tone he says, "To the late Rogers boy: tough break, kid."

His wife—I assume it's his wife—looks at him with disgust, but doesn't miss her chance to shoot the liquor, wincing at the burn. After placing the empty glass on the pool table, she looks around for her cue and chalk. Seeing this, her husband picks up the little blue cube and readies an underhand toss.

"Here, it's your break," he says as he lets it go into the air.

The chalk flies on a gentle arc to her. She sees it. I know she sees it, as she tracks it in flight. But despite staring right at it, she never lifts so much as a finger to catch it. The tiny cube, now inches away from her face, doesn't even register in a flinch. *Heads up, lady*, my mind is screaming.

Helpless, I watch as the blue chalk hits her square in the face.

"Jesus H . . ." she mutters. The chalk clatters on the floor and breaks into several blue chunks. "The fuck is wrong with you?"

Shock, then concern, then a flash of anger cross his features. "Me? You didn't even lift a finger, what the hell—"

"Everything okay over there?" Greg asks. The woman waves him off, slinking into their booth, the game of pool abandoned. Her husband moves in beside her, finally offering quiet apologies.

Kyle, train of thought derailed by the odd interlude, lifts his shot glass again, halfheartedly this time. "Uh, anyway, to Johnny Rogers."

"To Johnny," I echo, then sip. Over the rim of the glass I make brief eye contact with the bartender, and feel a little tingle of electricity across my scalp.

Greg sips, too. He's still looking at the couple, ruminating on what just transpired.

The uneasy tension in the room dissipates about as fast as cigarette smoke. Kyle eventually puts the shot glasses back on his tray and disappears through the kitchen door again, mumbling something under his breath.

From the karaoke-speaker-slash-jukebox, a singer croons a chorus over and over: "*all the best freaks are here.*" I can't help but concur as I try and fail to picture myself spending two weeks as Silvertown's only cop.

Chief Greg Gorman sighs once again. "I just cannot understand what the hell Johnny Rogers was thinking. What a senseless, preventable death."

I can only nod, remembering the night the kid's parents came home. The scream Mrs. Rogers unleashed upon the world when she and her husband pulled into the driveway to find Greg, me, and a dozen others waiting to greet them, the looks on our faces telling them more than anything said aloud after.

We had no answers for them. Not then, not now. We only had condolences.

Their "indoor kid," with a reputation for being a video game junkie who never went outside, had evidently decided to go on a hike while his parents were away. He went alone, with no gear and, for that matter, no experience. Told no one of his plans.

Out there in the wilderness, on damp mountain trails, he'd fallen—badly—and never gotten back up.

No one could have done a thing about it.

And no one could explain why it happened.

I lose myself in the whiskey and stare off to the middle distance.

When I finally look up, I catch Kyle checking me out in the mirror behind the bar as he shovels ice from a bucket into a cooler.

I smile at him, finish my beer, and raise the empty toward him in the universal signal for another round. Sure, Silvertown has its quirks, but the scenery is definitely growing on me.

"Hey Alan. What can I getcha?"

"Beer. Whatever kind, I don't care. Just cold. C-o-l-d cold. Kyle, man, you feelin' okay lately? I keep getting these raging headaches."

"Migraine?"

"Yeah! Fuckin' migraine. Cold is the only thing that works, man. This morning I opened the freezer and stuck my head in for, like, five minutes. Can't wait for winter. Cannot frickin' wait."

"Well, I'm fine."

"Huh?"

"You asked if I was feeling okay lately. I'm fine."

"That's good, that's good. Must be because you're indoors 'n' shit. Protection from the walls."

"Oh for fuck's sake, you're not blaming this on the cell tower, are you?"

"Naw, man! The town's freakin' out about that antenna shit, but guess what? They haven't even switched it on yet. One of the StellarComm techs told me. All the fuckin' nutters don't want to hear it, though."

"Finally some sanity around here—"

"Yeah, man. No, these migraines . . . they're from the airplanes, bro. Chemtrails."

"Oh, Jesus—"

"Kyle, listen, man. Hear me out. You know Spellman Field? They just started flying cargo out of there, which puts us guess where? Right under the goddamn flight path. I've seen the lines across the sky, like fuckin' God's cocaine or some shit. There's all kinds of funky stuff in there, man, and it's fallin' right on our heads."

# CHAPTER THREE

True to his word, Greg went on leave to visit his mother. He's been gone for two days and hasn't called to check in on me once. I'm determined not to call him, either.

Each morning I've arrived at the station at 7:00 sharp, and today is no exception. The chief has a strict morning routine, which I usually miss out on as I take the later shift. With him gone, though, the tasks fall to me. Unlock the front door, walk the building: gun locker, cells, and my cruiser parked in the small lot out back. That done, log in to the computer to see if anything relevant has come in overnight. Nothing ever does, but check anyway. To this routine I add making a pot of coffee and texting Clara to make sure she'll be able to volunteer today.

Her reply is quick.

Once the breakfast rush is over.

I shoot back Cool! See you then.

With all that out of the way, I step out onto the sidewalk.

The people of Silvertown still carry the somber weight of Johnny's funeral with them but are otherwise going about their lives. Shops are open, kids walk with their parents to the lone school.

"Morning, Sally," I say to a woman walking toward me at a brisk pace. She wears workout clothes and pushes a double-wide stroller. Her twins nap within.

"Greg back yet?" she asks, breathless.

"Next week."

A nod. She never breaks stride, heading off down the street.

Watching her go, I notice Geezer Willy standing on the corner, exactly where he is every morning when Greg usually opens the station. My first two weeks up here, before Greg and I staggered our shifts, the two of us would step out here each day and the first thing Chief would do is greet ol' Willy. I figure this is as good a place to start as any.

"Morning, Willy."

He's teetering slightly, walking cane wobbling in his ancient hand. "Morning, Officer. But I've told you, call me Geezer. Everybody does."

"Need any help across the street?" I ask, echoing Greg's daily exchange with the man.

"I'll manage," he replies, on cue, "in my own time."

He looks both ways, the very picture of vigilance.

No cars coming, but he doesn't budge at all. He's looking at me. No, he's looking past me.

"Now, isn't that a sight to behold?" he says.

I turn, and in that moment the sound of several large diesel engines reaches my ears. What I see is strange even by Silvertown standards. Coming up Main Street from the west is a caravan of US Army vehicles. Eight of them, each one identical to the last.

They roll through town at a snail's pace, and just when the lead truck reaches the center of town, the driver suddenly stops. Soon enough they're all stopped, blocking the entire road. It's like a scene out of a movie, and I half expect soldiers to start jumping out with guns in hand. None of them move, though, save for the driver of the lead vehicle who simply rolls his window down.

"Looking for the old base?" a man from town asks him, referring to an abandoned training facility a mile up the road, vacated years ago. "Gonna tear it down finally, before anyone else gets hurt?"

"We're looking for Jim Creek," the soldier replies.

I don't know who that is. For one awful second I think there might be a fugitive who's rolled in with all the tourists. Or, perhaps more likely, some AWOL soldier. I take a step closer, stopping at the back of a small crowd that's formed on the edge of the sidewalk.

"Jim Creek, the navy base?" the townsperson asks.

The army man nods.

"Hell, son, that's ten miles north. You're on the wrong mountain."

In that instant the other soldiers in the cab erupt into laughter.

"You assholes," the driver mutters to his companions. Cheeks red, he rolls his window up quickly and starts to move again. What follows is the longest sequence of three-point turns I've ever witnessed. It takes almost ten minutes for the whole convoy to redirect itself, and by the time they're finally gone at least fifty people are standing along the road, watching the spectacle.

"Okay, show's over everyone," I say, my tone light. The old police cliché earns me a few smiles and someone laughs, and the crowd finally disperses.

Barring any calls that need me elsewhere, I decide I'll spend the morning on foot near the station. At least until Clara shows up to handle the front desk.

Main Street runs east–west. Really it's just the state route, but everyone here calls it Main Street for the two-hundred-yard stretch through the populated part of Silvertown.

Most of the buildings date back to the late 1800s, the notable exception being the gas station at the western edge. Original brick facades still line most of the street.

It's all rather quaint, provided you can ignore the fact that at least half the structures are empty. I stop before one of these derelicts and put my hand up against the dusty window to peer inside. The interior is all shadow and gloom. Dusty floors of torn-up hardwood and bare foundation. Trash and cobwebs in every corner.

"The old head office," someone says.

I turn toward the gruff voice. The old man, Willy, has ambled up behind me. He has a pinched face and a huge red nose.

"Offices?" I ask.

"Conaty Mining Corporation," he says, then taps the base of the brick facade with his cane. "Technically they still own it, I think. Would rather leave it as an eyesore than sell it."

"Huh."

"Deep pockets and a vindictive streak will do that." He smiles, a bit sadly.

"It's Jupitas, right? You're Willy Jupitas?"

His eyes twinkle as he nods. "That's me. Resident dinosaur, at your service. But I told you, everyone just calls me 'Geezer.'" We shake hands, and with a tip of his tweed driver's cap, he turns toward the street. After a thorough check that no cars or army caravans are coming, he finally makes his way across the street toward the bakery opposite us.

On a whim, I follow him and open the bakery door. Unlike the empty office across from us, this is a storefront I know well. *Flour Child* is the name on the door, and the Woodstock-themed interior lives up to that moniker.

The plan forming in my head is to buy pastries for myself and Willy, sit down with him by the window, and over breakfast he'll regale me with interesting trivia from the town's past. But he barely spends twenty seconds inside. A coffee is waiting for him on the counter, along with a grease-stained bag containing his usual. With one last tip of his cap, Willy is back outside and ambling down the sidewalk again.

"Morning, Officer," the woman behind the counter says to me. She has frizzy salt-and-pepper hair and a beak of a nose. From the signs of wear on her tie-dye T-shirt and the scuff marks on the peace-sign pendant around her neck, I suspect her hippie bona fides are all in order.

"Hello again, Reyann," I reply. My third visit in three days.

The shop specializes in oversized bearclaw donuts shaped, of course, like Big Foot's signature footprint. I order one, plus a small coffee to go.

Reyann shakes her head slightly, as if disappointed.

"What'd I say?" I ask.

"Really, Officer. Those are for tourists," she says with a sigh. "I like you, Whittaker, so I'll finally let you in on a town secret: my scones are where it's at. They will rock your world."

"Sign me up. A scone would be great."

"It's on the house," she says, "if you'll help me out with something."

"Of course." For a moment, my spine tingles with a twinge of excitement. Could there be something afoot in quiet old Silvertown?

"Raccoons," Reyann says, casting a furtive glance toward the back of the shop. "I try to compost everything I can, but those little masked monsters keep getting into the bin and making a huge mess of the alley. I've tried everything. Could you . . . ?"

"Could I . . . ?"

She lifts her shoulders, almost imperceptibly. Her eyes get a little watery, too, and I realize the predicament she's in. Trapped between a strong desire to treat the animals humanely, and yet at her wits' end for finding such a solution.

"Tell you what," I say, "I've got a contact in Animal Control. Let me see what I can do." I wink at her and take a bite of the scone. God, it's good.

It's a white lie, though, about my "in" at Animal Control. I could definitely *use* a contact in that department, and this is a great opportunity to introduce myself. Bonus points if this inquiry ends up with me making friends with the person who bakes scones this good. "Wow," I say through the mouthful I just popped in. "Awesome."

"World rocked?"

"Very much so."

"I grow the rosemary myself," she says, beaming, then waves as she returns to her oven.

Back on the sidewalk, I'd be lying if I said there wasn't a spring in my step. As starts to the morning go, today's has been pretty great.

Part of the daily routine Greg has established is a drive from Silvertown down to the bridge at Keller's Gorge, to look for disabled vehicles or any other obstructions that might otherwise "impede the flow of tourists."

So barely an hour after that mind-blowing scone, and thirty minutes after installing Clara at the front desk of the police station, I've traded walking the beat for driving my cruiser.

And now, at this exact moment, I am in deep shit.

My police cruiser is skidding sideways down the mountain road.

By the calendar it's still a week until autumn, but no one told the leaves. They started falling in droves the day after Johnny's funeral, as if the trees were in mourning, too, or so half the town has taken to saying. After three days of that the roads are blanketed in great circular patches of red and yellow.

Across this slippery carpet my cruiser now glides.

Traction control alerts flash on the dashboard. I strain against the wheel, fighting for control. Trees line the right side of the road, but just ten feet beyond them is a two-hundred-foot drop. On the left there's a sheer rock face where the mountain was cleaved to make way for this very road.

In the middle of all of this sits a man, his butt right on the double yellow.

I catch a glimpse of him, there in the center of the lane, head between his knees, oblivious to the car sliding toward him at high speed. He hasn't even looked up.

My brain regains control of my muscles. Right foot moving from brake pedal to gas. I goose it, one hard tap, and the front wheels fight for purchase, then catch. The car lurches more than I want. I overcompensate, and now I'm spinning the other way, facing backward. Not two feet from my window the man glides past, still oblivious. Two-foot difference and he'd have been smeared halfway to Granston.

With a shudder and an awful grinding noise, I'm off the road. Gravel roars under the tires, spraying up the quarter panels. The car is careening toward the rocky wall. I clench my teeth and brace for an impact that doesn't come.

Everything goes still. Peaceful, you might even say, once I kill the engine. My breathing slowly returns to normal. The motor ticks like a failing clock.

I'm going to catch hell for losing control of the car. Greg warned me about it before he left. Said it's the most common problem we have up here in the fall. State Route 177's unofficial name is Slippery Slope for good reason. "City folk like you can't drive on fresh fallen leaves." I took offense at that. I pointed out the potholed, damp streets of Oakland that I cut my teeth on, and how that must count for something. But Greg just laughed.

And the thing is, he was right. About all of it.

Yesterday it was a brand-new Land Rover full of hikers trying to finish the "lake loop"—Lake Forgotten being an optional last on that list. And today . . . it's me. I've lived here for two months, and in that time I've driven this road a hundred times at least. I should be able to handle some leaves. *In my defense, Chief, I'm not used to rounding a bend to find a man sitting in the road.*

Speaking of which . . . I blink away the dregs of my adrenaline and look for him, half expecting to find the man in the road was an apparition.

Nope. Still there. A weekend warrior, gray-haired head between designer denim knees, sitting right on the double-yellow line.

Apparently I'm not the only one who's lost control today. A Harley-Davidson is wedged between two trees about twenty feet away from him. All bright chrome, red paint, and polished leather. The exhaust still pings and clicks, cooling in the misty morning air, in concert with my Dodge. The bike is mere inches from going over the side.

"Hello there," I call when I feel confident my senses have fully returned. "Are you injured, sir?"

He looks up, then starts to twist toward me and thinks better of it. His helmet lays at his side, and I can see a scuff mark across its otherwise gleaming surface.

I try again, stepping out of my cruiser and onto the road. "Silvertown police. I'm Officer Whittaker. Are you injured?"

He shakes his head this time, and kicks at a pebble in a way that is so childish I almost laugh. "Pissed about my bike," he says.

"Umm . . . yeah. Looks like a nice one."

"Missed the turn," he adds.

"Okay," I reply, maybe a little too skeptical. "Kinda hard to miss."

"Messed," he corrects with a sudden forcefulness. Wounded male pride, maybe. "I messed up the turn, took it too fast."

"But within the speed limit, I'm sure."

He nods slowly.

"And you're sitting in the middle of the road why, exactly?"

The question briefly pulls his attention from the motorcycle. He glances at the pavement around him, the leaves, the yellow lines. He picks up his helmet and examines the scuff mark across its side.

"I guess I could move," he says, finally.

A sudden image appears in my head of him stumbling over to his bike, disoriented, only to slip and fall into the gorge. A fate not unlike that of the boy, Johnny Rogers. The thought makes me shiver. "You know what? Just stay put. How about you tell me about your Harley?"

Keep him stationary and talking, that's the best option. He starts to rattle off the model name and some no-doubt-impressive stats, looking at the bike rather than me. I turn away and fire up the radio clipped to my shirt.

"Clara? It's Mary."

There's a click about three seconds later. "Still can't believe I get to do this. So cool. Ahem. Uh, go ahead, Officer Whittaker. I read you."

"This one's serious, Clara."

"Sorry, sorry. What's up?"

"Another accidental off-roader down here on 177."

"Not again," comes her reply, referring to the SUV from the day before.

"Afraid so. These leaves are catching people off guard." Including me, but I withhold that footnote. "Do you have a pen and pad? Here's what I need you to do; write it down. First, call Doc and see if he can come down here and have a look at the guy."

"Not an ambulance?"

"I don't think it's that serious, but Doc might have a different opinion. Anyway, he can get here a lot faster than an ambulance from Granston."

"Okay. What else?"

"We'll need a tow truck. A flatbed, for the motorcycle, so you'll have to call down to Granston. Check the notepad on my desk, I think I've got the name of the one the sheriff's office uses. Gamble and Sons? Gimble? Something like that."

"I'll find it. Motorcycle, huh? Is it a local?"

"No, not a local. One of the . . . what do you call them? Sons of Brand-archy."

"Oh, joy. If only they'd spend half as much on riding lessons as they do on accessories . . . Hang on, Mary, another call coming in."

While waiting I produce a few orange cones from the trunk of my cruiser and set them at either side of the bend, weighing each down with a rock in case the wind picks up later. The cones blend in with the leaves, though, so I add a few road flares for good measure. With the early arrival of fall, I wonder if the town has a streetsweeping service that comes through, and when they're scheduled to start. Probably worth contacting them and moving the date up to . . . immediately. I jot a note to that effect on a small pad I keep in my breast pocket. Greg probably has all the details in his head, but I'm determined not to call him, so some detective work will be required to find out who the city has a contract with and—

The radio crackles. "Mary?" Clara's voice sounds different, the semisarcastic charm replaced with a stark seriousness.

"Go ahead, Clara."

"I can barely get anything out of this woman. She's hysterical. Something about Old Mine Road, that's all I could understand."

I glance at the biker. Despite my advice to stay put, he's standing now. Pacing near his motorcycle, actually, with a cell phone pressed to his ear. Probably talking to his insurance agent or telling a buddy back at the office about his brush with death. At least he's off the road.

"Sir? Tow truck is on the way. A doctor, too, just in case. I've got another call to respond to. You'll be all right here?"

He offers me a thumbs-up, not breaking his conversation.

"Well, then," I mutter under my breath. "Have a nice day."

Back in the cruiser I press Clara for details, but there are none to be had. A woman phoned in, terrified or deranged or stoned, Clara couldn't be sure. "Maybe all three," she adds with a touch of judgment. "Might even have been a prank call. All I could get was Old Mine Road, then she hung up on me."

*When it rains, it pours*, I think. Still, could be worse. Greg could have been on leave the day Johnny Rogers died. This is a picnic compared to handling something like that on my own.

"Copy that, Clara. On my way," I say.


The only way to reach Old Mine Road from where I skidded off the asphalt is to head back up the mountain and through downtown.

As I approach the old buildings I can't help but try to imagine what it was like here before everything changed.

On first moving here I made the same assumption just about everyone makes about a place called Silvertown. Yes, there's an old silver mine here, but it was abandoned more than sixty years ago. What remained, however, was the company that owned it, and despite closing the mine they continued to grow and prosper. Until Greg stuck his nose where it didn't belong.

He still hasn't filled me in on all the details, and I haven't pressed too much. I know there were convictions, resignations, and even a suicide. When the dust settled, Greg was the only cop left in a town with no chief and no mayor. The scandal had claimed them both. The new head of the Conaty Corporation decided (out of spite, evidently) that Houston would be a better home for their headquarters. As a result, Silvertown's population plummeted from more than four thousand to just seven hundred or so practically overnight. Hundreds of houses and dozens of businesses remain empty to this day, not to mention all the Conaty warehouses, processing plants, offices, and labs. Empty shells to the last.

Which brings me back to the main issue dividing this place: those who sided with Greg after the whole Conaty scandal, and those who don't. Half the town thinks Greg's a hero for what he did. The other half think he should've backed off, that he's responsible for Silvertown's economic collapse. The only small consolation is that all the really pissed-off folks left years ago. I don't know how he survived their hostility. From what I've heard it was ugly. Really ugly.

Someone new actually moving here, as I did two months back, is the rarest of rare occasions.

As I drive through I find my gaze drawn to the faces of those out on the sidewalks. Earlier, before work hours, the number of people walking around almost makes the place seem normal. But after that initial rush the number has dwindled. One man buys groceries at the Gas-N-Go. Another walks his dog. Two women peruse a display of orchids outside the small flower shop. They stand close together, engrossed in quiet conversation as they browse. Gossip, probably. And they seem happy, I guess, but they're not quite smiling. Not yet. The shadow of Johnny Rogers's death still looms over Silvertown.

At the sight of my car I can see them look up, hopeful perhaps that I'll stop and join the gossip session.

Oh, who am I kidding?

They'll ask where Greg is. If he's made it to Virginia safely. When he'll be back. *Can you handle things on your own*, that's what they'll really be asking, with doubt in their eyes.

Every fiber of my being wants to stop, though. I want to win them over. I want to be part of the Silvertown community, more than anything.

But there's the hysterical woman on Old Mine Road to think about, just now. Better to let the town know I'm on important police business. Doing the job. I pop the siren on and press a little harder on the Dodge's gas pedal, ignoring concerned looks as I clear Silvertown proper. The huddled collection of buildings are in my rearview in less than ten seconds. The two women in front of the flower shop watch me go, and there will be rumors even before I round the bend, of that I have no doubt.

Old Mine Road splinters off Route 177 about halfway to the peak, like a loose thread from an old rope. It's a cracked mess of pavement that worms through four miles of misty forest.

As I drive I try to remember everything Greg told me about the road—and what lies at the end of it—when we came up here a month ago to escort a state pollution inspector on his yearly visit.

Once upon a time the road extended all the way to the old silver mine, but that hasn't been the case in years. Now it ends at a small parking lot that serves both the trail and the Masonic campground, neither of which see much use for their intended purposes.

The trail is a mile and a half of flat, muddy path with barely a twist or rise to speak of, ending in a fenced-off area where the mine entrance used to be. It's nothing like the mines you see in an adventure film. This place is filthy and sprawling. An industrial mine, in other words, but with all the equipment gone it's just a flat patch of cleared ground in front of a cleaved hillside and the huge, concrete-sealed tunnel.

As for the campground, well, there're better options up by the lake, ones that you don't have to be a Mason to legally use. Places that aren't downwind from a polluted old mine, too. Double bonus!

I say legally because the Masonic Lodge owns the land, and anyone else camping there would technically be trespassing.

Other than that one hike up to the mine with Greg and the inspector from the state a month ago, our visits here have all been extremely brief. Nothing more than a turnaround in the parking lot once a week to look for, as Greg likes to say, anything out of the ordinary. So far, all we've ever found is ordinary.

But today, of course, there is something off: another vehicle parked in the small gravel lot. It's a late-model Subaru, and grimy as hell.

I park the cruiser several car lengths away and get out.

The air is cool and thick, smelling of dirt and old growth, and there's a tension in it I sense somewhere deep down. Without thinking I've loosened my Beretta in its holster. I tilt my head down and to the left, reaching up at the same time to activate the radio. But there's no Greg to update, and I chastise myself under my breath. "Get it together, girl. Not going to convince the town you can handle things if you keep looking for Greg, too."

My gaze sweeps the tree line, then the lone car. Oregon plates, which is not so out of the ordinary. A Big Foot sticker on the bumper, which is definitely at home here. Probably purchased back in town.

But the car's not empty, as I'd first assessed. A small movement behind the driver-side window catches the sun. A lock of blond hair. Someone's inside, crouched way down. Perhaps a kid.

I make a wide approach, palm still resting on my pistol. The person in the front seat is looking the other way, toward the trail. My eyes drift in that direction, but everything's quiet. Quiet is the norm up here, so that's not so strange.

"Hello?" I call out.

The head of blond hair moves, but only from being spooked, not to look at me. Instead of going to the driver-side door I move to the front corner. With one fist I rap twice on the hood.

Now she looks.

Blue eyes, wide with terror and red-rimmed from crying. Tears have left clean jagged lines down tanned and dusty cheeks. Her body moves in little jerking motions, fighting to get her breathing under control.

Her hands are white-knuckle tight on the steering wheel. Eight fingers all pressed together like a row of teeth.

I make a twirling motion with my free hand. *Roll down the window.*

She shakes her head. *No fucking way.*

Then she turns back to the trail and, with great effort, uncurls her right hand from the wheel and points.

My gaze follows her shaking finger to the empty trailhead. A narrow dirt path leads off into a little cleft between two low rises covered with ferns.

Not a damn noise, save for the wind. A little breeze that whispers through the foliage, coming down from the mine, carrying a smell. Faint, but there. Metallic.

I hold my palm out to her and mouth "Stay here," as if she'll do anything but. Her eyes flick from my face to my service weapon and back. Finding reassurance in one or both, she gives the barest of nods.

At the trailhead I radio again, barely remembering to ask for Clara instead of Greg.

"Go ahead, babe," she says.

I keep my voice calm and low. "There's a hiker up here and she's pretty spooked about something on the trail."

"What do you mean, 'something'? Some asshole attack her?" Instantly there's a hard edge to Clara's voice.

"Not sure. She's uncommunicative. I think . . . I better go check it out."

"Shouldn't you have backup?"

"I should, yes, thanks for the procedure reminder. Don't think this can wait another week."

"Sorry, I meant . . . I don't know what I meant. Just be careful, okay? You may not know this about me, but I fended off a mugger once. As a result I take this kind of thing very seriously."

I take a deep breath, realizing we're both out of our comfort zone here.

"It's all right," I say. "I shouldn't have snapped at you like that. Last time I went after a suspect without backup it did not end well, so we both have reason to be touchy. But let's not jump to conclusions. For all I know this woman up here was spooked by a raccoon carrying a scrap of day-old pastry. So . . . just stay by the radio, okay?"

"Of course!"

"We'll be in constant contact. If there's something to this, trust me, I will get anyone and everyone who can assist me to swarm on this place."

Clara agrees.

Recent rain and the early arrival of fall have left the trail muddy and leaf strewn. Here and there I can see fresh footprints, presumably from the woman in the Subaru. Long strides, a sprint back to the car. And, more faintly, two additional sets heading up the trail at a casual walk. Hers and another, slightly larger. A boyfriend, maybe? Or did someone follow her?

Maybe Clara was right. Perhaps this was a botched assault of some kind. Maybe the woman in the car actually did tase the bastard, or gave him a face full of pepper spray, and he's going to be up here somewhere nursing his ego. Been a long time since I cuffed someone, and the thought holds serious appeal.

I follow the tracks, deciding for now to keep their presence from Clara.

Off to my right comes the soft babbling of the slow, thin stream that carved this little cleft. Despite the many years since the Conaty Silver Mine closed, all the crap they dumped in it back then still designates the water as polluted, and there are signs just visible through the trees warning as much. When Greg and I escorted the government inspector, he took samples and later said the signs need to stay up. *Do not drink or swim*, they warn. Maybe once that notice made sense, but now? It's too narrow and shallow to swim in, and no one in their right mind would drink the murky stuff. But, as Greg is fond of saying, "Regs is regs."

The trail turns slightly, heading up the hillside and away from the gurgle of water. Silence creeps in again, save for a few birds up high in the taller trees. They stop their chatter as I pass, though. Quietly watching, ready to take flight if I'm judged to be a threat.

A quarter mile on I find him.

He kneels in the middle of a clearing, his back to me. A place where four western hemlocks lean together, forming a sort of natural cathedral with a central opening where sunlight pours in. In a movie the shaft of light would be illuminating him, but not so here. Instead he hides in near-darkness, and the circle of light instead shines down on a mess of camping gear spilled from an oversize backpack.

The man still wears his own pack, so the one on the ground must be the woman's. She ditched it and sprinted in terror, but he . . .

He's on his knees, facing toward the mine and away from me, arms flat at his sides with his palms turned upward, as if in meditation. There's something very wrong about that pose. The stillness of it. The calm.

I draw my pistol, crouch, and scan the tree line. All quiet. Keeping to the edge of the clearing, I creep slowly around to the right.

I go far enough to be sure because there's a part of me—the relent-lessly optimistic part—still hoping he's just brooding over a camp-fire or, hell, even praying. The rest of me knows the truth, though. My gut tells me something about all this is dreadfully wrong.

When I move far enough to see him in profile, the sight chills me to the core. Then the smell hits me. My stomach heaves. I bite it back. Force myself to look.

His chest, from collar to stomach, is open and steaming in the cool air of the clearing. Ribs poke out at sickening angles from a mess of blood and muscle and torn clothes. It's as if something has ripped its way out from within his torso. A demon unleashed.

The evidence against such a fantastic theory is all there, though, waiting for my shock and revulsion to recede. Clothes shredded by claws. Teeth marks. It's all right in front of me. Huge paw prints in the mud finally force my brain back to reality.

A bear did this. A big one.

"Shit," I mutter. "Shit shit shit." My hand goes to my radio, and I almost say Greg's name. "Clara, you there?"

I wait, my eyes darting to every noise coming through the forest.

"Here, Mary! Are you okay?"

"Yes," I manage. "But only just. There's a . . . There's a body."

"Oh no," Clara replies. "Oh, honey, what now? It's not another one of ours, is it?"

She means another resident of Silvertown. Another Johnny Rogers.

Everything about his death suddenly returns to mind, images merging with the fresh corpse kneeling before me.

Johnny Rogers, lying facedown at the base of a twenty-foot drop on the side of the mountain, legs splayed at impossible angles.

This hiker, belly torn open like a soft-boiled egg, guts dangling.

I bite back another wave of nausea.

Clara's voice yanks me back. "Mary? Talk to me, please. Was it—"

"No, Clara," I say. "Not one of ours. A hiker from out of town. Bear attack, I think. Listen, get Doc up here, wearing his coroner's hat."

"Oh God."

"Keep it together. We'll handle this, okay?"

"Okay."

"Doc first. Then call over to O'Doherty's. Tell Kyle to come, with the appropriate firepower for something like this. Just in case the animal is still in the area. There's no sign of it now, but I don't want to take any chances." My Beretta isn't enough. But more than that, I have no experience with wild animals, especially of this sort.

"Got it. Anything else?" she asks.

"There will be more, but we need to make sure the area is safe first. Tell them to hurry, please."

"I'm on it, Mary. And please, be careful!"

"I will. Keep me posted."

She signs off.

"God dammit, Greg," I mutter, "hell of a time to go on leave." He'd have experience with something like this, surely. My mind churns with everything that needs to be done. Animal Control will need to be contacted. Maybe the Ranger Service. That's just to deal with the bear. There's still the hiker to consider.

I stand still for a moment, trapped between two choices. Stay with the body, or return to the woman at the trailhead. She's scared out of her wits, but she's safe in her car. My fear is if I leave the body, the bear will come back and drag it away, or worse.

In the end it's a compromise. I circle the clearing, making a load of noise to scare off the potential lingering bear plus any other animals that might be smelling dinner right about now. Then, I head back to the woman in the Subaru.


We sit side by side in the dirt, backs against the driver's-side door of my cruiser. She sips from a water I found in the trunk, her hands still shaking as she raises the bottle to quivering lips.

Neither of us have yet spoken. I simply went to my car and she followed. We both slumped here and stared at the trail. She with the water and me with the Beretta. After five minutes of dreadful silence I'm about to ask the basics—name, where are you from, and so on—but I settle for the classic.

"Tell me what happened."

The reply comes slowly, as if she's trying to remember something from years ago. "He just stood there," she says in an even, quiet voice that belies her shaking hands.

I nod, solemnly. Then I wait, but she doesn't continue, as if that is all there is to it.

"Didn't turn to run?"

"No."

"Play dead?"

"No. He just stood there. He was . . . he was . . . smiling."

A raking sob courses through her, and I wait it out, considering her words. When she finally calms down I ask, "And you? What'd you do?"

She glances at me as if I'm a moron. "I ran!" Her gaze swings back to the trail. "God dammit, Jeff, you . . ."

Grief drowns the words. She's sobbing, snorting back the worst of it. I put an arm around her, grip her shoulder, and try to picture the scene. The pair of them out on a guidebook-inspired nature hike, hoping to snap some cool pictures of a silver mine out of some John Wayne film for their social media profiles. They get to the clearing and stop for a drink of water. Maybe she's set her pack down and is fishing in it for a granola bar, and then he says, "Wow. Check out the bear." She looks, then reacts like any sensible human would: drops her shit and runs like hell. Probably assumes he's on her heels and then glances back to see he's not moved an inch.

He doesn't run. He doesn't even play dead like some people think they're supposed to do. Doesn't yell or make aggressive movements like you're *actually* supposed to. Nope, he's just standing there letting a bear—a savage brute of a bear from what I saw in that clearing—stride toward him.

He was smiling, she said.

That's weird.

I'm not a big fan of weird.

In my experience, "weird" usually means someone's lying. Maybe she pushed him down to buy herself some time. How's the saying go? *You don't have to be the fastest, just don't be the slowest.* Something like that.

But she doesn't look the type. And this is not the time to press. People in shock aren't the most reliable of witnesses.

I change tactics. "Is he . . . I mean, are you, were you, married?"

"No," she manages.

"Dating?"

"Yeah."

"Is there someone we can call? Family of his?"

"I . . . I don't know."

"You don't know if—"

"We only met a few weeks ago."

"Okay. That's fine. We'll figure it out."

She nods.

"Is the car yours or his?" I ask.

"His." She swallows, hard, and her next question is choked out. "Are you going to leave him out there?"

I pat her hand. "Coroner's on the way, and some others with hunting gear. Still, it might be better if you waited in the back of my car. Is that okay? You stay put and I'll go make sure Jeff isn't . . . alone."

She stares at the trailhead, her lower lip quivering. Finally, she nods.

I am getting her situated as Kyle and Doc pull up in separate vehicles. A modified Jeep and an unmodified Volvo, respectively.

"Wait here," I tell the young lady, and close the door.

Kyle parks first. His old Jeep looks like something out of a Mad Max film. Whip antenna, intake snorkel. Winch on the front, armored gas can and spare wheel side by side on the back. The whole thing has been coated in black bed-liner usually used to protect pickup truck beds. The "paint job" was done by Kyle himself, and it shows.

The vehicle creaks as he steps down. He smiles at me and I smile back. No further communication needed, I guess. Things had progressed rather quickly after we drank that toast to Johnny Rogers at the pub. I found myself back there the very next evening, and without Greg seated beside me Kyle and I talked until closing, and then some more in the alley behind the place where I learned all about his Jeep, among other things. The next night, I was back again, and that time we didn't part ways. A rapid escalation, I admit, but a welcome one. We're keeping it all on the down low.

He wears a camouflage cap over his shaggy brown hair, along with a matching vest. Jeans and a flannel complete the hunter's outfit. Oh, and the shotgun, expertly held.

"Clara said it was a bear. That true?" he asks.

"Yeah. Big one, I think."

"Damn. That's gotta be a first up here. A sighting is one thing, but an attack? Christ."

"Thanks for coming," I say.

He nods, then gives me a little wink. A wink as in "I can handle a bear," or as in "I really enjoyed having sex with you last night and wouldn't mind doing it again sometime"? Hard to say. Both options lift my spirits.

Meanwhile Doc unfolds himself from his boxy silver wagon. If one's car is the extension of the man, these two are the textbook examples.

Dr. Frank Ryan. Psychiatrist by trade, and as it happens the only Silvertown resident with a doctorate of the medical variety, and so has the distinguished honor of becoming the de facto town doctor. Like me he's relatively new to the area, having moved into the old Smiley mansion a year back, give or take. He runs his practice from the front room of the place, advertising it on the local public access channel constantly.

The town's too small for a full-time shrink, to be honest, but he doesn't seem to care. Town doctor, though? Apparently he grumbled about that for the first few months, according to Greg. Not his area of expertise, not what he signed up for, et cetera, et cetera. From what I've seen, though, the role has really grown on him.

He wears what he always wears: a gray tweed jacket that hangs loosely despite his large frame. A bow tie, plaid shirt, and dark slacks complete the uniform. The one difference today is the kind of boots you'd expect to see on an English gentleman enjoying a fox hunt. Big green rubbery things with a yellow stripe up the center. The only thing that could make them more perfect would be a price tag dangling from the side.

"Doc," I say in greeting. He towers over me. Over Kyle, too. Six-foot-eight if he's an inch. Wide at the midsection, way too thin everywhere else.

"Sheriff," he replies, "I hope this isn't another bogus call. I've had enough of those for one day."

I'm not a sheriff but he always calls me that. Part of the small-town fantasy, I guess. "Bogus? Wait, are you talking about the biker?"

His eyebrows lift and he turns his head slightly to one side, talking to the ground beside me instead of me, his words quick and just this side of a mumble. "There was no biker. There was no bike. Mile marker thirteen was quiet as a library. I canceled an appointment for what I can only assume was some kind of hoax. I really don't appreciate being the butt of a joke."

"Whoa, calm down." I spread my hands. "No hoax, Doc. There was definitely someone there. I thought he might have a concussion. Sorry if it was a false alarm. The dude must have gone with the tow truck." Only, that wasn't possible. A tow truck would need to come up from Granston, which takes an hour on a good day. Had the idiot pulled his bike from the tree and continued riding?

I file that. On my list of things to worry about right now it's far below murderous bear.

"Well," I say, "you'd better come take a look at the victim."

"How bad is it?"

My skin goes clammy at the memory. "Bad" is all I can muster.

He glances at Kyle, who adjusts his grip on the shotgun.

"Want me to take point?" Kyle asks me.

I nod, grateful. Doc follows me, seemingly unperturbed by the prospect of what awaits us farther up the trail.

Before the parking lot disappears from sight, I take one glance back at the woman sitting in my cruiser. She offers me a brief wave, her face unreadable. I wave back, then fall in behind the two men.

At the clearing, Kyle wastes no time. He doesn't even glance at the body, trusting my assessment of the state of the hiker. Instead, he continues on past the man and out the other side of the clearing, following the animal's tracks.

"Be right back," he says over his shoulder.

Doc approaches the hiker, stopping a good ten feet away. He pulls a handkerchief from one pocket and a small digital camera from another. The cloth serves to cover his mouth and nose as he begins to snap some photos for evidence. Then, with great reluctance, he walks a circle around the victim. There is only the briefest instant where he seems to look at the wound. Most of his attention is instead grabbed by the strange smile on the man's face.

"Terrible," Doc mutters, voice muffled by the cloth. He stops beside me and puts the handkerchief away. "Okay to move him?"

"If you feel you've gotten enough photos, I think that would be wise."

He returns the camera to his pocket and rummages through his satchel until he finds a folded-up black body bag from within. Then he seems to realize what the task entails and hands it to me. "Maybe we should wait for Kyle."

"Yeah. Good idea."

A silence begins to stretch, becoming something awkward.

"It doesn't make a lot of sense," I say, if only to fill that void.

Doc nods. "It is unusual, a bear coming this close to town. First time I've heard of such a thing, anyway."

"No, not that. The hiker."

"What about him?"

"Why didn't he run? Or play dead? His companion says he didn't even defend himself. Isn't that what anyone would do? Instinctively, I mean?"

A long pause stretches as Doc considers this. He rubs at his chin, and slowly begins to nod.

"Well," Doc says, "yes, theoretically. Fight or flight is about as simplistic as you can get when it comes to the primal behavior of human beings. There are many others. Danger avoidance, seeking sustenance, et cetera. And, of course, such reactions can be interfered with, even altered."

"You mean, like, with alcohol? Drugs?"

He glances at me, then back at the body. "Yes," he replies carefully.

"There are other ways?"

Doc takes his time, thinking carefully before he finally nods. "I was speaking more about conscious effort."

"Meaning what?"

"Consider a zookeeper, for instance. Any human being of sound mind would flee, or perhaps fight when faced with a tiger or a bear like this one. But with enough training and focus, that behavior can be tempered, even controlled."

"Huh. But it was probably drugs, right? I mean, c'mon. What are the odds that this guy works in the bear den of the Seattle Zoo?"

Doc shrugs. "I'm just giving you possibilities, Sheriff. Perhaps he worked at an animal rescue. Who knows? Finding out is your area of expertise, not mine." He shoves his hands into his jacket pockets and shrugs again. "If you want my opinion, Psych 101 information about primitive behavior won't help you here, Sheriff. In my estimation, the bear is what we should be worried about, not its victim. The most likely explanation is that this man was simply caught off guard and froze in panic. Ah, here's Kyle."

I glance toward the eastern edge of the clearing as Kyle emerges from the trees. He's got his shotgun held casually, and shakes his head when our eyes meet.

Kyle stops opposite me, the three of us making a sort of circle around the victim.

"Found a track leading away. The bear is long gone. What now?" he asks me.

"Can you help us move him?"

"Whatever you need."

"I'll need to see if he's got a wallet and phone. After that . . . listen, we can work together to get him down the trail, but I wonder if you two might wait for me to take his companion out of here before he's brought into the parking area."

The two men exchange a glance. Doc checks his watch before giving a resigned shrug.

"No problem," Kyle says for both of them.

# CHAPTER FOUR

On the drive back to town I ask her name.

"Katherine Pascoe." Her hands have stopped shaking, the look of shock replaced by numbness that matches her voice.

"Tell me again about what happened."

Her response takes a while to form. So long, in fact, I think maybe she didn't hear me. Her wide-eyed gaze remains fixed on some distant imaginary point.

Eventually she says, "We were hiking."

I glance at her, expecting more, but she doesn't elaborate.

"Just hiking?" I prompt.

"Yes."

"And then?"

"We saw a bear."

*Whoa, slow down,* I think. *You're gonna bury me under this avalanche of information.*

The lopsided conversation goes on like this for the duration of the ride. At first I chalk this up to shock, then perhaps cold detachment, but as the trees whisk past us I change my mind. This is one seriously introverted woman. She doesn't offer anything unless I press for it, and it takes the entire drive to get precious few results.

Katherine is a grad student at the University of Washington, and met the deceased at a book signing. They'd come up this way without a real plan, just a weekend of adventure and brewery hopping. They'd started down in Seattle and worked their way up to Granston, where they'd toured a new brewery and gastro pub.

While there, some idiot had given them the stellar advice to hike up to the old mine near Silvertown. This, I assume, was an innocent practical joke. One that proved fatal, but I decide to withhold from Ms. Pascoe the news that the silver mine is a dud and her boyfriend just might have died because of someone's warped sense of humor.

All that takes twenty minutes to extract, and maybe fifty questions from me. My eyes itch, bleary from lack of sleep.

At our tiny police station I preempt Clara's questions. "Later," I mouth, at her inquisitive look. "Brew some coffee, would you?"

While she tends to that I take Katherine by her arm and guide her to one of the four holding cells. She explained on our drive back, at my constant prompting, that she couldn't head home in Jeff's Subaru even if she wanted to. No license, never learned. So she'll stay put until we can contact his family and figure out what to do. Maybe put her up at Mrs. Kensington's B&B when the shock wears off.

"I'll just be right over there at my desk," I say to her. "Clara's making coffee. Just hold tight for a bit, okay? We'll sort this out."

Katherine nods, sitting down gingerly on the cot.

I plop my own butt at my desk, gulp some of the terrible coffee, and run the deceased's driver's license along with the Subaru's plates. My fingers drum impatiently on top of the computer's mouse as an icon spins.

And spins.

Despite all the talk around town, I have no idea if the big new cellular data tower on the mountain is working yet. In addition to wireless service for phones, it also has these microwave antennas that look like bass drums, providing fast internet as long as you have a similar antenna on your roof and line-of-sight to the metal monstrosity. The tower's disguised, quite poorly, as a pine tree. Not even a variety of conifer native to the Northwest, as Greg pointed out to me.

Some thirty seconds pass before I've got information on the deceased. Date of birth, Social, last known address. The poor guy was only twenty-four. An absolute shame. Then his driver's license photo pops up. It was smudged and worn on the actual ID, so much so I paid it no attention. But here on the screen it's crystal clear. I lean back, momentarily speechless. The charming half grin, the welcoming blue eyes, the scruffy beard . . . He looks exactly the same here, posing for a Department of Transportation camera, as he did staring into the jaws of a bear that was about to gut him from stem to stern. I mean the look on his face is identical. Disinterested, a little smug maybe. "Aloof" is the right word, I think.

I print the document, yawning as the page is spat out of the machine. Then I call Doc.

"What now, Sheriff Whittaker? I have a calendar to stick to. Appointments. Paying customers."

"You know I'm not a sheriff, right?"

He chuckles dryly. "Of course."

"Then why—"

"A little experiment. I thought it would be interesting to see how long it would take you to correct me. Two months to the day, as it turns out."

"And is it?"

"Is it what?"

"Interesting."

"Not especially."

I shake my head. What a specimen. "About the hiker. What's our plan?"

"I've spoken with the county medical examiner. She's sending a team from the coroner's office to collect the remains. Kyle's waiting with the, er, with him, until they get here."

"Did you ask them to do an autopsy?"

"Hah. Right."

"I'm serious."

He's silent for a second. "I really don't think that's necessary."

"Why not?"

"Mary, I don't think there's been a more obvious cause of death since Marie Antoinette's."

Maybe it's the stress. Maybe the lack of sleep or my soured stomach. Maybe it's the implication that I don't know how to handle this, but good-old-Greg would. Whatever, my temper overpowers my innate need to forge partnerships. I lower my voice. "I am serious, Doctor Ryan. The family of the deceased is going to want an answer as to why their son chose not to run from a fucking bear. And if he didn't have a little ganja or who-knows-what in his system it begs the question: Was he really just 'frozen in panic,' as you put it, or is she perhaps not telling us the entire truth?"

"Now just hold on a second. Calm down." He lets out a long breath. "This isn't like you. Are you all right?"

Pinching the bridge of my nose, I say, "Sorry, Doc. Just tired. Don't worry about me."

"It's my job to worry about you."

"Technically it isn't. I have my own doctor."

"I meant in the sense of being a medical professional—"

"I'm fine."

"This has been a stressful few weeks. For all of us. First that tragedy with John Rogers, then Greg goes on leave, and now this—"

"Dude. I said I'm fine."

"But tired," he says suggestively.

This stops me short, and I wish it didn't because he picks up on it.

"There are excellent remedies for that, Mary. Some of the newer sleep aids are—"

"No, really, I'm fine. Sorry for snapping at you."

I say my goodbyes before he can ask about my relationship with my mother or the specifics of my dreams. Winning the town's trust and friendship is one thing, but when it comes to Doc—or Pastor Osman for that matter—I think it's best if they don't know my every problem. Besides, there's no reason why I can't call the coroner directly. Introduce myself. Greg will be proud.

"Clara?" I call out. She doesn't reply.

The duty desk is in a small front room, and from where I sit, I can hear the little television on in there, tuned to the news. I walk over.

Clara Givens is leaning back in the chair, watching the little antique TV. She's got purple-and-pink hair this week, shaved on one side, and a nose ring. A sleeve of tattoos covers her left arm.

"Clara?" I ask again.

She raises one hand in response, her attention on the television. I glance at it. On the screen, there's some investment show on, and before I can tell her to switch it off I realize the person talking to the reporter is Mrs. Sandra Conaty, chief executive of the global company that used to be headquartered here.

Conaty is saying something about a streamlining of the workforce. Corporate executive talk for layoffs.

"Of course," the interviewer says, "you already streamlined your workforce when you moved from Washington State to Texas, didn't you?"

Conaty brushes the comment aside. "That was before my tenure as CEO, but yes, departing our headquarters there did provide an ancillary benefit of shedding deadweight."

"Nice," I note. "She seems like a lovely person."

"If Lizard People are real," Clara says, "and I'm not saying they are, but I'm not saying they aren't, either . . . she'd be hiding scales. Guaranteed."

"Good thing Greg ran them out of town, huh?" I reach past her and turn the volume down. "Fascinating stuff, but I need you to help me with something."

"Sure thing," Clara replies. Instead of walking back with me, she pushes her chair with both feet, wheeling all the way from the front desk to mine, then spins and looks at me earnestly, hands clasped in front of her.

I hand her the printout. "Mr. Jeffery Hall, our recently departed hiker."

She glances at it, frowns. "Damn. He was smokin' hot."

"Shh. His girlfriend is in the other room."

Clara gives me a concerned look, lowering her voice to match mine. "Was it awful? I bet it was. I hate the sight of blood."

I meet her gaze and hold it. "One of the worst things I've ever seen."

She puts a hand on my shoulder and squeezes. A silence stretches. Outside the roar of a Harley grows, rattles the windows, then fades. Clara releases my shoulder and puts on a brave face. "How can I help?"

"I need to call the coroner. While I'm doing that, could you please look through the, um, deceased's phone and wallet? I have his driver's license, but we need a relative we can call. A close friend. Anything."

"What about the girlfriend? She doesn't know?" she asks, jerking her chin toward the holding cell off to her left.

"They haven't been dating that long."

"Yet she followed him out into the wilderness."

I sigh. "Now now, don't judge. Besides, she's been through enough for one day. Let's give her a break. Going through his things is the easier route."

Clara nods conspiratorially. Then her nose wrinkles. She says, "I've got a shift at the diner in two hours."

"You'll make it, don't worry, I just . . . I'm shorthanded, ya know?"

A nod. "I get to go through his stuff, huh? Badass."

"Yes, you do. Wear gloves, please."

"You may count on me, Mr. Holmes."

At the bad British accent I roll my eyes, shooing her away toward the evidence locker. She navigates her chair in that direction without another word. Watching her go, I wonder if we have the budget to hire her. Doubtful. Greg warned me when he hired me that, because of the diminished size of Silvertown, the county sheriff has been pushing every year to close our department and let them handle the "minimal needs" of this place. They have a point, too, Greg admitted, but for some reason every year the state has declined to make the change.

"Instead they just keep cutting the budget, which is worse if you ask me," the chief had said.

"Hey, Clara?" I call out. I can at least float the idea, and then browbeat Greg into putting in a request for staffing.

She glances back at me, an eyebrow raised.

"If you want, I could put in a word with Greg. See if we can't bring you on part-time."

"Would I have to handle the front desk?"

"Well, yeah. But I'm sure—"

She's already shaking her head. "Thanks for the offer, but the idea of dealing with everyone who walks in here isn't for me."

"You work at the one diner in town. Wouldn't it be the same people?"

"That's why I work the grill. I could never wait tables. Or front desks."

I frown. "Sorry, I didn't know it would bother you. I can get another volunteer until Greg's back."

Again a shake of the head, this time more emphatic. "A few hours here and there is fine, I just couldn't make a career out of it."

"Okay. Fair enough."

She gives me an apologetic smile and returns to her task. Letting Clara get her curious hands on some genuine police evidence seems a small price to pay to keep her volunteering. Besides, it's not like the items are from a crime scene. So I let it go and turn my attention to the phone.

After navigating the county's government-grade phone menu for several billion years, my call finally reaches the coroner's desk.

"Shipman," the man says by way of introduction. I write the name down on my pad of useful contacts as I reply.

"Hi. It's Mary Whittaker, Silvertown PD."

"Silvertown? Usually it's Gorman who calls us."

"It's a team effort up here now."

He doesn't respond to that.

"Listen, about the victim in the bear attack—"

"That request just came in, and you're already on my case? We haven't even collected the body yet."

"I know. I mean, I figured. When you do look at him, though, could you do a full toxicology screen and send me the results?"

"Bears aren't poisonous."

I say, "But they could be diseased."

Silence again.

"Look, truth is I'm interested in the, er, pharmaceutical aspects of the report."

"Of the legal or illegal variety?"

"Both, and quickly if possible."

"Well, I surely will try, boss!" he says with a mock hick accent. Then he adds, "It is Friday, you know." The call ends abruptly.

Somehow, I come away from this call with the impression I'm not going to get answers until Monday at the earliest. On the pad of paper beside my phone, below the name Shipman, I jot down: *Don't boss, does not react well*, and underline it. The pad is close to full with such observations, and despite the chat with the coroner going a little poorly, this little nugget of wisdom will aid me next time.

I yawn and lean back in my chair, considering other options. Maybe drive back up to Old Mine Road and poke through the Subaru. Look for what the media love to call "drug paraphernalia." Or, I suppose I could just ask Ms. Pascoe in the next room. She's warming up to me, as long as I prompt her with constant questions. Plus she doesn't seem to be especially attached to the deceased. Maybe she'll come clean if there's evidence that drugs are involved.

No, I think. She really has been through enough. It can wait until morning.

The phone rings. Clara glances at me from the table by the evidence locker and I hold up a hand. "I got it," I add, suppressing another yawn. Then, into the handset, "Silvertown police, Officer Whittaker."

"May I speak with Chief Gorman, please?"

My heart sinks, and not just because they've asked for Greg.

This is a voice I know. Barbara Rogers, bereaved mother of the late Johnny.

"Sorry, Mrs. Rogers, Greg's still on leave."

"Oh. Yes, of course. I'd forgotten." After the slightest hesitation, there's a renewed confidence in her voice. "You're going to ask me if this is an emergency, and the answer is no. I just . . . I need to speak with him. I'd hoped he might come by."

"Is this something I can help you with?" I ask with a little trepidation. I want to help her, more than anything. But there's the hiker to consider, and his girlfriend in the cell. *You can't be everywhere*, my old boss once told me, *so stop trying*. I guess I can't help it.

She says, "You're familiar with Johnny's case?"

The death of Johnny Rogers is practically all Greg and I talked about before he left. I wasn't there when Greg found the body, but I've read his report. Studied the photographs. Tried to drink those images away. "Greg has briefed me, yes."

"Perhaps you could come by, then."

Not a question. Not that I'd refuse if it was. "Sure, of course. I'll be right over. Do you need me to bring anything?"

"No," she says firmly. Then, completely monotone, "I mean that. Please do not bring any more flowers. We have more than we know what to do with. I've had to ask Rachel to stop accepting orders if they're intended for our doorstep."

I'd delivered a bouquet myself. Just about everyone has. "I, well, we all just want to . . . we're all mourning with you, Barbara. It's the least we can do."

"Well," she says, "you might be able to do something that will actually help. Please come by and I'll explain."

This doesn't fill me with eagerness, but I agree all the same. Her son is dead. She's entitled to special access, to favors. Until Greg's back, anyway.

# CHAPTER FIVE

Barbara and Daniel "Buck" Rogers live in a large brick two-story home that should probably be designated as a historical landmark. The place is a century old, not that you'd ever know from looking at it. The couple keep it meticulously maintained.

Buck is as charming and amusing as his nickname suggests. Former astronaut, of all things. He now lives in semiretirement. Fishing most days, and on the others traveling around the world talking to everyone from school kids to CEOs about space. He and Barbara were at a conference in Paris when their son passed away.

That had been on a Saturday, almost two weeks ago now. The couple had returned the following Monday. Oblivious to their son's passing, they'd learned the news by finding half the town standing on their front lawn in tears. Greg, myself, and Doc were on the porch, waiting to explain—or try to, rather. I shiver again just thinking about it.

Buck himself had done the whole tough-alpha-male thing. Buried his son, thanked all the mourners, then gotten right back to work. Can't fault him. I'd have done the same, I think, not that I've a kid of my own to lose. I just know the M.O. of losing yourself in your work when life becomes too real.

Barbara meets me at the front door. Her salt-and-pepper hair is swept back in a severe bun and she wears no makeup. Her hands are clasped in front of her at the waist, pale against a simple black dress. Her face is as still as Lake Forgotten itself. Without so much as a word she leads me into what can only be described as the parlor.

The sun has come out and streams in brilliantly through three large windows. She takes one chair and gestures for me to take the other. On the sofa opposite are a sleeping bag and pillow, ruffled with recent use. She must not want to sleep upstairs where her son's room is.

A silence falls. Dust swirls in the sunbeams.

In a flat, matter-of-fact voice, Barbara says, "You've lived here, what is it, a month now?"

"Two, Mrs. Rogers," I correct, gently.

"Please. Call me Barb. Had you met my son?"

I nod. I'd come here ready to be a shoulder for her to cry on, to be swept up in her grief. The way she moaned at learning of Johnny's passing, and the raw emotion on display at the funeral, that was the Barbara I expected, not this . . . this automaton. It's unsettling. "I met him several times. He helped me stuff envelopes for that fund-raising drive—"

"Can we agree that my son was a good boy?"

This question seems primed to open a door I thought Greg had closed already: the suicide theory. I answer carefully. "I suspect a mother's opinion is biased, but my own impression is that yes, he was a good kid. No, not just good. A great kid. Everyone thought so. Look, if the insurance company is giving you a hard time, have them call me. No one in this town thinks your son took his own life. None of the usual signs were there. No note. No depression or problems at school. Nothing. He was a happy, bright, wonderful kid."

Barb looks down at her tea. Her eyes glisten but she holds it together. "It's not that."

"Then what? I'm here for you."

She steels herself. "Hiking," she says.

"What about it?"

"I don't understand it."

I hold my breath, because no one understands it.

At my silence she goes on. "Other than for school, Johnny rarely left the house. I know it's the way the world is now, but he was always looking at one screen or another. Before you think this reflects poorly on my parenting, we tried taking those confounded things away. He would just switch to books, or playing chess with his father. I once forced him to go outside and play, desperate for him to behave like any other kid, and you know what he did? He sat on the steps under the awning just out back and read a novel."

"An introvert," I say, thinking of Katherine Pascoe.

But she shakes her head. "It's not that. He had plenty of friends. But they would engage one another via their phones, or gaming machines. Ex-Box or whatever it's called."

"An agoraphobe, then?" Of course I had heard about the kid's lifestyle, holed up in his room playing games for hours on end, but no one had gone so far as to suggest this, at least not to me.

Again Barbara shakes her head. "We feared that. Had him tested a few years ago and then again when Doctor Ryan moved here. But, the assessment was that it was not a phobia. He simply disliked the outdoors. *Intensely.*"

This last word she says, well, intensely. No other way to put it. I nod my understanding.

"So . . . why the late evening hike, then?"

"This is what I wanted to talk to Greg about. Because no one else will listen, but I know he would."

"He would," I agree. "And I'm here to help, too, if I can. Greg and I have talked about this quite a lot, Mrs. Rogers."

It's the question that's been on everyone's mind, truthfully. Why does a boy with no interest, desire, or aptitude to hike and camp suddenly walk out of his home and off into the woods at nine one Friday evening? He tells no one where he's going, takes nothing with him but the clothes on his back, and gets a mile up the nearby ravine before slipping and falling to his death.

The explanations whispered around town are as varied and

strange as the people living here. Everything from sleepwalking to following a ghost to—

"Is it possible," she asks in that terrible even tone, "that he was tricked into doing this? The promise of meeting a girl? Some kind of prank by one of his friends, gone awry? A dare born of peer pressure? Or perhaps even something more malicious?"

I study the floor. I can't fault her for wanting an explanation. The problem is there will only ever be theories. Her son is gone, and so he cannot tell us the real reason.

I say, "Greg looked into those possibilities. There were no prints here except the three of yours. No signs of entry or really any indication at all that someone else was here, invited or otherwise. His friends, that we're aware of, were all accounted for. All we have is the video from your security camera and the neighbor's account."

The footage, from one of those fancy doorbell cameras, shows Johnny Rogers walking out their front door and straight across the street, into the woods. His path took him past a neighbor's yard, and he saw him trudging into the trees at a calm, leisurely pace. He thought nothing of it. And why would he? It was just a kid exploring, perfectly normal behavior on a mountain like this. Maybe the hour was weird, but not weird enough to worry over.

"The thing is, Officer, he spoke with his friends mostly via the computer," she says. "Or texting." This word she almost spits out.

"I know," I say patiently. "We sent Johnny's phone and laptop to a digital forensics specialist at the county sheriff's office, just in case, but as of yet there's been no indication that anything was amiss."

"As of yet," she repeats numbly.

"It's Greg's professional opinion," I go on, "which I share, that his friends had nothing to do with this. They're all—we're all—shocked beyond words, Mrs. Rogers. Barb." I let that sink in. It sounds rehearsed to my own ears, but she doesn't seem to notice. "Unless," I add as a tingle runs up my arms, "there's something else? Something you remembered, or found?"

She shakes her head, not at my question, I think, but at some internal debate. "I'm just having a hard time understanding. This was so out of character for him. So . . . *random*. I wondered . . . when I called I'd planned to ask Greg to take another look through Jonathan's room. A closer look. If there's anything that might suggest drugs, or alcohol. Anything that could have clouded my son's judgment . . ."

Her words echo what I'd said to Doc about the hiker, almost exactly. Another shiver flashes up my spine. "Greg was rather thorough," I say, and instantly see the disappointment in her features. "But, maybe a fresh set of eyes would help? Unless you'd rather wait for Greg—"

"Thank you, Mary." Barely a whisper. "I'd appreciate it if you had a look."

"Of course." I eye the sleeping bag on the couch. "How about you wait down here?"

She nods once, takes a careful sip of her tea. Her eyes are focused on the steam curling up from her mug.

Upstairs I enter Johnny's bedroom.

A typical teenager space. Posters on the wall for various staples of pop culture: *Mass Effect*, *Stranger Things*, and half a dozen others. I only vaguely recognize them.

The floor is hardwood, original from the look of it but gleaming like the rest of the house. In fact, everything's been thoroughly cleaned and tidied. I wonder for a moment if Barb did that herself, or if she'd had a service come in and do it.

In Greg's report there were a number of photographs of this space. I'd been so focused on the death itself, and the reactions of both parents and town, that I didn't really look at it from the perspective of the kid. In hindsight, there are signs everywhere that he treated this place as his own little cave.

The bed itself looks stiff and almost unused, shoved into one corner. The main attraction here is the sofa, which is well worn and piled with cushions and blankets. It sits only a few feet from a large flatscreen television. Beneath the screen on a double-deck stand are several game consoles and at least six controllers in various colors.

A thought occurs to me, and I cross to a shelf on the adjacent wall where dozens of games are shelved in seemingly random order. Most are unknown to me. Greg has a list of all these in his report, I recall, but I don't know if anyone has really looked into what they are. Seems a bit of a stretch to blame video games for this, but I file that away for further examination anyway.

There's a small desk by the window with a simple lamp and a pad of lined white paper. Ballpoint pens in a plastic cup. Probably where he did his homework. The window looks out on the mountainside, or would if the blinds weren't drawn and covered in dust. So he wasn't sitting here pining for the great outdoors then.

Johnny's school backpack hangs from a hook on the back of his door. I unzip and open it, looking for a laptop or iPad despite knowing we already bagged and removed such devices. I do find a graphing calculator, but that seems harmless enough. It's sandwiched between textbooks and spiral notepads. I thumb through the latter. Pages and pages of neatly handwritten class notes. No convenient letter from a friend daring him to survive a night on the mountain. No suicide note. No anything, really.

He was a nice kid. Every fiber of my being says so. A homebody, sure, but that's not so strange these days.

I walk down the hall toward the bathroom. Hardwood creaks underfoot, giving way to marble tiles that gleam in the midday sun.

On the sink there's a blue plastic cup, faint imprint of Johnny's lower lip still visible. A toothbrush rests beside it. I check the medicine cabinet but there's nothing remarkable. Floss, aftershave, deodorant. All the usual suspects.

For Barbara's sake I look extra closely at everything, then sigh. She wants to hear something that might explain, but the truth is there's no explanation coming. The kid screwed up. Was probably just tired of being cooped up, finally, and wanted some fresh air. We'll never know why he went out that night. Maybe, *maybe,* he drank a shot of Dad's whiskey just to see what it's like. This perhaps clouded his judgment just enough.

Only there'd been no trace of alcohol in his system. No drugs, either. They'd run the tests twice just to be sure.

"Still," I mutter, "can't hurt to double check."

I walk back out into the hall and, on a whim, decide to look through the other rooms. Maybe the kid had a stash in the back of the linen closet. It's thin, but the more time I spend up here, the more Barbara will be reassured I did my best.

A wall of towels and bedsheets greets me. In the back I find a stash . . . of more towels. I close the door and move on to the guest room. Perfectly made bed. Unadorned dresser. Neither looks like they've been used in five years. I poke around a bit but there's nothing here, either.

Master bedroom? I wonder if Barbara will be pleased or insulted if I check there. But she's downstairs and hasn't made a peep so, okay, might as well be thorough.

I think back to Greg's report. He'd gone through this room after the body was found, and then again after the Rogerses returned from Paris. In the report Greg's focus was entirely on the wet bar Buck keeps in the corner. The father had verified all the bottles appeared to be at their proper levels. "So sure?" I'd asked Greg. He told me patiently that Buck had spent six months aboard the International Space Station. "The man knows how to keep track of supplies." Hard to argue that.

I decide to look through it all the same, even if it's a waste of time. No, I remind myself. I'm giving Barbara some peace of mind, and that's no waste. And who knows, some extra effort might pay dividends. Maybe she won't sound so disappointed the next time she calls the station and I answer instead of Greg. A woman can hope.

In the master bedroom I'm struck again by the exactness of it all. The flawlessly made bed, decorative pillow perfectly centered. The dresser with an elegant lamp and a bottle of perfume spaced evenly across its gleaming surface. Barb, Buck, or both run a tight ship here.

Everything's where it should be, clean and tidy.

My mouth twitches at this thought. This happens to me sometimes. On the verge of an important idea it's like my cheek muscle knows before my brain does. I feel the quirk and wait for the thought, but for now it remains out of reach.

I check the master bathroom. It's spotless, too. I pry open the medicine cabinet. The Rogerses are in their early fifties and reasonably healthy. Not much here but ibuprofen and cold remedies. A bottle of prescription medicine called Donepezil, prescribed by Dr. Ryan for Buck. I'm not familiar with it, and quickly google the name on my phone. In reading the results I get that little twitch again. The drug can improve mental function in people with Alzheimer's.

I didn't know Buck had the disease, and can't help but wonder if there perhaps had been some changes here in this household that drove Johnny to go out that night.

As theories go this one is utterly dire, and completely unfounded. I close the cabinet door a little too hard in frustration.

Back downstairs I tell Mrs. Rogers that I didn't uncover anything new.

She takes the news with nothing more than a tightening of the mouth.

I ask, "Did Johnny have a playroom or a man-cave type of space? Somewhere to hang out other than his bedroom?"

"No, nothing like that."

"Okay. Well, I'll tell you what. Now that I've seen your house firsthand, I'll take another look at the file when I get back to the station. Compare the two. Who knows, maybe we missed something."

Her eyes glisten, but still no tears fall. Holding back the grief until I leave, I assume. Such a change from the wailing wreck she'd been a week before. "Thank you for stopping by," she says after a moment.

I think she means it. Hard to tell. All the vibrancy has gone out of Barbara Rogers and I'm starting to wonder if it will ever return.


Halfway back to town my phone rings. It's Kyle. Bartender, co-owner of the Bait & Tackle, Mad Max Jeep driver, and my lover as of three nights ago. "Hey there," I say. "Did they come and collect the body?"

"Yeah, all set there."

"Where are you now?"

"Still up here. Figured I should follow those tracks as far as they'll go and see if I can find anything."

"Want me to join you?"

"Already finished."

"What'd you find?"

"Jack squat," he says. "Found some fur that confirms it was a black bear, which is what I figured. Plenty of them in the area even if sightings are rare. Attacks even more so, but I guess not totally unheard of. Anyway, the tracks cross the stream, then up over the eastern ridge. Rocky terrain. I lost the trail there. That bear's long gone, Mary."

"Good. What the heck was it doing here in the first place?"

"I dunno, global warming? Strange weather screwing with its instincts. Or something."

This is a new one. Leave it to Silvertown to turn climate change into a conspiracy for bear attacks.

"When's the last time an animal like that was even spotted around here?" I can't recall anyone mentioning a bear, but I've only been here a few months. Kyle is born and bred.

"Kenny claims he saw one up at Two-Shits about four years back. It just ran off, though."

"Claims, huh?"

"Yeah, well, this is my brother we're talking about. No tale too tall for that guy. He says he saw Big Foot once—like, *legit* saw Big Foot—so take it with a grain." Kyle shifts the phone around and lowers his voice. "How you holdin' up, babe?"

Wow. Already I'm "babe"? Not sure I'm into that.

"I've had better days," I tell him.

"Want some company later?"

I consider it. My cheeks get warm at the memory of our first night together. Urgency and sweat. His teeth on my earlobe, my fingernails in his back. "Tempting, but what I really need is some sleep. Rain check?"

"Hell yeah. Holding you to that."

"You'd better. See ya."

He hangs up.

As I drive, my thoughts drift back to what he'd said about the climate messing with the bear's behavior. My brain went to Johnny when he'd said that. Why? Something about staying indoors, or hibernation? "Climate," I mutter. "Maybe not so crazy after all, huh, Mary?" I chew on my lip, lost in thought.

The movement in front of me barely registers in time. Someone's stepping off the curb not fifteen feet ahead. I slam on the brakes. Tires shudder. My body heaves forward, the snap of the seat belt locking makes me grunt.

The Dodge lurches, rocks, stops. My heart pounds in my chest. I'm pretty sure I just ran someone over, and it takes a second before I can even look and see.

I raise my eyes to find Geezer standing at the nose of my cruiser, not a foot from the bumper, with a quizzical look on his wizened face. He's got his palms resting on his walking cane and sort of a glare in his eyes. In fact, he's scowling. I've never seen him scowl.

I step halfway out of my car. "Willy? What are you doing?!"

"Eh?" he asks. "Taking a walk. That a crime all the sudden?"

"I . . . Jesus, Willy, I almost killed you. Why'd you step in front of the cruiser like that?"

He glances down at the car as if it's the first time he's ever seen it. He scratches at his ear. "Well, I don't . . . uh . . ." Suddenly the confusion is gone. His scowl returns. "Pedestrians have the right-of-way in this state, Officer. Best remember that!"

Then he *harrumph*s and continues across the street, not bothering to look in either direction.

For a good ten seconds I just stand there, dumbfounded. Adrenaline pounds at my temples, slowly receding as the old man ambles away. Had I just come inches from killing someone? God, how that would go down. Vehicular manslaughter, distracted driving. I feel so tired my eyes itch. What if he'd waved at me, signaled his intent to cross, and I'd just totally missed it?

I need rest and I need it now, before I make an unforgivable mistake.

My fault or not, part of me wonders if Willy has any family here. Someone to take care of him if, or when, his facilities start to fail. That day might come sooner rather than later, if this little incident is any indication.

I make a mental note to ask Greg—damn it, make that Clara— to look into whether Willy has any relatives we can contact who might be able to help. Or at least what kind of care options are available.

Later, though. Right now I need a giant wad of carbohydrates in my belly, preferably in the form of pizza, plus maybe a glass or three of wine, followed by the sweet embrace of a good night's sleep.

"Welcome to Silvertown. What can I getcha?"

"Hmm? Oh. Uhhh . . . nothing. I'm waiting for someone."

"That's cool. No problem. What happened to your nose?"

"I . . . tripped. Um, can I use your phone?"

"Isn't that your cell phone on the bar."

"The battery's dead."

"Screen's on."

"What? Oh. Yeah. I mean the reception. No signal."

"The screen's on because it's ringing, actually."

" . . . "

"Aren't you going to answer it?"

"Hello? Yes. No I can't find— Yes. Understood. Yes, ma'am. Bye."

"Who was that?"

"None of your business. I'll be going."

"What about the person you're waiting for?"

"Huh?"

"You said you were waiting for . . . Hey, I'm talking to you—Okay, bye then, stranger. Thanks for visiting Silvertown. Don't let the door hit you on the way out. F'ing weirdo."

# CHAPTER SIX

When you want pizza in Silvertown there's really only one option: the gas station. When I discovered this I very nearly declined the job, as I practically live off the stuff (it is, to me, the one and only superfood). But, as it turns out, they make a surprisingly good pie.

"A large this time, Kenny," I say. "But you'd better make it cheese in case she's vegetarian."

"She who?"

"Long story. Ask your brother."

"Ah, Kyle's bangin' some new chick? Wait, are you buyin' her pizza because he broke her poor widdle heart?"

I'm about to correct him, but decide neither my sparkling reputation nor Kyle's slightly-less-so needs any additional attention just now. "Nothing like that," I call to him from the row of coolers. "Got a hiker at the station. She had a run-in with a bear this morning."

"No shit? Mauled?"

"No shit. And no, she's okay. It's her boyfriend the bear went after."

"She a vegan?"

I get on my tippy toes and make eye contact with him over bags of Doritos. His face shines red as he leans over heated rollers where shriveled hot dogs tumble infinitely. Kenny's the greasy, wiry version of his brother, Kyle. Today he looks even thinner than usual. Almost sickly. "Bears don't like vegans?" I ask.

"The cheese," he says, nodding at the pie in the big metal oven.

"Oh. Right. Crap. I didn't ask. If she is . . . more for me, I guess."

Kenny clucks his tongue. I may not have a reputation in Silvertown for one-night stands, or even for being a member of the police force, but Kenny knows my metabolism. Since about age ten I could eat just about anything and the weight doesn't stick. Even dressed for duty, armored vest and all, people say I'm too thin, that I could stand to put on a few pounds. I sure as hell do try, honest.

A freakish metabolism is something Kenny and I have in common.

"You know, I saw a black bear up at Two-Shits about four years back," Kenny's saying as he tends to the oven. I mumble my familiarity with this tale, but he goes on. How the beast had made eye contact with him across the placid waters of Lake Forgotten, and then Kenny had reached for his hunting knife, and the bear, clearly impressed by the length of the blade, turned and fled. No metaphor here, no sir.

"Is that where you saw Big Foot, too?"

"Now, now, Officer, I sense a bit of skepticism in your tone."

I grin at him. "It must be difficult."

"What must be?"

"Trying to convince people of a true Sasquatch sighting in a town positively buried in Sasquatch bullshit is like . . . I'm too tired to think of an analogy."

He says, "Well, I know what I saw. And it was up there by Fort Curtis. The old army base."

The base, which closed more than three decades ago, is on the opposite side of the mountain from the silver mine. Between it, the old mine, hundreds of shuttered old houses, and the mess of abandoned Conaty Corp. facilities, Silvertown overflows with tailor-made settings for tall tales.

"Hey," I ask, "speaking of that. Remember that army convoy that came through this morning?"

"Yep. Morons."

"Someone asked them if they were coming up here to tear down Fort Curtis, 'before anyone else gets hurt.' What was that about?"

Kenny makes a farting noise. "Classic Silvertown B.S. Ask Kyle, he loves to spread that rumor."

"Okay. I will. What was the base for, though? I've heard everything from secret super-soldier experiments to a torture black site."

"Shit." He laughs. "Truth is they trained soldiers for wilderness survival. Boring, I know, but the truth usually is."

And this coming from the guy who says he saw Big Foot. I let it slide. Of course, half the town loves and perpetuates such stories. Good for tourism, assuming you think becoming the next Roswell, New Mexico, is a tourism goal worth pursuing. The other half are either retired or would prefer some real jobs make their way back here. Yet another half—yes, three halves, math is not my strong suit when I'm this tired—are just waiting to be old enough to move away, like Johnny Rogers and all his friends no doubt dreamed of doing.

In the end I pass on all the fancy bottles, settling instead on a boxed wine.

As he rings me up, I take a closer look at him. "You okay, dude?" I ask. "You look like you've lost some weight, and no offense, bud, you didn't have any to lose." His lips are so dry and cracked I want to buy him a tube of balm right then and there.

He just shrugs, though. "Allergies," he says simply. "New meds killed my appetite, but at least I can breathe."

I get behind the wheel again, and immediately my mind conjures up the face of Willy Jupitas standing at my front bumper. Hyper-aware now of my lack of focus, I drive the last hundred yards to the police station at a snail's pace, scanning the sidewalks for anyone who might decide to suddenly step in front of my car. Fortunately everyone else is behaving normally.

At the station I find the front desk deserted. Clara comes out of the break room at the sound of the door, though.

"Oh good, just in time," she says.

"Do me a favor," I say over her. "Call down to Granston and find out—"

Clara's grabbing her purse and she gives me an apologetic look. "Sorry, babe, I've got my shift at the diner now."

"Oh, damn it, I forgot. I'll handle it. You go. Shoo."

"Thanks. Hey, are you okay? You look . . . befuddled, I guess."

"Just had a close call with Mr. Jupitas. It shook me up."

"With Geezer? What happened?"

"Don't know, really. He stepped out in front of my car. It was almost suicidal."

"We're talking about the guy who takes ten minutes to cross the street most days?"

"I know, that's exactly what I thought. It was like that hiker." The words are out before I really know what I mean.

"Mary?" Clara asks. "Explain?"

"I didn't think about it before, but now . . . Willy and the hiker. Neither one recognized the danger they were in. Didn't even flinch."

Clara frowns. "I think you might need a night off, Mary. That's one hell of a connection to make."

"I suppose you're right." I shake my head.

"Besides, Geezer is like a hundred years old. Probably just didn't see you."

I nod.

Clara squeezes my shoulder. "Look, I've gotta run. I'm sorry. We'll talk later."

"No worries. How's our patient?" I ask as she's opening the door to leave.

Clara's eyes dart toward the cells in back, and she lowers her voice. "Quiet. Like, *really* quiet."

My understanding nod turns into a yawn. One of those eye-watering, couldn't-stop-if-you-wanted-to kind of yawns.

"You need some rest, Mary," Clara says.

"Don't I know it."

Clara holds up a finger, then fishes around in her purse. She comes up with a prescription pill bottle and tumbles one of the pale blue tablets into her palm before handing it to me. "Take that," she says. "They're supposed to be amazing."

"Supposed to be?"

"Just picked them up yesterday, but I spaced on taking one last night. Anyway, my sister swears by them, so I asked Doc for a scrip."

I pull a face. "Taking someone else's prescription medicine is usually a terrible idea."

"My sis said they'll be OTC soon. Doc confirmed it. Harmless and extremely effective." This last she does in a mockery of Doc's voice.

When I still hesitate, she folds my fingers around the object and says, "Seriously, Mary. You're pushing too hard, with Greg gone and all this other shit. Go get eight hours. The town will still be here."

"I . . . okay, I will. Thanks, Clara."

She waves and heads off to her actual job, grilling burgers and frying up onion rings at the town's lone diner.

The pill I pocket and try to forget about, tempting though it is. Sleep via medication is always a last resort, for me.

I move slowly through the station. Despite Clara's reassurances, I still can't quite shake the idea that there's some connection between the hiker and old Willy. I just can't for the life of me imagine what it is. Halfway to my desk my stomach emits a loud grumble, reminding me of the pizza I'm still carrying.

In the break room I take two red plastic cups from the cabinet and fill them with white wine from a box. One I set beside the pizza, the other I take a healthy gulp from. The golden liquid calms my thoughts, like sunlight poking through thick clouds. Sipping, I wander over to Greg's desk and thumb through Johnny's file again. It's thin. Pictures from the ravine, mostly. But a few of the house. The boy's room. Scribbled notes from interviews with his friends and teachers.

One photo catches my eye. A picture of Johnny's bookshelf, stocked with far more video game cases than books.

At my desk I search online for each game, scanning the images and synopses that pop up. I'm not exactly sure what I'm looking for, and almost give up, but the second-to-last game in the row is apparently some kind of apocalyptic wilderness survival simulator. It occurs to me then that *if* the boy shelved his games in order of when he bought them, that means this title, *Bug Out Bag*, would be a very recent addition. Could it be that playing this game inspired him to give the real thing a try?

I jot a note to research the game further, specifically to see if it was something his friends played, too. It's not much, but if it eases Barb's mind it'll be worth it. The effort feels like genuine detective work, and I'm quite pleased with myself.

Another rumble from my gut tells me enough's enough, though. I grab the pizza box, the wine box, and some paper plates, then head to the one occupied holding cell.

Katherine Pascoe lies on the stiff bunk, hands clasped over her belly. She stirs as I enter, and at the whiff of food she's sitting up just as I'm sitting down. I hand her a cup, then a plate with a slice of pizza. The lack of meat makes it an abomination in my view, but she tucks right in.

"Good," she says between mouthfuls.

"We've got a world-class Italian restaurant here in Silvertown."

"Really? What's it called?"

"Gas-n-Go."

She grins halfheartedly, and for a while we feast in silence. Not because we're stuffing our faces, although the rate at which we demolish the large pizza is damned impressive even by my lofty standards. No, it's more that she's both in shock and the quiet type, and I'm too tired to think of anything to say. For a while, at least.

"You want the last slice?" I ask her.

"No."

"Well, I'll take one for the team, then. Never leave a slice behind. Police policy."

She doesn't laugh, but there's another brief grin. Progress.

I shrug and polish off the remains of the meal. "Listen, Katherine, I don't have a big place, but you're welcome to my couch. Or there's a B&B that I'm sure has a room open—"

"What about here?" she asks.

"This is a jail cell," I point out.

"It feels . . . safe."

"Well . . . sure. Why not? Whatever makes you comfortable."

"Thanks."

Delicately, I broach the subject of her boyfriend. "Can I ask you something about Jeff?"

She gives a little shrug.

"We're just trying to understand what happened," I say. "Why he didn't, you know, run, or play dead."

"I don't know why."

I nod, understanding. "Is there anything . . . what I mean is, did he work with animals or something? At a zoo or—"

For a second my question perplexes her. But after a moment she shakes her head, definitively.

"An animal lover, maybe?"

Another shake, less sure this time.

"Look, Katherine, we're a team here, okay? You can talk to me."

A lift of her shoulders. Then she swallows, hard, and focuses intently on the floor of the cell. "The first time he came to pick me up, he freaked out at my roommate's dog."

"So he loves dogs?"

"Freaked out in a bad way."

"Ah." I picture the scene. "Is it a big dog?"

"A pit bull mix, but before you get the wrong idea, she is the sweetest dog ever."

"Did she growl at him or something? Maybe he's got something about him, a scent or whatever, that the dog—and the bear—"

She shakes her head. "She never had a chance to even sniff him. Jeff got one look and boom, he was waiting in the car outside."

"Jeez. He say why?

A shrug. "Told me later he hates animals. A phobia or something."

"Still, you went hiking."

"Didn't think we'd see a bear."

So much for Doc's zookeeper theory.

"Okay," I say. "Get some rest, we'll talk more tomorrow, okay? We'll figure this out."

Ten minutes later she's asleep.

With food and Ms. Pascoe taken care of, I move back to my desk and just sit for a while, listening to the sounds of the station and trying to recapture my earlier revelation. That idea that Willy showed the same lack of fear that our deceased hiker displayed. I try to regain that mindset, to force myself to agree with it. As is often the case, though, the combination of time and white wine has given me a chance to reconsider. It seems too much of a stretch, now.

I leave the cruiser's keys hung on their hook inside the station and pull my jacket on, determined as always to walk home and, in the process, acclimate.

Country music spills from O'Doherty's across the street, mingled with the voice of someone singing along on the karaoke machine. Other patrons erupt in laughter at a particularly cringe-worthy note.

Without thinking I take a step in that direction, every fiber of my being drawn to the prospect of company and conversation. I'm imagining it as I step off the curb and onto the street. How I'll dispel any rumors about the hiker, showing I'm on top of the situation. I'll flirt with Kyle a bit, too, maybe let one thing lead to another . . .

I stop. Not tonight, I'm forced to remind myself. I've got a date with the inside of my eyelids tonight, and it's a date I need to keep. With an effort I turn back to the sidewalk and put one foot in front of the other. Repeat, and repeat again. It's only when I'm half a block away that the siren call of the tavern starts to drift from my thoughts.

The few storefronts that have actual tenants are all dark, even though it's only 8:00 p.m. Most have been closed since five. There's the flower shop, Petal to the Metal, which experienced quite the burst of sales for the Johnny Rogers funeral. What a strange business that must be, I think. A few doors down is the quaint bookstore, Tales Well Told. The owner, an appropriately bookish man named David

Acaster, sits hunched at his desk near the window of the cramped space, illuminated by a single lamp. Before him is one of those magnifying glasses mounted on an articulated arm, and he's very intently focused on a tiny object held in one hand as he dabs paint on it with a brush held in the other. The magnifying glass makes one of his eyes look six inches around. I wave at him, but he doesn't see me.

I round the corner and come upon the diner, which as far as I know is actually named Diner. Greg calls it The Greasy Spork, more to annoy its owner than anything else. It's a great spot—1950s chic, with stainless-steel outer walls and those porthole-style windows. Inside, the booths are clad in red leather and there's a jukebox at one end filled with classic records of the era. None of it is in what you'd consider pristine condition, but compared to most places here it's damn well kept.

A few people are inside eating. Viewed in profile from out here on the sidewalk, their presence gives the place a wholesome vibe that is straight out of a Norman Rockwell painting. Walking by, my nostrils fill with the wonderful odor of Clara's freshly fried onion rings, the house specialty, and even my pizza-filled stomach emits a yearning grumble at the prospect.

Clara's just visible through the narrow opening between the counter seating and the kitchen. She waves at me as I stroll past. I wave back, grateful for her help today. Kyle's help, too. Even Doc's. At least I've won three of them over, and soon maybe Barbara Rogers can go on that list. Just six hundred-ish to go.

"Six-hundred-ish. Right," I say to myself, picking up my walking pace. I know exactly how many people live here, because when I moved into my cottage I heard the number a dozen times or more: I was resident number 666. Some thought that amusing, but some gave me dark, superstitious glares. It didn't exactly help ease my arrival. But now, with Johnny's passing, we're back to 665. No one's mentioned that yet, at least not to my face, but I'm willing to bet it's a topic of conversation.

Past the diner the storefronts are all dark. Not as in closed. These are entirely vacant. Dark alleys run between some, but they're not like the alleys Oakland had. Those were home to the homeless, or to the hoods dealing drugs. These are simply dark, yet somehow just as menacing. I get the feeling some haven't been explored in years, except maybe by raccoons.

Abruptly the row of buildings ends and so does the sidewalk. I trudge through fallen leaves, no sound but my soft footsteps and a mild breeze that whispers through the branches. As the sun finally sets on Silvertown, my thoughts are all over the place.

Some part of my brain keeps lingering on what Kyle said, about climate change messing with the bear's instincts. I wonder now if there is actually a connection between what happened out there and what happened to Johnny Rogers. Perhaps he'd seen the same bear, only instead of standing still he'd run and, in the process, tripped and fell into the ravine?

I get that twitching of my mouth again. This time I try to focus on it. There's something to this, I just can't see what.

The dead hiker. His girlfriend, asleep in a cell.

Johnny Rogers, and his poor mother.

Something about their grief that is, I don't know, wrong, somehow? I shake my head at that. *Wrong path, Mary.*

What, then?

A hiker who is terrified of animals fails to run from a bear.

And Johnny, the screen-addicted boy who never left his room, suddenly decides to go hiking? If nothing else, they were both acting out of character, at least according to their loved ones. But that doesn't mean there's any connection.

Still, I can't shake the thought. Something about this is off. "It's Silvertown, Mary," I can hear Greg telling me. "There's always something off."

"What a day," I mutter to the pavement. And just think, only seven more to go before Greg returns.

Far ahead, just before a bend in the road, a pack of coyotes emerges from the trees.

I stop dead, instantly on alert, watching.

As a kid growing up in San Luis Obispo, years before we moved to Oakland, my nights were often shattered by the sudden wild braying of coyotes. Around age eight my father explained to me that they weren't laughing, as I'd thought, but celebrating a kill. That every time I heard that noise, I was actually hearing the result of one of our neighbors' cats or dogs being torn to shreds.

My dad's a bit of an asshole, but that's another story.

It's been years since I've heard, or even thought, about coyotes. I had no idea they were even up here.

One by one they cross the dark asphalt, eyes glowing as each looks at me in turn. I wait there at the side of the road, hand on my pistol, until they're long vanished into the undergrowth.

Not five minutes after entering my house I find myself staring at the bathroom mirror, glass of water in one hand and the sleeping pill Clara gave me in the other. On any other night I wouldn't give a sleep aid like this a second thought. But tonight? After the day I had? I think maybe it's a good idea. Otherwise I'm likely to lie in bed, staring at the ceiling as my wired brain tries to process every-thing going on. I'll get my second wind, and be up half the night like that.

"Screw it." I pop the pill, wash it down, and climb in bed.

The med really works. Knocks me straight out.

So much so that it feels as if a scant second has passed when I'm yanked fully awake, several hours later, by what I immediately take to be an earthquake.

A deep rumbling pulses through the walls of the cottage. The back door rattles on its hinges. Adrenaline floods my body, starting a war with the sleep aid that neither side quite wins. Before I know it I'm on the floor beside my bed, on hands and knees, panting from fright and only half conscious.

The shaking ends abruptly. Everything goes quiet.

"What the hell was that?" I mumble, and stagger to the bedroom door. I stop under the jamb, trying to remember if that's safe in an earthquake or not. My head clears a little. The clock says 1:39 a.m.

I run a hand over my face, willing my nerves to settle. I'd been dreaming of a bear, a big black one, strolling toward me down Main Street, and all the townspeople just standing there welcoming it with open arms—

Mumbling from outside. Hard to make out, except the last part, because it's my own name: "Mary Whittaker."

"Kyle? That you?" I call out. Only, that voice didn't sound like Kyle's. Or did it? "Kyle?"

I hear steps heading around back.

Which finally triggers a coherent thought. The back door had rattled. It doesn't rattle when it's bolted, which means I forgot. I curse my fatigue and stumble along the dark hallway toward the back of the little house. You always hear about those small towns where nobody locks their doors. Well, this place isn't like that. Silvertown has its share of quaint, neighborly people, but with so many folks passing through, we do have a bit of a problem with break-ins.

Having heard my name out there, though, it's not theft I'm worried about. Last thing I need tonight is a drunk Kyle pawing at me while I'm half asleep. I might make unwise decisions.

I reach for the handle. "Not tonight, dude. Go home. I'm—"

The door bursts open. It cracks into my hand, sending bright pain up my arm. I stumble back.

A dark figure looms on the top step. Black boots, designer jeans, leather jacket, and gray hair.

Kyle doesn't have gray hair.

I recognize this man a second later. The biker from mile marker thirteen. The one sitting in the middle of the road who started my day yesterday. It was the thunderous exhaust of his Harley shaking the house, not an earthquake.

White gauze stained with blood is taped across his nose. Had his nose been broken this morning? I can't recall. I don't think so, but my brain's full of fog.

His eyes are cold and narrowed.

I shake pain from my right hand. "Can I help you?"

"Mary Whittaker," he says, his pleading, apologetic voice totally at odds with his murderous glare. He takes a step forward. "I'm so sorry! I can't stop."

The words are just this side of insane, but before I can challenge him something slips from his sleeve into his hand. A bottle of some sort. In his other hand he holds a rag. He sprays something onto it. Two pumps of mist. Vinegar smell hits me, eye-wateringly strong.

His eyes hold mine as he wraps the damp rag around his fist.

"I'm sorry," he repeats meekly. "I wish I could stop."

"So stop, then. Right there."

"I can't." He steps toward me.

"You picked the wrong house, asshole." This doesn't come out as tough as I'd hoped, and the pill I took has left me sounding like I've just downed half a bottle of tequila.

He crosses the threshold, technically first-degree trespassing now, leveling a glare on me that has me stepping back despite myself. It's the disparity between what he's saying and what he's doing that terrifies me the most. My heart's racing, but my limbs are heavy as lead.

He snarls, winding up. His wrapped fist sings through the air between us. I'm rooted in place, body ignoring brain.

The fist hits string and glass, tangling in the shitty old chandelier hanging over my breakfast table. His strength tears the whole mess of 1970s kitsch right out of my ceiling. Plaster rains down. Glass beads shower the floor. His hand is snared, only for a second.

One damned second, but it's enough.

Something finally clicks in my head. I turn and run.

Boots stomp loud behind me.

I take a sharp left into my bedroom. No time to close the door, he's right on my heels. Two steps in I dive headlong across my bed, misjudging distance, smashing into my nightstand, sending the table lamp flying into the wall. The drawer handle digs into my scalp, warm blood flowing. I roll just as the insane biker crashes on top of me. He grasps my face with his rag-wrapped hand, covering my mouth and nose. Strong medicine stench. I fight to hold my breath. The bastard's heavy. Spittle sprays from his mouth as he tries to smother me with that cloth. My fingers fumble and find something cold and hard. The neck of the table lamp. I smash it into the side of his face. The biker grunts and balls his free hand into a fist. Before he can throw the punch I hit him again, this time square on his broken nose. Half the bandage covering it is torn free.

He howls in pain like an animal. Sneezes. Blood sprays into my eyes.

I knee him, aiming for the groin but missing. Still it shifts his weight, and I roll from under him.

I can barely see. Blood stings my eyes and I'm not sure whose it is. The room is almost pitch-black. I scramble to my feet and run with arms outstretched, feeling my way to the bedroom door.

There. I grab the handle.

And slam it closed, sealing us both inside.

Hanging from a peg on the back of the door is my gun belt. My sweaty fingers, still stinging from the door he kicked against them, fumble at the Beretta's handle.

Footsteps behind me. He's on his feet again and coming. Boots on hardwood, relentless as a zombie.

Stomp.

"I . . ."

Stomp.

"CAN'T . . ."

Stomp.

"STOP . . ."

"Go to hell," I say.

The pistol barks. Its muzzle flash illuminates his wild bloodshot eyes and the neat, round, red hole that's appeared in the middle of his forehead.

As blood and brain slap wetly across the window behind him, the fucker crumples to my bedroom floor.

# CHAPTER SEVEN

I'm rooted in place. Standing there, the literal smoking gun in my hand, too wound up and confused to do anything.

My knees give out. The room swims as I sort of half fall, half sit. I try and fail to make any kind of sense out of what just happened. Why this guy came here at all, much less to try to . . . to try to what? Kill me? Kidnap me? I figure that cloth, still wrapped around his hand, is soaked with chloroform, and wonder how I can test for that. I don't know the first thing about chemical analysis.

And what the hell was he saying? Why couldn't he stop attacking me in my own home?

I run through our encounter on the south grade road early yesterday, but the conversation is hard to recall exactly. Not a lot had been said, I remember that much. He seemed okay, upset about his stupid Harley more than anything. And then by the time Doc had arrived to check on him, he'd left. What had I done to warrant this?

I'm speculating. Shouldn't do that. Facts are what's important.

Blood and brain are dripping down my wall.

My own head is pounding, no doubt a result of the strange cocktail of sleeping aid and massive adrenaline come-down.

"Shit," I mutter as the ramifications of all this start to manifest into three words that every cop dreads: "officer involved shooting."

I just killed an intruder. Entirely justified, but I've got some prescription sleeping drug in me that I don't have a prescription for, not to mention a bit of white wine still sloshing around in there, and on top of it all I'd had a run-in with this son of a bitch yesterday. It's not going to look good. It's going to bring questions, or at least rumors. Folks might wonder if this prick and I hadn't hit it off, that maybe I'd given him my address and told him to come up and see me sometime. Rumors like that are absolutely the last thing I want.

A sound breaks my train of thought. More footsteps outside.

The gun is still in my hand, and I tighten my grip on it, ears perked.

"Hello?" someone calls out from the driveway. An elderly woman. One of my neighbors, I think, but which one exactly I'm not sure. "You okay in there? I heard . . . I thought I heard a gunshot."

"I'm okay," I say back, raising my voice to be heard. "There was an intruder."

"Should I call the police?"

"I am the police."

A pause. "Well, yes, I know, but . . ."

"Everything's under control," I say. It sounds highly unconvincing to my own ears.

Must not have convinced her, either, because seconds later I hear the woman mumbling into her phone. Hard to catch it, but the words "break-in" and "shooting" are clear enough. I wonder who she's talking to. I'm the police, and my phone didn't ring.

A 911 operator, then. Those calls go to the state patrol and are routed from there. Someone will be calling me shortly, I expect. After they call the station. And after they call Greg, no doubt first on their backup list. They'll get to me eventually, though.

The room's getting a bit blurry as I wait for the phone to ring.
Sound fading.
Eyes heavy.

I'm awoken by a pounding at my door and a heavy fog throughout
my mind.

The room swims into focus. Dead man on the floor, streaks of
gore on the wall behind him. The beginnings of a terrible odor.

Pushing myself up to one elbow, I mumble something about
needing a minute. It's a minute too much.

The front door is kicked in.

Loud footsteps echo in my front room. Half of me wonders
where my pistol ended up, the other half is trying to remember
where the clock is. All I'm able to manage is sitting up and wiping
some drool from my chin before an older man in uniform fills the
doorway to my bedroom.

My first thought is Greg, but the uniform's the wrong color. The
badge the wrong shape. This is someone else.

He's got a revolver pointed at me, but lowers it when he sees my
face.

"Mary Whittaker?" he asks.

"Yessir," I say like a fresh cadet.

"Sheriff James Davies, Granston County. Drove up when no one
here responded to a 911 call. Are you injured?"

I start to say no. Then I think better of it and rub the back of
my head. I'd rather he think I fell than that I was in a drug-induced
stupor.

Sheriff Davies is the textbook example of a cop. Mustached,
white as white bread, probably wears aviator sunglasses when on patrol. From his midsection I'm guessing doughnuts are also involved
in the equation.

He crosses the room, taking care not to touch or disturb anything until he reaches the body. He checks for a pulse, but it's a

perfunctory effort. Death is not up for debate here. Davies stands, studies the splatter on the wall, then glances at me. "Anyone else in the house, Officer?"

"Not that I'm aware of," I say. "I mean, he came alone. Pretty sure anyway."

"Any idea who he is?"

I quickly explain about my encounter with him on the road the day before, and that he broke in, mumbling apologies even as he attacked me.

"And you fired in self-defense?"

"I did."

He glances around, nodding all the while. "I'll back you up on that. Apologizing for what?"

"Excuse me?"

He helps me to my feet, then to a chair in the corner. "You said he apologized."

"Oh," I say. "Honestly, Sheriff, I have no idea. It was like he was sorry for attacking me. He was stoned or something. Acting really weird."

It's 3:21 a.m., I note, finally able to focus on the clock. In my experience there are few headaches worse than the one you get when chemically aided sleep is interrupted, never mind twice in the same night. Today is going to be a nightmare.

"Sure you're not hurt?" Sheriff Davies asks. "You don't look so good."

"I have a first aid kit in the bathroom."

He eyes me. "No offense, but you need a professional. There are two EMTs outside, they can look at you."

"Really, I'm fine."

The skeptical look remains, but he nods and turns back to the room. With his phone he snaps pictures of the body, the wall, and the smashed table lamp. Then he takes a pair of blue gloves from his belt, and an evidence bag from one pocket, in which he carefully places the rag my attacker had wrapped around his hand.

Finally, he leaves the room. By his footsteps I can picture him searching the rest of the house, which doesn't take long. Most of this time is spent in the kitchen, examining the back door and the busted chandelier. More photos are snapped.

His path takes him back to the front door. I hear him exchange words with someone, and fear he's making an announcement to my neighbors about what happened. But a few seconds later he returns, a couple of paramedics on his heels. They followed him up from Granston, evidently.

The male of the pair helps Sheriff Davies load the body onto a gurney, while the woman comes over to examine me. I don't have the energy to tell her not to bother. We say nothing to each other as she shines a light in each of my eyes, then feels my scalp. If the lack of a bruise or lump is a concern, she doesn't mention it. Maybe Davies told her about the chloroform, and the working assumption is I got a few lungfuls during the skirmish, hence the state I was in when they arrived. Satisfied I'm in no immediate danger, she shifts focus to helping the other two.

Ten minutes later the paramedics are gone. Davies and I sit in my front room, sipping tea, which he made.

"I know Gorman's on vay-cay," the man says. "He and I go way back. I helped him with that Conaty thing some years ago."

"I'll let him know you were here," I say, wishing he'd leave.

"It's not that, though please do tell him hello for me. What I wanted to say is, if you need me to cover for you today, or hang around and help out—"

"No," I reply, without even really considering it. "I'll be okay. Nothing much happens up here and this . . . this is just paperwork now." He seems about to protest. "Really, it's no big deal. Thank you so much for coming up."

"I suppose I should be getting back," he says reluctantly. Then he waves vaguely toward the rear of the house. "And don't bother with the paperwork. I'll file the report on this, Mary. Procedures, you know. Can't be you who files it, considering the location and the vic . . . the, err . . ."

"I understand."

"There might be an inquiry, but I doubt it. Depends on if your trespasser had a spouse or a lawyer, I guess. Anyway you should know in a few days, and certainly no judge will want to see you before Greg gets back, if at all. Uh, you sure I can't help you clean up the . . . you know."

"Really, it's fine. I'm not . . . this isn't my first rodeo."

This gets a grunt of respect from the older man. "You were SFPD, is that right?"

"Oakland."

"Oakland, yeah. A tough beat I'm sure." He waits, but when I say nothing he softens his tone and says, "My offer stands, Mary. Call me if you need anything."

Palms on knees, the sheriff pushes himself to a weary stand. He nods at me with, I think, a profound understanding of what I've been through, and heads out the door.

The house is finally quiet again.

Three cups of coffee and two toaster waffles later, I break out the cleaning supplies and set to work bleaching the ever-living shit out of my bedroom wall and window. Whereas the photos of Johnny Rogers and the sight of the mauled hiker had bothered me, this mess has no effect. Maybe it's because the crud came from a complete bastard who tried to kill me, or maybe it's because I am beyond tired and completely strung out.

By the time sunlight makes its way into my room, the job is reasonably complete. The back door is still an issue, but I can live with leaving it dead-bolted for now. I shower and put on my uniform, ready for whatever the day feels like throwing at me.

It can't be worse than yesterday.

"Hey friends. Welcome. What can I getcha?"

"Moscow Mules all around, barkeep! Hey man, we heard, like, is it true there's an old army base up here? We heard they found a kid's body there back in the 1980s. Like, murdered, and that's why it was shut down. Is that true?"

"Not . . . exactly."

"Meaning what? C'mon man, you can tell us."

"Look, the four of you gotta keep this to yourselves, okay? Folks around here would prefer that city slickers just stop in for Big Foot stickers and crystal healing shit and then fuck off back down the mountain. They want to keep the truth buried, just like that kid."

"So there was a body found! Holy shit."

"Not . . . exactly."

" . . . meaning?"

"Here's your Mules."

"Oh, damn, okay. C'mon. You can't say 'not exactly' like that and not tell us more, man."

"Four Moscow Mules comes to . . . lessee, twenty-five times . . . carry the one . . . that's a hundred bucks."

"What? One hundred dollars for four . . . Oohhh-kay, I get it. Fine. Here . . . Sara, do you have . . . ? What about you, Rick? It's cool, I'll cover you man, but you owe me. All right, here's the hundred."

"Thanks."

"Well? C'mon. You said not exactly. What'd you mean?"

"What I meant was they closed the base because they didn't find a body."

"What?"

"As in, a kid went in and never came back out. And this town wants to keep the story buried because . . . the truth is, no one knows who the kid was. No one was reported missing. But the cameras don't lie, know what I mean?"

"Ohhhh hooooo ho, damn, holy shit, serious? It's on camera?"

"Just the gate camera. Security. A buddy of mine showed it to me. He was military police, and right after that happened he got shipped off to Japan. Anyway, you see a kid walk in, right past the guards . . . like they can't see him. And the kid never comes back out."

"Fuck me . . . that's crazy."

"Look guys, that's all I can say. If you'll excuse me? Got other customers. Enjoy the drinks, and . . . hey, keep all that to yourselves, cool? Right on . . . How you doing over here, Suz?"

"Good, thanks. Um, Kyle, a word in private? I thought they closed that base because of budget cuts?"

"They sure did, yeah."

"So what's with the tall tale? That's not like you."

"I don't know. Started doing that a few years ago. I was in a bad mood and spun some bullshit about a disappearance to some nutter, and the next summer this couple wanders in and asks about it, so I added to the tale. Next summer after that I threw in the army base for fun, and so on. This is the third group that's asked about it this year. Kinda cool, right? How legends are born. I figure in a decade there'll be a line out the door, maybe even a Netflix movie."

"And the hundred dollars?"

"Call it a gullibility tax."

# CHAPTER EIGHT

As I step out the front door that morning I find myself wishing I'd taken Greg's advice and parked the cruiser at home. A police car prominently displayed in my driveway might have convinced my attacker to abandon his insane plan. Assuming he had a plan at all. But more than that, I also wouldn't be faced with the long walk to the station now. My throat is slightly bruised, as is my neck and shoulder. My head hurts from a combination of alcohol, that sleeping pill, and some good old-fashioned blunt force trauma.

The walk does wonders, though. It's a calm morning, not a cloud in the sky, and by the halfway point I'm almost enjoying myself. Fresh fallen leaves crunch under my boots. Birds are chattering high in the branches above. It occurs to me that for the first time in perhaps forty-eight hours nothing weird is happening. No coyotes crossing my path. No owls flying over in perfectly straight lines.

No one trying to kill me. That's always a plus.

The plan had been to get straight to the office and the business of police work. The plan upon reaching the edge of town, though, is more food. I stop in at Diner for a second breakfast. "Turkey and avocado scramble. Hash browns extra crispy. Coffee. Water," I tell the waitress, a robust and sour woman called Ashley Gilbert.

"Well, good morning to you, too." She pulls back the menu she'd been about to hand me. She eyes me, and then seems to notice my injuries. The question is on her lips but the glare I give her seems answer enough for now. With a shrug she walks away, trading barbs with a couple of elderly men seated along the milk shake bar with newspapers spread out before them.

I've picked a corner booth, the one that lets me look out on downtown's only intersection, with a view all the way up to the station. Greg and I sit here often, because he feels the view alone means we're basically on patrol.

So I watch the town come to life while I sip my coffee. I do this not in hopes of spotting something out of the ordinary, or catching sight of some event that requires my attention. It's the opposite, actually. For some reason I just want to bask in the normalcy of it all. From this spot, with the sun just starting to rise above Two-Shits and bathe the eastern-facing walls of the town in golden light, Silvertown does indeed feel normal. Quirky, sure, but in a charming way. In that way a small town is supposed to be quirky. As opposed to the introverted-kid-who-went-hiking-alone quirky. Or the dude-who-sits-in-the-road-after-crashing-his-Harley-and-then-tries-to-kill-me quirky. Or the . . . *fuck, let it go, Mary.* I really need to sweep all that crap aside and treat this for what it is: a new day.

The meal arrives and I wolf it down, lost in thought as I shovel hash browns into my bottomless pit of a stomach.

It's only when I'm back out on the sidewalk that I realize I didn't speak to anyone inside, other than when I'd ordered my food. Not the two old men reading their newspapers, or the four teens giggling as they played with a Ouija board, or the woman in the corner with the hoodie. She'd held a napkin in front of her nose the entire time I was there, waiting for a sneeze that never arrived.

None of them looked at me. In hindsight, maybe they were deliberately not looking at me. By now the whole town probably knows that something went down at my house last night. Not all the details, of course, but enough to get the rumor mill running at full capacity. The diner would have been a great opportunity to put on a brave face, assuage fears, and generally let people know I'm handling the situation. If only I'd thought of this when I was in there. Instead I just sat and stared out the window in uncharacteristic silence. This'll likely put the rumor mill into overdrive. "She was in shock," they'll say. "It was like she was hoping Greg would come driving down the street and set things right." Something like that. I suppose there's nothing to do about it now.

Hell, I didn't even glance in the kitchen to see if Clara was working. She'll be pissed if I didn't say hi. But turning around, walking back in, and switching on the old Mary charm would just make me look even more out of sorts.

I resolve to do better. I'm going to be upbeat today and make my mark on this town.

By the time I reach the next shop I force myself to feel as if I've left not just the diner, but what happened last night, behind me. *You are Silvertown's only cop*, I tell myself. *Compartmentalize, stow it, and get back to business, Mary.*

Sally Jones walks past me, her cute bob of red hair radiant in the morning sunlight. She's a part-time Realtor and a full-time mom. It's weird to see her without her babies, though. She has twin girls, still in diapers. I smile every time I see her with that double stroller she's always pushing around. I don't care who you are, you can't not stop and coo over those adorable little munchkins. Today, though, she's walking beside a man I've never seen. A tourist from the look of him.

"Morning," I say, tipping my hat like John friggin' Wayne.

"Good morning, uh, Officer," she replies.

Doesn't she know my name? I've met her like ten times. Whatever. I refuse to let it bother me. I march on, entering the station at 8:00 a.m. on the nose.

The place is dark and whisper quiet.

"Ms. Pascoe?" I call out. No response. Leaving my coat on its hook, I weave my way through the small office toward the cells. The door to hers stands open, and no one's inside. "Katherine?" I try,

louder this time. There's a rustling sound from the rear of the building. Only storage rooms back there, and the old drunk tank from the
days when Silvertown had nearly six times its current population.

Feeling the hair rise on the back of my neck, I make my way
toward the sound. There are three storage rooms, doors all closed.
Beyond them is the drunk tank, its door propped open by a little
rubber wedge as the space needs perpetual airing out.

Another rustling sound, definitely coming from in there.

The grimy little cave hasn't been used in . . . well, I have no idea
actually. Certainly not since I moved to town. The room is like a
communal shower. Yellowing tiles separated by grout gone black
with mildew. I round the corner with my pistol drawn, not quite
remembering when I unholstered it.

When I see her I immediately put the gun away.

She sits in the corner of the small room, wet hair dangling in
front of her face. Her eyes are closed, her body dripping wet. Stark
naked. Clasped in her hands is her phone, from which dangles the
white cord of a pair of earbud-style headphones.

"Katherine?" I say it twice, quite loud the second time, and her
head finally snaps up.

She covers her breasts with one hand, embarrassed and startled all
at once. With her other hand she yanks the headphones from her ears,
dropping the phone in the process. It clatters loudly on the tile floor.

"You okay?" I ask. I don't avert my eyes, instead I'm looking her
up and down for signs of trauma.

"Wanted to take a shower," she says, defensive and shivering.

I glance around. There's an old bar of soap beside her, but other
than that and a bucket in the far corner that reeks of bleach, the
room is empty. Her skin is dotted with droplets of water.

"Then why are you—"

She grimaces. "No towels."

"Honey, this isn't a shower, it's a . . . never mind. Wait here."

A quick march to the front of the building and I reach the bathroom, within which there's an actual shower with soap and towels.
I grab two of the latter and return to her, deciding for now to hold

back the information that there's a real shower in the front of the building. She accepts my gift gratefully, and I turn away while she wraps one around herself and begins to towel dry her hair.

"Do you have a change of clothes?" I ask.

"In the car," she admits.

Kyle was kind enough to tow the vehicle here so it wouldn't have to sit at that old dirt parking lot overnight. Within ten minutes my guest is dressed in clean clothes and gratefully drinking a cup of Mr. Coffee. From the car she also grabbed a box of granola bars, one of which she tears open eagerly. It's only then I realize I should have brought her breakfast from the diner. Too late now, I guess.

For the time being I leave her to her meal. Sometime this morning I'm going to have to figure out how to get her home.

On the middle of my desk is a sheet of paper. A Post-it Note is attached with the words "the deets you asked for—good luck" and Clara's signature. On the paper itself is contact information for the deceased hiker's parents. I scan it quickly, hoping they'll be the answer to my Katherine Pascoe dilemma, but unfortunately the couple lives in Salt Lake City. I decide to hold off for an hour before I call them with the news.

It's Saturday, and that means a stream of folks will be driving up from the city to see Lake Forgotten and buy some Big Foot trinkets. Freshly fallen leaves still blanket the twisty mountain road, but with any luck the cones I placed at that first hard corner will engender some caution. I don't think I can deal with another accidental off-roader on Slippery Slope, especially since the last one tried to kill me.

The one plus about that bastard assaulting me in my own home is that Sheriff Davies is the one who'll have to write the report. I'm the victim (a word I detest, but in police parlance it's the appropriate one) in this case. Still, I expect he'll want a detailed account from me, so I begin the process of typing something up.

I'm about halfway through this when I hear the front door open and shut.

"Back here," I say. "Is this an emergency?"

There's no reply. I glance up from my screen but can only see the back half of the reception area from here. No one responds to my query. With a bit of irritation I walk over, only to find the station entirely empty. Outside the window, Katherine Pascoe is walking away down the street, backpack over her shoulder.

I step out onto the sidewalk but she's already too far away for a polite shout to get her attention. Back inside, I check the cell she'd slept in. She's made the bed and taken all her personal belongings with her. Even the towel I gave her has been neatly folded and placed atop her one blanket.

"Not even a note, huh?" Maybe she's more embarrassed than I thought at my seeing her naked. Perhaps she's super religious or something.

*Shit.* Only then do I realize that I gave her my cell number but never got hers. *Stupid stupid.*

I'm back out the door at a jog, elbowing past a couple walking their dog. The little terrier yaps at my heels, its owners grumbling at my rough passing before realizing who I am. Then they step well aside, thinking better of voicing ire at a police officer in a hurry.

At the corner I stop. Katherine is nowhere to be seen. The Gas-n-Go is diagonally across the street from me, and I wonder if maybe she went there. Buying a toothbrush, perhaps. But she wouldn't have packed up all her stuff and made the bed were that the case, would she?

Movement on the left catches my eye. The little used bookstore, Tales Well Told, has just opened. Through its window I spot her browsing a shelf.

The bell above the door jingles as I enter, and the owner, David Acaster, gives me a tired nod from behind the register. David is seated at a small desk, reading, with an old orange cat curled up in his lap. Steam curls from a chipped mug at his elbow. The cat obscures most of what is undoubtedly a Grateful Dead T-shirt, judging by the tie-die and dancing bear. He's cleaner cut these days, and pretty snowy up top, but if you told me David was at Woodstock back in the day, I'd believe it in a heartbeat.

"Something wrong, Officer Whittaker?" he asks, one white eyebrow arched.

"Morning, David," I say, pleased he at least remembers me. I caught a shoplifter here during my first week on duty. "No, nothing wrong, just need a word with . . ." I crane my neck and spot Katherine in the rear of the shop. I nod toward her, and Mr. Acaster inclines his head that way, giving me permission, not that I need it.

"Katherine?" I say when I'm right behind her.

She turns and looks at me quizzically.

"Um," I say, at a loss for words suddenly, "I just . . . I was wondering where you'd gone. Are you leaving?" I nod toward her backpack.

"Oh. Oh, sorry. Yeah."

I wait, but as is her style, no details are offered. I say, "It would be good if I had your contact information before you leave town. In case I have any further questions, I mean."

She shakes her head, admonishing herself. "Sure. I don't know what I was thinking." Almost at random she plucks a beaten-up old book from a shelf labeled MYSTICAL/OCCULT. I wait as she pays for it and then say goodbye to David and his cat.

We walk side by side back to the station. Once there Katherine fills out a contact form for me. That done, she smiles at me and turns to leave.

"Do you—" I start, not quite sure what to make of her behavior. I swallow and try again. "How are you getting back?"

"My sister," she says.

"Oh. Okay, good. I just . . . I didn't know. You could have said."

She looks at me, brow furrowed, as if this concept of telling someone about something has never crossed her mind before. For a few seconds her gaze grows distant, and then she snaps out of it. "I guess I should have. Sorry. I don't know why . . ." and her voice trails off again.

A sober silence fills the room for a few seconds. Then Katherine Pascoe tightens her mouth apologetically, turns, and leaves. No thank you, no farewell. Just Katherine's still-damp locks disappearing out the station doorway.

"All the best freaks are here," I recite, suddenly reminded of the song playing in O'Doherty's the other night. With a shrug, I get back to work.

Despite my determination to have a good day, the phone call with the dead hiker's parents ends the plan before it can really even get started.

Mr. and Mrs. Hall hear the sad news about their son, Jeff, via speakerphone in their living room. Their grief is dreadful but short-lived, as Mr. Hall quickly turns to anger and finger-pointing, demanding answers. Who was he with? Are there signs clearly posted warning visitors of the dangers of bears? Why the *F* not?

It goes on and on. I manage to remain patient and levelheaded throughout, but only just. We leave things on what I can only describe as a suspicious note. They're going to fly out, they're going to want to talk to everyone from me all the way up to the governor, they might even bring a private investigator if we don't have some *f'ing* answers by then.

People grieve in different ways, I remind myself, taking solace only in the fact that it will probably be at least tomorrow, if not Monday, before the couple arrives. I hope by then they'll be over the initial shock and a little more reasonable.

I lean back in my creaky old wooden chair and take stock. It's hit me, quite suddenly, that I'm in too good of a mood. Last night someone tried to kill me, and yet just minutes ago I was strolling down Main Street all sunshine and rainbows. It's easy enough to pin this on shock, or stress, or the very unwise popping of a prescription pill. Perhaps even a combination of all three.

But I also think, deep down, that I'm in a good mood because I'd got the better of that asshole. I'd killed a man who was trying to do the same to me, perhaps with even more evil intentions to play out before that. I'd defended myself, I'd been brave, just as I'd always hoped I'd be.

In other words, I feel like a grade A badass. A little spring in my step could be allowed, couldn't it?

Now that I think about it, the answer is no, as the phone call with the hiker's parents has proved. Two deaths in as many days in this quiet mountain town, both on my watch, is going to raise eyebrows. I've got my work cut out for me.

The door to the station jingles open and Kyle steps in, dressed for his shift at the Bait & Tackle rather than his bartender look, not that the two are much different. He looks harried, alarmed, but the expression turns to relief when he sees me.

"Jesus, Mary, I just heard. You okay?"

"Heard what?"

"About what happened last night. The . . . the guy in your house. Holy shit."

"Oh yeah, that. I'm fine, really."

He's staring at me like I've just stepped off an alien spacecraft. "You're not fine. You're in shock. I'll get Doc over here."

"No." The word's a little harsher than I intend, and the tone seems to only add to Kyle's concern. I try again. "I am fine. Really. Just . . . look, between us, I feel kinda . . . I don't know, powerful. I defended myself, Kyle."

"You did more than that," he says, but there's a smile playing at the corner of his mouth. That's pride, I think. And something else, too. A glimmer in his eye I recognize.

I stand and walk past him, locking the front door and setting the OUT OF OFFICE sign to indicate just that. Then I stroll past Kyle again, letting his eyes follow me as I make my way to the back where the storage rooms are.

He gets the hint.

In a room used for storing cleaning supplies, paper towels, and printer paper, I lay the man down on the hastily cleared table and let him deal with his own disrobing while I strip out of the uniform.

Naked, I climb up over him and resist the tug he gives me. He wants an embrace, he wants to see my eyes. Two nights ago our mouths never parted while we made love, but I need something different now. I turn and face the door, away from him, and with a few adjustments he's inside me and I'm doing all the work.

"Slow down," he breathes.

Not today, I think, staring at the door, then with my eyes closed, fulfilling myself with total abandon. It's over quickly. I've barely broken a sweat, and unlike our previous encounters I skip the sensual process of coaxing him back for round two. Instead I leave him there, panting, glistening, then calling out to me with more than a little confusion.

Not ten minutes after I locked the front door, I'm back and opening Silvertown Police's headquarters for business. Kyle emerges from the back room a few minutes after that, glancing around expectantly. "Who came in? Did they suspect anything? Didn't hear the door."

"No one came in," I tell him, back at my desk already.

"Oh," he says, confused. "You got up in such a hurry, I thought . . ."

"Just have a lot of work to do, actually. You know?"

From his expression I gather he's not taking this at face value, and for a second I'm tempted to reassure him. I decide instead to let the boy stew a bit, wondering what my intentions with him are. It's a relationship tactic I've seen a hundred times, be it friends or characters in films, but one I've never tried myself. I've had a fair number of lovers in my life, but one thing I've never had is makeup sex. No games, not even a single argument. Maybe I've been missing out.

"Well, okay. See ya later, I guess?" he says from the door, though his eyes are begging me for a rematch.

"Bye," I say, with a grin I can't quite manage to hold back. He returns the smile, though a little sheepishly, and leaves.

I don't exactly know who this new Officer Mary Whittaker is, but I think I like her.

Paperwork ensues. By 10:00 a.m. I'm already thinking about lunch despite having had two breakfasts. I decide I should get out into the sun and patrol on foot for a bit. Be seen, answer questions if people have them. The incident at my house last night has already spread like a virus through Silvertown, I'm sure of it. Might have even made the morning headlines down in Granston. Gossip I can handle, but the idea of a news van or two arriving fills me with dread. Slick-talking so-called reporters and their camera teams. One of the draws of this place over a city like Oakland is the distinct lack of those parasites.

I'm halfway out the door when the phone rings. "Silvertown Police," I answer.

"Greg?" the caller asks.

"Do I sound like Greg?"

A pause. "No, sorry. It's Mary, then?"

"That's right."

"Hi, Mary, my name is Milton Skinner, don't think we've met. I live up on Silver Glen Lane—"

"Is this an emergency, Mr. Skinner?" I ask. Silence stretches.

"Er, well, I'm not sure. It's about my neighbor, Sally Jones."

My mind is yanked back to earlier, when I passed her on the sidewalk. "Sally, yes. I just saw her here in town. What's the problem?"

"You saw her in town?"

"That's literally what I just said."

"Ohhhh-kay," Milton Skinner replies. "We got off on the wrong foot here, Mary. Maybe I should call back."

I take a deep breath. "Sorry, no. I've just got a lot going on. Go ahead. You were calling about Sally?"

"Thing is, Officer, I can hear her babies crying, which is saying something, because she lives a hundred yards from my porch and they are inside her house. They've been at it for a while, actually. I thought maybe she'd had a fall or something and they're too young to know what to do, but if you saw her in town . . . I just . . . well, I thought I'd call it in."

Suddenly his name registers in my head. Greg has ranted about him several times. The proverbial concerned citizen, calling in at least once a week to report something that, more often than not, should be ignored or at least handled by someone other than the police.

As far as I know he's never once been right about something he's phoned in, but I hesitate. Sally's presence on the sidewalk, without her adorable twins, and with a stranger to boot, had been odd. "How long have they been crying?"

"An hour and a half. Maybe closer to two."

"Okay. Thanks, Milton. I'll check it out."

"Do you want me to go over there and have a look?"

In my mind I picture Sally, home now, trying to feed two whining toddlers, and a creepy old dude peering in through the window.

"No," I tell him, "I'm just a few minutes away. I'll handle it. Stay put, though, in case I need a statement."

"A statement?! Well, okay. Of course, Officer Whittaker! I'll be here."

I won't need a statement, but concerned citizens do love it when they're acknowledged. He sounds positively chuffed when he says goodbye and good luck, like he's just ratted out some neo-Nazis to the FBI.

*Sally Jones*, I think, grabbing my belt. It's easy to imagine how this will go. Your typical small-town quaint misunderstanding. Sally probably hired one of the local teens to watch her kids for a few hours so she could show an old friend around town, her only crime being that she neglected to inform Milton Skinner of her plans. And the babysitter, being a sixteen-year-old, was probably taking selfies while the kids ran wild. I'd bet money on it.

Before heading to Silver Glen Lane I take a quick circuit of downtown, hoping to spot Ms. Jones, but there's no sign of the woman or the stranger she was with, so I head on up the mountain.

Silver Glen Lane is one of the last streets to intersect with Route 177 before the main road's final winding stretch up to Lake Forgotten. It's your typical narrow, curvy lane, cutting a path through two nearly solid walls of trees. Driveways splinter off here and there, most disappearing behind the old growth, the actual homes well back from the road. You don't move up here to listen to the sound of cars driving by, that's for sure.

Sally lives about halfway down. She's one of the few single mothers in the area, and with twins to boot, but everything I know about her indicates she handles her situation with a natural deftness, exuding positivity all the way. The term "rockstar mom" unfortunately jumps into my head.

Sure enough, though, I can hear the wailing kiddos before I'm even out of the car. They sound absolutely awful. Hoarse from screaming, scared out of their wits. A chill runs through me as I pound on the front door.

"Ms. Jones? Hello?" I call out. "Silvertown Police. Open the door."

No reply save the crying.

I try the handle, find it unlocked, and step inside. I can tell immediately just how wrong my theory was. There's no babysitter here.

The twins are there in the front room, on the floor. One is sitting in a saggy diaper, bawling her eyes out. The smell of it hits me a moment later. The other is standing on the back of the couch, her hands against the large view window, as she tries to grasp the dangling handle of the window blinds. Her left arm is covered in dried blood, but she's not crying. Not anymore, at least. From the way her face looks, I think that's a recent development.

"Oh, children," I say, going to them without hesitation. "It's all right now. I'm here. I'll find your mom, okay?"

After a quick search of the house to confirm there are no adults present—nor any inattentive teens for that matter—I spend the next half hour just calming the pair, and dressing a shallow cut on the climber's left hand. In the kitchen I discover that a glass has fallen and shattered on the floor, which caused the injury, judging by the trail of blood droplets leading from there to the living room.

Soon enough I've got them seated in fresh diapers at the dining room table, munching on Goldfish crackers and sipping milk.

"Now what?" I ask the two kids. They both ignore the question, content with their snack.

I can't think of what to do except wait for Sally Jones to return. It's not like I can leave them here while I go looking for her.

Although . . .

I search the woman's garage and find what I need. Two car seats, stuffed in a corner. I install them in the back of the cruiser, and several minutes later I've got the children safely secured. The seats are designed for infants and way too small for the toddlers, but with some wrangling I make it work.

"The jig is up, kiddos. I'm taking you downtown," I say to them.

"Let's hope this is the only time you ever find yourself in the back of a police car, huh?"

Both of them look on the verge of restarting their terrible cries.

From the house I grab their gigantic double stroller, spend five minutes figuring out how to fold it, and another five squeezing it into the Dodge's trunk.

"Siren on?" I ask, starting the car.

One of the kiddos starts whimpering.

"No siren, then. You got it."

I drive back to town. The twins, exhausted from their tearful morning alone, are lulled by the gently curving mountain road and instantly fall fast asleep.

It's only when I pull up in front of the station that it hits me: What the hell am I going to do with two toddlers?

For several minutes I sit in the car, contemplating my options, the children sleeping soundly in the back. Do I leave them in a cell like I did with Katherine? Right. Brilliant idea. I can't drop them at my place, which is technically a crime scene until Sheriff Davies says otherwise. The obvious answer is to find their mother, Sally, read her the riot act for leaving her kids unattended, then hand them over with a glare that will keep her from doing something like this ever again. But finding her means scouring the town, going into every shop. Knocking on the doors of all her friends, maybe even checking the trailheads and campgrounds. That's a lot of getting in and out of the car, muscling the kids out of the back, wrestling with the huge stroller. It's going to be brutal, but it has to be done. Just thinking about it starts a headache growing behind my eyes. Caffeine's wearing off, probably. That will be my next problem to address.

I drum my fingers on the steering wheel. For some reason the thought of Katherine Pascoe, the hiker, keeps floating around on the edges of my mental debate. How she left so quickly. How little she said whenever I spoke with her, and the way she'd so eagerly tucked into some gas station pizza.

Just then my phone starts buzzing in my pocket, and when I fish it out and check the caller ID, the name triggers something in my brain, like a door being opened.

*Clara. Clara!*

"Christ on a stick, get it together girl," I mutter to myself. Why am I sitting here thinking about wrestling a double-wide stroller from the trunk of the car all day when I could have called Clara?

"Hey there," I say, pressing the slab to my ear.

She's talking before I get the words out. *Where are you, are you okay, what happened last night, everyone's talking, did you shoot someone,* and several more phrases I don't quite catch. It all kinda blurs together in front of my suddenly pounding skull.

"Dude, Clara, chill out," I tell her, a little more forcefully than I intend. "I'll tell you all about it later. For now I need . . ." I trail off, the words elusive. What did I need, again? The answer is hazy all of a sudden. Damn this headache.

One of the children starts to fuss.

"Mary, is . . . is that a kid with you?" Clara asks.

Her question jogs my foggy brain. "Yes. Two kids, actually. Sally Jones's twins. I've got them in my car because their mom left them home alone this morning."

"Sally?"

"Yeah."

"Sally's here. At the diner. I was wondering where her kids were."

I sit bolt upright. "She's there?"

"Uh-huh. Having coffee with some strange guy."

"Holy shit. Okay. Don't let her leave, I'm on my way."

I throw the car in gear and make my way to the diner. It takes me all of thirty seconds to get there and I park on the street right in front to make sure everyone can see me.

Clara has smartly led Sally to the door, and nudges the woman down the two steps to the sidewalk as I'm coming around the front of the car. With a look of confusion and concern aimed at me, Clara retreats back inside. Customers watch me from every window. Familiar faces. I ignore them and focus on the mother in front of me.

She's smiling.

I'm not. "Sally Jones, I need to have a word with you, right now."

Too loud, I realize belatedly. Inside, the diners' forks and spoons freeze midair and all eyes are turned to me. Sally points to herself like a schoolkid getting called to the principal's office, then sheepishly follows me to the car. Once we're a few feet away from the diner, I lay into her.

"Tell me there was supposed to be a babysitter, Sally."

Her brow furrows but the smile comes back. "What's that supposed to mean?"

"Sally Jones," I start formally, which wipes the grin from her face, "I'm tempted to arrest you for child neglect."

The look of bewilderment on her face is enough to make me want to slap her back to reality. It's as if I've spoken to her in Swahili. "Neglect?! But," she stammers, eyes darting to the kids in the car, to me, and back, "but they were fine when I left them."

Did she really just say that? I tilt my head and step right up into her face. "Fine?" I ask. "Sure, for about five minutes probably. You've been gone for hours."

"Well, this man needed directions. I couldn't just say no." As she says the words a note of doubt creeps into her voice.

I close my eyes and speak with deliberate slowness. "How does 'directions' turn into lunch with a stranger? Why couldn't you say no? For that matter, why'd you open your door at all? Who is he? Who needed directions so goddamn urgently that you left your twins at home alone, where one of them cut herself on broken glass?" It all comes out in one breath.

Sally Jones is staring at her kids now, her lower lip quivering. Tears begin to fall, and she's shaking her head. "I don't know. I don't know!" And then she's bawling, on the verge of collapse. People in the diner begin to stand, probably thinking I've just informed the woman of a death in the family.

"Look," I say, "come with me to the station and we'll sort this out, okay? Can you do that?"

She turns back and is looking, I realize, at the man who needed directions. He stands at the corner of the building staring back at us. With my index finger I point at him and do a "come here" gesture. He moves slowly through the diner, ignoring the confused looks from the rest of the people inside, and joins us on the sidewalk.

"What's the problem, Officer?"

"Who the hell are you?"

My tone has him backpedaling, glancing at Sally. "I just met her. We were—"

"Not what I asked." I glance over my shoulder at Sally. "Sally, go check on your kids." Can't believe I have to tell her that, but it works. She moves off. I turn back to the man. "Let's try again. Who are you?"

"Rob. Rob Key."

"From?"

"Miami. Florida."

"That's a long way to come just to lure a woman away from her children."

"Lure? Whoa, Jesus, hold on." He raises his hands, palms out, as if I've drawn my weapon. "*Lure?!* Okay. Look. There's no need for . . . I'm here looking at some properties. Factories. I work for Coca-Cola and thought we might be able to convert one of the old facilities here into a bottling plant. For water."

"Your next sentence better get to the point, sir."

He actually laughs at that. The nervous kind of laugh. "I took a wrong turn. The road wasn't on the GPS. I was about to turn around when I saw Ms. Jones there, at the end of her driveway getting her mail. I stopped and asked for directions. She kindly offered to come with me into town, show me where the old factories are, the works. A grand tour. Then I mentioned being hungry and we ended up here for breakfast."

Mr. Key stops there, eyeing me as I eye him for signs of deception. I can't find any. "And her children?" I ask.

"Genuinely, I had no idea she had—*has*—kids until this moment, Officer. She didn't mention them. Not once." His eyes dart to Sally, then back to me.

"You expect me to believe that this kind woman, who famously dotes on her little ones to a fault, just hopped in your car and left them entirely alone?"

His hands lift even higher. "It's what happened. I don't know what else to tell you."

A silence settles over us as I weigh all this. The warmth of the day has given way to clouds, and a light rain begins to fall, tapping on the hood of my cruiser. Sally is standing beside the back door, one kid in each arm, watching me.

From the corner of my eye I can see all the faces in the window of the diner. Twenty or so people, including Clara, all quietly judging how I handle this, no doubt already imagining what Greg would do. Comparisons will follow. I decide I don't care. My performance is not the primary concern. It's Sally's children, then Sally, then this douchebag from Miami.

"ID?" I ask, holding out my hand.

He gives me a Florida driver's license. Name and address noted, I offer it back but hold it tight when he tries to pull it away. Our eyes meet. "Don't leave town," I advise, "until I've cleared you to do so."

"Okay?" he says, making it sound like a question. A question of my authority, or perhaps even my sanity.

"Got a business card?"

He hands me one.

"The number, is it current?"

A nod.

"Okay then. Shoo."

"Officer, when do you think I'll be cleared to leave? I'm due in Lake Stevens this afternoon for—"

I shoot him a cop look. One that lets him know that he'd better drop it and move along. It registers, and with slumped shoulders he turns and marches back into the diner, muttering something about what a weird-ass town this is. Since I can't argue the point, I let it slide. There's a chance, albeit a small one, that I just cost Silvertown a Coca-Cola factory and the jobs that it would bring.

He shoulders his way back to his table. Through the windows, I can see Clara in the kitchen, watching him pass. She stares daggers at him, breaking her gaze away only once he's reached his table.

Clara takes her apron off and pushes out of the kitchen, weaving a path through the dining area that keeps her well away from the man. From all the patrons, really.

"Mary," she breathes as she reaches me, gathering me into a hug. As we part she puts a hand on my forehead, then my cheek. "Are you okay? I heard what happened."

I nod to her, lowering my voice to match hers. "Right as rain, actually. I know it sounds weird, but there was something . . . empowering about it. Was that how you felt?" I figure if there's one person in Silvertown who knows this feeling, it's Clara.

She shakes her head, though.

"I mean, a bit? Mostly it just reaffirmed my belief that you can't trust anyone." She glances over her shoulder at Rob Key. "Least of all strangers. What the hell's going on?"

"I don't know. Sally left her kids alone. Why, exactly, I'm still trying to figure out."

"But why'd you bring the twins with you? What if it had taken you all day to find her?"

I start to respond, then hold back, realizing I have no answer.

"You could have called," Clara adds. "Any of us would have stayed with them while you tracked her down."

"I handled it," I say. "Just like I'm supposed to. No need to drag anyone else into this mess."

She squints at me. "That doesn't sound like you at all."

"Maybe you don't know me as well as you think."

Clara pulls a face. "And that *definitely* doesn't sound like you." She places her hand on my forehead again. "Look, we all process stress different ways. Least, that's what Doc says in our sessions. Are you sure you're good? You don't need anything?"

I nod again, hug her, and tell her to get back to work. Clara is the closest thing to a friend I've got in Silvertown, and I know that this hug should make me feel good, but it . . . just doesn't. "We'll talk later."

"Okay."

As for Sally Jones, I'm still at a loss. She's unapologetic as I drive her and the children back to her house. In fact, she pays me almost no attention at all, spending the entire time half-turned in her seat, cooing baby talk to the kids and fussing over the bandage one wears. She's the model parent, like nothing happened. Like she didn't just abandon a pair of two-year-olds to their fate so she could chaperon a complete stranger around town. If it had been Brad Pitt scouting film locations I could maybe—just maybe—understand. But Rob from Miami? No way. Something else is going on here.

Turning onto her road I start a mental tally of all the weird shit that's happened in the last few days. No, scratch that, I have to go back to Johnny's death if I'm going to do this right. Cause aside, there's no denying Silvertown has seen a spate of crappy decisions from a cross section of inhabitants that, to me, have next to nothing in common. Spectacularly crappy. Lethally crappy, in at least two cases. Maybe three.

Johnny and his ill-advised nature walk.

The hiker and his lack of fear in the face of a wild bear.

The wannabe Hells Angel who tried to chloroform me and paid the price.

And now, Sally Jones.

There's a part of me that wonders what might have happened to these two children if the nosy neighbor hadn't called and reported their crying. The optimist in me thinks that surely Ms. Jones would have come to her senses before too long and rushed back to them. After everything else that's happened, though, I'm not so sure.

At the house, Sally takes the two kids inside and then comes back for the stroller, which I've removed from the trunk for her.

She thanks me, pushing the bulky thing into the back corner of her garage. Then she gives me a small wave of goodbye.

Instead of heading back inside to her children, though, Sally starts to walk off into her yard. Fetching a toy? Turning on a sprinkler? I wait to see. She just keeps walking.

She's a hundred feet away when I finally call out to her.

"Sally? Where are you going?"

"The neighbors. I figure I should apologize for the worry I caused."

"And you're leaving the kids alone inside while you do that?"

I'm too far to see her expression clearly, but her sudden gasp has "oops" written all over it. She runs back, one hand over her mouth.

"Oh my gosh, I'm so sorry. I'm not thinking clearly."

"I noticed."

"Am I in trouble?" she asks shyly.

"You tell me," I reply. "I still don't understand what happened here."

She places one hand on her forehead, checking her own temperature, then shifts her fingers to rub at one temple. "Maybe I'm coming down with something. I genuinely don't know what I was thinking, Officer. Then or now."

"Call me Mary, okay?"

"Of course." She looks up at me, gauging my anger, perhaps. Then her eyes continue up, past me. She's staring off into the distance. I turn to see what she's looking at.

There, on the mountainside, in plain view of her house, is the new cell phone tower. A giant, poorly disguised artificial tree, beaming its signals right into her front window.

I shake my head, turning back to her.

"Look," I say, "I'm not going to call CPS on you or anything, just . . . I don't know, please be more mindful. I can't stay here with you all day and help watch them."

At this she looks truly baffled. "I'd never ask you to. I'll call my aunt, or the kid who sits for me sometimes, so I can lie down."

"That works," I reply, wondering why I thought my help would be her first port of call. "I think . . . I think we're all still a little off-kilter since Johnny . . ." I let that trail off.

Sally rests a hand on my forearm and gives me a little squeeze. "Thanks," she says, and then she's heading inside, already offering cheerful words about snack time to her kids.

As if nothing happened.

# CHAPTER NINE

"I'll check in on you later," I mouth to Sally, stepping off her porch and onto the gravel driveway. Through the window she smiles and makes one of the girls wave cutely at me, as if all is right in the world.

Though I can't quite bring myself to consider this situation resolved, I think I can safely file it as "under control." At the car I glance up the hill toward the next house, just visible through some trees. Milton Skinner is watching from his big bay window, and raises one hand in a gesture of thanks. I nod to him, though I'm not sure he'll see it from this distance, and make my way back to the road. At the end of the narrow lane where it meets the state route, I stop and consider my options. On a whim I turn left, away from town.

Sunlight streams through the tall trees, making the yellowing leaves on the alder trees practically glow like beacons amidst their evergreen neighbors. A sign indicates two more miles to Lake Forgotten. At the last intersection before the lake there's a small coffee stand appropriately called Last Chance. I pull in for an americano and a blueberry muffin top.

Ten minutes later I'm parked in the small dirt lot near the lake, with a grand view of its placid waters and the two snow-dappled mountain peaks rising steeply above.

For all the grief its Two-Shits nickname earns, I have to admit the scene is quite beautiful. Even the section of rockslide just beyond the far shore, where part of the Two Sisters collapsed ages ago and slid all the way to the water's edge, looks impressive.

There's no one else around. I crack the window and sip my coffee, with only the crisp air and the sound of birds to keep me company. The muffin top is chocolate chip instead of the blueberry I'd asked for, but today doesn't feel like a day to be picky, so I eat it with undiminished zeal.

Once the view wears off a bit, my mind starts to drift to last night. The man in my house, his rag-wrapped hand and those murderous eyes. What keeps returning to my mind, though, is what he'd said to me. *I wish I could stop. I can't stop.* What was that all about? Can't stop assaulting people in their homes? Can't stop his urge to kill? He was too clumsy to be some sort of serial attacker. I quickly jot a note to look into the man's background, just in case.

Then, of course, there's the *why* part behind his words. Why couldn't he stop? Drugs? Mental problems? Little green aliens controlling his brain?

I shake my head, vigorously, to banish this train of thought from my mind. The dude was nuts and got what he deserved. Roll credits. Leave the why to the journalists and forensic psychologists. I stopped him, that's what matters.

Before me the lake is dazzling. Sunlight dances on inch-high waves. A pair of deer wander out from the forest's edge, approaching the water with all due wariness. One drinks while the other keeps watch, then they trade roles. Seeing them and the simplicity of their lives somehow clears my head.

It's nice to just sit and not think about the attack. Or anything, really. That's not to say my mind isn't all over the place—far from it— but nothing seems to hold my attention when competing against this view. I wonder if maybe that's what they meant when they named this Lake Forgotten. A place to forget about everything else.

I sit there until the muffin is gone, and wash it down with the last sip of coffee.

Snack consumed, I say goodbye to the landscape and start back down the mountain. The brief respite has done my mind-set a world of good, but I half expect to find the town in flames or overrun by zombies as payback for me taking ten minutes to veg out.

The road twists and turns, following the contour of the mountain. It's an odd road in that its corners are banked like a racetrack, and this only made sense to me when Greg explained its construction back on my second or third day up here.

Turns out, back in the 1950s they'd decided to build a telescope up here. An odd choice given the region's typically cloudy skies, but the budget was approved for political reasons and that was enough to get the project started. Step one was a decent road all the way to the selected site. Not just any road, though. They were going to be hauling a big mirror up here, and that sort of equipment can't be put under too much stress. The truck that would deliver it needed to be able to maintain a relatively constant speed and minimal g-forces, even in the curves. So the road to Lake Forgotten is inclined in its turns, though not to the extremes of a true racecourse. Still, it's enough that it unsettles you the first time you drive it, and also makes it an ideal road for thrill seekers, hence the constant stream of motorcycles up here. Once every summer there's even a herd of exotic Italian cars that makes the pilgrimage, or so Greg tells me. Open season for writing speeding tickets, I expect.

Plans for the telescope were scrapped in favor of a mountain in Southern California, which makes way more sense. Half the road, though, had already been built. West of downtown it's normal, but from just east all the way to the top, it's some world-class twisties.

In town I stop for gas and instantly recognize the Volvo parked at the other pump in our two-pump town.

"Heya, Doc," I say as the fuel starts to flow.

He glances at me, raises one eyebrow. "Sheriff," he says, tipping a nonexistent cap. "Just fueling up for my drive to Portland."

His older-model silver Volvo wagon is immaculately clean, as if straight from the showroom. Its only adornment is an oval-shaped sticker on the back window. White, with black letters: 140.6. A distance runner's sticker, presumably from a previous owner, unless it means inches instead of miles. To my eye Doc doesn't look like he's run a day in his life.

"What's in Portland?"

"A conference. The annual Neuroscience Society gathering."

"Good for you."

"Quite a night you had last night, eh?"

"Heard about that, did you?" I cross my arms, trying to play it cool. Just another day on the job.

"Hard not to. The newspapers and media are all over it."

"Right. The *Silvertown Gazette*'s web page must be getting hammered—"

"No, not ours. The big ones. 'Top Seattle lawyer shot dead by small-town cop,'" he quotes. "That's headline stuff, Mary."

Top Seattle lawyer? I try to mask my surprise at this detail.

Doc is eyeing me for a reaction. I feel like an insect under a specimen jar. "What's Greg think about it?"

"Greg?" I ask. "I doubt he's heard about it, unless it's been on CNN."

He squints at me. "You mean you were involved in a shooting and didn't think to call him?"

I open my mouth to argue, only to close it a second later. Doc's right. I hadn't thought to call Greg. "He's visiting his sick mother," I say, knowing how lame it sounds.

There's a click as his gas tank reaches capacity. Doc replaces the handle, then ducks between the two pumps to stand closer to me. "I'm sure you can't discuss details, but . . . are you okay?"

"Fine," I say.

"It's just . . . you mentioned being overtired yesterday. I hope that didn't affect your—"

"Nope, I'm good. And it was the other way around. *You* mentioned me being overtired, Doc. I said I was fine, and you know what? Slept like a log last night, except for the encounter with that . . . what'd you say, a lawyer?"

He nods. "Oh! I see . . . You didn't know him? Just a one-night stand, then?"

It's all I can do not to smack him. "What the hell are you talking about? The bastard broke in and attacked me."

"Oh!" He steps back, hands raised. "Sorry, Mary, I didn't mean . . . I didn't . . . the articles—"

"They're not saying *that,* are they?"

"No! No. They didn't specify."

"Wait, so that was your own theory, then?"

"I didn't mean anything—"

"Like hell you didn't. Tells me way more about you, though, Doctor Ryan."

"I'm so sorry."

"Maybe you should analyze your own shit for once."

He closes his eyes and holds up both hands, defeated.

"Forgive me. I assumed, and made an ass out of . . . well, just me in this case. Whoever he was, I'm sure—"

"It was that crashed motorcyclist, Doc. The one who I tried to get you to go see? The one you said wasn't there?"

"Again, I apologize."

"Yeah, well, have a safe trip."

After an awkward few seconds, Doc gives me a sheepish nod and turns to leave.

"Hey Doc," I call out as he's halfway folded into his boxy wagon. "You treat any broken noses yesterday?"

For a second he stares at me, expressionless in the face of my non-sequitur. Then he shakes his head, thinks better of asking me why I want to know, and drives off for his fancy conference in Portland.

It's only then that I realize I'm now the lone cop in a town *with no doctor.*


Driving to the station I kick myself for not thinking to ask Doc to call on Sally Jones. Her behavior this morning is worth his attention. Bipolar is my guess, or something along those lines. Maybe she stopped taking her medication recently.

Of course, Sally's medication needs are none of my business. Still I think Doc should know about the incident. I call him and leave a voice mail when he doesn't pick up.

Back behind my desk for what feels like the tenth time that day, I take a stab at clearing out the email in-box. Most of it is crap. Alerts for things that are technically nearby but have no bearing on the goings-on here in remote Silvertown. I usually read these anyway just for the nostalgia of being part of a much bigger police force. The effort has only paid off one time so far. About a month back, two kids assaulted an old lady and stole her car down in Granston, and in their panic to avoid being caught they took a right instead of a left turn, which brought them up here to Silvertown. Granston police blocked off Keller's Bridge near the base of the mountain, effectively trapping them up here, and then let me and Greg know. Took all of five minutes to find the two youths, both fifteen, who sadly had done a Thelma and Louise into a ravine just north of the bridge rather than face the consequences of their actions.

Today I can't bring myself to care. Not about the teenagers, that was a true shame. No, today I can't get interested in this list of general alerts. I file them all.

One message, sent to me specifically, does catch my eye. A copy of Sheriff Davies's report regarding the incident at my house, which he's BCC'd me on out of professional courtesy. I skim it. Can't really bring myself to look at the pictures too closely. It's my fucking house and I was the one who pulled the trigger. I do scan the deceased's bio, though, and sure enough it's right there in black and white: Rhod Mitchell. Attorney-at-law for Dawson & Wendig, a prominent Seattle firm. High-power business lawyers. I learn all this by googling the place and checking out its website. My attacker was a partner there and has his own section on the "Meet Our Team" page. Specialized in corporate law and finance, enjoyed riding motorcycles and spending time with his wife and two children.

I slump back at that bombshell.

Wife. Two kids. "Shiiiiiit."

I feel no remorse for pulling the trigger. But still . . . these details paint a part of the picture missing before now. I want to think of that son of a bitch as a son of a bitch, not a human being. Not a father.

"Well, kids, your dad was a turd. Sorry, but that's the truth," I say to the screen, resigning myself not to lose any sleep over it. I just hope I don't have to face them in a courtroom someday soon. I don't want to look into their eyes.

I'm about to close the page when I notice something else. Near the top of the screen there's a rotating list of testimonials, changing every few seconds. Quotes about the amazing credentials of the firm. One in particular catches my eye. Not the quote itself, but the name attributed to it: Sandra Conaty. Or at least I think that's what it said. The damn cycling banner won't let me scroll back.

It could only be *the* Sandra Conaty, the woman on the news the other day. CEO of Conaty Corporation, the very company that Greg ran out of town.

I click around a bit and find a "Clients" page. Sure enough, among the hundreds of other recognizable brand names, there's Conaty Corporation. "Huh," I say aloud, not quite sure what to make of it. On the one hand it's a connection. Tenuous, but still a link. Conaty is a gigantic global enterprise, though. True, both the family and the company have been gone from Silvertown for years, but it makes sense they'd continue to use a big Seattle law firm. Hell, they probably have lawyers in every state and several countries, too.

"And yet . . ."

They're gone because of the efforts of Greg Gorman, and by extension, the Silvertown Police force, which last night was yours truly. Had Rhod Mitchell been at this firm back then? Worked on the case? Could some lingering resentment toward the town be behind his drive up here?

My mind runs a bit wild with possibilities. I'm suddenly imagining him drugging me not to assault me but to tie me up and lecture me. To tell me what really happened, as a consolation prize for Greg being out of town. He'd tell me how Chief Gorman had

it all wrong, and ruined all those careers for nothing. Or, hell, that
the conspiracy theories are right. That the Conatys have some secret
facility in Silvertown where work continues to make super soldiers
for the government, or study UFO wreckage. *Uh-huh, yeah, that's
gotta be it.* All the harebrained theories I've heard since arriving swirl
around in my brain.

Or maybe he just works at the same firm. Maybe he heard about
Silvertown when someone mentioned the old client and what had
happened, or maybe . . . just maybe . . . he was only here because
of the perfect road with racetrack-quality curves. Maybe this run-
down backwater town was the last thing on his mind.

"Ugh," I mutter, and close the message, thinking that if I'm not
careful I'm going to become just like Kenny, seeing Sasquatches
where there are only squirrels.

No, the most likely scenario is that this midlife crisis man—one
of the Sons of Brand-archy as I'd correctly guessed—was on a weekend ride, and in trying to play the part of consummate badass he'd
probably taken some tainted substance from actual bikers and his
pharmaceutically twisted brain had said "go after that cop, she's the
reason you wrecked your precious bike because she only put up the
cone *after*."

All I know for sure is that "wife and two children" almost certainly
means this encounter is not going to go away quickly or quietly.
There will be questions, claims of trigger-happy police, perhaps a
formal investigation and paid leave, in my future. I wonder what
Greg's reaction will be, and how the hell he's ever going to leave me
on my own again.

"Hi, Chief, welcome back, sorry for the media shitstorm and the
lawsuits," I whisper to my desk.

My desk does not respond.


The afternoon passes uneventfully.

I remain in the station, filing some paperwork and tidying up
the place a bit. Only one person stops in: Rob Key, the water scout

for Coca-Cola. He asks permission to leave town so he can make an early flight back, and I grant it, if only because looking at him now I can't see how he could have possibly been charming enough to get Sally Jones to leave her precious children unattended for two minutes, much less two hours. Clearly the fault is on Sally's side of things in this case. She wasn't right in the head. Nothing else makes sense.

Still, I make sure he knows I've got his contact info and will inform the local precinct where he lives of what transpired. He swallows at this but nods and even does an awkward little bow as he departs.

At five I walk home. It's a warm evening, the weather still not quite sure which season it is. Passing the diner I glance in the windows, half expecting to see Mr. Key still here, contrary to our last exchange. But, alas, no. The place is half-full, just the usual crowd. I'm almost past the window when I think to wave at Clara, only to realize she's not in the kitchen. Already gone home, I suppose.

Past the shops and empty buildings I wander along the quiet stretch of asphalt. No coyotes cross the road this time, but I do spot a few eagles up in the high branches, their heads shifting back and forth as they scope for snacks.

Only one car passes me. A black SUV with tinted windows. It slows as it comes alongside, paces me for a few seconds, then continues on. Can't help but wonder at that. Someone who thought they knew me? A perv checking me out? I'm still in uniform so that seems unlikely.

Whatever. They leave and I'm glad for it. The silence tonight is kind of wonderful.

I'm half expecting to find news vans all parked in front of my house, after what Doc said about the headlines, but then they would have been at the police station, too. Their lack of presence is welcome all the same.

Still, once inside I can't quite decide what to do. The sheriff didn't expressly tell me to vacate the premises pending investigation. I'm not even sure there will be one. Yet the house still feels like a crime scene to me, and my gut is telling me not to stay long.

So I shower, change into civilian duds, and pack a bag with my uniform and some essentials. Half an hour later I'm retracing my steps back to the station. If Katherine could sleep in a cell, so can I.

I pick up a gas station pizza on the way, eat alone like a complete loser, and my head has just hit the pillow when my cell phone rings.

"Hey Kyle," I answer, wondering if he'll want to come by for a rematch of our earlier escapades. I have a sudden vision of me handcuffed to this metal bed, him waggling the key at me and telling me I've been a very naughty officer. All the daydream needs is some *bow-chicka-wow-wow* music and I just might make myself puke.

His voice is raised over a loud background. "Whatcha up to? You should come on over to O'Doh's." The pub. From the sounds behind him the place is packed.

"I was just about to hit the hay."

"It's eight p.m."

"Don't judge. I had a long-ass day."

"Well, okay, sure, but just about everyone's here, Mary, and they're all talking about you. I thought maybe you might want to dispel some rumors. You know how this place gets. In an hour they'll have it that you fought off a pack of werewolves last night."

"Let 'em. I'll be a goddamn legend."

"Mary, c'mon."

"So it's just these rumors, not because you want to see me?"

"Well, yeah, that, too. Been thinking about you all day. Since we . . . well, I mean—"

"Look at you, getting all tongue-tied. How cute. Okay, fine. Give me ten."

"Cool. Seeya." He hangs up.

I stand and glance at the metal bunk. Mentally I rearrange the fantasy. It's set at his place now, and he's the one cuffed to the headboard.

Better. Maybe even tempting.

"The beast with two backs," I mutter, getting dressed again, smiling a little.

# CHAPTER TEN

O'Doherty's is in rare form.

Which is to say, busting at the seams with people, and almost all of them locals.

Every booth is full. People are standing along the back wall. There's even a drunken man trying to share the tiny stage with the massive sound system. He's crooning with a spectacular lack of skill about how all you zombies should hide your faces.

It's like all the shit that's happened since Johnny was laid to rest has finally shaken the town out of its state of mourning, and everyone decided it's time to get together and be normal. Well, Silvertown-normal.

I try to play it cool, hanging up my jacket and taking pole position at the bar, but before my butt's on the stool there's a sort of recognition that ripples through the room like a belly flop on a placid lake. It's the opposite of everything going quiet. People are raising their beers to me and shouting their hellos over the karaoke-slash-jukebox thing. A few pass me and give me a hearty pat on the back.

The stool next to me is suddenly occupied by a keenly interested Miles Osman, the local pastor. Normally I'm opposed to clichés, but Miles is exactly what you expect for a small-town preacher. It's like Ned Flanders grew a pair and then became a used-car salesman. Pencil-necked and festooned with thick lenses in unfashionable frames, he rests an elbow on the bar, his fist gripping a frothy pint of Guinness.

"Mary, hello! How are you holding up?" he asks.

I nod at Kyle, whose grin is saying *look what I dragged you into, sucker!* "Corona," I tell him.

"Put that on my tab," Pastor Osman adds.

"Make it two then," I say, and I hope my expression tells Kyle to make it snappy. "Thanks, Pastor, I'm doing fine. It's not as big a deal as it seems. The media's just . . . you know."

Several others are hovering now, beers in hand, sensing the story is coming out. The room gets a little quieter.

"It's true then?" one of the women standing nearby asks. "That lawyer attacked you in your house?"

I nod, to her but also to Kyle as he places two bottles in front of me. "Yeah, it's true, but it's all over now. Nothing to get excited about."

Someone barks a surprised laugh. "You killed the fucker, though, didn't you? I mean c'mon, Officer, that's worth getting excited about."

"Unfortunately lethal force was necessary, yes."

This sends another ripple through the crowd, some nodding understanding and others gasping their surprise. It's easy to forget that death is a big deal in a small town. Three of them in as many weeks is positively huge.

I sigh. "Really, it's not a big deal. Go back to your drinks. Enjoy yourselves."

This has precisely the opposite effect of what I wanted. They're having none of it. The pastor channels that as he taps his pint with a fork. "Mary, please. A man assaulted you in your home, and he's . . . paid the price for that. We have a right to know what happened."

"A *right*?" I snap. The aggression in my voice hits him like a backhanded slap. "It happened in my private residence, Pastor. You have a *right* to know whatever information the Granston sheriff decides to release. Anything else is at my discretion."

The warmth and energy drains from the room, and for several seconds everyone's looking at their cups. The song from the karaoke machine has ended, and nothing follows it. Above the bar the muted TV is still playing Doc's awkward commercial, making me wonder if that thirty seconds of stilted hilarity has been on since the last time I was here, playing over and over again. At least it's still muted.

Pastor Osman, no doubt used to strong reactions when poking his nose into other people's business, is unfazed. His smile exudes understanding and compassion. "I just meant in the sense that, currently, you're our only police officer. I'm a small-town guy but I've read the news enough to know the term 'administrative leave' often comes up in situations like this. We just want to know what will happen next."

"Nothing. Nothing is happening next," I say tersely. Then I take a deep breath, faltering under the weight of all their downcast eyes. A man was shot right here in their little town, with me at the center of it, while the cop they've known and trusted for years is a thousand miles away. I guess I understand their anxiety. *And*, I remind myself, *I'm supposed to be trying to win them over.* Telling them all to butt out of my business isn't helping in that regard. I swallow back this urge to push them away and force myself to address the room.

"Look, sorry, it's been a long couple of days. I've heard from the sheriff and, while there may be an inquiry at some point, his report has cleared me of any wrongdoing. Even if they want me to come down and answer questions, it would be after Greg returns. So, relax, all of you. I just want to enjoy my drink in peace, okay, everyone?"

Some accept this right away, returning to their own conversations. A small shift in the room's social gravity away from me, and it's enough to restore some balance to the situation. Gradually things return to what passes for normal here.

The pastor takes a healthy swig from his pint glass, contemplating the dark brown liquid. "Can I ask you about something else, Mary?"

"Shoot," I say, in a tone I hope says otherwise. He soldiers on, though.

"While it may also be none of my business, I should mention that Sally Jones is a parishioner at the church and, I think it's safe to say, a friend. Any chance you could help me understand what happened with her this morning? I've only heard secondhand—"

"You'll have to ask her, Miles. We might not have much in common, but a respect for confidentiality is something we both must share."

He eyes me for a moment, and I can see the realization dawn inside him that, were the roles reversed, he wouldn't reveal to me something told to him in confidence, either. He nods respectfully.

Kyle, standing just within earshot, has been wiping the same glass with a cloth since I sat down. We make brief eye contact and he pulls off the stealthiest wink I think I've ever seen. I lift my bottle to him in a silent cheers, sip, and study the familiar Corona label.

"Which way did you say those bear tracks went?" I ask him. "I might go have a look in the morning."

He sets the overly polished glass down and studies me. "I can handle that for you."

I mull this. Sip at my beer.

"Or," he adds, "we could go together."

"I don't need an escort."

He's only slightly more surprised by this response than I am. "Sorry," I quickly add. "Not sure where that came from. I just want to be sure it's gone."

"No one's mentioned seeing it."

"That's good, I guess."

"But," he adds, "Jojo and Edgy saw some ATV tracks up on the ridge over the old mine."

"Who and who?"

"Sorry, force of habit. Josh Dent and Alex Carr," he explains. "They run the mechanic shop behind the Gas-n-Go."

"Oh yeah, sure," I say, though I can't recall ever meeting them, much less hearing their nicknames. Greg has handled maintenance on his old cruiser since, well, forever, and mine's only a few months old, so I've had no reason to visit their shop. It's a dingy building tucked back behind the gas station, with an old faded sign that just reads DENT & CARR AUTO MECHANICS and a barely legible phone number. And here I'd thought the name was just a cheesy attempt at humor. Beneath all that it says SORRY, NO BIKES in freshly painted letters. I see it every time I go for my gas station pizza, which is pretty much daily, but never really thought much about it. "Surprised they don't fix motorcycles, too. Seems like it'd be easy money up here."

At this Kyle and the pastor share a significant glance with each other, which takes me aback. "Am I missing something?" I ask.

Kyle's chuckling as he moves off to fill another order, which leaves Pastor Osman to answer, and that has the man blushing. He stammers, trying to find the words.

I try to stop him with an upheld hand. "I think I get it."

"They wouldn't get along well with the biker crowd," Miles says anyway.

"Yeah, dude, I definitely get it. *Comprende*." No sense forcing the straitlaced pastor to state the now-obvious.

Someone's paid actual money to coax that famous Rick Astley song from the sound machine, bringing groans from half the patrons. At least no one has picked up a microphone to sing along. I might have had to make a public decency arrest.

"ATV, huh?" I call out to Kyle, raising my voice over the music.

Kyle nods, setting a pair of shots in front of a couple at the other end of the bar. "S'what they said. Not so odd, this time of year, but it's worrying, given the bear situation. Be a shame if we lost another tourist."

This has others seated nearby nodding in concerned agreement. Tourists—be they hikers, bikers, or "conspiratards" as I once heard someone call them—have been the lifeblood of this town ever since the Conatys left.

Kyle goes on. "Makes me wonder if we should put signs up or do an alert of some kind."

"And by we you mean me," I reply.

He looks puzzled, one eyebrow lifted high. "No, I mean we. Like how you rallied all of us to help with the hiker. Or how you enlisted us all to help direct traffic for Johnny's funeral. You know, a typical

Mary Whittaker–style team operation. Clara could print something up, she's good at that, and we could all pitch in to post them around the popular spots."

His words are like a splash of cold water across my face. I sit there, mildly stunned, and not quite sure why.

"Mary," he starts. "Something's up. I realize we haven't been, um, hanging out very long, but this isn't like you."

I'm about to tell him that he doesn't know me well enough to say that, but he holds up his hands. "Wait. Before you respond, just think about what we talked about the other night. About your brothers? About what happened to you in Oakland?"

I think back to the first night Kyle and I made love, ignoring the sex part for once and focusing on our afterglow conversation. He wanted to know about my past. About why I left Oakland.

"Must have been pretty bad to make you decide to move here. I mean, no one moves here. Not willingly."

So I'd told him, but I'd started with my childhood. Growing up with four older brothers, you'd think that would make me hyper-competitive and fiercely independent. "That's so not me," I'd explained. "No, my thing was teamwork, since my earliest memories. Mom wanted me to clean my room? I'd go convince one of my brothers to help. Or all of them."

"You had them wrapped around your cute little finger," Kyle observed.

"It wasn't like that. Okay, at first, yeah, but that only works to a point. No, it was more like . . . I just always make things a team effort. It's better that way, isn't it?"

"Teamwork makes the dream work?"

"I could arrest you for that. Lame cliché in the first degree," I said to him, punching his arm.

He grunted a laugh. "What's this got to do with Oakland?"

And so I'd told him the whole sordid tale. How I'd found the perfect partner, how we'd made such a great team.

"Then one day we're chasing this armed suspect who's just gone into a home and barricaded the front door closed. I was ready to pursue, but it was my partner who said we should wait for backup. But I knew there wouldn't be time, not if we both remained together out front. So I said it. Said we should split up. Cover the front and back, keep the suspect penned in."

"Smart play," Kyle observed.

"Yeah, I thought so, too, but it was like pulling teeth to even suggest it. And look what happened. I went around back. The perp came out the front door only seconds later, guns-a-blazing. Probably saw me go and figured the odds were even now."

"Shit. What then?"

"Zach, my partner, took a round in the gut. Missed his organs, didn't miss his spine, though. He's paralyzed now, in case you're wondering. That's on me."

"C'mon, you can't—"

"It's on me, Kyle. We should have stuck together." After that he smartly knew it was time to drop it. Just wrapped his big arm around me and we fell asleep in the silence that followed.

Now, Kyle is watching me as I replay our conversation. He leaves his point unsaid: *Should have kept it a typical Mary Whittaker team operation.*

"Yeah, well, maybe you don't know me as well as you think, Kyle. Maybe you got your read wrong. I need some air."

Kyle again shows his intelligence and lets it go. Before I know it, I'm up out of my chair and out the door in what I hope is not too much of a huff. With gravel dust rising from my heels, I make my way to my crusier and lean against the driver-side door. I'm staring at a beat-up old junker parked next to me, replaying Kyle's words in my head.

*Typical Mary Whittaker team operation.* I see my distorted reflection in the junker's window and then something clicks and I stop cold.

"Typical until this morning," I mouth to the warped doppelgänger.

For a time I can do nothing but stare at the pattern of decay on the car door. Rust and metal. That's how the brain is supposed to work, isn't it? Gradual decay, or just gradual change if you're lucky. Not this, though. This happened overnight.

"So what changed?" I ask the door. "Why didn't I call 911 after the attack? Why'd I take Sally's children instead of securing a sitter or . . ."

My voice trails off as I think of a half-dozen other moments today where I'd shunned teamwork and gone it alone. Hell, I hadn't even been the one to call the sheriff and get him to my house. A neighbor had done that. Furious with myself, I open the cruiser and shove myself into the bucket seat, slamming the door closed behind me.

"What changed?" I repeat, racking my mind. "What the fuck changed?!"

The answer seems suddenly obvious.

There must have been something on that rag wrapped around the lawyer's hand. Not chloroform but . . . something else. I try to recall the report that Sheriff Davies submitted. I'd been too focused on the revelation that Rhod Mitchell had a wife and kids to pay any attention to the forensic analysis. Had one even been included? I can't remember. Probably not. Too soon for that.

I pull out my phone and send a reply back to the sheriff, asking if he can send the info as soon as it comes in. "Just curious" I tuck in at the end. *Not because of any side effects, pinky-swear!* As if that would even occur to him. Kyle might be able to spot a change in my behavior, but not Davies, whom I spent all of an hour with just after ending someone's life in my own home.

Then the dreaded four letters, *P. T. S. D.,* creep into my skull. It's a real problem. I've seen others suffer from it enough to know that much, but I've also seen it used as a pat diagnosis to clear a case from the files of overworked therapists. I've seen cops fake its symptoms, too, earning not just a pat diagnosis but some serious paid leave as well.

"Fuck," I mutter, head in my hands. I can't imagine exploring the post-traumatic theory. Not now. Not while I'm here alone.

There's a knock at the window.

"Mary?" Kyle's voice, concerned.

"Just a sec," I call out. I twist the key to engage the battery and roll down the window.

"You all right?" he asks when it's about halfway down.

"Yeah," I say.

He nods, still concerned. I realize he's not here to check on me. "What is it?" I ask.

"Mr. Wilkinson came in. He says Clara never showed up for her shift."

Hugh Wilkinson owns the diner where Clara works. "Sure she did. I saw her there this morning."

"For her second shift," Kyle replies. "He said she had two today, but went home after the first and never came back."

My response is automatic, incongruous with the sinking feeling in my gut. "She's at home. Decided against working a double but forgot to call. Okay? Mystery solved."

Kyle just turns around and heads back to the bar and I find myself leaving the cruiser and following him. Kyle holds the door, concern radiating off him. For me, or Clara, I'm not quite sure. Both of us, probably.

When I enter the bar Hugh is waiting just inside. He says something, but I can't hear him over the karaoke machine, which has started up again.

"Someone turn that shit off!" I shout.

The sound vanishes a second later. All eyes are on me now.

"Hugh, she probably took a nap and forgot to set her alarm. Or got a headache. Or a million other things that don't require police attention."

"That's just it," Hugh says, with his hat literally in his hand. His fingers rub at the worn old Seahawks logo in the middle of the cap. "I went by her place. It's on my way, so no big deal. But . . . Officer, listen, the front door was open."

"Unlocked?"

"No, *open*. All the lights were off, but her door was just standing wide."

"Did you go in? Touch anything?"

His eyes get very, very large at all the implications behind this question. It takes him a second to respond, and when he does his voice is shaky.

"A few steps, that's all. I called out for her, but there was no reply. So I came here. To the station first, I mean. Then here."

Kyle shifts at my side. "Want me to round up—"

"Just hang on," I say, pressing both palms downward on the invisible tension rising from the room. My cheek twitches, some revelation lurking under the surface of my thoughts. I push it away and try to focus. "No need to panic, guys. She probably went out and didn't realize the door hadn't latched behind her."

Kyle looks unconvinced. Hell, *I'm* unconvinced. With everything that's happened in the last few days, I'm certainly not going to rule out another strange occurrence in Silvertown. But I don't exactly need the townspeople freaking out, either. I try for a reassuring smile. "Everyone go back to your drinks. I'll head over there and find her."

Kyle opens his mouth, but I shake him off and start walking back to my car.

As I open the car door, Kyle calls out to me. He's on the sidewalk in front of O'Doh's, across the street. "Mary, what the hell?"

With one foot in the car, I turn to him. "Dude, relax. The wind blew her front door open."

"It's just—" He starts, pauses to gather himself, and tries again. "This is what I was talking about earlier. It's not like you to go it alone."

"Um, newsflash? Greg's out of town. I am alone."

"You're not, though." He takes a few steps into the street. "We're all happy to help."

"Help with what? Look, I know the last few days have been insane, even by Silvertown standards, but that doesn't mean I need to get a posse together every time someone forgets to lock their door."

He's crossed the street now and stands just a foot away from me. "Why are you shutting me out all the sudden? Shutting all of us out. Ever since that creep last night—"

"Um, weren't you and I having sex just a few hours ago?"

"You know what I mean, Mary."

"Okay," I say, "okay. Truth is I'm trying to prove myself to this town. That I can handle things without Greg." I can see he's not buying this, so I place a hand on his chest. "Go back inside. We'll talk about it later. Right now I need to check on Clara."

Kyle nods, at first skeptically but then with more conviction. "Call if you need backup. Deputize me if you have to."

"I will," I say, though I don't believe my own words.

He steps back and waits there in the lot, watching me drive off.

I round the corner and accelerate past the gas station. Kyle's words rattle around in my head, partly because they so closely match what Clara said to me outside the diner earlier, but more than that they're an echo of my own thoughts only minutes before. And yet here I've done it again. Gone solo without even considering the alternative. I told everyone else to stay put while I handle things myself. Completely contrary to the "typical Mary Whittaker team operation," as he so aptly put it. Ever since I killed that biker it's like I've lost my instinct to build a team around me, or join up with—

*My instinct.*

I slam on the brakes. The cruiser skids to a halt in the middle of the main drag. Luckily the street is otherwise empty. For a minute I sit there, listening to the thoughts swirling in my head.

This tornado of memories all spiral around a single idea, one that I couldn't see before simply because I wasn't looking at *myself.*

Ever since we found the hiker I knew this had something to do with instincts. But I'd been so fixated on the fight-or-flight idea that I never really paid much attention to what Doc had said regarding primal behaviors. "There are many others."

Instead of running for his life, the hiker just sat there and let the bear attack him. But what if it wasn't a malfunction of his fight or flight response? Katherine Pascoe had said he hated animals as a general principle. He was intensely afraid of them. Wanted nothing to do with them to the point where he waited in the car to pick her up rather than have to be near the roommate's dog. Then, suddenly, here in Silvertown, that's flipped around completely, and at the worst possible moment.

Then there's Sally Jones, helping out some nobody in total opposition to her intensely strong maternal instinct to care for her own damn children.

Willy Jupitas, stepping in front of my car the other day like there was no danger in it at all. Easy at the time to chalk it up to his age or my distractedness. Now, though . . .

Let's not forget *me*. My natural drive to become part of a team, or form one when none exists. That's been me all my life. And now, ever since that prick tried to kill me, I've been doing the polar opposite. Striking out on my own with no support.

"Oh my God," I say to the dashboard, as other such cases flash through my mind. One in particular escapes my lips, "Johnny Rogers. Holy fucking shit."

The dead teenager. A homebody. A gamer who detested the outdoors. Suddenly he's hiking, alone in the wilderness with no skill for survival, leading to a fall that ended his life.

What's the connection? I rack my brain. We're all on the same mountain. Bombarded by radiation from the new cell tower? Drinking the same water? What?

I cast about, trying to think of other examples that might help. Everything out of the ordinary that's happened recently. The woman in the bar playing pool. Her husband had tossed the chalk to her and watched it smack straight into her face. I remember her shock. As if she was surprised that she could do nothing but take the hit.

And what about the lawyer-biker? I rack my mind, trying to make that fit. But no, I think he was something else entirely. A different kind of insane. I can't see how his behavior fits. Even his crash on the road earlier that day lacked the kind of weirdness the rest of us are experiencing. He'd been upset about his Harley, sure, but was that really so strange? The thing must have been one of his most prized possessions. So maybe he was what he appeared to be: a creep.

There was his broken nose, though. And what he'd said as he attacked me. That was odd.

"Still," I say aloud, "doesn't fit." I drop him into a different mental room for later processing. That douchebag isn't important right now. It's my friends—the citizens of this weird-ass little town—who matter.

And one of them needs me right now.

I step on the gas, glad once again that Greg let me have the brand-new cruiser. The Dodge's tires don't even squeal as the car roars forward into the night.

Buildings begin to blur past. I throw the lights and siren on just so this moment matches the urgency I suddenly feel. *Something* is messing with people's instincts here—mine included—but right now there's something more important to solve.

"Clara," I say to myself.


My only Silvertown friend lives in a neat little craftsman-style bungalow about a half mile outside town, one of many in a row, all built in the mid-1950s.

I pull up in front of her house and get out, leaving the engine running and the light bar strobing its brilliant blue-red flashes across the surrounding trees and homes.

Her place is as kitschy as they come. Flowers hang in pots all along the front porch, along with about twenty different wind chimes. They play their discordant songs as I approach. The harmonic notes just more than a whisper in the light breeze. The front door is closed now, but whether that's because Clara returned or her boss shut it after his visit, I'm not sure.

I take a step toward the porch and stop myself. The revelations I had in the car are still bright in my mind, as is the conversation Kyle and I had. If some chemical on that rag last night, or knocking my head against the wall, has screwed up my brain somehow, I need a way to remind myself of this fact.

Once again I kick myself for not really listening to Doc when we stood in that clearing beside the dead hiker. He'd dropped another little nugget of wisdom there when he spoke of how a zookeeper can consciously override the most basic of human instincts, over time and with constant effort.

I'm short on time, but I have to do something, otherwise I'll keep slipping into autopilot. There's got to be some way to jolt my mind back on track. But what?

A simple solution comes to me. Before heading up to the house I move around to the passenger side of the cruiser and grab a black permanent marker from the glove box. Cap between my lips, I write on the back of my hand in thick black letters:

### YOU NEED HELP

I underline *help* just to hammer the point home. With any luck, seeing this every few minutes will override whatever's causing me to go it alone.

Which, I realize as I'm walking up the front steps, is exactly what I'm doing right now. *Relax,* I tell myself. *One thing at a time. You don't even know if anything's wrong yet. Clara could be inside right now, sipping wine and watching TV. This is nothing but a routine check until proven otherwise.* If that happens, I'll call someone. I'll call Kyle.

I rap on the front door. "Clara?" I call out. Then again, louder, knocking with more urgency. I tap the doorbell a few times for good measure, and as I do so I can clearly read the large block letters written on my hand. The words *you need help* written there so boldly. Anyone else who sees it is going to think I've gone nuts, which only reinforces the message, so whatever.

The door remains closed, the house silent and dark. I walk around the side, switching on my flashlight as I go. The beam sweeps through uncovered windows, their frames casting crosses onto the interior walls. Out back Clara's got two reclined lawn chairs and a high-end barbecue incongruous with the rest of her somewhat shabby belongings. String lights hang around the perimeter of the space—little white ghosts and orange pumpkins that I suspect have less to do with Halloween and more to do with Clara's personality. Other than these, the whole place is dark.

I knock on the back door. Twice for good measure, calling out my presence per procedure. There's no reply. No movement inside. No sound at all, save the wind chimes.

Back around the front, I try the handle and, sure enough, the door opens right up. Technically I'm not supposed to enter the premises, but then again "technically" and "Silvertown law enforcement" are often two separate things. One of the perks of a small-town force. Besides, Clara's a friend and I'm concerned about her, and her boss did report her missing. Unofficially, sure, but there's that "technically" line being a bit blurred again.

I step in.

Hardwood creaks underfoot. The place is warm and smells like vanilla incense. I check the kitchen, and nothing's out of order. Stove's off, no food left out as if she bailed midmeal. Just a normal, if quirky, kitchen.

On the table by the front door there's a cradle for charging a cell phone, and it's empty. There's also no keys and no purse.

I tap the flashlight against my leg, thinking. Either Clara left just like any other day, or someone went to a lot of trouble to make it look like that. Problem is, neither scenario would include leaving the front door wide open. And none of this explains why she didn't show up for work.

On a whim I step outside and tug the door closed behind me, careful to make it a light gesture. I turn and watch the door as it swings shut. The motion is smooth. No creaks or resistance. Despite me barely pulling it, the door rotates all the way until it taps lightly against the frame, and I hear the latch click into place.

"There goes the wind theory," I mutter. Next I try walking out and not tugging on the handle at all. I stand there for several minutes to see if it will move on its own—some doors do, if a breeze is circulating through the house. But here, nothing. The door stays right where I left it.

Okay, then. She takes her phone and purse, she turns off the lights, she leaves. Plain forgets to close the door. Not that unusual. Perhaps she left this door open earlier in the day to let some air in, exited via the back, and forgot the front was still open. An understandable mistake, not so odd really. Plus, if her departure had been early enough in the day there'd have been no reason to have any lights on.

I'm pleased with this train of thought. Other than the fact that she's not answering her phone, it makes pretty good sense to me.

Until I spot the control panel for the security system. It's mounted on the wall by the front door, and it's off.

Instantly my assessment changes. Because although leaving home in a forgetful mindset might include also forgetting to arm the security system, I've been ignoring whose house I'm standing in. Scatterbrained or not, Clara takes her personal security very seriously. She might forget a jacket, or her driver's license. She wouldn't forget to arm the security system.

I set my jaw, determined now not to find excuses to explain this all away. I need to figure out where she went, and why she didn't phone her boss. This last could be explained easily enough. A scheduling goof. Maybe she thought she had the day off. Wrote her calendar entry on the wrong day. Anything.

As to where, well, Clara's a grown woman and can go where she wants to. None of her boss's business. But I'm her friend and I'm a cop, so I can make it mine.

Crossing the street, I rap on the front door of the house opposite hers. It's a little late in the evening, but after a few seconds an elderly woman opens the door and looks me up and down. "Yes?" she asks.

"Good evening, ma'am. I'm Officer Whittaker, and wondered if I could ask you a few questions about your neighbor Clara?" I gesture toward the house across the way.

"Oh. Yes?" She's timid and stays half-hidden behind the door.

I realize she's wearing a nightgown and I try to ignore it, not wanting to make her uncomfortable. "Have you seen her today?"

Her nod is sharp and brims with judgment. "Over there," she says flatly, with a thrust of her chin to a place diagonally across the street. Not Clara's house, but a place maybe fifty yards farther along the road. Turning, I see a dirt lot full of twenty or so parked vehicles, mostly lifted pickup trucks. Behind the makeshift parking lot a greenbelt gives way to dense forest. The old woman continues. "She

was hanging out with those weirdos. The loud ones with their ridiculous trucks. Laughing and smoking." I turn back to her in time to
see her mouth the word "pot," with a sneer.

"Hmm. And after that?"

"They all left together."

"Left?" I ask. "Left how? Their trucks—"

The old woman squeezes her eyes shut, as if tapping into a deep
well of patience. "They didn't drive away, obviously. They walked
into the woods."

"The woods," I repeat, scanning the tree line beyond the greenbelt. "What's back there?"

She sneers. "How would I know? Unlike those kids, I pay attention to the signs."

The way she says "signs" bring sudden goose bumps to my arms, because it sounds like she means mystical signs from above rather than the
"keep out" variety. I'm about to ask her to clarify when she stops me.

"May I get back to bed?" the woman asks.

I nod, thank her for her time, and cross to the dirt field clogged
with lifted pickups. They're all Fords with Idaho plates, I note. Even
from a distance I can see bumper stickers proclaiming the virtues of
gun ownership and hunting. Not usually the weed-smoking types,
but these days who knows? It's no different from drinking Coors,
now. Maybe not in Idaho, but here certainly.

A single old streetlamp casts stark yellow light that swims from
the moths circling the bulb. Everything else is lost in shadow. I stop
for a moment to let my eyes adjust.

Most of the trucks are old and beat-up, but one is brand spank-
ing new. A huge F-250 with all the frills, not a scratch on it despite
the small fortune that's clearly been spent on upgrading its off-road
capabilities. On the back window is a modified Starbucks logo, with
the iconic mermaid woman wielding two pistols, and the words
"guns & coffee" around the outer circle. On the tailgate is a Jesus
fish mowing down a Darwin fish with an assault rifle.

"Nice," I mutter, and press into the space between the two rows
of vehicles. There's no one around, just as the old lady said. Foot-

prints in the soil imply a large group, mostly wearing hiking boots I think, though I'm no expert. Greg would rattle off the makes and tread patterns, I expect. I check the time, and in doing so spot the words written on my hand.

## YOU NEED <u>HELP</u>

"Fuck! Forgot already." I slip my phone from my pocket and try Clara's number first. Still no answer. Then I call Kyle. He picks up on ring number one.

"Find her?" he asks.

"Not yet."

Kyle waits expectantly.

Uttering my next sentence feels like pushing open an ancient rusted gate. My brain does *not* want to go here, but focusing on the words written on my hand pushes me through the mental barrier. "Could use some . . . help, I think."

"Name it. Anything."

I explain about her empty house and the trucks, and what the old woman said. Kyle's concern matches my own.

"Can you give me fifteen minutes to close the bar? I can meet you there. I know the lot you're talking about."

"Thanks, Kyle."

"No worries, babe. See you in a few."

He disconnects and I'm left turning over the word "babe" in my mind a few times. Deciding that while I don't love it, I also don't mind it as much as I thought I might. I turn to take in the scene once again. The tiny dirt parking lot suddenly feels very quiet. Across the street, the old woman's house is now dark, though there is a sudden movement of the curtains at the front window when I glance that way.

A chill is in the air. Light breeze blowing up the mountain. Stars fill the clear sky, making the towering trees feel that much more oppressive. A silent, black wall that feels utterly impenetrable.

I flick my flashlight on and walk to the line where the lot ends and the greenbelt begins, scanning the edge of the wilderness. All the footprints indicate the group moved east from here, straight into the trees along a . . . well, not really a path, but more of a trampled stretch of dirt and ferns, winding off into the darkness.

An owl hoots nearby. Then another one, farther away. I swallow. There's a third noise, deeper in the woods. Not an owl, but a braying laugh that carries on the evening wind. A dog of some kind? Coyote?

*No, idiot, that was a drunk.*

As my ears adjust I also make out the rhythmic pulse of a bass drum. Heavy guitar. More laughter.

And just beneath all that, something like a scream. Of delight or terror, I honestly can't tell. I'm moving through trees now, pistol drawn, my arms crossed at the wrists to keep weapon and flashlight aimed as one.

A dull metallic creak suddenly erupts from under my foot. I step back, sweeping my beam downward, then let out a slow nervous breath. Half buried by leaves is a chain-link fence that's been pushed over. Dense growth has all but consumed it, and the rest is covered in rust. On my left there's a solid flat object attached to the fence. I sweep my boot over it, revealing a sign that looks at least forty years old, probably more. It had been white, once upon a time. Now it's practically turned to dust. Even so, the words are still legible:

NO TRESPASSING

U.S. GOVT. PROPERTY

"Pay attention to the signs," I mutter, understanding now what the old woman meant.

The sign in question, and the fence it's affixed to, are half consumed by the forest. Which means there's no expectation whoever is out here would know about the warning. I file that.

I crest a small rise. The path becomes twisty, vegetation closing in around me the deeper into the woods I go.

After a minute I catch a glimpse of flickering light through the dark trees. A bonfire, and a big one at that. The sounds of partying fill my ears, blotting out all else. Nearing the edge of the clearing I slow my pace, every sense on full alert. My eyes scan the fire-lit faces, looking for Clara, but from here I don't see her. Just strangers. Mostly men with beards and ball caps and plaid shirts. A tribe if there ever was one.

More details begin to register. They sit on camping chairs and coolers. Beer bottles are everywhere, as are red plastic cups and cigarettes. The smell of pot hangs in the air, too, though faint. Not really the heavy drug crowd, after all. On that my instinct was right. Which is a shame. Potheads are mellow in my experience. Drunken gun freaks? Not so much.

Speaking of guns . . .

In my limited view I already count four. Rifles of various size and make, leaning against trees or slung over shoulders, as if another civil war might break out any second.

I keep back in the trees, flashlight off, making a slow circle of the gathering. There's no sign of Clara, so I shift focus to looking for the ringleader. No one stands out, but my gut tells me there has to be someone here in charge of this. Such events don't happen spontaneously.

Off to one side they've erected a tent, and it's a big one. Fancy, I'd call it. Perhaps that's where the tribe leader holds court. There's a row of kegs in front of it, and several more weapons lean against them. Three shotguns and—of all things—a motherfucking crossbow.

A sudden rush of anger brings bile to my throat. Silvertown is no paradise, but I've no doubt these people will leave a gigantic mess out here tonight, rolling out tomorrow morning with no more thought than they'd have exiting a Porta Potti. Someone else's problem. It's a mentality I can't stand, but I have to tamp down my bubbling rage because, far as I know, they've yet to actually break any laws. Can't fault them for trespassing given the state of the sign. But, on the other hand, there *is* technically a sign. Probably several. Which means I can be a hard-ass stickler if I need to. What's more, there had better be enough open carry permits for everyone toting right now. Whatever it takes, I just want to find Clara and make sure she's okay. At the very least I need to know if she's here, or if they've seen her. Armed with the eyewitness statement from the old woman, it will be interesting to hear what these people have to say.

I flex my fingers on both pistol and flashlight, plotting my move.

Go in mean? Pointing my gun in people's faces, shouting for Clara?

Or go in friendly? The smiling local law enforcement just making sure everyone's having a good, if safe, time. Oh, and by the way have you seen . . . ?

Then there's a wait-and-see approach. Stick to the shadows. Spot Clara first, maybe learn all I need to without ever making my presence known. Perhaps she's friends with these people. Old college chums. Nah, I think. That's fear talking. Clara's all *Alternative Press*, not *Guns & Ammo*.

I settle for friendly, striding in from the trees into full view with a grin on my face and my weapon holstered. "Evening, friends."

The effect borders so closely on the comedic that it's all I can do not to laugh. Everyone turns to me. The music stops within seconds, needing only that classic vinyl needle scratch to be any more perfect. Spliffs disappear, as do the beer cans held by the younger-looking participants. I file that, too.

The whole party just shuts down at the sight of me, like I've pressed a pause button.

Except, that is, for a few precious seconds of extra merriment by those in the tent, who of course have not seen me yet. There's some laughs and chatter that dries up when they realize everyone outside has gone quiet.

"Something wrong, Officer?" one of them asks. A guy near me, a beer bottle in each hand. He has a buzz cut, freckles across his nose, and a sort of captain-of-the-team swagger.

"Maybe," I say, forcing my voice to be calm but loud enough to carry. "Maybe not. Had a report of excessive noise, so I came to check it out."

"Excessive noise. That a crime?" He puts a little chortle into this, raising his voice to show off for his audience.

"Yes, it is," I say. That shuts him up. I can already guess the next question, so I cut it off. "But that's not why I'm really here. We've had a missing persons report in the area."

Several of the men in the crowd cast spooked glances at one another. One of them, a heavyset youngster with shaggy hair, looks sidelong toward the tent before catching himself. He swallows.

Casually as I can, I move my hand to the butt of my pistol. There's a tension in the air that wasn't there a second ago. "A woman," I say, raising my voice a bit more. "Brightly colored hair, nose ring. A local who lives nearby. Goes by Clara. Anyone here by that description? Any of you seen her?"

Nobody says a word.

"In fact," I add, "I have an eyewitness who says she saw you talking to her in the parking lot. Ring any bells?"

No one moves.

Except for one. The big guy who glanced at the tent. He does so again, or starts to. Before his gaze swivels too far he catches himself and tries to turn the motion into a kind of "let me ponder the mysteries of the universe" glance, turning his chin up toward the stars and rubbing the back of his neck with one hand. His eyes, I can see now, are bloodshot and watery. He's seated in a portable folding chair.

"You," I say, getting his attention. "What's in the tent?"

All eyes turn to him now. The youngster swallows once more, then manages to look surprised. "Nothing," he says. "Beer. Chips."

"It's the snack tent," someone off to my left adds.

"The snack tent," I repeat.

The young man in the chair nods, emphatically.

"A tent designated for snacks. Show me?"

Now a hesitation. Again he swallows. Then, with great reluctance, he pushes himself out of the chair and starts to walk to the tent, glancing back at me several times as we go. When he reaches the tent he steps to one side, as if to say his job here is done, only then noticing I've stopped about ten feet from the structure. I nod at the flaps.

The youngster shrugs and pulls one side back, then gestures for me to enter, like a footman motioning his queen to enter the carriage. Several of the onlookers chuckle at this.

I shake my head. "You first."

Once more his Adam's apple bobs. But he turns and goes in. I don't think he's scared, at least not of anything immediate. More likely they've got a shitload of drugs stashed in here and he's not keen on being the one to get all his friends arrested for possession.

I follow him, and as I step under the flap of the tent it's like I've stepped on a switch. Behind and all around me there's a flurry of activity. I turn in time to see the backs of every other member of this gathering as they run for the trees. They leave their chairs, their drinks, everything but what they can haul under one arm, behind. Some of them are laughing as they flee. I've no doubt that in another thirty seconds I'll be hearing the sounds of all those Ford trucks firing up their engines.

Frowning at the thought of all those inebriated drivers heading down Slippery Slope, I turn back to the heavyset man, half expecting to find him gone, too. And he is, at least partially. He's literally on hands and knees, crawling under the staked-down side of the tent off to my left.

I let him go. I'm here for Clara and don't really relish the idea of trying to make a few dozen drug arrests while she's still missing.

It's clear right away that she's not here, though. The tent is empty of people. True to the dude's word, the place is indeed a makeshift pantry for snacks and alcohol. There's huge cases of beer, several bottles of harder stuff, and box after box of bulk-packaged chips, hot dog buns, and so on. Enough for a whole weekend, I estimate, even with the size of the group.

Yet they've just up and left it here, along with the expensive tent. Why?

"Drugs," I voice. Has to be. But there are none visible. Of course only true idiots would leave their stash in plain sight, but then again they doubtless chose this location so they could party without prying eyes, so why hide them?

Then there was the way the dude glanced at the tent when I mentioned Clara. Why would he have done that, if the tent was empty?

I take a second to look at the improvised room again. There's the crates and cartons of food and drink. Several untapped kegs in one corner. Boxes of paper plates and plastic cutlery. Boxes of ammo, too. All this sits around the edges of a square Persian rug, ten-foot on a side, that's been laid on the ground, presumably to keep the dust or mud to a minimum.

I step onto the carpet and reach for the nearest stack of beer cases. Then I freeze, and look down at my feet.

There should be dirt and leaves beneath this carpet, but I've stepped on something hard and . . . not flat, not exactly, but flat-ish. I retreat and kneel down, drawing my gun. With my free hand I grasp the edge of the rug between thumb and forefinger, and lift it up.

Concrete.

"The hell?" I whisper, peering farther under the rug. As I lift the carpet higher, I realize this is big. Much too big for a random pad of concrete in the woods.

Throwing caution to the wind I heave the carpet aside.

In front of me, on the ground in the middle of this nondescript forest on a mountain in the Cascades, is a ten-foot-by-ten-foot concrete slab with a hatch in the center. A round, steel hatch, painted dull blue. It has two handles on one side and a large hinge connecting it to the concrete on the other.

Across the center, faded stenciled letters read:

U. S. AIR FORCE

A few seconds pass wherein I simply stare in completely stunned silence. "What the actual fuck?"

# CHAPTER ELEVEN

Metal groans as I twist the two handles to the left. They're ancient and haven't seen oil in years, certainly. But to my surprise the hatch itself swings upward quite smoothly.

Flashlight between my teeth, I shove the big metal door all the way open. Beneath it is exactly what I expected to find: a hole, leading down into darkness, with a metal ladder embedded into one side.

"Clara?" I call out. "It's Mary Whittaker. You down there?"

The words echo back up through the concrete tube. It's the only response I get.

"This is Silvertown Police," I shout, louder. "We're coming down."

The "we're" bit is a nice touch, I think. Holstering my gun, I begin to climb. It's hard to see with the flashlight held in my mouth, but the ladder seems to descend about twenty feet, and in no time my foot finds another concrete floor. I step off the ladder and go back to the classic tactical stance: gun in one hand, flashlight in the other, wrists crossed for support and stability.

The space around me is not a room, but a tunnel. It has a flat floor and a curved ceiling that forms a half-circle about ten feet high. Pipes and bundles of wire run along the length, secured every fifteen feet or so by thick metal braces.

"Hello?" I call, fruitlessly. The place is clearly deserted, and has been for decades. Probably since the end of the Cold War. A memory comes to me, then. A passing comment made by Greg during my first day on the job, when he'd rattled off all the places in the area that contributed to the "conspiracy theory charm" Silvertown enjoys. It had been a long list. The Masonic campground, the closed pharmaceutical factories, the old army base, and "even a few moth-balled Minuteman silos." He'd said they were locked up tight. I wonder if he knows about the fallen fence, the rusted signage, and most of all the entrance I just used. Maybe this last has only recently been discovered and subsequently cracked open.

From somewhere farther down this passage someone suddenly laughs. A bright, friendly, mirthful laugh. Distant but distinct.

That's Clara's laugh.

I open my mouth to call to her, then decide against it, because I can hear music now, and other voices. Slowly, quietly, I make my way along the corridor, gun and flashlight pointed at the ground ahead of me. On a whim I click the light off and wait a bit for my eyes to adjust. The place is absolutely pitch-dark, or seems that way at first. But after about thirty seconds I realize there's a thin line of light coming from under a door at the far end, maybe forty feet ahead.

I continue on and find my assessment to be exactly right. There's a metal door. In its center is a faded square where some signage used to be, long since removed. Hopefully not a warning of radiation risk. Above the door is a light bulb behind a wire-mesh bracket, turned off. In my mind's eye I can picture it strobing red, warning of imminent attack or launch, or the need to evacuate.

These thoughts I banish with a shake of my head, because Clara's laugh has just reached my ears again, much more clearly now. Just on the other side of this door, in fact.

I grasp the handle and yank it open, releasing warmth and light and music. A smell hits me hard. The fog of weed being smoked, of sweat, of sex, and other things I'm loath to discover the source of.

Music blares from a small speaker. A band I don't know, something heavy and bleak, which mingles ominously with the voices of the six or seven people in the room.

None of them notice me. They're all seated on ratty old mattresses, arranged in a square facing in on one another. In the center of that square is a patch of dusty concrete floor littered with the proverbial "drug paraphernalia." Vials of liquid, bags of powder, strange chemical smells. Light comes from a few candles placed around the room, plus a camping lantern in one corner that blinks erratically as its battery clings to life.

The walls of the room are covered in scrawled messages. Some carved with knives, some in spray paint, and the rest in permanent marker. Faded messages, and fresh ones, too. There are dates, with some of them going back years. Decades. One says "Vader was here— 7/1/77," with a badly drawn caricature of the famous movie villain.

*Focus*, I tell myself, and adjust my grip on the flashlight. It's only then that I notice the words written on my hand. *You need help*. Yes I do, goddammit. And once again it's like the very concept has been wiped from my brain. Is that even possible? I make a mental note to google it. *No, moron, you need help, remember from five fucking seconds ago?* I take a deep breath. Asking Doc might be better than an Internet search. He is a shrink, after all, and from what we discussed when we found the hiker's body, he knows a thing or two about instincts and what might affect them.

Later, though. Right now I have a friend to rescue.

"Clara?" I call out. My voice is more tentative than I'd like, and goes unheard above the loud music, which thumps from a surprisingly powerful speaker the size of an egg carton. The device rests atop a cooler nearby. I cross to it and take a moment to find the power switch, then flip it off.

The conversation in the room continues for a few seconds before everyone realizes the music has died. They turn to the speaker almost as one and, seeing me, react. Eyes go wide. One of the young males abruptly stands, as if I'm the ghost of his long-dead grandma.

"Everyone stay calm," I say in a soothing voice.

"It's not what it looks like!" the young man says, voice high with panic.

"Stay calm," I repeat with force. "I don't care about your drugs, I'm just here for—"

"It's not drugs," the boy says. And he is a boy, I think. Sixteen, seventeen tops.

I click my flashlight on and turn it toward him, causing him to throw one arm up to block the glare. "Dude, you think I was born yesterday?" I ask him.

Beside him a woman—scratch that, a girl, she can't be more than seventeen either—comes to a slow stand, skinny arms outstretched, palms facing me. "It's true," she says.

My stance swivels to shine the light on her. "Save it for later. I'm just here for my friend Clara. Dyed hair that's shaved on one side. Nose ring? Seen her?"

"Oh yeah!" another of them says excitedly. "Clara! She's cool as hell. Um. She went down into the silo with the others."

"What others?"

"The rest of the club." He says this as if it's patently obvious.

"You've got thirty seconds to explain, short stuff, before I let you explain it to a judge." It's the oldest empty threat in the police officer's handbook but hot damn does it work on kids.

Despite his obvious terror, Short Stuff launches into an explanation.

"We're from Idaho," he starts.

"No shit. Saw the license plates and, to be honest, I don't care. Tell me about this club. Then tell me where Clara is."

He swallows and tries again. "UrbEx," he says, and immediately registers my confusion at the term. "Urban explorers. We find abandoned places and—"

"—explore them," I say, finishing his sentence. "Get to the point."

"Well, we heard about this old missile silo from another club, and convinced James's brother to bring us here. James is our club president. His brother is Adam, he's up there partying with all his college friends."

Urban explorers? That makes a weird kind of sense, I think. "Well, Adam's not up there anymore," I tell him. "They all bailed when I showed up. Sorry to say."

"Bailed?" Skinny Arms asks. "Fuck. How do we get home?"

"We'll worry about that later," I tell her. I give myself time to take a deep breath. "Okay, none of this explains the drugs, but you're kids and I'm not here for—"

"They aren't, though," the girl insists again. She kneels beside the center area of the room and gestures, so I swing the flashlight there and take a proper look. "Just some stuff we borrowed from the chem lab at school. To test dust samples."

Short Stuff is nodding. "For radiation."

"Radiation?" Suddenly the word "silo" registers in my brain.

He nods even more vigorously. "Rumor has it the air force left a warhead in here somewhere. Another club picked up traces on their Geiger counter but couldn't pinpoint it. That's what James said, anyway."

"Only we don't have one," Skinny Arms adds. "A Geiger counter, I mean. So we thought, screw it, we'll take samples of the dust and—"

"Right," I say, "Okay. Hold that thought. Honestly it sounds like total horseshit to me—relax, relax. Right now I don't care. And I don't have the manpower to figure out if you've broken any laws by coming in here, anyway. Probably a dozen of the federal variety, but I'm of a mind right now to ignore all that on the condition that you tell me where to find my friend Clara."

"I'm here," a voice says from the darkness beyond the youngsters.

She strolls into the room with a smile on her face, flanked by two college-aged boys. One is quite handsome if you ignore the ravages of acne, and the other a bit overweight and sporting some of the thickest glasses I've ever seen. Geeks, I think. Nerds. Incongruous with the partying crowd above. Incongruous with Clara, for that matter. The semihandsome one is staring at her with puppy-dog eyes, I note.

"Heya, Mary," Clara says, coming over and hugging me. "I see you met the group."

"You know these kids?"

Clara grins. "No. Well, yes. For a few hours now."

I take her by the elbow and turn her to face me, making sure I have her full attention. "Everyone's been worried sick, Clara!"

She seems genuinely shocked to hear this. "Why?"

"You didn't show up for work, for starters. Your front door was open. This just the morning after someone tried to kill me in my home. All our calls and texts, ignored."

Frowning, Clara fishes her phone from the pocket of her dusty jeans and shows the black screen to me. "Turned it off."

"Why?"

"James said it would interfere with their equipment."

"And you believed him? A kid you just met?"

At this Clara looks almost hurt. The surprise on her face is genuine. "Why would he lie?"

"To lure you into a dark, hidden place where no one would ever find you?"

The boy starts to protest, but I hold up my hand to silence him, my focus never leaving Clara. She scrunches her nose. Her eyes dart left and right several times as she ponders this strange and foreign concept. Except it's not strange and foreign to her, not in the slightest. Clara's the survivor of an attempted mugging. She's wary of strangers. It's why she spends her time working the grill at the diner instead of waiting tables where the tips are. Hell, she keeps a Taser in her car and a small can of pepper spray attached to her key chain.

"They're just kids, Mary. Explorers."

"Again, so they claim. And even if true, it's quite possibly illegal for them to enter this place."

"James said they have permission."

"Did he," I say, and throw the boy a stern glance.

Instantly he's rubbing the back of his neck, studiously looking at the floor. All the color has drained from his face.

"Well," he stammers, "not exactly permission, I guess. More like—"

He goes on, mumbling his excuses, but I'm not listening. Neither is Clara. We're staring at each other, and I can see she's finally realized something's wrong here. The expression on her face is exactly how I must have looked sitting in my car outside O'Doh's.

"I don't know why I—" Clara begins, then stops herself, sensing that I might have an explanation. I do, sort of, but this isn't the time or place for it. All I know is, whatever is affecting me appears to now be affecting Clara, too.

"Okay. Okay," I say to James. "Enough. Pack up your stuff. Let's find your brother and get you guys out of here. We'll overlook all of this provided you stay away from this place. Hear me?"

I get a wide-eyed nod as my answer. Good enough.

"Get to it, then," I say to him, gesturing toward their science gear.

Twenty minutes later we're back in Clara's house, waiting for coffee to brew.

The teens from Idaho found James's older brother had not, in fact, left them high and dry in a missile silo. They'd tried, but at the exit of the parking lot they'd been met with the business end of Kyle's shotgun. He'd held them there, not knowing what the hell was going on but absolutely sure that *something* was.

"I'm so glad you showed up," I tell him now, across the chipped surface of Clara's small kitchen table.

"Thought you were going to wait for me," Kyle says.

"I think that was my intention, but I forgot."

"Forgot?"

"I'll explain in a second."

He nods, impatient but willing to wait for some answers. As Clara fiddles with her French press, I start planning out what it's going to take to build a fence around that silo entrance. Chain-link and razor wire? What about signage? As I take the offered mug, I see the words on my hand again and kick myself, mentally. I don't need to build a fence. What the hell am I thinking? Call the air force and tell them kids are urban exploring that place and someone's going to fall or get lost or whatever. Lawsuits likely. That'll get them up here by Friday.

"Hey, Clara?" Kyle asks, raising his voice to reach her in the adjacent room.

"Mm?"

"I didn't know you played guitar."

She pokes her head out of the kitchen.

Kyle's turned in his seat, gazing into her living room, where three electric guitars are mounted like trophies above the fireplace. They're not new. Far from it, actually. Each is scarred and battle-bruised from excessive use.

"Oh. That," she says. "I don't. I mean, I tried, but I'm terrible."

"Then why'd you buy three?"

"Inherited," she says, back in the kitchen now. "Along with a big-ass amp that's out in the garage. I took lessons, really gave it my best shot, but . . . not my thing, I guess."

She comes in with a tray of steaming mugs and takes a seat. The three of us sit there for a moment, sipping the excellent coffee.

"They were my cousin's," Clara says. "Not the mugs, the guitars. He toured with Quiet Riot if you can believe that. Reunion tour about, geez, ten years ago?"

Kyle's eyebrows shoot up. "Seriously? I used to love them. Hell, still do."

"Eighties hair-bands are the shit, aren't they?"

The pair of them fist-bump, then sip coffee in near unison. For my part I feel like the third wheel on a first date, only vaguely aware of the band or their music.

"You need help," Kyle says suddenly.

"The hell I do," I start, then realize he's reading the words from my hand. I dip my chin and give my brain a few seconds to over-come what my instincts tell me. "I absolutely do," I finally say. Then I point to the words. "This is what I wanted to talk to you two about."

"Help?" Clara asks.

"No. Not exactly," I say. "I have a theory about everything that's been going on. The start of one, anyway. It's out there, but this is Silvertown so . . . that seems appropriate."

"I'm listening," Kyle says, leaning forward. "This is some kick-ass coffee by the way, Clara."

"Life's too short to drink anything else."

"Amen to that."

"So here goes," I say, and wait for their full attention. "Clara, can you see the similarity between what happened out there and what happened with Sally Jones earlier today?"

From her puzzled expression, the answer's no. I go on.

"Sally is a textbook example of a helicopter parent. Agreed?"

They both nod.

"This morning, though, she leaves them alone and goes on a tour of Silvertown with a total stranger."

I've got their attention now. Neither says a word, they just wait.

"Then I find you, Clara, out in the woods—no, in a missile silo of all things—with a bunch of kids you've never met before."

"Oh, they're harmless, Mary."

"That's not the point. Or, rather, it is exactly the point."

"Huh?"

I turn to Kyle. "You've known Clara much longer than me. Would you say she's the type of person who jaunts off to strange, dark places with complete strangers?"

"Hell no," he says instantly.

A confused expression forms on Clara's face. She's looking at Kyle, then at me, then somewhere in the distance. "Yeah . . . that's true," she says slowly. "But Sally left her kids alone. Babies. That's totally different."

"Uh," I reply, "I wouldn't say totally."

"She left her kids in danger. I was just having a laugh."

"A laugh with strangers. In a creepy, old, possibly radioactive missile silo no one knew you were in."

Again that confused look. "I don't know why I did that, Mary. Honestly. It didn't even occur to me until you brought it up."

"And that's my point. Because I've been having some issues of my own. And I didn't realize it until Kyle said something at the bar an hour ago. Though it was just an echo of something you said even earlier, at the diner, Clara."

"What I'd say?"

"That I didn't need to do everything myself." I point at Kyle. "Or, as Kyle put it, that I'd stopped with my 'typical Mary Whittaker team operation.'"

Clara's quick to brush this aside, but Kyle's features are as if chiseled from stone.

"Ever since that guy attacked me last night," I add, "I haven't been myself."

"It was empowering, you said."

"This is more than that, though. I have to really, really think about it, but when I do I can recognize this change inside me. I bet if you do, you'll see it inside yourself as well."

'I guess so," she says haltingly.

"Yeah," Kyle says, nodding. "I think you're right."

I glance at him. "You're feeling differently, too?"

He shakes his head, slowly at first but then more firmly. "Nah, I just mean in you. I noticed the change. Couldn't articulate it, though."

"Hold on," Clara says. "You said you started acting differently ever since that guy attacked you."

"Yeah. Specifically he put a rag coated in some chemical over my mouth."

"But nothing like that happened to me."

I give a slow nod. "True. Hadn't thought of that." It's a dent in my theory. One of many, really. "Nothing like that happened to Sally, either. At least that we know of."

Clara's eyes go wide. "Meaning? Are you saying he attacked her, too? Or did it without her knowing? Wait, are you saying he did something to me? Like, while I was asleep or . . . ?"

I shake my head, before she can get too worked up. "I'm not saying that."

"But it's possible."

"I . . . no. I mean, yes, but I just don't think that's what's going on here."

"So what is?" Kyle asks, after a brief silence.

We all sit there, staring at the table.

"The cell tower?" Kyle asks.

I groan.

"What?" he asks. "I'm not one to buy into a Silvertown conspiracy theory but . . . I mean, c'mon, something's causing this, and that giant antenna is new. The timing has to mean something."

I grimace and shake my head. "This would be going on all over the country, then, wouldn't it? Those towers are everywhere."

He shrugs. "Maybe no one else has put two and two together yet."

"Let's call it a distant possibility, then. What else could be causing this?"

"Runoff from the mine?" Clara suggests. "In our water?"

"The mine's been closed for ages, hasn't it?"

"True."

Kyle leans in. "It's not part of the water supply, anyway. Silvertown's comes from snowmelt, far as I'm aware."

Clara tilts her head, conceding the point.

Kyle nudges me with his elbow. "You have a theory?"

I hesitate. Trying to put my thoughts into words makes it all seem like nonsense. I feel like I'm just falling into the Silvertown trap, finding a conspiracy where none exists. Or worse, inventing one. Making connections that aren't really there.

"No," I say as casually as I can. "Just trying to think it all through."

He nods, sips his coffee. Clara does the same, and for a while we all sit and ponder.

Okay, so Clara and I are acting strange but Kyle seems his usual self. Another point against my theory. I consider the other examples from the last few days. The hiker? Okay, so he froze when faced with an angry bear. Is that so bizarre? Not really, I admit. Willy Jupitas walking in front of my car? People get absentminded sometimes, do they not? Especially in their later years . . .

"Mary?" Clara asks. "You're doing it again."

"Doing what?" I ask.

"Excluding us," Kyle says for her. "C'mon. Think out loud. What's your theory?"

I sigh. "My theory is that this town might finally be getting to me."

"And?" he prompts.

"It's nothing," I reply. "Really. I just need to not be so gung-ho about proving myself while Greg's gone. I do need help, that's the simple truth. I need you guys. And as long as the three of us agree something is really going on here, I can . . . I mean . . . we . . ."

"We're a team," he says, and pats my hand warmly. "Don't worry, we'll keep reminding you."

"Thanks."

He nods at me. But he doesn't look entirely convinced. "I still think there's something to this, Mary, even if you've talked yourself out of it."

"Maybe you're right. I need to think about it more. And I really need to get some sleep," I say. Neither of them voice opposition to this.

"Tomorrow, then," Clara suggests. "Breakfast at the diner. We'll figure this out."

We say our goodbyes to Clara only after she promises to lock her door, activate her security system, and call me first thing in the morning.

"Want another sleep-aid?" she asks me at the door. "They really do work."

"I'm good," I tell her.

Outside, Kyle walks me to my car. We embrace, and our lips find each other's. The kiss lingers, starts to become something more. It's me who pulls away first.

"You can stay at my place," he says, voice husky, hands firm on the small of my back, pressing me to him. "If you need."

"Sleep, Kyle. Sleep is what I need." I sigh and move to rest my head in the crook of his neck. And there's my left hand, resting over his heart, the words YOU NEED <u>HELP</u> practically shouting at me.

"That's all I meant," he says with mock indignation. "Any insinuation otherwise—"

I press a hand to his lips. "Fine. Okay. Let's go."

I follow him home, and we're lucky it's late because his place is on the top floor of the same building O'Doherty's is in. Right across the street from the police station. At this hour, no one's around to see me climb from my cruiser and walk to Kyle's.

We kiss briefly under the little lamp above the entrance. It's an inset doorway just to the left of the pub's front door, leading straight into a set of narrow stairs that provide access to the three apartments above the pub, each one floor above the last. Kyle's is on the fourth, and last, story.

He lets me in and we kiss again.

"I was serious about sleep," I say when we break, breathless. My voice is husky like his was, betraying my words, but I guess my eyes are serious because Kyle watches them, and he nods.

"Works for me."

In bed I lay propped on an elbow, watching him brush his teeth in the bathroom just beyond.

"Hey," I ask, "is Kenny okay?"

"Whaddya mean?"

"I don't know. When I saw him at the gas station he looked . . . thin."

Kyle leans out the door and studies me for a second. "I know he looks like a tweaker, but he's clean. Swear." His head vanishes again.

"Thinner than usual, I mean. And his lips were super dry."

Kyle's bedroom is simply furnished. The queen mattress is on the floor. There's a low table on the adjacent wall with a flat-screen TV on it and a PlayStation. One of the games stacked beside it I recognize.

"Hey, you play *Bug Out Bag*?" I ask him.

"The game? Used to. It sucks. So unrealistic."

Below the window on the adjacent wall is a cheap dresser, flanked on one side by a floor lamp and on the other by a tall gun safe, suitable for holding several hunting rifles.

"How many guns does one man need?" I ask, eyeing the metal box as he comes back into the room.

He glances that way, then at me, and gives a sheepish smile. "Actually," he says, "it's pretty much empty right now. Kenny's cleaning them for me. It's kind of a thing for him. He's fine by the way. Kenny. Far as I know."

" 'Pretty much' empty? Care to elaborate, sir?"

"Just a single pistol, Officer. For self-defense."

"You better have a permit for it."

"I . . . uh . . . gee, Officer, not exactly."

I assume he's joking, because I was joking, but to my surprise he opens the safe. Makes a show of it, in fact, with no attempt to shield the combination from me. From inside he removes a holster and belt. Even in the dim light I can tell it's old, the leather cracked in places, yet it still has an air of being lovingly maintained.

Inside the holster is a pistol I've seen in dozens of movies, but never in person. "Is that a Luger?"

"Yep," he says, proudly. "Want to hold it?"

"It's really unlicensed?"

He stares at me, and his face scrunches up in an almost comedic admission of guilt. "I mean, I think so. This old fogie gave it to me to cover his bar tab, few years back. He sort of implied I should keep it on the down low. Figured it would be best not to find out."

"Yeah, of course. You wouldn't want to find out it's a Nazi murder weapon or something you've been slathering your fingerprints all over."

Kyle shrugs, a little too amused at the sarcasm. He offers the weapon to me, grip-first.

I shake my head at him. "No, I don't want to hold it. Pretend I never saw it, okay?"

He puts the old gun and its holster back in the safe, spins the lock, and crawls onto the bed.

Ten minutes later, with Kyle spooned against my back and his warm breaths tickling the hairs on my neck, I fall into the best sleep I've had in days.

# CHAPTER TWELVE

The sound of rain against Kyle's window stirs me awake. Soft gray light pushes in around the edges of the blinds. It's just enough to see the crumpled sheets and discarded clothes. Funny, I think, how the aftermath of a night of sleep isn't too different from that of love-making.

Careful not to wake him, I slip from under the covers and gather up my things. The idea of a warm shower is practically enough to make me salivate, but I decide against waking him. I want to cross the street and be inside the station before anyone notices I was here.

The clock on my phone reads 6:12 a.m. There's no messages, and only one text: a note from Clara, thanking me for rescuing her from the silo and offering to buy breakfast as a show of gratitude. "We are still getting breakfast, yes?" the message concludes. She sent it only a few minutes before. I reply:

busy morning ahead. make it lynch and you're on.

Followed by:

*lunch! ducking auto convict.

Her reply is two emojis: a face crying with laughter and a thumbs-up.

I leave Kyle's place on the top floor of the narrow old four-story building. I always thought living so close to work would drive me nuts, but as I slip out the little side door next to the pub's entrance and walk quickly across to the station, I can appreciate the benefits.

I go inside only long enough for a shower and a cup of coffee. Fifteen minutes later I'm in the car, feeling energized and ready to roll.

Last night as I fell asleep—which didn't take long—a plan of sorts started to take shape in my muddled brain. More of a credo than a plan, I guess. A mantra that I repeated to myself several times before drifting off. "Look into everything, no matter how crazy." And that's exactly what I intend to do today. Before lunch if possible. I want to have something solid the next time Clara, Kyle, and I talk.

Because although I'm convinced now that at least some of Silvertown's residents—myself included—are having behavioral issues, the question is how? Why?

I take my time driving through downtown. There are no cars around yet. Just a few people out for morning walks, either alone or with their dogs. None of the shops are open, at least not for business. The door to the kitschy crystal-healing and occult gifts shop, called The Dark Wheel, stands ajar. The sight of its open door gives me a little knot of dread, but as I drive by, the owner of the store, a soft middle-aged man with jet-black hair flowing to his shoulders, waddles out butt-first, sweeping a broom left to right as he goes.

He's about to sweep the dust into the gutter when he sees me and thinks better of it, fishing a small bronze dustbin from his back pocket as if he carried it everywhere. I stop and roll the window down.

"Morning," I say.

"Greetings," he says theatrically. "It's Officer Whittaker, yes?"

I nod. "Sorry, I'm still learning names. Can't believe we haven't met yet. You are?"

He crosses the empty street to stand by my door, offering a hand. "Damian Blackwood," he says with a little bow.

I shake his hand, grinning despite myself. It's the man I saw wearing a black trench coat, that night after Johnny's funeral. "Not your given name, I assume?"

He replaces the dustbin handle-first into his back pocket and makes a zipping motion across his lips. "All part of the persona."

"Your shop," I say, eyeing the window displays, "must do pretty good business in a place like this, huh?"

"Oh," he says, "you can't even imagine. People will buy anything, to my constant yet well-concealed amusement."

"As long as you're not promising results."

He turns slightly and points to a sign above the door. More of a crest, cast in bronze. It looks very old. The image depicts a vaguely Egyptian figure, one of those ones with the head of a dog, holding an ankh in one hand and some kind of laurel in the other, all surrounded by a star with yin-yang symbols at the points. Above all this a phrase is carved, in Latin: *Nihil hic actu operatur*.

"What's it say?" I ask.

"It says 'Nothing here actually works,'" he replies.

I laugh gleefully. "That's awesome."

"The store pays the bills, yes, and . . . well, allows me to focus on my own, err, hobbies."

"Ohhhkay. Bit weird. Not going to ask."

With a sheepish grin, Damian knocks twice on the hood of my cruiser and wanders back to resume his sweeping, the knowing grin never leaving his face.

I drive on, my skin feeling just a little clammy at the way he said "hobbies." The sign is pretty good, though. No doubt about that. What it must be like to go through life on the right side of an inside joke. These last few days have felt like the opposite of that.

Leaving both the town and the dwindling morning rain behind, I make my way up the winding mountain road, stopping again at Last Chance coffee to refill my travel mug, but instead of continuing on up to the lake I take a right. This road is new, only one lane wide, and serves a singular purpose. Leaning forward as far as I can, chin pressed against the steering wheel, I glance up at the steep mountainside. It's densely forested. A wall of green. There, in the middle of all that lush nature, stands one tree about twice as tall as the others, and so obviously fake it's almost funny. The cell phone tower is too thick, its branches too stubby, and it's painted slightly the wrong shade of green. Then there's the rectangular panels that protrude from its upper reaches, an array of drum-shaped antennas, and a few satellite dishes mixed in for good measure.

I drive on, following the access road for a good half mile around hairpin corners and rutted dips. At one point I have to get out and unlock a gate. It's weak as far as security goes. Just a pair of thick metal poles attached on hinges at either side and padlocked in the middle. The key is on my cruiser's key chain, carefully labeled by Greg. I swing the gates open and pull the car through, deciding to leave the barricade open behind me, since I don't plan to be here long. The road goes on another few hundred yards before coming to the base of the "tree."

The tower, some three hundred feet tall, sits on a concrete pad about twenty-five feet square. Surrounding this is a high chain-link fence with barbed wire on top. There's a whole slew of beige utility boxes just within the perimeter, some as big as a car. They all sport signs with various warnings: risk of electric shock, primarily. The whole place hums with the current running through it.

It's early still and the sun is low, illuminating only the top of the tower, which is about twice as tall as the trees around it. Up close it's almost comical how wrong the thing is. The color's off, the branches look hilariously stunted, and the height is . . . well, ridiculous. Another detail occurs to me: it's totally unaffected by the wind.

My phone rings. I glance at the screen, hoping to see Kyle's name, but instead I see the indicator that this is a forwarded call from the Silvertown Police station number. When no one's at the office it gets routed to Greg's or my phone, depending on the day, but with him gone it's set to go to me exclusively.

"Silvertown Police, this is Officer Whittaker."

"Uh, hi, yeah, this is Sean Dennis with StellarComm?"

The StellarComm logo is all over the gear behind the fence I'm standing next to, and I'm guessing I triggered an alarm coming in here. "How can I help you, Mr. Dennis?"

"Well I'm up here on the access road to our tower there, and the gate is wide open. Unlocked."

"Okay, and?"

"Well no one else but me should be up there today, so . . . well, I just thought you might want to know. I was going to head up to do some maintenance, but if someone's up there . . . I guess I thought you might . . ."

"Come on up, Sean," I say. "I'm the one who's up here. I left the gate open."

"Oh. Oh!" He sighs, a relief that is gone just as quickly as it appeared. "Wait, how come you're there? Did something happen?"

I kick a pebble away from my boot. "No no. Just a routine visit," I say. "Come on up."

A few minutes later his white van rolls into the small parking area in front of the fence. It's a Ford utility model with window-less sides, a StellarComm logo writ from front to back in huge letters.

Sean Dennis steps out and closes the door, but doesn't cross to me. He looks to be about eighteen years old, rail thin and with a hawkish face covered in acne. He pushes a pair of well-worn glasses up to the bridge of his nose, glances at the tower and the equipment at its base, then finally steps to me and offers a hand.

"Mary Whittaker," I say, shaking.

"Hi. Uh. Hello, Officer."

His hand is cold, and trembling a bit. Instantly I'm on alert.

"Maintenance?" I ask.

"Yeah," he says, almost embarrassed. "Nothing's wrong with it. Just the regular weekly site review."

"On a Sunday?"

"I work weekends," he explains. "Perks of being a newbie."

I nod, and make a sweeping gesture toward the tower. "Don't let me stop you."

He seems reluctant to move, as if me watching him work is going to reveal some trade secret, which I suppose is possibly the reason. But I just stand there. After a few awkward seconds he moves to the back of his van and starts to rummage around.

"Tell me about this place," I say.

"Okay. Uhhhhh, like, what do you want to know? I just started two months ago, so I'm not sure how helpful I'll be." He emerges from the back of the van with a satchel full of tools and one of those steel clipboards, but instead of a pad of paper forms it's got a tablet computer attached to the front.

"Anyone but you ever come up here?"

"Not since it was switched on," he replies, unlocking the small gate that leads inside the fence line.

"So it is on, then?"

"Well, yeah. Of course it is. For about a month now. Aren't you getting better signal lately?"

I shrug. "I suppose so. Some people aren't." From his expression he takes this personally. I decide to go a step further. "Ever get a headache from working so close to these things?"

He squints at me, as if trying to decide if I'm being serious. "No. Why would I?"

"Some people claim it gives them headaches."

The corner of his mouth twitches back, but he suppresses the smile before it fully forms.

"That amusing?" I ask.

Sean lifts his shoulders, lets them fall. "People say that everywhere. We heard all about it in training. Some techs have even been assaulted."

"What, here?"

"Not here, just . . . in general." He opens a panel on one of the boxes, checks some LEDs inside, then snaps it closed again. "I've seen people posting online saying, 'The 5G is giving us all cancer!' Thing is, you get way more radiation from the sun than any of this stuff. But no one wants to hear that. No one wants to know that there have been studies where they put people next to antennas that were on, or off, or some that weren't even real. No one could accurately tell if the antennas were transmitting or not, at least any more than they could guess heads or tails. Still, people blame their headaches on these signals, not their bad diets and lack of hydration."

The speech sounds a bit rehearsed. Something right out of his StellarComm training manual, I assume, or just overheard in the break room. Doesn't make it any less true, though.

"What about bloody noses?"

He just shakes his head, amused and a little annoyed now, too, I think.

"Changes in behavior?"

At this he glances at me, and for the first time there is something like curiosity in his gaze. "Like what?"

"Like, say, making a successful lawyer and family man break into someone's home and try to kill them? That kind of change in behavior."

His face scrunches up. Complete bafflement. "Huh?"

"Don't you watch the news?"

"Not if I can help it."

"Fair enough," I say. "Thanks for your time."

He offers a sheepish wave and returns to his tasks.

"Oh," I add, halfway to my car. "You ever see anyone else up here?"

Sean Dennis shakes his head. Slowly at first, but then with more conviction. "Just you cops."

I nod, turn away. Only then does the plural register. "Cops . . . more than me, you mean?"

"Yeah, that other guy, he was here once. Well, at the gate, leaving when I arrived."

"Remember his name?"

Sean thinks on this a moment before finally shaking his head.

"Older guy, gray hair, bushy mustache?"

The kid squints at me now, still shaking his head. "No, younger, like you. Black hair. I think he was Mexi . . . sorry, Latino."

"Same uniform as mine?"

"No. No. Like a dark blue, I think. I don't really know, he didn't get out of his car. Just waved at me."

I frown, unsure what to make of this. "What about his car? Black, like mine?"

Sean shakes his head again. "White," he says.

A state trooper, then. Odd they would have come up this far, but not completely weird. In Washington an officer of the law has full policing rights anywhere in the state, though agreements among agencies usually put some polite restrictions on that. As such they do usually check in with us when they come through on patrol. Could be they did just that, of course, only via a direct line to Greg. There'd have been no reason for him to let me know. I make a mental note to remind the chief he should insist they use the main station line, assuming they really are calling his personal number. "How long ago was this?"

"Uhhh . . . two weeks? Yeah. Two weeks, time before last."

The same weekend Johnny Rogers died. Surely that's a coincidence. I tell myself as much, at least. And it makes even more sense that Greg neglected to tell me a state trooper had come through, as we would have been too distracted with that investigation. For all I know the call is still sitting in his voice mail, unheard.

I thank the boy again and get in my car. Before leaving, on a whim, I jot down the make and model of his vehicle, as well as the license plate number. None of my "something's fishy here" detectors are going off, but I'm not entirely sure I can trust my brain right now, as evidenced by the words scrawled on my hand.

At the intersection with the state route, I pull in once again to Last Chance, opting for a decaf this time. I ask for a blueberry muffin top again, making sure they give me the right one. The same two teenage girls are working the small booth today, both gossiping in hushed voices as they work the espresso machine. *OMG* this and *LOL* that.

"Anyone else come through this morning?" I ask. "Hikers, I mean, headed for the lake?"

"Just that weirdo from StellarComm," the blond one says.

"Weirdo how?" I ask, intrigued.

The brunette girl replies, "He said if we ever wanted to check out the tower, he could show it to us. Guh-Ross!"

"Like we didn't know what he meant. Also, last time he was here, I saw he had a porno mag on his dashboard. I mean, seriously? So frickin' gross."

My personal opinion is that he'd genuinely meant to impress them with the tower, and not any innuendo. "Just him? No one else came through?"

Blondie shrugs. "Saw some station wagons turn off that way as I was opening this morning. They didn't stop for coffee." Her chin indicates the left turn at the intersection. While the right turn goes up to the cell tower, the left goes off into forest, downhill.

" 'Wagons' plural?"

"Uh-huh. Three of 'em."

"What's back there?" I ask, glancing toward the road.

The girl wrinkles her nose. "Beats me. Trees?"

Her friend speaks up, though. "Some old trail. It's all overgrown, though. I think there's a ghost town way down there somewhere."

A ghost town. That's a new one. Not only does Silvertown have an abandoned military base and a toxic mine site, apparently we've got a ghost town, too. Of course we would. "Interesting. Thanks." I leave them with a five-dollar tip, eliciting big smiles, and head back to my car to drive away. Out of curiosity I take the left and follow the weather-beaten road into the trees. It only goes about two hundred yards before transitioning into a lumpy gravel trail.

After about a mile of twists and turns, I come to a sort of clearing. There are indeed three station wagons parked off to the side. One has a tiny sticker in the back window that reads SILVERTOWN HISTORICAL SOCIETY. I place my hand on the maroon hood. Cool to the touch. From one of the pockets on my belt I find a piece of chalk and use it to mark one of the tires. This is more out of habit than anything. One of the oldest police tricks in the book, primarily to know if someone has been parked too long in the same place. That's not a concern here, but if the cars are parked here tomorrow it might be nice to know if they camped wherever they are, or left and returned.

Back in my cruiser I pull an old paper map from the glove box. It doesn't take long to find this stretch of road, nor to find the dotted line continuing from the dead end. A walking trail. I trace its winding, erratic path with my finger. Sure enough, nearly six miles into the forest there's a marker for a historical site. Trinity, it's called. This is a new one to me. I google it on my phone and sit for several minutes reading about the place. More of a settlement than a town, really. According to the site, there was a "general store, saloon, and several brothels," all-purpose built to serve prospectors, but the location turned out to be inconvenient once the silver mine was dug. People gradually moved to the rapidly growing nearby Silvertown, which was much easier to access from the mountain's base.

I read on, finding blog posts from the historical society. The term "ghost town" is used generously. It's really just a collection of decrepit, disused structures, all rendered inaccessible to any tourism by six miles of treacherous, poorly maintained trail. And though it's not expressly stated, I get the sense the historical society's preservation efforts are more for their own satisfaction and not to turn the site into another stomping ground for tourists.

Map folded again and tucked away, I set off once more, though less sure now of where I'm going to go next. The cell tower theory seems like a dud. All the other options seem too much like the plots from episodes of *Ancient Aliens*. Next thing I know I'm going to be at the county airport, asking about chemtrails.

Without any real sense of purpose, other than simply to keep looking, I head on down the highway, through a quiet downtown, and all the way to Keller's Bridge—the westernmost point of my jurisdiction.

The old iron bridge marks the spot where Silvertown ends and Granston begins. It's a rusted, ugly thing that looks about twenty years past its maintenance date. Greg is convinced a tired trucker is going to bump into it one night and send the whole thing down into the river some fifty feet below. One of us comes down here every day just to make sure no one's broken down on the span, as it is the only way in or out of town.

There had been an effort back in the 1980s to replace the bridge with a modern steel-and-concrete version, but like the planned telescope at the mountaintop, work was scrapped when 90 percent of the residents moved away in the wake of the Conaty fiasco. Not enough tax-base to justify the cost. "The state is just waiting for the town to die, now," Greg told me on our first visit to the bridge together.

What they'd managed to build before that happened was large concrete pylons on either side of the river. They're still here today, like two monuments to the shifting winds of politics and economy in Silvertown.

As for the river, it's not much more than a trickle right now. In spring I'm told it gets quite full and swift, but with all the snowpack already long melted, not much makes its way through at this time of year.

I scan the rubble of the nearly dry riverbed, noting only a few items of trash among the rocks. Definitely an eyesore, and I resolve to come back later with a trash bag and some gloves.

A sound begins to register in the very edges of my hearing. A low humming, vaguely reminding me of the noise that the Harley had made outside my window the other night. This is not far from the mark, as thirty seconds later I'm treated to the sight of at least fifty motorcycles crossing the bridge and heading up the mountain. Not Harleys this time, though, but an armada of high-strung sports bikes. Ducatis and Kawasakis. Even a few of the new electric sort go humming by.

I watch the riders. Most have their faces hidden behind tinted masks on their helmets, but it's obvious they're all taking in my presence and assuming the worst. Their dream of a day storming up and down the twisty mountain road has been dashed by the local five-oh. Well, good. I don't much feel like unwrapping some eighteen-year-old from around a tree today.

Which reminds me . . . there is one thing I could check out while I'm down here.

After the horde of riders passes, I drive back in the direction of town. It's a short trip to mile marker thirteen. Red and yellow leaves still blanket the road here, but they've been crushed to mulch in the center of each lane. The sports bikes appear to have gone through in single file to avoid anyone racing over anything freshly fallen. Smart move.

I park in the same place where I'd spun out two days ago, kill the engine, and sit for a while.

This is the spot where I met him. The man who tried to kill me. The man who I killed. For a minute or so I can't remember his name, then it comes to me: Rhod. Rhod Mitchell. Lawyer. Father. Wannabe badass.

The road's completely quiet, so I get out and stroll across it, stopping at the spot where Mr. Mitchell was sitting when I almost ran him over. I think about what was said that morning, trying to remember the exact words and coming up a bit short. "*Pissed about my bike*" was the most standout quotable moment. He'd sounded so childish.

At Old Mine Road, Doc had accused me of a false alarm. Said he'd come down here to find no one, and moreover, no bike.

I cross the second half of the road and step into the dense trees and ferns that come right up to the asphalt. There's maybe five feet of flat ground before things slope off sharply into a valley carved by the river. I can just hear the waters below. Ahead of me is the wishbone-shaped tree in which the Harley-Davidson had been wedged, front wheel slowly spinning, exhaust still ticking with heat.

Careful where I step, I approach the tree and look at it closely. Sure enough, there are deep gouges where the bike slammed into it. Chunks of the tree's tan flesh are exposed where all the bark has been scraped off. In places there is red paint left behind by the motorcycle, the color of blood in this shadowed place.

"Maybe he pushed it on through," I think aloud. "Forced it over the side. A total write-off for the insurance company."

Leaning into the V made by the tree's forked trunk affords me a nice view of the valley. The meandering river, barely five feet across in places, growing to as much as fifty in others, snakes a path between the cleft where two mountains meet. There's ours, and there's the one on the other side. A low and uninteresting neighbor called Mount Berdeen. Dense trees stretch from its peak all the way down to the river's edge. The land over there is almost all national forest, patrolled by state rangers. *Almost* all. There is a patch of land about a mile distant, upstream and set on a hillside overlooking the more idyllic part of the river. Sitting nestled in the trees, just visible from where I am, is a large home. A mansion, really, and built in a very modern style. All straight edges and massive windows.

The place is probably worth more than every home I'll ever own put together, and the bitter part of me bets that it's used only two weeks out of the year. I wonder who owns it, and how they came into their money. But a bigger part of me couldn't give a shit. Just another rich asshole, no doubt.

Directly below me the ground slopes sharply down to the water. I see no sign that the Harley had been shoved through. The ferns all look pristine, and the tree trunks that cling to the side of the hill are untouched.

I step back from the tree. Stopping here hasn't been a total waste. I've confirmed the motorcycle had been here. Which means I didn't imagine my first encounter with Rhod Mitchell, not that this had ever really been up for debate.

What else does it mean, though? That he'd been here, obviously. Sitting in the road, pissed about his bike, talking on his phone. He'd said something to me that didn't jive, I recall. "I missed the turn" is what I'd heard. Then he changed "missed" to "messed," like I'd heard him wrong. I don't think I had, though.

But there's no turn here to miss, other than the bend in the road. Even with the leaves blanketing the surface, it's impossible not to see as the mountain frames it on both sides—steep wall on the right, drop off on the left.

So he'd "messed" it. Okay. Weird phrasing but perhaps under-standable after a crash like that.

And later he'd broken into my home and attempted to assault me, apologizing as he did so and telling me that he couldn't stop.

Between those two events, though . . . what had happened? He'd gotten his nose patched up by someone. Which is strange, and not just because Doc hadn't seen to him. It's strange because there was no indication he'd smashed up his nose when I saw him. Not only had this dude had his nose patched up after I'd left, he'd injured it, too. So what was that all about? And who had patched him up? Dr. Ryan's the only show in town for medical treatment, but by the time he got down here our Mr. Rhod was gone along with his precious wrecked bike.

Whether he "missed" or "messed" the turn, that's just an oddity. But the nose is tangibly weird. I file that, a little self-aware at how many things I've been "filing" lately. Pretty soon here that mental filing cabinet is going to overflow, unless I start finding some answers.

I turn my thoughts to the altercation at my home. He'd arrived, vroom-vroom, kicked in my door, and—

The line of thinking stops me short. A detail I'd missed. I'd heard a beefy motorcycle just seconds before he'd broken in, but the next morning when I'd left there'd been no bike outside. The sheriff hadn't mentioned one either, or even asked how the dead man had arrived at my place. I guess I'd assumed it was obvious, and the bike had been taken away. Only, when would that have happened? Sheriff Davies hadn't brought a tow truck with him, surely.

So what had happened to the bike after Rhod had arrived at my house? It didn't drive itself away. This thought sends a tingle of electricity right up my arms. What if he hadn't been alone? This possibility had not occurred to me before. I think back, wishing once again I hadn't taken that sleeping pill because much of that whole night is blurry as a result. Had I heard the bike departing? Faced with someone trying to kill me, listening for such a sound had not been high on my radar.

All right, so perhaps Rhod wasn't alone. Maybe whoever patched his nose rode with him, then fled when they heard the gunshot? The thought is too speculative for my taste. I don't even hang on to this theory, I just drop it. What I need to do is find out what happened to the Harley. I need to talk to my neighbor, the one who called in the assault. Maybe they heard something.

Opening the door to my cruiser I'm yet again faced with the words written on my hand. The reminder prompts me to call the sheriff. It's his direct number and there's no answer, so I text him instead.

**Mary Whittaker here—where is Rhod Mitchell's motorcycle? Would like to take a look at it.**

Holding the phone as I wait for a reply, my hand and its prophetic message seem to shout at me. I decide to call Doc. He'd said something about traveling to Portland for a few days to attend a conference, yet he still answers on the first ring.

"Greetings, Sheriff," he says.

"Doc," I reply. "How's the conference?"

"The conference? Oh, yes. It's boring. So boring I'd almost forgotten about it. I'm in my hotel room trying to take a nap, actually."

"Well, sorry to interrupt."

There's a pause, perhaps as he's levering himself out of bed. "No problem. 'Trying' was the key word in that remark. I hate hotel pillows. Too soft." He stops talking and a silence begins to stretch, quickly becoming awkward and then uncomfortable. "You called for a reason, I assume?"

"I did. It's about the hiker who died."

"Coroner's report come back?"

"Not until tomorrow," I reply, realizing I'd totally forgotten I was even waiting for it. I rub my temples with thumb and index finger, trying to will my brain to start working properly. "I was thinking about what you said. About instincts."

Doc doesn't say anything, just waits to see where I'm going with this. But as the silence starts to drag on he prompts me.

"What about them, Mary? Has something else happened?"

"No," I reply. "I mean, yes. Sort of. It's just little things. People are acting strange and I'm trying to get my head around it."

"Welcome to Silvertown," he says. It's the same thing Chief Gorman says whenever something odd happens, and it makes me wonder if one got it from the other, and who said it first.

"No offense, Doc, but it's disheartening to hear such a pat response from you."

"Oh, how so?"

I shrug, even though he can't see me. "I expect that kind of dismissiveness from the average Joe, but not a shrink, I guess. Aren't you all about looking into the strange and making it intelligible?"

"Well, now, Mary, there is some offense." He takes a breath.

"Look, a town like ours, it has a kind of gravity to it. Happens all over the place. Amityville. Loch Ness. Salem. Roswell. Once the reputation gains traction it starts to attract certain people to it. The situation intensifies and grows. Perhaps in Oakland someone talking crazy would be a thing to pay special attention to, but in places like Silvertown . . . it's harder to spot behavior of legitimate concern. Scientists call it a signal-to-noise ratio, and when it comes to strange behavior, Silvertown has a lot of noise."

"Fair enough," I say. It all makes sense, but I'm still not satisfied, so I try a different tack. "Still, I was hoping you could explain—"

"I thought I'd just explained—"

"Not that. I'm talking about when we were at the hiker. You said something about how there are things that can interfere with reactions. Like fight or flight stuff. Remember that?"

"Yes."

"Well, what'd you mean?"

"The usual suspects, I suppose. Drink enough vodka and you'll be driving the wrong way on a one-way street trying to bat away the oncoming headlights. If that hiker decided to drop acid in order to enhance his connection with nature, could be he thought that bear was a friendly unicorn."

"But that's not a change in his instincts."

"Of course it is," Doc replies, emphatic. "Such behavior is driven by sensory input. How you react to a cute and fluffy dog with its tongue wagging is quite different from how you'd feel when confronted by a frothing, snarling Doberman. Which one you see, no matter what's actually there, informs your instinctive reaction. A change in our senses results in a change to our most base behaviors. They're inseparable."

"You sound like an expert."

"Hardly. As I said before, this is Human Psych 101 stuff, Mary. No offense."

I guess I deserve that. "Fair enough. Okay then, what about on a larger scale?"

A pause. "How large are we talking here?"

"Uhh, like, the whole town, pretty much?"

"Is this a hypothetical situation, Mary?"

"Like I said, people are acting weird and I'm just trying to sort it out."

"Well, as I said, this isn't my area of expertise. If you'd like I can contact some of my colleagues—"

"What about the cell tower?" I ask.

That stops him short. This pause is the longest yet. Long enough to make me think perhaps I hit the nail on the head. But Doc's response is not what I hoped.

"That seems highly unlikely to me. But, once again, not my field. I'd suggest you contact the company that installed it—"

"I already spoke to their field tech. He said definitely not."

"Which only makes you think perhaps you're onto something."

I wince. "Guilty. A little bit."

"Well, I can't fault you there. Industry is not where you go when you want truthful answers. Academia is what you want. Call someone at the university and ask. Might be you really are onto something there."

As he speaks my phone has begun to vibrate with an incoming text.

"Thanks, Doc. Good advice. Look, gotta run. Enjoy your conference."

"Cheerio," he says.

I tap the screen to view the message. Messages, in fact. It's a rapid storm of replies from the sheriff.

no mitchell motor bike

assume towed after crash

assume arrived on foot your place

checking wth local tow co's

more son

*soon

My phone suggests "Thanks very much!" as a reply so I fire that off, the gears in my brain already turning.

No bike. Yet I'd heard one. I guess one possibility is simply that someone else had ridden by, entirely unrelated. But I'd heard it pull up beside my place, and stop. Hadn't I?

Damn that sleeping pill. My mind had been seriously fogged that night. There is, I have to admit, a strong chance I dreamed that noise.

I drive back to town and stop in at HQ to spend some time reading Wikipedia about cell towers, various broadband and wireless technologies, and on down that big rabbit hole. Before I know it I'm reading about packets and code-division, millimeter-wave spectrum, and a whole slew of other things beyond my comprehension. That's okay, though. I'm just scanning, looking for anything about effects on human behavior. But all I manage to find is a page about "WiFi sickness," an imagined malady people attribute to their home network routers. The page has a massive edit history, and I spend a few minutes looking through the changes people have made to the content over the last few years. It's like a war between the sane and the insane, fought in little skirmishes over verbiage. "Imagined malady," for example, had been changed several hundred times to "well-documented phenomenon" and then back, as two users of the site tried to assert what they felt was the truth. It's not hard to see why there are those who would look at such efforts and think someone's trying to cover something up.

Sitting back in my chair, it occurs to me this is a dead end. Even if that tower has such an effect, why would it only be happening here?

Clara calls. "You, me, lunch at the Diner. Now."

"Rain check? I'm right in the middle of tracking down a lead." Not entirely true, but not really a lie, either.

"You need help, remember? We all agreed to lunch. To talk about all this some more."

"Make it dinner, then. And don't worry, the message on my hand is helping. I just spoke with Doc and the Granston sheriff. By dinner time I might actually have some new info for us to talk about."

"Hmmm," she breathes. "Okay. But at least stop by for your food. I'll box it up."

"You rule," I say.

"I know."

"Be there in a few."

It's a promise I keep, stopping in just long enough to give Clara a hug in exchange for a Styrofoam container that smells like fried-batter heaven. Kyle hasn't arrived yet, but Clara says she'll say hello for me. It'll have to do for now.

From the diner I drive up to Old Mine Road again, shoveling onion rings into my mouth as I go. On the way the pimply young man from StellarComm passes me in his white van, offering a sheepish wave as we zip by each other.

Midafternoon is kind of glorious up here. The sun spends all morning on the eastern side of the slopes, but right around 11:00 a.m. it finally rises above Two-Shits and, for the rest of the day, casts a warm and dappled glow over our side of the mountain. Combine that with the autumn leaves on the ground and the whole world seems to glow with a friendly warmth.

In the parking lot where I found Katherine Pascoe cowering in her car, I take a slow walk and examine everything. Kicking aside rocks and leaves in the hopes of finding some critical clue I missed before, but in the end I discover nothing. So I hike up to the spot where the bear attack occurred.

Approaching the clearing where we found the body, I begin to feel nauseous. Just the memory of that scene is enough to trick my mind into seeing it again. Smelling it. I hesitate at the edge of the space, leaning against a tree as I wait to vomit. It never comes up, though. After a few minutes the sensation passes, and I continue.

The police tape I put around the location has all blown off and wrapped around a nearby boulder, so I kill a quarter-hour replacing it. The deceased's parents will be arriving sometime later today, and they won't be too pleased if they come up here to find the scene in such a state, the implication being their son's death is a low priority, or worse, being handled sloppily.

Back in the lot I'm halfway into the driver's seat of my car when a distant sound stops me. For a moment I think I've imagined it, but then it comes again. A sort of hollow thud, like someone striking a drum with one of those padded drumsticks you see in marching bands. I wait, ears strained, but the sound doesn't return. Still, I'm pretty sure I didn't imagine it, and it wasn't natural, so I get back out again.

The parking area is utterly silent, save for a light wind rustling nearby branches. I make a slow circle in place, looking for anything that might hint at the source of the noise, but there's nothing. Trees surround me, save for the trailhead leading to the site of the bear attack, and the entrance to the Masonic Campground opposite.

I walk around my car and over to the rusty metal gate that blocks the gravel road leading to the place. The barricade is identical to the one keeping traffic away from the cell tower. Unlike the cell tower's gate, though, there's no key on my key chain for this one. We probably have an extra key for it back at the station somewhere, but I decide to simply walk around the barricade instead. The gravel road isn't long, and besides, the sun is out, and I'm a California girl at heart.

The path—calling it a road would be generous—is deeply rutted and ill-maintained. It's also devoid of any tire tracks or footprints. During my whirlwind first week on the job Greg had mentioned something about this place and its owners, the Free Masons. That storied, secretive organization that factors into countless conspiracy theories right alongside the Illuminati. From Greg's perspective it's just a club for making professional connections. "All the perks of religion without the deity business," he'd said. For whatever reason they'd all but stopped coming up here in recent years. The various fees and taxes remain paid up, though, keeping the property on their books and off-limits to everyone else.

It's only a quarter mile to the campground. I stop at the end of the path and survey the place briefly. Weeds and grasses poke up everywhere, but I can still see the various plots where RVs can be parked or tents set up. There's a few Porta Pottis off to one side, padlocked shut. Opposite them is a row of picnic tables and a few concrete grilling areas, charred black from years of use.

Farther on, just visible through the trees, there's a pond. Its placid surface is a murky green, and even from here I can see the little circular eruptions of ripples as insects land and take off again.

Wild blackberry bushes surround the stagnant pool of water, their branches so heavy with the fruit that they droop to the ground. The dirt is littered with the little berries, rotting away.

Through the tangle of blackberry I spot a hint of blue. Not sky, though. This is a bright, unnatural blue, like a piece of fabric or plastic, maybe, about thirty feet past the pond. Curious, I walk around to the right, but can see no way to get to whatever it is.

Then I try the left, and about fifty feet along I find a narrow trail that leads through the thorny bushes.

Unlike the dirt road, there are footprints here, and they seem pretty fresh to me.

Cupping one hand beside my mouth, I call out, "Hello? Hello?!"

There's no reply. No sound at all, really. Insects and a few birds. Whatever that drumbeat I'd heard before was, it hasn't happened again.

I make my way through the branches. They're thorny as hell, snagging on my shirtsleeves and grabbing at the legs of my pants. I pause, consider going back to the car for some gloves. This idea I discard as paranoia and carefully push a branch aside so I can duck past it. As I do so, the words on my hand make their mantra-like statement to me once again. *You need help.*

"I'll be the judge of that," I tell my past self, and continue on.

One second I'm squirming through the undergrowth, the next I'm in a small circular clearing, maybe twenty feet across. It's so perfectly circular, in fact, that it must have been carved from the blackberry thicket with a chain saw.

Off to one side of this is a domed camping tent. A nice one. Dark red with yellow zippers and cords.

But I ignore it for the moment. It's the center of the clearing that has my attention.

Here someone has built a pyramid out of plastic blue barrels. Big ones. Ten- or twenty-gallon, I think.

On the sides of the containers are white stickers covered with printed words and icons. Three stand out to me immediately.

A triangle with a skull and crossbones inside, the word "poison" below.

Beside it is another triangle. Inside this one is a wavy line with a dotted line above it. Nonsensical save for the word printed below: CORROSIVE.

At the very top, in bold print, is the last detail that matters: POTASSIUM FLUORIDE.

There's a rustling sound from across the clearing.

Someone is in the tent.

"Hey Kenny. Can I get you something? You look like you could use a good meal, man."

"Nothing, bro. I'm good. Just came by to ask you something. Do you know about this?"

"I can't read that from here, hand the phone to me. Hand the fucking phone to me, Kenny. I'm not going to drop it. Thanks. Moron. You call Mom, by the way?"

"'Course I did. The big five-oh. Damn. She gave me shit about not making her a grandma yet. Like who wants to be a grandparent at fifty? Anyway, read that, Kyle. Seriously read it. Did you know about this?"

"'StellarComm'? That's the cell phone company, right? They built the tower up the mountain? What about 'em?"

"Read it, man."

"I did. Corporate vision, some bullshit about sustainability . . ."

"Not that, bro. Look at the bottom."

"Contact us . . . technical support . . ."

"Dude, here. Look. See, right here? 'StellarComm is a wholly owned subsidiary of' . . . Dun dun Duunnn! 'Conaty International.'"

" . . ."

"Conaty, Kyle!"

"Yeah. So?"

"You don't think that's odd?! After everything that happened with them, the way Greg ran them outta town. Here they are, secretly building our cell phone tower? C'mon, you gotta admit that's suspicious."

"I don't know about 'secretly.'"

"It is, dude. Fuck, you're blind sometimes. Greg's gonna lose his shit when he gets back. I gotta show this to the guys. Later, bro."

"Uh . . . okay, later. Hey, don't forget about the Octoberfest planning thing tonight."

"Can I skip it? You know I don't like to plan things."

"Hell no you can't skip! You're on the committee! And there's the taste testing, which I'm footing the bill for. Free booze, Kenny."

"All right, all right. I'll be there, jeez."

# CHAPTER THIRTEEN

My pistol is drawn and held in both hands before I can even think about it. I aim it at the ground in front of me.

"Silvertown police," I say. "Come out of the tent, please."

I inch forward and to my left, trying for a better view over the top of the chemical containers. The front of the red tent is open, its occupant on hands and knees, as if searching for something inside. A man, I note, from the hairy butt crack poking out between jeans and T-shirt. His body stiffens at my words, the movement stops.

"Nice and slow," I add. I keep my pistol aimed at the ground in front of me, having not quite decided yet if something illegal is going on here. My gut says yes, but with everything that's happened over the last few days, I'm not sure how much to trust my gut.

He starts backing out, wiggling as he extricates himself from the tent. He's thin but muscular, with some tattoos visible on his upper arms. What we'd call a tweaker where I come from. His shoes, I notice, are caked with mud and appear to be regular old running shoes, not the usual trail boots I see up here.

I try to glance past him, get a better look inside the tent, but the sun is facing me and glinting bright blue off the fluoride barrels.

The shadow inside of the tent is impenetrable, and I decide I'll get a better look when he's outside and standing well away.

Finally he's out, coming to a shaky stand with his back still to me, hands outstretched and open, even though I didn't ask. That's good. I love when people do that. He wears faded blue jeans and a white tank top.

And he wears something on his back that I need a moment to comprehend. Recognition hits me after several seconds: it's the aluminum frame for a camping backpack, sans the actual backpack part. Dangling from it on both sides are orange bungee cords.

I clear my throat. "Turn around, please."

He does, a little too swiftly. The orange cords flap around his sides with the motion, then come to rest.

We stare at each other for a long moment. He at my gun. Me at his broken nose.

His broken, bandaged nose.

That can't be coincidence. I flex my fingers on the pistol, shift into a shooter's stance. "Mind telling me what you're doing out here, sir?"

His eyes are bloodshot, dark rings circling them. He's so thin I can see veins under the skin of his forehead, along his neck. There's a strength to him, though. Skin and bone and muscle, nothing else. Well, the beard and mustache, in a style I'd call "hobo chic."

His jaw moves, gesticulating, as if chewing my question to see how it tastes. When he's ready to answer, his eyebrows move first, climbing up that veiny forehead. Then his jaw starts to work its way open, and he lifts his hands slightly, turning them over with something almost like a figure skater's flourish. It draws my gaze, which is the point, I realize, too late.

With a snap kick he sends the pyramid of empty potassium fluoride barrels tumbling toward me. The single barrel on top flies at my head, end over end. It's not completely empty, after all. A few handfuls of its contents remain. White powder is thrown out in a billowing cloud as the barrel sails through the air.

I dive to the side, throwing an arm up and, in the chaos, accidentally discharging the Beretta.

There's a thunderous crack, then another sound, almost as loud. A deep and echoing *DOOM* as the bullet strikes the empty barrel flying toward me. Then I hit the ground, arm across my face. It's a good thing, too, as I feel that cloud of white powder wash over me. It reeks, stings my nose, like spoiled bleach, if such a thing even exists. I gag, rolling through the mud and leaves away from the barrels, the tent, the man.

I stagger to my feet, eyes burning, lungs full of that acrid chemical. Somehow I've managed to keep my gun, and I swing it in the general direction of the man, sure he's about to kick it out of my hand.

But no kick comes.

I try to blink the sting away, then swipe my sleeve across my eyes. A mistake. The sleeve is covered in white powder, too, only adding to my misery. The stinging sensation goes into overdrive, tears pouring down my face. Back in training I experienced pepper spray. Volunteered for that, eager beaver that I was. A quick spritz to see what it was like. Promised myself never again. It was absolutely awful.

This stuff is worse.

I heft the gun and fire into the sky. Once, twice.

"Do not move!" I shout. I hope maybe he can't see me in the cloud of white his kick produced, can't tell that I'm basically blind.

But then I get the answer. Not in the form of a kick, or even a gunshot, but in the sound of an engine starting.

A motorcycle. Not a Harley, though. Nor a sport bike. Something in between.

I press my eyelids together as tight as I can, hold my breath, and rush across the clearing. My foot strikes one of the empty barrels, making another deep *DOOM* sound, though not nearly as loud as the first.

It takes a force of will to stop, but I know I have to, otherwise I'm going to go headlong into a tangle of thorny blackberry bushes from which I might never escape. I stop and blink my eyes, over and over, fighting back the burn. When I finally look up the world is blurry, seen through the awful lens of tears. My throat burns, too. My lungs.

The engine revs, and through the hazy shapes of blackberry vines, I see the man begin to move away on a big four-wheeled ATV.

I stagger after him. It's no use, of course. I can barely breathe. My eyes are all but useless. The world looks like I'm viewing it through a window smeared with Vaseline, but that's not even the real problem. I simply can't keep up with an ATV on foot. My car's too far away to be of any help, not that I could drive it through the blackberry bramble even if I wanted to. So I drop my pace, listening to the sound of the engine fade.

The broken-nosed tweaker is getting away.

In the middle of the narrow path between the thorny bushes, I stop and bend at the waist, closing my eyes and spitting into the dirt. Not quite retching, though I would if I could. After a minute or so I can see again. There're deep tire tracks in the damp earth, easily followed. I jog along, gun still pointed at the ground in front of me. The rider—Captain Tweaker, I'll call him—is long gone, the ATV's throaty engine no longer audible, but I have a feeling he might not have been alone up here. Those chemical containers must have been heavy when they were full, and it seems unlikely to me that one person could have lugged them all the way up here.

As for the barrels . . . what the fuck? What's a man doing in the middle of a blackberry bramble with nine big drums of—what was it?—potassium fluoride? I think that was it. I've heard of those two things separately, but not together. What the combination might be used for I have no idea. But given the man's appearance and how well hidden his little hideout was, I'm pretty sure it has to do with drugs. Meth, most likely.

I reach the end of the trail, and instantly an answer presents itself. Well, more like a theory. A better one than the meth angle, at least.

The trail doesn't so much end as become a single-lane road. Over the span of thirty feet it widens, and the ground transforms from dirt to asphalt. Old, potholed tarmac with weeds growing from its myriad cracks and wounds.

Two lines of muddy tracks go straight down the middle of this, the knobby pattern of the ATV's big tires clearly imprinted for fifty feet at least, before they finally fade away.

But it's not the road that provides the source of my new theory. It's what's beside it.

There's a concrete foundation, fifty feet on a side, all fenced in with razor-wire topping a chain-link barricade.

And inside this, like some trapped titan, standing on steel legs three feet around, is a water tower.

It's elevated up from the ground about twenty-five feet, the tower itself that tall again. It's painted green to blend in with the forest. Trees surround the whole thing, blocking it from view on all sides save this one.

Stenciled in block letters across the giant container's midsection is:

SPUD

I almost laugh. If the water tower were painted brown instead of green it would look a bit like a giant potato standing on its end, with its rounded top and bottom and cylindrical middle. But the lettering makes sense. It's the county utility district acronym, I see it every time I get my water and natural gas bill.

That they had a water tower up here is news to me, but I suppose it makes sense.

There's a gate at one corner of the fence, standing wide open.

"Hello?" I call out, though I'm reasonably sure I'm alone. I walk up to the gate, spotting the pair of bolt cutters on the ground beside it when I'm still ten steps away. They're black metal with red plastic handles, the cheap sort of tool you'd find at any chain hardware store.

I kick the tool aside, not wanting to touch it in case I'll need to pull fingerprints, and step onto the concrete foundation, then inside the fence itself.

Pipes run up into the water tower from beneath its center point, along with several others that come up from the ground at the corner opposite me. I can feel a slight but clear vibration through my feet. Water, pumping in or out. Maybe both. I wonder what the source is, and if it feeds into Silvertown. The stream coming out of the old mine is polluted, but there's plenty of small lakes and rivers around, not to mention the snowpack when there is one. Doesn't really matter, I guess.

Though the road outside the fence is in ill-repair, the foundation and the tower itself are immaculate. Well maintained, I suppose is the term, because it's obvious to me at the same time that all this has been here for a while. Ten or even twenty years, I'd guess. Some cracks in the concrete, a few scratches and dings here and there. But it's far from derelict, unlike so much else on this mountain.

Even the lettering on the tower looks freshly painted. There's no rust on any of the pipes, either. Not a single little white blob of bird shit to be seen anywhere.

I look at the ladder running all the way to the top of the tower, and try to imagine the scrawny figure of Captain Tweaker scaling all the way up there with one of those big barrels under one arm. Seems impossible.

I glance at the ladder again. At the base of it are two more blue barrels of the fluoride chemical.

These are both sealed. I walk to one and put my foot at the top of it, trying to push it. It barely moves. Has to weigh forty pounds at least, I think.

It hits me, then: the frame of a backpack that dude wore, bungee cords dangling. He was strapping these barrels to his back.

This guy wasn't cooking meth in a tent in the forest. He's some kind of eco-warrior. Or, I suppose, maybe the opposite of one. Eco-terrorist?

One time when I bought a bottle of water at the Gas-n-Go, Kenny went on this rant about how Silvertown stopped putting fluoride in the water a few years back, after one of the town's myriad conspiracy theories managed that rarest of feats: a majority of folks here believed it. People became convinced that fluoride in their drinking water was evil, and voted to stop adding it, despite mountains of science pointing to its benefits.

So here's this dude, sneaking around, breaking into the town's water supply and adding the fluoride himself. Could have been doing it for months for all I know. With the Masons letting their campsite go unused, Captain Tweaker's little trove of supplies in the bramble might well go unnoticed until next summer, or longer.

It's a decent theory. Holds water, I think, and almost smile.

Except, really, it doesn't work at all. There are three problems:

He assaulted me.

He ran when I told him to stay put.

And he had a broken nose.

It's this last fact that I find the most disconcerting. Two men have attacked me now in as many days, and both had broken noses.

If I learned one thing about police work from my partner in Oakland it is this: "Coincidences aren't."

The other two flaws in the theory are less disturbing, but perhaps worse in the grand scheme of things. The man's reaction implies something quite a bit more sinister than wanting to help the town with its dental issues. Potassium fluoride could just as easily be poison. I'm no chemist, but the labeling on the barrels certainly looked dire. For that matter, the contents might not have even been what the barrels claimed. Maybe the fucker was dumping pure cocaine into the water. *About a billion dollars' worth, Mary?* All right, that's going way too far into fantasy land, but still . . . it could have been any one of a million white powders. Hell, it could have been something purely meant to gum up the pipes.

I look up the length of the ladder, tempted to climb up and poke around. My guess is I'll find some kind of access hatch, its padlock also cut. But I doubt I'll learn anything more.

No, right now I've got a bigger priority: find Captain Tweaker.

The road he took off on has to lead somewhere, and if I drive fast enough I might be able to meet him at the other end. There is, after all, only one road that gets you off this mountain. I picture him roaring around the last corner before rejoining the state route, thinking he's got away with it, only to find me leaning against the side of my cruiser, smiling with my arms folded. Like something out of *Dukes of Hazzard.*

I pull my phone out, launch the maps application, and wait. There's a little icon representing my position in the center of the screen, but the rest is blank. I zoom out. More of the same. It's then I spot the little indicator at the top corner, telling me what I should have spotted already.

**No signal.**

# CHAPTER FOURTEEN

I run back to the car, ignoring the thorny branches as I go. Ignoring the man's tent, and the spilled empty barrels, the white powder on the ground.

All of it will have to wait.

In the car I grab the map from the glove box again. It only takes me seconds to find Old Mine Road, the parking lot, and even the Masonic Campground. No pond, but after a small gap I spot the line representing the disused road, which the map indicates is called Meridian Lane. I follow the line as it winds its way through the backcountry, well away from Silvertown. Finally it bends and works its way back, rejoining the state route just this side of Keller's Bridge.

I throw the cruiser into gear and spray dirt and pebbles as I leave the trailhead parking lot.

Meridian Lane. I ponder this, sure I've heard the name before. After a minute I vaguely remember seeing the faded sign. There are not many roads on this mountain, and between Greg and me we make it a point to drive along each of them over the course of any given week. But Meridian Lane Greg told me not to bother with. When I'd asked about it, he'd said . . . what? What had he said, damn it? I feel like it had something to do with utility access, which makes sense, given the SPUD logo on the water tower, but this could just be me connecting dots that don't exist.

*You need help.*

The words practically blaze at me as my left hand, curled around the Dodge's steering wheel, comes to twelve o'clock, right in the center of my vision.

I unlock my phone and call Greg for the first time since he went on leave. But nothing happens. There's still no signal. "Huh," I muse. Should be full bars here, closer to town. The big fake-tree tower is just up the mountain from me, clear line of sight.

Rejoining the main road, I flip the sirens on and step on the gas. Six miles between here and the intersection with Meridian Lane, but the guy on the ATV has a good five minutes' head start. His road is curvier, though, and from what I've seen quite badly maintained. Mine, on the other hand, is banked like a racetrack. This just might work.

Before I'm even halfway I spot a vehicle coming up the mountain and recognize it seconds later as Kyle's Jeep. He slows down, one hand out the window urging me to do the same. So I do, and kill the siren.

Soon enough we're parked on the road, blocking both lanes, our cars pointing in opposite directions. Luckily there's no one else around.

Before I can say anything he speaks, more urgency in his voice than I feel, and I feel quite a lot. That's not a good sign at all.

"Are you after him?" he asks, breathless.

"The dude with the blue barrels? How do you know about him?!"

He pulls a face. "Huh? I'm talking about Kenny," he says. "Are you after Kenny!?"

"What the hell would I be after your brother for?"

The response seems to deflate him. He sighs with relief. "Is your phone working?" he asks.

"No signal," I tell him. "Speaking of, can I use yours?"

Instead of answering, he glances up the road, shaking his head and swearing under his breath. "No signal for me either. It's happening to everyone, actually. That's why I'm out here instead of at the bar."

"What do you mean? And what's it have to do with Kenny?"

"I think he and some of his stupid friends did something."

"That doesn't sound good."

"No it does not," he agrees. "Wait, this isn't what you're riled up about? What's with the flashing lights? And what's with the white powder all over your face? Who's this Blue Barrel Man?"

I hold up a hand. "Tell you later. Go on about Kenny. But be quick. I'm literally in hot pursuit right now."

"Shit. Okay." He gestures up the mountain. "My brother came by the bar, all agitated. He'd found out something about that company. The one that put up that cell tower."

"You mean StellarComm?"

"That's them, yeah."

"What'd he find out?"

Kyle seems to brace himself before speaking again. "They're owned by Conaty."

"Conaty?" My mind reels, trying to connect dots and failing. "That's not going to go over well."

He nods. "Exactly. He was going all conspiratard about it. Like they're listening in on our calls, still out for revenge against Chief Gorman. He was really worked up. You know how he can be."

"I kinda don't blame him. That's suspect even to me."

"Well, then he said he needed to show it to his friends. Half an hour later, *boom*. Everyone loses signal. Me. All the customers. Folks I talked to outside. Everyone."

I glance in my rearview mirror, but despite how big and out of place that cell tower is, we've parked at one of the few points on the road where you can't see it.

Kyle jerks his chin at my car. "Go. I'll find Kenny. Hopefully all they did was flip the power switch, and if so, I'll try to get it back on."

"Thanks," I say. "Good luck."

"You, too. Sure you don't need help?"

"Finding Kenny is helping. Don't worry, I got this." I wink at him as I floor the gas pedal. The tires give a satisfying little chirp, and then I've got the sirens back on, and Kyle is receding quickly in the mirror.

I pass mile marker thirteen, half expecting to see the ghost of Rhod Mitchell sitting in the road, shouting "I'm sorry! I can't stop!" as I roar by.

But there's no one there. Just asphalt and leaves.

A mile farther on is Meridian Lane. There's no sign for it, and the intersection comes at the center point of a sharp curve, on the inside, with dense trees huddled right up on its edges. Blink and you'd miss it. Don't blink and you'd pay it no attention whatsoever.

I slow and take the turn, then drive another hundred yards or so before I spot an obstacle. There's a low gate across Meridian Lane, a feature that seems to be the theme for today. First at the cell tower, then the Masonic Campground, and now this.

This one is just two elongated triangular frames of steel tube. Where they meet in the middle, a sign gleams in the sunlight stating in no uncertain terms that this road is for utility access only. Drooping from behind this are loops of thick chain, and I can just make out a padlock holding it all together.

I skid to a stop in front of the barrier. Captain Tweaker must have gotten through here somehow, which means he can get back out again, so I angle my car into a sideways position to block as much of the road as possible. I leave the lights flashing and the engine on.

Beyond the gate, Meridian Lane goes up a hill and then down again, giving me a view of only fifty yards or so. Between the locked barricade, my car with its red-and-blue lights flashing, and the pistol on my hip, I figure I've got this guy dead to rights.

But after two minutes pass and nothing happens, I start to lose a bit of that confidence. He should be here by now. I study the ground in front of the gate. There's no ATV tracks across the leaves on the road, but he had a tent up there and, for all I know, made the drive up to the water tower days ago.

"Or this isn't the route he took," I say to myself. It was an ATV, after all, giving him access to game trails and any one of a number of firebreaks. An unlikely approach, sure, but not impossible.

Several more minutes pass uneventfully.

"Shit," I say. I'm going to have to go up there and find him. Which means figuring out a way to open this gate. There's bolt cutters in the cruiser, and I don't see any way around using them. The posts to which the gate is attached are right beside thick trees, providing no room to squeeze through.

"Fine," I say to the gate, "have it your way." I walk to the back of the cruiser and pop the trunk. As I'm there, something small and white flashes by in the corner of my eye, toward the main road. I glance in time to see an albino squirrel dart across the lane and disappear down the steep mountainside across the state route. I marvel at this for a second. How many squirrels in a million are albino?

As I'm staring at the spot where the animal disappeared, a new detail emerges. A long groove in the dirt at the roadside. I squint, and realize it's actually two long grooves, about three feet apart. ATV tracks, I've absolutely no doubt.

"Gotcha, you bastard," I breathe.

Leaving the bolt cutters where they are, I slam the trunk closed and walk into the woods. The tracks run more or less parallel to Meridian Lane, weaving around trees where necessary. I follow them back to the state route. Kneeling, I examine the treadmarks in the muddy area just before the tarmac. The grooves are deep, and the walls crumble to the touch. Fresh, then. So Captain Tweaker left Meridian Lane somewhere just before the gate, wove a path through the trees, and emerged here.

Only, once back on the state route he didn't go left or right. Instead, he drove straight across and over the drop-off on the other side where that squirrel just vanished.

Feeling childish, I check both directions for traffic. The bend in the road here provides little visibility, and because of the twisty nature of the little-used road, people often take it at high speed. But all's quiet just now. Only my footfalls and the chirping of birds are sprinkled over the constant sigh of wind through the branches high above.

On the far side of the road I move to the little berm that marks the drop-off, and lean out over the side, wincing slightly at what will greet me. But unlike the point at mile marker thirteen, where Rhod's Harley became wedged in the tree, the mountainside here turns out to be less of a cliff and more of a slope. A forty-five-degree incline, if that.

It's more than the angle that surprises me, though. At this particular point, where the ATV tracks leave the road, there's a gap in the trees perhaps six feet wide. Ferns grow in the span between, many of which I note have broken fronds. The ground is littered with these, and they're all trampled. Not just by the ATV, I realize, but also by several tire tracks in varying sizes and freshness. Dirt bikes, maybe? Or . . .

"I missed the turn," I say, repeating Rhod's words from when I'd found him sitting in the road, three miles up from here.

I walk back to my cruiser to kill the engine and lock the doors, leaving the lights blinking away for now. From below the front-passenger seat I grab a bottle of water and a pack of almonds I keep stashed there for times when stopping for a bite to eat isn't in the cards.

Then I set off on foot, following the tire tracks down the mountain toward the river. For the most part the trail is a straight shot, and the farther I get from the road I notice less and less effort has been made to conceal it.

Nearer the river, as the ground levels out a bit, large boulders and dead trees have accumulated, and the path begins to wind around them as a result. In places it becomes harder to follow, but on foot and going slow, I've got plenty of time to study the landscape and find its signature markings.

At the river the path turns, heading northeast now. Upstream. The riverbed is almost dry this time of year. Just a trickle of water barely six inches deep that splashes and froths around a wide bed of rocks, from tiny polished pebbles all the way up to boulders larger than my car. Most of them are bleached white from a summer's worth of sunlight.

As such it's not hard to see the spot where the ATV crossed to the other side. There are two rows of rocks nearly black from water splashing off the vehicle's tires. Which means Captain Tweaker tore through here only minutes ago.

I make my way across, almost slipping twice on a mossy patch in the middle. The far bank is more of the same. Dead logs, ferns, and boulders that give way to dirt and trees the higher I climb. It's steeper on this side, causing the trail to follow the contours of the landscape. The woods are denser, too, with a different mixture of trees, given the south-facing slope and its abundance of sunlight.

It's close to noon now and I'm sweating under my uniform, breathing hard. I guess I can skip leg day this week, I think ruefully, as my thighs begin to burn from the exertion.

I hike. And hike. And hike. Half a mile since crossing the river, I'd guess, before I stop to catch my breath and take a few healthful swigs of the water while I sit on a fallen log.

My phone still shows no signal. That worries me. Especially in light of what Kyle had said about Kenny and his friends. I stand and move to the edge of the trail, peering across the valley and up the slope toward Lake Forgotten. I think I see the spot where the atrocious fake tree should be, the StellarComm cell phone tower. *A Conaty Company.* But there's nothing there. Just the real, actual trees. Maybe I've got the location wrong, but I don't think so. It should be there.

"That's not good," I mutter, trying to picture myself arresting Kenny. I hope it doesn't come to that.

One thing at a time, though.

I get back on the trail, jogging now.

It goes on and on, snaking ever upward. Then, abruptly, the trail levels out onto a plateau and just ends. I'm so focused on the ground in front of me that I almost run into a wall of leaves blocking my path.

"Fuck," I whisper, my heart pounding.

"Wall of leaves" is a more accurate description than I want it to be. This is an actual wall. Covered in ivy, yeah, but still a man-made wall. Eight feet high.

Taking several steps back, I stand on my toes and try to see anything over the top, but it's too high. I turn my focus back to the tire tracks I've been following. The ATV's path runs right into the wall. Or, rather, under it. A secret gate?

Curious, I put my hand on the wall and push. Nothing happens. Then I use my shoulder, and throw all my weight into it, digging in my heels. There is only the slightest hint of movement, but it's enough to confirm my theory. A concealed gate. How goddamn interesting.

Glancing left and right, I see corners in equal distance to either side, so randomly I choose left and walk to the end, peering around the edge.

More wall leads to another corner. A hundred feet long, this stretch. But beyond it is not only forest now. There's a road, too. A single lane of paving stones, forming a sort of grid pattern that, I think, must have been very expensive to lay. The road is long, too, stretching off far to my left before it becomes too obscured by trees to see.

I creep along and as I get closer I realize it's not a road at all. Despite the length, this is someone's driveway. It's right about then I notice the camera atop the wall. It's at the corner, and tracks me as I walk.

No point in creeping now, I decide. I stand upright and try not to let the little black rectangular box irritate me as it rotates to keep me in view.

Rounding the next corner, the house comes into view. "House" is barely the right word, though. No, this is something that needs a few adjectives and perhaps a solid f-bomb to describe it. Fucking Huge Mansion. That works.

It's visible in the distance, sprawling and modern. Delicately arranged rocks cover one wall, lacquered hardwood another, the next entirely in frosted glass. Everything at right angles.

A fountain marks the spot where the driveway ends, making a circle around the gently splashing water I imagine is full of koi or something. There's a red Ferrari parked off to one side, some leaves on its otherwise flawless curves. Just in front of the vehicle is a six-car garage, all the doors closed. I guess the Ferrari wasn't good enough to park inside and can't help but wonder what else is in there.

But well before all this is the gate. Another goddamn gate.

The driveway passes under its black iron span, the two halves of it meeting in the middle at an ornate crest in gold: a lion's head. As gates go this one is damned impressive, making a nice exclamation mark on the day's theme, I suppose.

I walk up to stand in front of it, then notice the small black box that protrudes out over the driveway on my left. There's a button on it, as well as a speaker and a small camera like a single, beady black eye.

With my thumb I press the button, and wait.

Seconds pass.

Then a crackle. "Yes?"

"Officer Mary Whittaker, Silvertown police."

"Yes?"

I glance at the camera. Did they not hear me? I lean in, making sure my badge is visible to them. "I am in pursuit of a man riding an all-terrain vehicle, and have reason to believe he is on the premises."

A pause.

"Yes, and?"

The voice is vaguely familiar, but the one thing I'm sure of is that it's not Captain Tweaker. The tone is too low. Too calm and snooty.

I glance at the Fucking Huge Mansion again, wondering what kind of approach to use. This home must be the massive one I glimpsed through the trees earlier this morning when looking for Rhod's motorcycle. From there it had been impressive as hell. From here, even more so. Whoever lives here, they're loaded.

I decide to be polite, to cater to their wealth. "Would it be all right if I entered the grounds and had a look? And before you ask, no, I don't have a warrant. This is an active pursuit. The suspect might be dangerous. I'm asking because it's the polite thing to do, but you should know that I do have the authority to come onto your property in a situation like—"

There's a dull clang and then the hum of a motor. The gates begin to swing open.

I nod at the camera. "Thanks," I say.

They don't bother to reply.

This slight I ignore, and soon I find myself walking down the paved lane, cataloging new details as I go. The house is angular in a hyper-modern style, but the layout is classic, weirdly reminding me of the White House. Two wings stretching to either side, with a large central section in between. Ruining the balance of this is the six-car garage, which juts off the east wing at a right angle.

The red Ferrari parked in front of it is not the classic sort, but a recent model. So new there are no plates on it yet, not even the dealership logo stand-ins. I suppose I could take down the VIN, but as of yet I can't see any reason why I need to.

I stop at the fountain, which is circular and of a classic style, in contrast to the modern lines of the house. No fish swim within its waters; in fact the water is crystal clear. Lights are arranged around the base of the central rock formation, which water tumbles down in a soft bubbling cascade. It must look quite impressive at night, I think.

For a time I stand there, listening, half-expecting a servant or groundskeeper to come out and greet me. Perhaps offer to show me around. But there is nothing save the sound of water trickling down the sides of the artfully arranged rocks, some wind stirring the surrounding forest, and very distantly the babble of the stream in the valley.

I look along the length of the structure, figuring I should explore the grounds first, then knock and ask some questions. But there's no obvious way from here to the back of the property, and the place in the wall where the ATV's tracks disappeared. That ivy-covered wall huddles right up against the house on either side, and I have no doubt it spans the property's entire perimeter.

The front door, then, I suppose. I walk up and resist the temptation to wipe the sweat off my brow.

I reach to knock, but as my knuckles swing toward the surface there's a click and the door whooshes open with incredible speed.

Three people stand before me. Two men and a woman.

All have bandages over their noses.

And the man in the center is someone I know.

"Run away, Mary," says Chief Greg Gorman. "Please! I can't stop!"

# CHAPTER FIFTEEN

"Get away from here, Mary!" Greg shouts, even as he's reaching to grab me. His eyes are wide in terror, but most of his face is obscured under a bandaged broken nose.

"What the fuh—"

This is all I manage before I hear the scuff of a shoe behind me, and then a cloth bag is drawn over my head, surrounding me in darkness.

I try to claw it away, but before I can move more than an inch my legs are yanked out from under me and my arms are grabbed at each wrist. I don't so much as fall forward as am propelled there, onto the floor. My brain is still trying to reconcile the face of Greg, not yet even close to processing the fact that a zip tie has just tightened around my wrists, and another around my ankles.

"I'm so sorry, Mary!" Greg rasps in my ear. "I can't—"

"No talking!" someone barks.

Greg instantly stops.

"What the hell—" I begin, my voice betraying my state of panic.

"Subdue her, Senator!"

Someone kicks me in the stomach. Air rushes from my lungs in a great "oomph," and as I fight to draw breath, the hood is lifted just enough for a gag to be shoved into my mouth. I suck air through my nose, squirming, trying to see, trying to shake the bag from my head. It's no use.

Expertly my belt is removed. Pistol, baton, everything. Gone.

I'm lifted bodily from the floor and marched deeper into the house. The front door slams closed. Commotion all around me.

The word "senator" registers, but this baffling detail is swiftly dashed away by another.

Greg Gorman. He's here, with them. Nose broken. Grabbing me and talking just like the biker did when he entered my home. What the hell is going on?

"Put her in there," someone says. I hear a door opening. The people carrying me make a hard turn, and then I'm thrown to the floor.

The door slams shut, and there's the turning of a lock.

For a second everything is quiet. I focus on my breathing, and try to squeeze the tears from my watering eyes. My stomach is a big knot of hollow pain. The bag around my head reeks of sweat and mildew.

After a while—maybe a minute, I'm not really sure—I'm finally able to uncurl from the fetal position and roll onto my back. My mind feels like it's at war with itself, so many thoughts tearing through, seeking attention and answers. I suck in air through my nose, work my jaw, and somehow manage to spit the gag out of my mouth. It wasn't tied around my neck, I realize, just a rag stuffed in to keep me from screaming.

Why? I wonder. Is there someone in the house who might hear, someone they don't want to hear?

Worth a shot. I open my mouth, rear back for the biggest earth-shaking scream I can muster, only to have it die on my lips as heavy metal music begins to blare at me through speakers in the ceiling. Skull-crushingly loud. Bass that rattles my jaw. Screeching guitar. No way could I be heard over that, which I suppose is the point?

Maybe that means they're watching me. Well, fuck them, I'm not going to lie here like a pig trussed up for the firepit. I heave my knees up to my chest, whip my arms down my back, and bring them around from below me. It's grueling work, and for a second I think my wrists have become stuck on the bottoms of my shoes, but then something gives, and my hands are in front of me again. Still zip-tied, but in front of me.

That's got their attention.

A key rattles in the door.

I push myself to a stand and grit my teeth, grabbing the hood over my head with both fists and tossing it aside. I glance around, looking for anything I can use as a weapon.

It's a bedroom, I think, or supposed to be. But it's been emptied except for a thin mattress on the floor.

In front of me the door is opening. I square up on it, bringing my hands up. How I'll fight with my wrists and feet bound is not really the issue here. I'll figure something out. I have to.

The figure in the door is shadowed by a bright light behind them. I wait, coil as best I can, ready to swing.

"Please forgive me, Mary," Greg Gorman says, advancing into the room. His voice has a nasal quality to it because of the bandage. It was him on the speaker at the gate, I now realize. "I can't stop."

"Oh, yeah?" I spit. "Why the hell not?"

He hesitates, but only just. "I'm not in—"

"No talking," someone behind him says. "Subdue her, now."

Greg's hand instantly comes up, and there's a click. A little dart shoots across the room, wires trailing behind it, and then the electricity hits my body.

The world goes white.


Time has passed. I know it has. The world is still white, but also hazy now. It moves too much, spinning and twisting, first left, then right. Back again. A high-pitched ringing assaults my ears. My whole body tingles.

The first coherent thought I manage is simply: *Greg.* I try to say the name, but nothing comes out, not even a moan.

I close my eyes and wait for the dizziness to pass. Gradually, new details and sensations begin to register. Pain across my thighs, ankles, biceps, wrists, chest, forehead. Each the same, a pressure, a . . . a . . .

I'm bound, I realize. Not like before, not the zip ties, but thick straps. Nylon or leather, something like that. And they hold me to a chair.

My chin is held firm by a tight bracket made of metal or some hard plastic. I don't have enough control of my body yet to try to test the strength of any of this, so I catalog it, working toward a mental picture of the situation.

And the situation is not good. I'm bound tightly to a chair, barely able to move. My mouth doesn't seem to want to work, even if I could open my jaw. It occurs to me my uniform is gone. They've removed it, along with my Kevlar vest, leaving me in an undershirt and underwear. No shoes or socks, either.

The bag is back over my head, too. The difference now is that there's a brilliant white light shining on my face, bleeding through the fabric. I can feel the heat of it. Reminds me of a dentist's lamp.

My heart is racing, pounding in my still-ringing ears. I put all the focus I can muster into breathing, aware of each heartbeat, willing the time between them to grow. Soon I achieve this, and the ringing in my ears fades, too.

There are voices nearby. Two men, I think, speaking in low, con-spiratorial tones.

One has a very slight accent, so slight in fact I cannot immedi-ately place it. Asian, perhaps? The other voice I know.

But it's not Greg.

It's *Doc.*

My head swims once again. Pain and confusion all mixed to-gether. First Greg, now Doc. Who else is involved in this shit show, I wonder, as a fresh anger grows inside me. I channel that rage, use it to push all the questions from my head.

I strain my ears, picking out words.

". . . use the liquid."

"There's no time," Doc replies. "She'll be here soon and—"

"It's our last chance to verify the results. Do it. I have to coach the senator . . ." the possibly Asian man is saying. His words fade.

Doc replies in his mumbling way, too hard to make out. The tone is emphatic, though.

The other man's response is clipped, harsh. Almost barked. I catch only this: ". . . need verification, so do it. Now."

When Doc replies, there's no fight in his voice, no argument. Just pure acceptance of an order.

I hear a door close. Footsteps coming toward me.

I close my eyes and will myself to be calm, to appear asleep.

The bag is pulled from my head. My eyes, though shut, are filled with a glow, as if I were on a beach and facing toward the sun. The heat is intense.

My urge to squint is reflexive, unavoidable, so I roll with it. Slowly try to turn my head, then make a small show of thrashing against my bindings.

"It's no use," Doc says. "Try to remain calm, Mary. It's for the best." He moves around me, checking the straps, and then his fingers are against the inside of my wrist, taking my pulse. This places him in front of me, obscuring the light.

I blink, try to look at him. Acting is not something I've ever really tried to do, but now seems like a good time to start. "Thought . . . you . . . were at conference . . ." I stammer.

He shrugs, as if we're old friends having a polite conversation. "Well, you know, that wasn't entirely a lie. It's a small conference, and not in Portland but here at the senator's mansion."

"Who . . ." I start.

"All will be revealed," he says, smiling a little. "We weren't expecting you here."

"Happy to disappoint you."

Doc's smile turns slightly sad.

The door opens again. Someone backs in, slightly hunched over. It's Captain Tweaker. He's carrying a metal tray with a syringe on it and a small, unmarked glass bottle. Tucked under his arm is an iPad, or something like it.

Doc turns and takes the tray from him, placing it on the table beside my chair. He pokes the needle into the bottle and draws a clear liquid into the chamber.

"Don't worry," he says soothingly. Then to Captain Tweaker, "Pulse a hundred ten, blood pressure a hundred forty over ninety."

"Got it," Tweaker says, tapping at the screen in his hands.

"You took her weight and height when she was out?"

"Yup."

"With or without her clothes?"

"Without. I'm not an idiot."

"Don't use that tone with me."

Tweaker dips his chin, cowed. "Yes, sir," he replies, and it's like I'm hearing a different person. The casual bad-boy tone is gone, replaced by an almost military deference.

Doc nods, satisfied. "Be ready with the timer. We're doing the oral method, not injection."

"I understand."

"Where's Ang?" Doc asks.

"With the senator. But he'll be ready, he said to tell you if you asked."

"Very good."

Doc lifts the needle toward me and I don't need to act now. I thrash against the straps. It's totally useless, but I don't care. I have to fight. I can't let them do this.

Through clenched teeth I say, "You'll go to jail for this, Doc. All of you. You'll—"

"No, no," he says, smiling again. "Not with both you and Greg here. Now relax, Mary. We're almost done."

With an almost tender gesture Doc reaches up with his free hand and grasps my chin around the edges of the bracket. Then he squeezes at the sides of my mouth, a surprisingly strong grip that, despite all my effort, forces my lips to part. Not much, but enough.

Doc presses down on the syringe's plunger and a clear liquid fires into my mouth. The aim is perfect, between my teeth and straight down my throat. It happens so quickly and forcefully that I'm not ready for it. Before I can gag it out, Doc clasps his gloved hand over my mouth and presses hard, forming a seal. Then he jabs me in my side with a thumb. It's unexpected. Something about the placement and force of this causes me to swallow involuntarily.

"Good," Doc says. He glances over his shoulder. "Start the timer."

Captain Tweaker obediently taps the screen of the tablet, then twists it around and holds it with both hands against his chest. The number 73 fills the display in giant numerals, replaced a second later by 72, then 71.

Doc assesses this and gives a short nod. "Plenty of time," he says. "Clear the path and call it out."

The skinny piece of shit steps backward out of the room, keeping the iPad's display facing Doc the entire time, even when he moves around the corner into the hallway outside.

64 . . .

63 . . .

"Mr. Ang!" Tweaker calls out. "One minute!"

"Mmm," someone replies, sounding far off.

That name again. Ang. Where have I heard it before? Another detail to file, though my rapidly growing mental file isn't going to matter if I don't get the hell out of this chair.

The goddamn display says 57 now. Seconds to live? Seconds to . . . what?

I want to scream at Doc. Grab him by the collar of his ill-fitting shirt and shake some answers out of him. *What did you give me? What the fuck is going on here, and why are you and Greg involved?*

Doc has moved behind me now, and suddenly the chair I'm in lurches into motion. He's wheeling me, I realize. For some reason this scares me more than anything else that's happened. This room is a known place, but out there . . . I can't even begin to imagine where they're taking me, or why.

The cold fingers of panic begin to twitch around the edges of my mind. This in turn sends my own fingers—the only part of me I can move—into a fluttering blur of motion. I twist and bend, contorting my hand, trying to pull free from the bindings and then, desperately, probing for the clasp that holds the straps so tight. It is out of reach, of course, but I don't care. I strain. Groan with the effort.

"Just relax," Doc says. "There's nothing to worry about."

46 . . .

45 . . .

We move down a dark hallway, Doc pushing me as if I'm a piece of furniture being delivered. Captain Tweaker is in front of us, walking backward, the iPad always facing Doc, the numbers ticking inexorably toward zero.

Many doors, all closed, line the passage. Doc ignores them all, making straight for the last one, walking without panic and very much with purpose.

Before Tweaker reaches that last door, it swings open. A new person, silhouetted against a window, holds it aside, letting us through. A woman, I think. Doc turns my chair before I can get a good look at her.

The room is a study, or home office. Big oak desk. Walls lined with books. I can do little more than swivel my eyes, trying to read their titles as we pass, but all I get is a general impression: legal tomes, biographies of former presidents, a few classic novels.

There's another door ahead. Tweaker pushes it open with his foot.

37 . . .

36 . . .

Doc wheels me into a small room, long and narrow. Probably once a closet, I guess. Ten feet long and five wide.

The woman in the study approaches. She's holding a finger to one ear. "He wants to know if she swallowed it."

"Of course she did," Doc says.

"Are you sure?"

"Yes, I'm sure. Just tell him we're coming."

She nods once, then backs away.

Doc presses a button on the wall just inside the small room, and the whole thing lurches. A low electric hum comes from the walls.

Not a closet then, but an elevator. Going down.

When the doors open I'm wheeled backward into a sort of man

cave. Wine bottles, a humidor for cigars, a dartboard. But just a few feet inside there's a plastic swoosh from behind me, and the tone of the wheels on the floor changes from carpet to something like laminate or vinyl. Two thick plastic curtains brush past my ears and close before me as Doc guides my chair into what I can only assume is a psychotic's murder cave.

The walls, ceiling, and floor are all lined with plastic sheeting.

A long groan escapes my lips.

Doc raises an eyebrow at this, curious. Maybe even concerned. But he does nothing to help me.

Then I glimpse the benches along the side walls. A microscope, racks of test tubes and machines. I can only guess at their purpose.

I see a row of small refrigerators with glass doors and samples inside, color coded.

Several laptop computers line the desk above.

There's a safe with a fancy biometric lock.

Captain Tweaker lets us pass him and now follows us, still holding the tablet toward Doc. I can see the timer again.

16 . . .

We move through the laboratory. Doc walking backward, pulling me. Tweaker following. His head is bowed like a monk, eyes fixed on the iPad in his hands. Their steps are in sync, matching the seconds that tick away.

Suddenly Tweaker glances up, seems to see me for the first time.

"I'm sorry about this—" he says. I can only stare back at him, momentarily dumbfounded by the sudden change in him. Attitude, posture, everything. He's like a different person.

"No talking," Doc snaps. "Be absolutely silent now!"

Instantly the man's head bows again. In the blink of an eye he's Captain Tweaker again. Why? Fear?

11 . . .

10 . . .

Another door, another room. This one's small, I guess, just from the way the sound echoes. Or rather, how it doesn't. Doc spins me around.

The space is absolutely empty save for a simple desk, upon which rests a computer screen. Behind this, on the otherwise unadorned walls, are two large speakers built into the surface.

Tweaker holds the iPad out slightly, emphasizing its eight remaining seconds. He sets the tablet on the desk beside the computer, using a kickstand built into its case to keep it upright for Doc—or me—to see. Then he turns and leaves the room.

Doc arranges me in front of the computer screen, and then his footsteps are receding. Before he closes the door, I hear a dial twist. A loud hum begins to emanate from the speakers.

The door closes.

4 . . .

3 . . .

2 . . .

1.

The countdown goes blank.

There's just the computer screen, the hum from the speakers, and the blood pounding in my ears. My jaw starts to quiver, my imagination running wild with the terrible, nightmarish things they're going to force me to watch.

Finally the display comes to life.

Against a black background a woman's face appears. Elderly, hawkish. Vaguely familiar. She has a tight bun of silvery hair. She seems to be looking right at me.

"You will do whatever I say," she says in a calm, almost bored voice.

The image changes. Same woman, but outdoors now, her hair down.

"You will do whatever I say," she repeats.

Another shift. Indoors, candle lit.

"You will do whatever I say."

Outside overcast, from her left.

"You will do whatever I say."

In a car, streetlights throwing shadows over her wrinkled features.

"You will do whatever I say."

Smiling at me, quiet voice.

"You will do whatever I say."

Full of rage. Shouting.

"You will do whatever I say!"

Left side, right side, from behind, in shadow, through a curtain, on a windswept plain, in an alley.

"You will do whatever I say. You will do whatever I say."

The screen goes black, but the voice continues. Over and over. Different volumes, different tones, but always recognizable as the same person.

"You will do whatever I say. You will do whatever I say!"

I can do nothing but watch and listen.

On it goes. On and on and on.

And with each repetition I think to myself, *Like hell I will.*

# CHAPTER SIXTEEN

I think *Like hell I will,* but I don't say it.

I wish I could claim this is because of some sense of defiance or bravery. They are part of it, but mostly I remain quiet because I'm too stunned by how bizarre this all is.

After being tased and dosed with who-knows-what, there was a small part of me that still hoped all this would turn out to be a profoundly bad prank.

That hope diminished as they wheeled me to this room, but part of me still clung to it.

Not anymore, though. This video has finally convinced me otherwise.

The film took some effort to make, for starters. To edit together. To have queued up on a computer, ready to start the moment the timer ended. Stuff like that takes time and planning. Money, too.

Which means, I realize, "bizarre" is the least of my worries.

Something big is going on here. Very big.

"You will do whatever I say."

She's back to her original version, facing me with a black background behind her. This time the woman doesn't repeat the phrase.

Instead there's a pause lasting perhaps thirty seconds, during which she just stares down the camera, eyes boring into mine.

Suddenly her features relax. She even smiles a little.

"You will be calm in this room," she says.

There's another pause. I wonder if I'm supposed to reply. But this is like a horrible game of Simon Says, and Simon didn't say reply, so I keep my mouth shut. As long as I'm bound to this chair, helpless, I figure the best thing I can possibly do is stay quiet and observe.

The moment they let me out, though, someone's going to get fucking hurt.

"You will not panic in this room," the woman adds. "You will not fight in this room. We're going to let you out now."

*Oh, good timing.* I coil, mentally, ready to strike the moment I'm able.

Behind me the door opens again, sounding a bit like an air lock. Soundproofed room?

I keep my eyes on the woman's face as two people come up to either side of me. They move around the table to stand on either side of the screen, facing me, as if acting as bodyguards for the monitor.

The man on the left is Doc, all six-foot-eight of him, bulging belly and thin arms and legs. Bushy graying beard. I feel nothing but a burning hatred at the sight of him, but I force my eyes to stay forward, face as placid as I can make it.

On the right is the Asian man. I'd seen him in silhouette before, and painted a picture in my mind of what I can only describe as a villain from a James Bond film. Which was the one with the weird dude in the no-tie suit? *Dr. No?* I think that was it.

My mental image was way off, though. This man is spectacled, with unkempt hair and a soft figure. He wears a tacky Hawaiian shirt under a white lab coat. Cheap, ill-fitting jeans and a pair of white running shoes complete the . . . well, "look" would be generous.

"The man to your right is Mr. Ang," the woman on the screen says, challenging my perception that the video is a recording. If it is, it's extremely well timed.

She goes on, her gaze suddenly intense. "You will obey his every command, unless it contradicts with any command of mine. Blink if you understand."

I blink.

Mr. Ang is watching me. His mouth twitches, on its way to a smile until he gets it under control.

"The man to your left is Dr. Ryan," the woman says. "You will obey his every command, unless it contradicts with any command of Mr. Ang's, or mine. Blink if you understand."

A pecking order. Interesting. I blink again.

The woman waits, and I decide finally that this is indeed a recording. She has no idea how I am responding to all this. After a few awkward seconds, she leans forward and says, "Gentlemen, you may proceed with the test."

My heart seems to skip a beat at that. Her words, and the sinister tone. Anxiety courses through me. *What test? Isn't this the test? I blinked, didn't I?*

Doc walks over to my chair, and reaches for the strap at my wrist.

I tense, almost salivating at the prospect of getting to punch him right in the face. Break his goddamn nose and . . . a thought occurs to me then. Everyone else here has a broken nose, except for Doc and Ang. And me.

"You will remain calm and passive," Doc says. "Until myself, or Mr. Ang, say otherwise, you will speak to no one unless directly asked a question. Blink if you understand."

I blink.

The other man moves around the table and begins to undo the belts on the right side, starting at my arm and then my leg. Finally the strap holding my head back is removed, and the little cup that's been pressed against my chin is swung aside.

Doc, on my left, is kneeling and working on the leg strap. I could kick him in the face, but then my left hand would still be bound, so I wait.

He stands and leans over to work on the straps on my bound left arm, then pauses.

"Who wrote 'You need help' on your hand?" he asks me. Then he adds, "Tell the truth."

I answer immediately, with the first thing that comes to mind. "Kyle," I say.

"And why did he do that? Tell the truth."

The lie had been automatic, coming from seemingly nowhere. Now I have to roll with it. Despite everything, I still don't want Doc or this other bastard to know the details about what happened in my home the other night, and everything I've learned since. Rhod the Biker had been sent by them, of this I'm now sure. Greg had, after all, uttered the same strange words upstairs, apologizing that he couldn't stop. And his nose . . .

I try to affect the same tone Captain Tweaker had used earlier, when Doc told him to start the timer on the iPad. Not robotic, exactly, but something close to it.

"A private joke. Kyle wrote it in response to the intensity of our lovemaking the previous evening."

Straitlaced Doc averts his eyes. "That's . . . interesting. Why didn't you wash it off? Tell the truth."

"Permanent ink," I say. This at least is true.

He raises an eyebrow, then nods. He's blushing a little but evidently satisfied with my responses. He frees my left hand.

"Step out of the chair," Mr. Ang says.

I lean forward, balling my hands into fists on the armrests. I figure a quick jab to the testicles for each of them should start things off in my favor.

But what would that accomplish? I'm in my underwear, my belt is gone, and with it every weapon I have. I'd be in a room with a doctor and a scientist, neither of whom appear to be carrying weapons, and a house full of who-knows-how-many "henchmen," I guess is the right word.

As I slowly push myself to a stand I think through what I've seen here already. Where's the nearest door leading to the outside? There'd been floor-to-ceiling windows in the den above us. French doors opening on a patio, or just windows? I wish I'd paid more attention, but that damn timer had filled me with too much worry to put much thought into anything else.

"Follow me," Ang commands, and turns to leave.

Clearly these people think I've been put under some kind of hypnosis. That I'm going to do what they ask. Maybe I can buy some time if I continue to let them believe that. Choose a moment when I can get to my pistol, or the shotgun in my car.

Except my car is miles away and across a steep canyon. So my pistol, then. It could be anywhere, though. They could have tossed it into the trees, or buried it, or anything. So as tempting as it is to beat the shit out of these two, I force myself to calmly comply. I need a way out of here, then I'll act.

They lead me out of the small room and back through the lab. It takes all my willpower not to stop and study the equipment. I want to gather evidence, memorize all I see here in case it's important later. But Ang has set a brisk pace, and commanded me to follow, so the best I can manage is a few sidelong glances. There's a sharps container, and beside it a little stand for holding syringes. I glance the other way. On that table is a machine that barely fits on the surface. It's blue and has a glass front for viewing the work going on inside. I see only a brief glimpse, but it's enough. The machine is for making pills. A tray on the bottom holds the bottom half of the lozenges, clear in color. A small robotic arm sweeps across these, spurting a little powder into each. Above, the red top-halves of the pills wait to be pressed down, ready to seal the contents within. A box sitting beside the machine looks to hold about a hundred of the completed product.

Then we're back through the plastic curtains. Into the elevator, standing around awkwardly as it glides upward. Neither man says a word to me, but they both steal furtive glances. At me. At each other.

"Oral delivery," Doc mumbles to Ang, almost childishly excited all of a sudden. "It's finally working!"

"Yes," Ang replies. More reserved, this one, but there's a definite note of pride in his voice. "Though the timing is still an issue."

"So?" Doc asks. "A simple calculation and—"

"Too fiddly. But that's a hill to climb another day. Right now the important thing is to verify this version and move on to deployment."

*Verify? They're not convinced of my compliance,* I think. *Not yet. Not entirely.* Hence the test the woman ordered.

I stare straight ahead, doing my best to ignore them. All I have to do is play it cool and take my chance when it comes.

The elevator lurches to a stop. Ang opens the door.

The others are all there when we emerge, with something like regret in their faces. A look of sadness, almost. The look on Greg's face in particular fills me with a sudden anger, nearly impossible to tamp down. *He's sorry? Can't stop? Bullshit.* I tense, my fists balled so tight my fingernails start to break the skin of my palms. I want to lash out, but more than that, I realize, I want answers.

Ang misconstrues my sudden rigidness, and speaks calmly into my ear.

"Do not be afraid," he says. "You're doing very, very well." We push through the group, who part like reverent cultists.

"Follow," Ang says to them, and the reaction is immediate. Movement all around, behind us.

Someone starts to speak, but before the sound can become a word, Doc snaps at them. "No talking!"

The group falls silently in behind us as Doc and Ang guide me down the hallway.

My eyes go immediately to the front door, but before I can even think about making a break for it, Ang steers me in the other direction.

Into the main room of the massive house.

It's a sunken living room. Bleached hardwood floors, white throw rugs in several places, and sleek modern furniture throughout. A massive flat-screen television is affixed to one wall, currently turned off.

The main feature of the room, though, is the fireplace. It's right in the center, open on all sides. More like a firepit, really. There is open air above it for perhaps ten feet, then above that a stonework flume is built into the vaulted ceiling, rising twenty feet above us. As for the firepit itself, the surface is a bed of colored glass beads, presumably with burners beneath. There is no flame just now. Surrounding all this is a bench of the same stonework, knee-high.

"Form the circle," Doc says to those gathered. Not "a circle," I note, but "*the* circle." A chill runs up my arms.

Feet shuffle on the hardwood floor as the group takes their places. Some begin to talk in low voices. There's a casualness to their response, as if this were all completely normal. Their reaction, I realize, seems to be a manifestation of the tone of Doc's command, not just the meaning. Interesting.

"No talking!" Ang barks. Then under his breath to Doc, "You have to remind them."

Doc nods meekly, cowed by the reprimand.

Guiding me by the elbows, the pair lead me across the hardwood floor until we stand next to the firepit.

Fire is not something I've ever been especially afraid of, but in this situation, about to undergo some sort of test, my brain suddenly fills with nightmarish scenes. My hand thrust into the flames, skin and muscle boiling away to a sick barbecue odor. Or a red-hot brand, a satanic symbol maybe, sizzling against the skin of my arm. My stomach churns equally to both thoughts, and I bite back a sudden urge to vomit.

"Step up onto the edge, Mary," Ang says.

*Don't hesitate*, I tell myself. *They'll know the commands aren't working. Just play along, pick your moment, then run.*

But his tone, like Doc's before, is casual, and I bet I can use that. The tone seems to indicate the level of response. No need to rush in my obedience.

I step up onto the stone bench, then again to the thin ledge above it, one deliberate step at a time. Once on the ledge I stare at the firepit in front of me, knowing they'll turn it on any second now and ask me to . . . to what, to walk across?

"Turn around," Doc says.

I do.

The others have all filed in behind us, forming a half circle around a throw rug on the floor below me.

I'm facing them now, which is a hell of a lot better than facing the fireplace in my estimation. Perhaps Ang just wants me to make a speech. Proclaim my loyalty, or repeat some oath. It could be that the punishment for failing the first time is a broken nose.

There's eight people in all. Doc, Ang, Chief Gorman, Captain Tweaker, and four others I don't know. Only one of them is a woman, but her expression is no different from the rest.

My gaze returns to one of the men. An older gentleman who looks familiar in the way that all politicians seem to. Could this be the senator they keep referring to? Surprise, surprise, his nose is bandaged, too.

But that's not all he shares with the others—each has a weapon of some kind. Pistols in belt holsters, or knives, or Tasers. *Shit*, I think, my plan of making a run for it suddenly quashed. I can't imagine reaching the front door before one of them can draw and fire.

Only Doc and Ang appear to be unarmed, but that doesn't help me at all.

With an almost magician-like flourish, Doc leans down and pulls the white rug away, tossing it aside.

He steps back into his place within the half-circle and looks up at me. Between them all, the bleached-white hardwood floor beneath the rug has been revealed. It is not white, here, but stained red.

Stained with blood.

A fresh bead of sweat begins to trickle down my spine.

Ang lifts his chin. With a strong note of pride he says, "Keeping your hands at your side, and making no effort to turn away, fall forward to the floor."

My eyes lock on that red stain as Ang's words register. The trail of sweat on my back goes cold, and goose bumps rise all across my body.

Time seems to slow.

This is my moment. I know this, deep down. I have to run. Have to try. Outgunned, outnumbered, it doesn't matter. I must try.

It'll never work, though. Running is suicide.

I swallow. Can't hesitate to obey, but don't have to hurry, either. Just need to buy time, to think of a way out. I start to lean. Just a bit, like going on tippy toe to see over a crowd. My mind races. How to get out of this? Nothing comes to mind. Every last bit of me wants to turn now, to run, to get away from these fucking weirdos and . . . and . . .

I keep leaning forward. Have to sell this. Just need another second to think. So I tilt, giving them what they want to buy myself a precious moment.

*Think, Mary, think!*

*Reach the tipping point. Then put a foot forward, sprint for the door!*

Maybe I can make it before one of them can draw.

The floor keeps rising toward me, a little faster now. My toes ache from the pressure my body is exerting. Soon gravity will take hold.

Go for one of their guns? The woman, I think. She's slight and . . . her hand is on the butt of the weapon. It wasn't when Ang gave me the command, but she's moved it there now. Am I taking too long?

The others have hands on weapons now, too. A flicker of suspicion rippling through them. Doubt entering their curious stares. I keep tilting toward the bloody patch in front of me.

Two thoughts pass through me at once.

*I need to get out of this.*

And . . .

*There's no getting out of this.*

My body is betraying me, though. Or maybe gravity is. Because my controlled tilt is at the threshold now. The last possible instant where I can stop myself.

And I don't.

I'm falling. Slow, then fast. Then too fast.

There's no choice now. It's going to happen. Have to sell it.

I pour every last shred of conscious effort into keeping my hands at my sides. Every instinct within me says to cushion the blow, to turn away. And I can't. They'll know. They'll kill me. I keep my face forward. Hands flat on my hips. No idea how, but I do.

My toes leave the ledge. Free fall.

*Don't flinch, don't flinch, don't flin—*

I hit the floor nose first, and for a split second, there's only the sound of it. The crack of brittle bone, the wet slap of meat and blood. And the grunt that comes, involuntarily, from my lungs.

No pain, though. Not for that split second.

Then it arrives. Like a tidal wave. Like the sudden crack of a gunshot. Bright and searing and absolute.

Pain like fire. Lightning in the mind.

All thought blots out. Anguish instead. I scream. Then I stop. It hurts too much to scream.

Some time passes. I've no idea how much. I've curled into a ball, hands at my face but not touching my broken nose. Warm blood flows onto my palms. I'm coughing through my mouth. Tears that feel scalding hot well around my eyes.

There's a strange noise that manages to get through all this. I try to latch on to it, desperate for anything I can mentally anchor to that isn't the exploded star in the center of my face.

It's a popping sound, like distant gunfire. Or champagne bottles being opened.

No, not those things. I get it now. It's applause.

"Welcome," Mr. Ang says, "to the Broken Nose Gang."

# CHAPTER SEVENTEEN

Something about my nose feels strange. There's a fuzzy sensation there, as if I'm being tickled by a feather.

This makes me want to sneeze, but I can't seem to. My head feels like it weighs a hundred pounds, like it's been filled with something warm and numbing.

Pressure on my nose, now. Slight, then gone again, then it's back. A probing. A blotting.

I open my eyes a little.

Doc leans over me. His hands gloved in blue latex. He holds a cotton ball in metal pincers, dabbing at my face. It comes away stained red.

"She's waking up," Ang observes.

"It's okay," Doc mumbles. "I gave her a shot of Novocain."

"Give her more," someone replies.

"Let me handle dosages, will you?" Doc shoots back. "All of you, relax and be happy we have a new member."

I glance around, my eyes and my head clearing a little. The rest of the "gang" are in a circle around me, watching. Greg, Tweaker, Ang, and the rest. They look . . . sad, as if they've just witnessed an old friend fall ill.

Ang glances at the lone woman among them. "Proceed with the plan," he orders her. "This has been a distraction, but we still must be ready."

She glances at her watch. "They're expecting me in half an hour, does that still work?"

Ang shakes his head. "Phone them and stall." He jerks his chin toward me. "She won't be a problem now, but we still have preparations to make and we're behind schedule. None of this will matter if the demonstration does not go as planned."

The woman frowns. "And if he decides to just cancel the order?"

"Give him a discount. Hell, tell him it's free. He'll wait if it's free. Now go load the van, and be ready to leave."

She nods firmly and disappears from view. Footsteps receding.

"And put your earpiece in!" Ang calls after her. "In fact, all of you put your earpieces in."

The group complies, instantly. Each retrieves a small object from under their shirt collars and puts it in their right ear. The devices are attached by clear, spiral-shaped cables that disappear under their hair and shirt collars. Just like you see bodyguards wear. Or secret service agents.

"Senator," Ang says, "you're with me. The rest of you, go back to your duties."

He turns and walks away. The older man with the fine silvery head of hair instantly follows.

I try to watch them go, lifting my head from the cold hardwood floor. It's the wrong time, though, because my nose collides with Doc's metal pincers.

Novocain or not, my world vanishes into another sizzling white agony.

*"O'Doherty's, Kyle speaking. Oh, hey, yes! Finally! Are you outside? Well fuck, where are you then? You said delivery by six p.m. No, tomorrow's no good, the event starts tomorrow. I need the beer now. Tonight. Uh-huh. Okay. How late are we talking? I've got the whole committee due to arrive any minute and they're all expecting a sample. Yeah. Okay, okay. Wait, did you say free? Seriously? That's kick-ass. Thanks! Of course we'll be here. For free booze? Hell yeah we'll wait."*

# CHAPTER EIGHTEEN

The pain has become a dull throb.

I groan and try to sit, only to find my hands are tied down. "What—"

"I'm here," a voice says. It's Greg, in the room with me.

I'm lying down now on a mattress. I can feel the tightness of the bandages across my face. There are other voices, muffled, outside.

I try to open my eyes but can't see much, they're too watery.

"Mary," Greg says. "I'm so sorry about this. I can't control . . . well, you know, now. You're one of us. We do as we're told."

I strain to see him, try to blink away the tears. It's no use. When I try to wipe at my eyes, the straps prevent the gesture.

"Why—" I start to ask.

"Just a precaution. Doc was worried you'd try to touch your nose. He said—"

Suddenly Greg stiffens, eyes on the wall beside me. He nods, as if hearing a voice in his head. The earpiece, I remember.

"Acknowledged: I will get Dr. Ryan," he says to whomever is on the other side of the line before standing abruptly.

"Wait," I say, but it's too late. Greg—the chief of police—my boss—is already out the door.

I've no real choice but to lie there and wait for my eyes to clear. When that happens I have to wait more for the room to stop spinning.

My whole head feels heavy and dull. My body lethargic. Medication of some sort. I wonder how long I've been out, and what time it is.

When Doc comes in a minute later I've already mentally braced myself for more tests. What will they order me to do next? I wonder. Shoot someone? Shoot myself? I'm okay with those, if only so they'll give me a gun.

But when he sits beside me the first thing he does is undo the straps holding my arms down. Without thinking I begin to rub feeling back into my hands.

"How do you feel?" he asks.

Carefully I swipe the tears from my eyes. "Like I drank a bottle of NyQuil."

He nods, watching my face carefully. "I've given you painkillers, and injected a numbing agent around your nose. It should get you through the worst of it."

"Thank you," I say, surprised at how heartfelt it sounds. A silence stretches between us, I suppose as he's waiting for me to get my senses back. I have to force myself to remember that they think I'm under some kind of spell. But no one's told me I can't ask questions. Before they do, I figure I should try.

"What's all this about, Doc?"

"The test?" he asks. "A crude method, I know, but we needed a foolproof way to make sure the treatment works. And, more to the point, to make sure you weren't already exposed to the old version."

"What the hell are you talking about?"

He smiles at me, almost fatherly. He's leaning in and delicately checking the edges of my bandaged face. So close I can smell his lack of cologne, his breath like cheddar cheese. I can see the dandruff in his hair. I want nothing more in that instant than to grab two fistfuls of his gray mane and ram my forehead into his nose. Fair's fair.

But I don't do this. I want answers. As long as he's buying my act I've got to keep him talking.

"It's Ang's invention," he says, "and it's going to change the world."

I look at him, meeting his gaze and forcing myself to have at least a little of the reverence Doc's voice holds. "Why isn't your nose broken?" I ask.

He brightens. "Ah, excellent question! I was one of those affected by version one."

"Doc, c'mon. I don't understand what that means."

Finally he leans back, satisfied my bandages are sufficiently in place. As he slumps against his chair he lets out a long sigh, perhaps debating how much to tell me or, I think, he may just be tired. He looks exhausted.

"It's like . . . immunizing someone against a disease. You can't un-immunize someone."

"Still not following you."

His chin falls in frustration. For a moment he casts about, trying to think of words that I'll understand. Finally he sits upright. "How would you describe me, Mary? *You will answer honestly.*"

Well, that's a gift horse I'll happily ride.

"Socially awkward. Frumpy. Stodgy. Tall and gangly."

"Okay, I get the—"

"Misshapen. Repulsive. Annoying."

"That's quite—"

"Flabby. Weak."

"Ah," he says with sudden vigor, snapping his fingers. "There! Finally at the heart of the matter!"

"Excuse me?" I ask, genuinely confused.

"Suppose I told you I used to be in perfect physical condition."

My eyebrows shoot up involuntarily. Doc sees this, gives a sheepish shrug.

"Ever notice the sticker on the back window of my car?"

"A hundred forty point six," I mutter, remembering it from the gas station. "That's like a joke, right? A play on the marathon runner sticker? Like you could really run that far."

He shakes his head. "I completed the Ironman triathlon twice, actually."

I pull a genuine face. "Bullshit."

"Honest truth, Mary. I did track-and-field in college, every sport you could imagine before that. Wrestling, swim team. Ever since I was a kid, exercise was in my blood . . ." His words trail off as he's momentarily captivated by his own memories.

"Okay . . . ?" I prompt.

He taps his breast with a balled fist. "It was a part of me, Mary. My drive to be active and athletic literally defined me."

I wait, now. Through the haze of medication and a dull, distant pain, I finally understand where he's going with this because of the changes I've recognized in myself. Connecting with people, building teams, and forging partnerships. It had been part of me. More than that. The core of my being. A defining trait. But no more.

So yeah, I know what Doc is saying. But I can't let him know that. I have to keep up this charade a little longer.

Lost in his own little monologue, Doc continues, "After I met Ang, after I really understood what he was working on, I tried the treatment myself. Version one. At first we thought it had failed. We almost gave up, in fact, but then Ang noticed I'd stopped exercising. Completely. Didn't think about it once. It was as if that part of me had been deleted. When he realized the effect his invention had caused, he knew he was onto something. It just needed to be perfected."

"What are you talking about?"

"Instincts, Mary. Instincts. A reversal of the core behavior within the hypothalamus—our animal brain. Whatever that instinct happened to be. Different for everyone. Difficult to pinpoint, to measure. But in time . . . "

He smiles at this admission, a little sadly. Then the smile fades.

"Very crude, version one. The instinct reversal is interesting but ultimately useless. Testing was needed. Data. It was the only way. We had to factor in so many variables. Account for signaling from the amygdala . . ."

He's descended into Doc Mumble Mode, talking out of the side of his mouth, more to himself than me now. But just as I start to tune him out the intensity floods back into him. His eyes light up and he looks at me again. "And now—now, Mary!—it works! How it's supposed to. Pathways aren't reversed, they're opened up, receptors primed. With proper timing the imprint is strong. Targeted. Amplified. We have to test to make sure, of course. The nose, the fall."

"So this . . . whatever it is . . . removes our instinct to break a fall?" I ask. "To flinch?"

"No, no, you don't see it yet. But you will, you will."

He's rocking back and forth a little now, almost giddy as he watches me make the right connections.

Pathways. Receptors. Imprint.

"*You will do whatever I say,*" I repeat. The woman in the video. I realize suddenly that I've seen her before. Where I can't recall, though. I try to focus on her, but my mind is still hazy.

Doc's fully rocking in his chair now, grinning like a child. "Yes, yes! Isn't that amazing? It's working, Mary. Finally. No more mistakes, no more guesswork. Now the real work can—"

"Hold on . . . what do you mean, 'mistakes'?" I ask.

His face goes red, eyes suddenly wide. Doc stammers for words, and is saved when the door opens.

Ang comes in, along with Tweaker.

"Let her rest, Frank, we have a lot of work to do."

"Of course," Doc replies. To me he says, "I'll be back to check on you. Once the painkillers wear off you'll be ready to join the effort. It's good to have you here, Mary. Get some rest." Then, very deliberately, he adds, "Do not leave this room or speak to anyone else but me or Mr. Ang."

An *order*. One he believes I will obey perfectly. He pats my arm, the very picture of confidence, eyes twinkling as he hoists himself from the chair and follows Ang and the thin man out of the room.

The door closes softly behind them.


I lay there for several minutes, listening to the sounds of the house. The electric churn of a dishwasher running, or a laundry machine. A garage door opens, and a car leaves. Farther off is the whine of a lawn mower. Or could that be the ATV? The sound grows quiet, then louder. Captain Tweaker patrolling the estate, perhaps?

As the sound lulls again something new is revealed. Voices. They're directly below me, I feel certain of this. So perhaps I'm not in the room where Doc dosed me with their drug or whatever it is, but in an upstairs bedroom. The space looks the same, but in these super modern homes, all the rooms kind of look the same.

In the empty, quiet room my mind begins to fill with questions. So many questions. They swirl like angry bees, as elusive as they are annoying. I need to think. Need to clear my head of this medicinal haze.

Pretending to stretch and work a kink from my neck, I scan the walls and ceiling, looking for cameras, sure they're watching me and that leaving me alone is some kind of test. I see none, though. Just a small motion sensor on the light switch, a fire alarm, and a small air vent. Any of these could hide a camera.

Then I recall Doc's orders, and figure I can follow them to the letter and still maintain my cover. I won't leave the room, or speak to anyone but him and Ang.

Slowly I rise, trying to keep my face still. Every little twitch makes the skin around my nose stretch or pinch, triggering a deep and distant pain dulled only by the pills. When they wear off it's going to be brutal, I think, hoping there's more painkillers to come.

There's a single window on the wall behind me, with vertical blinds folded closed. I tug the chain and they rattle, rotating to allow daylight in.

The window faces south. Spreading out below me is the back-yard, if you can call something so huge a yard. Grass stretches at least three hundred feet before reaching the ivy-covered wall surrounding the property. Beyond is the steep valley that, somewhere below, meets the river I crossed to get up here in the first place. In the distance I can see the mountain, and somewhere up to the left is Silvertown, Lake Forgotten, and Two-Shits. There's people up there, friends, perhaps wondering where I am. Wondering when their cell phones will work again, and gossiping about whatever strange behavior is the latest on a growing list. What will they do, I wonder, when the conspiracy du jour is that a missing-persons report needs to be filed on the town's only cop?

None of them know where I am, I realize. I went solo, again, and didn't think to tell anyone.

Doc's explanation still rattles in my head. Instincts. One is strongest. Then the treatment—version one, that is—reversed it. Hence Doc stopped taking care of his body.

I think back to the conversation with Kyle and Clara after we'd rescued her from the silo, when I'd been about to voice a similar theory. I'd given up on the idea at the last second as stupid, despite all the examples in front of me. Because I couldn't come up with anything connecting all of us.

"Mistakes," Doc said before he left the room. I rack my brain, trying to piece everything together. Unbidden I suddenly recall what Mrs. Rogers said to me about her boy, Johnny. *It was so out of character.*

But how? When? Surely Doc and his gang couldn't have grabbed him and injected Ang's concoction because there was no gang, not then. It's this new version that creates behavior like Rhod Mitchell's. Johnny, Clara, Sally, myself, we were all given the previous version. But how?

It hits me, then.

The sleeping pill Clara gave me. I took it that night, before Rhod attacked me. And ever since then . . .

Yet Clara was fine, at least until the next evening? Surely she'd taken one, too. I think back to our conversation. I was dead tired, not thinking clearly. But I think she said something about her sister swearing by them, and that she herself hadn't taken one yet.

But she must have that night, or the next. Because her behavior had changed, too. Hence the woman famously mistrustful of strangers went down into a dark abandoned missile silo with a bunch of teens she's never met.

And where had those pills come from? Doctor Ryan, of course. The only game in town for prescription meds. He'd tried to push those sleeping pills on me, too, come to think of it.

I try to picture the Rogers' house. The master bathroom. There'd been something there. No sleeping pills but something else. Alzheimer's medication, was it? I'd googled it, thought nothing of it, but now I can see a new angle. The meds improve focus, memory, reactions. Everything a teenage gamer craves to get the upper hand. The sort of thing Johnny might try while his parents are away.

It wasn't the cell tower or government nerve agents or satanic rituals. No, it was Doc Ryan's pharmacy that caused all this.

As I hold the vertical blind aside to gaze out on the mountain, there's those damned words on my hand, coming into focus once again.

## YOU NEED <u>HELP</u>

I stopped asking for help after I took that pill. I stopped teaming up with anyone, stopped being a partner, at least seeking such things out. And that was my defining trait, or as Doc had put it, my strongest instinct. Turned on its head.

It's not often that I kick myself for only being a B student, but standing here now I wish I'd paid more attention in Criminal Psych, and the various instincts the human animal is gifted with. There's got to be a bunch, and the more I think about it, the more it explains all the weird behavior around town these last few days. The woman in the bar, making no effort to catch the pool cue chalk. Sally Jones caring for a stranger instead of her own toddlers. Careful

Willy Jupitas stepping out in front of my car, as if not recognizing the threat it posed.

I'm willing to bet they all had recent prescriptions from Doc. Maybe not sleeping pills, but something.

"Diabolical," I whisper. Because it's perfect. With no pharmacy in town, Doc hands out everyone's pills, laced with Ang's proto-types. In our secluded town he can easily observe the results, for the simple reason that he's Doc and the population is tiny. Almost comically easy to keep tabs on people. And he doesn't even need to be secretive about it. Everyone trusts their doctor, and Silvertown only has the one. He could just ask. "How are those meds working out? Any *interesting* side effects?"

Activity in the yard interrupts my line of thought. Greg's come out the back of the house, along with two of the others. The three confer for a moment, then spread out. Greg himself strolls to the side of the house, disappearing from my view for a moment before returning just seconds later pushing a wheelbarrow full of paving stones. He guides it about halfway to the distant wall, then stops. The other two people join him there.

For a long few seconds they all just stand around, staring at one another. Greg's finger is pressed to his ear. Commands being given, I suppose. Once received, they all turn in unison and move to the wheelbarrow.

I watch, confused and a little morbidly fascinated, as the trio take the flat, square stones and carry them twelve paces—always twelve—out from the center point of the wheelbarrow, before plac-ing them in the grass. A circle begins to form.

Silvertown must really be growing on me because my first thought is of Stonehenge, and fairy circles. That sort of thing. There's some-thing very pagan about making a big circle of stones on a lawn, even if those stones are only the size of pizza boxes.

I half expect the shape to become a pentagram, but the supply of stones has run out, and the three walk back to the house after putting the wheelbarrow away. At one point Greg looks up at my window, and it takes every ounce of self-control I can muster not to step away from the window guiltily. I'm not violating Doc's rules, I remind myself. I'm one of them. The Broken Nose Gang.

Greg smiles and there is still that hint of apology in his expression. I smile back, giving him a little wave, trying to let him know I understand. After talking to Doc, it's clear that however complicit Greg's actions make him in all this, his mind is not on board.

The thought gives me a new and horrible perspective on what these people are going through. Their apologies—"I'm sorry, I can't stop"—imply something so much darker. They're aware of the loss of control. Prisoners in their own heads. Holy Christ, that has got to be a nightmare.

I'm hit suddenly by a wave of guilt over Rhod Mitchell, the biker—and the father of two—who I shot and killed. He hadn't wanted to break into my house, but some low-level part of his brain had been flooded with the urge to do so. He could do nothing but watch the whole thing play out, right up until the moment I shot him.

I begin to shake, violently, as a newfound rage boils through me.

Time to redirect my anger toward the people responsible for all this. Toward Ang, and whoever that woman was on the screen. She looked so damn familiar, but I still can't place it.

I let the blinds fall and sit back down on the bed, trying to think of what the fuck to do because another memory has just come back to me, something I'd forgotten about in all this insanity:

Captain Tweaker and his barrels, which he'd been emptying into the town's water supply.

*Holy shit.* There'd been debate, when I was bound in that room, about whether to give me the liquid version. Oh hell. What if the contents of those barrels had been laced with Ang's drug? Contaminate the water supply and boom, you have a whole town of people who appear normal but, with the right command from the right person, obey like robots.

Only, that can't be right. I think through the details of my own experience. Weight and blood pressure and pulse, then that timer with the oddly specific 73 seconds, which started the moment they sprayed that crap into my mouth. You couldn't put something like that into a water supply. Who the hell knows when anyone will consume it, and even if you could get them to do it at the right time, what then? How do you *imprint* the desired behavior on an entire town all at once?

So whatever Tweaker was dumping in the water, it wasn't Ang's creation. So what was it? And why?

My stomach lurches. The vision in my head changes. Instead of *The Stepford Wives* robotic slaves, what I now imagine is Jonestown. That death cult. Bodies in the grass, in the church, everywhere. They'd drunk the Kool-Aid.

Suppose what Tweaker had been putting in the water supply wasn't Ang's creation at all. What if it was simply poison? In one fell swoop, all evidence of the experiments would be wiped out. Left behind would be just myself and Greg—the town's only police—and Doc, the town's lone doctor, all agreeing on the same version of the story per the bidding of a voice in our ear. We'd say it was some outbreak or suicide cult or who-knows-what. Who'd think to check of a drug no one's ever heard of before, especially if it's long since left the system, its damage to the brain already done?

No one would. Christ, it's fucking perfect.

Except for one thing.

"They're not expecting me," I whisper toward the floor. For the moment, at least, they think I'm part of the gang. That's the only card I have to play.

If that is their plan, though—to hide here while Silvertown commits an unwitting mass suicide—then I may already be too late. Staying here, pretending to be one of them, waiting for the right moment to make some arrests . . . that's not going to cut it. People could be dying off even now.

I need to get away. Warn them. Save whoever I can.

Kyle. Clara. Sally and her twins. All of them.

I need to save Silvertown.

# CHAPTER NINETEEN

The problem with this goal is immediately obvious to me.

Even if they believe I'm one of them, the primary trait of membership in their gang is not the broken nose, but blind obedience. If I'm wandering around the house, they'll know instantly that I'm not under the spell, seeing as I was ordered to stay in the room.

On a whim I go to the door and try the handle, just to know if it's even an option.

Locked from the outside.

To quote Doc, *that's interesting*.

Either he doesn't trust my state of mind as much as he's letting on, or this treatment of Ang's isn't as foolproof as it seems.

I sit on the bed again, thinking the idea through. Perhaps blind obedience is not entirely correct. Reviewing everything I've seen and heard here, there are plenty of instances where Ang and Doc's "gang" seemed to stray from their orders. And one detail in particular stands out. Doc had to tell Tweaker a second time not to talk to me. And then, a few seconds later, Ang chastised the big oaf. "You have to remind them," he'd said.

Why, though? And I guess more important, can I use this knowledge somehow?

Instincts, as I understand them, manifest in the way we behave without thinking. Or, rather, *before* thinking. Flinching when something is thrown at us. Running from danger. There's the instinct first, then the rational thought after. We flinched, but the object being thrown was soft. We fled, but the threat chasing us was just an affectionate pooch. One governs our behavior more quickly than the other.

I think back once again to Doc's words as we viewed the body of the hiker. "Consider the animal handler," he'd said, perhaps giving away more than he should have. His point had been that with enough training you can overcome your instinctual behavior.

If that were true here, though, then why hadn't Greg just gone all Charles Bronson on Doc and Ang the moment his head caught up with what his body's been doing?

The answer hits me like a bolt of electricity: *The woman from the screen.*

I hadn't thought about her much until now. And suddenly it occurs to me that the only real rewiring of the brain they've tried to do to me here is to get me to believe whatever she says.

*You will do whatever I say.* Only once that has been absolutely baked in do the next instructions come. You'll do whatever Ang says, unless it conflicts. Etcetera.

Well, fuck, now that makes sense.

Her original command is the new instinct at the core of Greg, Tweaker, and all the others. When Doc tells one of them to do something it is her command that makes them comply.

But over time perhaps their brains start to erode this reflexive trust in the woman's original order.

Okay, Mary, that's great and all, but what does it mean? And why is the woman from the video at the heart of this, and not Ang himself?

I rack my brain, still sure I've seen her somewhere before. Not just seen, but her voice . . . I've heard her voice. Where?

After several minutes, though, I give up, the memory remaining just out of reach.

What I need to do is stop speculating and focus on getting out of here. The door's locked, which means I'll either need to force my way out or wait until someone comes.

I decide to wait. Doc will either come back and give me some task outside this room during which I can slip away, or he won't, in which case it makes sense to wait until everyone's asleep before I try to flee.

Back at the window I stand for a while and stare at the landscape. The valley and the mountain beyond beckon like an old friend, and it's tempting to comfort myself by picking out all the landmarks of Silvertown. That's not going to help me here, though, so I force myself to study the immediate surroundings instead, starting with the wall at the edge of the property.

Even from this side it's hard to spot the movable section that Tweaker used to vanish. It's the ground that ultimately gives it away. Two semicircles of gravel marring an otherwise flawless lawn. There's a large garden shed to one side of this patch, with track marks in the grass leading up to its door. The ATV must be in there. If there's only one such vehicle, and I can steal it, their chances of catching up to me are slim. *Good*, I think. The beginnings of a plan. Now how to get there? Between the shed and the house is roughly a hundred yards of lawn, sun-soaked and offering nothing in the way of cover. Other than grass, all I can see is the weird circle of paving stones, and the edge of a patio just below my window. Leaning until my forehead is against the cool glass, I can see someone's legs at the very limit of my restricted view. They sit in a lawn chair, and there's an assault rifle laid across the person's lap.

Okay, so much for a dash across the lawn. I'd just be target practice.

Movement in the middle distance draws my attention back to the wall. Someone's walking there. Patrolling the property.

Guarding against me trying to escape, or someone coming after me? The latter seems more likely, given that I'm supposedly part of the gang now. But on the other hand, anyone looking for me here is dishearteningly unlikely. Perhaps my arrival has simply put them on edge. They must have felt pretty safe and secluded here before I rang the buzzer at the gate.

The sun creeps across the sky with maddening slowness, but waiting for dark is my only option, I think. After some time I go and sit on the bed, then lay down to rest. The painkillers are strong, but I suspect they're also making me tired.

I've no idea how long I slept.

All I know is, when I finally sit up and rub at my eyes, the room's nearly pitch-black. The only light comes from a faint glow creeping in around the edges of the window blinds.

I smell something. My stomach reacts before my brain can identify the odor, sending a sharp pang of hunger through my gut. As my eyes adjust, I spot the source: a dinner tray in the middle of the floor.

Hunger gets the better of me. In a flash I'm out of the bed and wolfing down the contents of the tray. A room-temperature cheeseburger, corn on the cob, and a bottle of water. This last I chug until it's half gone, before realizing I should save some. I twist the cap back on.

Despite sitting here long enough to cool down, the burger and corn taste backyard-barbecue fresh, which makes sense. There's no restaurant in easy driving distance, and having food delivered would only draw unwanted attention to this secluded place. I might be able to use that, I think. A barbecue in the yard somewhere. There'll be tools, lighter fluid.

I go to the window and glance outside, peering through a gap in the blinds I make with thumb and index finger. A half-moon sits in the western sky, made hazy by thin clouds. Shifting yellow light from the first floor of the mansion casts rectangles out onto the grass. The glow flickers and waves, no doubt thrown by the big fireplace from which I took my nosedive. How quaint.

The most striking source of illumination outside, though, is the candles. One has been placed on each of the paving stones, creating a glowing dotted outline of their circular placement, which only serves to reinforce my earlier vision of some ritualistic purpose.

Kneeling down, I put my ear to the floor and listen. At first there's only the ambient sounds of a large home. Air circulating, water moving through pipes, and the even more subtle hum of electricity. But then I hear the muffled sounds of laughter, and voices in conversation.

They're distracted, I think. Eating. Not the best time to make my move. Best to wait until they're all asleep. Only, now I'm not so sure that's ever going to be the case, not if someone's sitting with a rifle on the back patio, and another is walking the perimeter. Those kinds of precautions are done in shifts.

Besides, I slept for hours. Time's not on my side, and here I am hesitating, napping even. I need to get back to Silvertown. Warn them. And then find a way to end this.

Time to stop worrying about cameras.

I try the door again, but of course it's still locked. Leaving the lights off, I kneel down in front of the handle and try to inspect it, figure out what I'm up against. Picking a lock is not something I ever learned how to do, but I watched my brother once, and he explained the basic principles. He had tools, though. I don't.

"Think, think," I whisper. There's a small bathroom in here. I haven't looked through it yet. Tools, maybe? Take the door off its hinges? I search under the sink and find nothing but a roll of toilet paper and three extra bars of soap. The paper I leave, but the soap I take. Back in the bedroom I remove the pillowcase from the pillow and stuff the soap inside, then tie it off. I swing it around a few times. The soap's not that heavy, but as weapons go it's better than nothing. If I can crack someone in the temple with this, I think they'll at least be stunned, if not out cold for a bit.

On a whim I take the towel that's hanging over the small bathroom's shower stall and roll it into a loose tube, stuffing it under the blanket on the bed. I arrange the pillow to be mostly underneath, too, and plump up the blanket where I can. Let them come in and think I'm still here, asleep. For a few seconds only, sure, but it's better than nothing.

Now what? Wait for someone to come to collect the food tray? Thump them on the head and make a dash?

Could be hours. Even until morning.

Go out the window? I cross to it again and peek through. It can open, and the screen on the outside looks flimsy, but the only place to go from here is down to the patio, which is illuminated by the expansive windows looking in on the great living room. Someone would see me. I study the ground below. What I can see of it, at least. There is the guy sitting with the rifle on his lap, but he's a good five feet to the left, so dropping on him is unlikely in the extreme.

I pace for a moment, then sit again, suddenly dejected. It's no use. I get one shot at this, and none of the options are good. I want to be well away from this place before anyone knows I'm missing. A fifteen-foot drop onto a stone patio is likely to leave me with a sprained ankle, maybe even a broken one, only to then be chased down into the valley. With no shoes or socks on, either. It's useless. But I can't think of a better idea.

I go to the window and pry with my fingertips, dragging it aside as slowly as I can, not wanting to make any noise. When it's finally open all the way I go to work on the screen, lifting the two plastic tabs at the bottom and trying to lift it out of the frame. The tabs are stiff, though, and the screen refuses to budge. I try harder, straining as much as I dare, ignoring the cool early autumn breeze on my skin and the sounds of the night. Crickets, leaves stirred by wind, and the babble of the low river somewhere farther off like a whisper.

And then another sound begins to register, so faint and subtle at first I think I'm imagining it. But the sound grows steadily.

An airplane, I think. Small one, prop engine. Can I use that? Light a fire, get their attention? They'll report it, and the National Parks Service fire response would come.

As the sound grows, though, it changes. Becomes more like a rhythm, or a pulse. Helicopter, then. The sound is growing by the second now. Police, searching for me?

There's a flurry of activity downstairs. I hear a door opening, and the voices get louder. From the yard below me I hear Chief Greg call out.

"Ang, it's them!" he says.

My heart skips a beat as I picture SWAT officers rappelling down from a chopper as a sniper in the doorway picks off the hapless, panicked members of the Broken Nose Gang.

But then I recognize Greg's tone. It's not alarm. It's expectation. There's a muffled reply.

The sound of the aircraft becomes a sudden roar, and the yard is illuminated by its landing lights.

Suddenly the ring of lit paving stones makes sense. They aren't for some kind of satanic ritual. They're a goddamn landing pad.

The vertical blinds before me begin to whip and twist as the great wash of the rotor buffets the back of the house. Shadows dance through the room, the light a brilliant erratic strobe, hitting my face like a physical force as I try to bat the blinds into position and hold them down. I can only hope no one aboard is looking this way.

I give up and crouch below the window. The sound of the helicopter is tremendous, drowning out everything else, and I realize this is the chance I've been waiting for. As distractions go it's magnificent. But not for exiting via my window.

Grabbing the pillowcase with the soap in it, I rush to the door. It takes one swift kick to get it open, wood splintering in the jamb where the latch had been. Between all the activity downstairs, and the thunderous wind of the helicopter, the noise is inaudible even to me. Going to have a hell of a bruised foot, but thanks to Doc my body is still loaded with painkillers.

A quick glance left and right. The hall is empty. I go right, toward the center of the house, running with the pillowcase held low and loose, swinging at my shins. Doors blur by on either side, all closed. I keep going. At the corner I peer around and then move again, finding the next leg of the hall empty as well.

Halfway down its length, the hall reaches the center of the great house and the walls to either side become railings. When I reach that spot I'll have no cover to either side, so I slow to a stop just before.

The span of hallway before me is really more like an elevated bridge looking down on the living room to the right and the foyer to the left. On the other end of this bridge the hall continues on, mirroring my side. But just before that there is one key difference: a stairway going down, ending in the foyer beside the front door. It's so damn close. Twenty feet, then down, then freedom.

Just one problem. I'll be completely exposed as I cross that twenty feet. Everything depends on how distracted my captors down below really are.

Outside the note of the chopper's blades begins to diminish into a dull rhythmic *whump* under a high-pitched whine, growing quieter by the second.

I get down on all fours and peek around the corner, looking past the fireplace toward the back wall of the house. It is comprised entirely of glass panels from floor to ceiling. I hadn't realized it before, but each panel is not just a window but also a door of sorts. They're installed on rotating pillars, allowing the whole back of the house to be open to nature if the occupant desires. They're all closed now save the middle one, which is rotated exactly halfway. Ang, Doc, and their broken-nosed henchmen all wait there, watching the spectacle of the helicopter landing.

This is my moment. All eyes on the helicopter, and whomever is getting out of it.

I should run, now. Get away. But I hesitate. My gaze is pulled outside as the rotor finally comes to a stop. The aircraft rests on the lawn exactly in the center of the stone circle. All the candles are still lit, a detail that, despite all that is going on around me, I find stunning. Then I notice the pattern in their flickering and realize they're fake. Little LED tea-light candles meant to mimic the real thing.

People are getting out of the chopper, but I can't see them from this vantage point. Ang walks out the back door, though, and I hear him call out a warm greeting.

"Welcome, Mrs. Conaty," he says. "Welcome."

And there she is. Sandra Conaty.

The woman who used to own this town. The woman, I now realize, from the video. The woman who'd said the words at the heart of all this: *You will do whatever I say.*

# CHAPTER TWENTY

To Ang, Doc, and all the rest, Mrs. Conaty says, "Prepare rooms for my guests. We've had a rough flight. The demonstration can wait until the morning."

Like dutiful staff, they all turn and set about their tasks. Even Greg—my boss, the chief of police, the man who brought down the Conaty family and drove them from Silvertown—hops to it.

I duck behind cover just in time. There's a flurry of activity as Conaty's wishes are seen to. People moving through the house. Back against the wall, I hold my breath and consider options. Crossing this "bridge" to the other wing seems out of the question now. My best chance has vanished.

Words float up from below. Conaty is talking to someone. ". . . for the use of your beautiful home, Senator." Then, "Have you all met before?"

A man's mumbled reply.

Then four clear words, from the senator. "An honor, Mr. Secretary."

Secretary? My mind races as my stomach goes hollow. This is big. This is really fucking big. I start to lean back, hoping for a better look at the guests. I need to see them. I need to remember faces. But a sound stops me dead. Footsteps on the stairs. Someone's coming up.

On tiptoes I dart back down the hall toward my room, quietly trying doors as I go. They're all locked, but from this side. Dead bolts, no doubt installed recently because who the fuck builds a mansion with six guest rooms that lock from the outside?

Choosing one at random, I flick the dead bolt and slip inside, closing it behind me. No way to lock the door from within, so I'll just have to hope no one notices. Maybe they won't, but what's definitely not going to go unnoticed is the smashed door to my room, with its splintered jamb and shards of wood on the carpet. Nothing I can do about that.

The room I find myself in is identical to my own, but on the north side of the hall. Its window blinds are open, and I can see the long paving-stone driveway snaking off through the trees into the distance, little pools of yellow from landscape lights dotting its length.

I'm alone, the bed empty. I check the bathroom just to be sure. No one here.

The room is like mine: a bed, nothing more. The bathroom contains the bare minimum of supplies. Soap, toilet paper.

I check the window. This room is, if anything, worse than my own. A similar drop, but with rosebushes waiting at the bottom, and nowhere to go except the well-lit circle where the driveway reaches the front door. Someone stands in that doorway, just a shadow. The woman I saw earlier, I think. Keeping watch. Armed, probably.

The fountain in the center of the driveway's circle glistens in the moonlight, patterns of light pushing up from beneath the water's surface to dance across the sculpted statue and the facade of the mansion. Beyond, the six-car garage is exactly as before. All doors closed, the lone Ferrari parked in front, its red paint glinting as light from the fountain plays across it.

Where would the keys be? Kitchen, hanging on a hook? In Ang's pocket, or on his bedside table? Of course, from what Conaty just said, this isn't Ang's house after all. It's not even hers. So perhaps the keys are with this Senator. No, I think. Who walks around their own house with keys in their pocket?

With a six-car garage I imagine a set of hooks mounted on a wall inside, probably even labeled so the senator doesn't have to suffer the inconvenience of trying to remember which key is for which supercar. The question is which wall? In the garage itself? His den? The kitchen?

The garage, I decide. Even if there are no keys, I can't go deeper into the house, not with all these people around. But I sure hope there're keys, damn it. The idea of roaring out of here in a growling red sports car, flipping Ang and all the rest of them the middle finger as I tear down the mountain, is tantalizing. But then I remember they have a helicopter, and rifles, and I wonder just how far I'd really get.

Someone's in the hall outside, walking swiftly.

I pad to the door and stand behind it. They approach. I hold my breath again. But the footsteps move past without breaking speed. I let out my breath, just long enough to realize they're only steps from discovering my escape.

Time to go.

I slip from the room. In the hall I find I'm four steps from Captain Tweaker, who stands with his back to me, staring at my door. He's frozen in place, on the cusp of crying out an alarm.

Yet he hesitates, steps forward. Pushes my door open, not with his fingers but with the barrel of a pistol.

I pad up behind him and swing the pillowcase. There's a dull thud, and as he crumples to the floor he lets out an involuntary sigh. His collapse is otherwise whisper quiet.

"Good thing you weigh almost nothing," I mutter, dragging him into the room.

Out of habit I check for a pulse, finding it quickly. Strong and steady. A brief temptation comes over me to strangle him, but the cop in me can't do it.

I take the gun and set it aside, then make quick work of binding his hands with the bedsheet. It's not much, but it's what I've got. The pillowcase weapon no longer needed, I remove two of the soap bars and, with the third still tucked inside, stuff it into his mouth, tying the fabric tight behind his neck. A passable gag that might buy me an extra minute when he wakes.

His pants and shoes are next. Good hiking boots and a pair of jeans. The boots are, surprisingly, too small for me, but the jeans fit okay as long as I leave the fly undone. Better than nothing.

The gun is a cheap Smith & Wesson nine-millimeter, the kind a homeowner buys at Wal-Mart to protect belongings no one would ever want to steal. I check the magazine, see the glint of brass. In the dim light I can make out at least three bullets, so I'll assume that much and cross my fingers for more. If I'm lucky there's a full ten plus one chambered. Now's not the time to empty it and count.

I search his pockets and find nothing else. No keys, no wallet, no phone. He does have an earpiece, but when I remove it the thing all but falls apart in my hand. The casing is cracked, and a bit of circuitry is visible within. The smack I gave him must have clipped the device, too. I hold it up to my own ear for a few seconds anyway, but hear nothing. I decide to throw it in the toilet rather than take it with me.

Before leaving, I flip the mattress on top of him. Anything to muffle his cries of alarm when he comes to.

I creep back down the hall. There's a lot of activity downstairs, but other than Tweaker I'm pretty sure no one else has come to the second floor. The nice guest quarters must be down there, somewhere.

With the smallest movement possible I take another look around the corner, down into the expansive living room. The fireplace is roaring now. Greg is out on the patio again, just visible from my vantage point. He's standing at alert, a rifle in his hands now. Guarding the house.

In the living room itself, Mrs. Conaty sits in one of the leather chairs, her legs crossed and a glass of wine in one hand. She's speaking with two men who sit across from her. Both wear expensive suits. One has dark hair and a thick mustache, face etched in a perpetual scowl, his skin visibly wrinkled even from here. The one referred to as Mr. Secretary? For the first time in my life I find myself wishing I paid more attention to politics.

The other man has a great mane of blond hair. His suit is fitted but worn casually. No tie, shirt open two buttons to reveal tanned, clear skin and several thick gold chains around his neck. His legs are spread slightly, and his arms are up on the back of the sofa. Absolute comfort, absolute confidence. He laughs and says something. Not quite loud enough to make out the words, but loud enough to hint at an accent. It's not quite British. European? Whatever the case, it's snooty. He reeks of money.

Behind the sofa are four more men, all standing rigid, hands clasped in front of them. Bodyguards, clearly. Belonging to the two men, or Conaty? I mull that and decide it doesn't matter. They'll kill me either way, of that I'm sure.

Ang walks in from the dining room area off to the side, carrying a bottle of wine. All eyes go to him.

I take the chance.

A dash across the walkway, past the stairs and into the hall beyond. Here I stop and press my back to the wall, forcing my pulse to return to normal, along with my rapid breaths. I strain my ears, but there's no sign that anyone below saw or heard me. Quiet conversation continues. Someone says something that elicits a brief polite chuckle from Conaty.

The older man—I assume Mr. Secretary—responds with a note of annoyance, but at this distance and over the roaring fire, the words are hard to make out. All I get is ". . . results that are better than cold hard cash?"

Conaty's response is smooth, controlled. I hear little of it, but a few words register. ". . . handful . . . maintain . . . live in constant doubt?" This last is louder, the words edged and forceful.

Mr. Secretary does not reply. Cowed, impressed, or bored I'm not sure.

I move deeper into the house. The hall on this side of the foyer is longer than the other section, but with fewer doors. I keep to the edge, gun gripped in both hands, pointed at the floor two paces in front of me. The first door I come to has no retrofitted dead bolt. Just a simple handle. I twist it and open it a few inches. Linens on shelves, only a foot deep. I push it closed and quietly let the handle go.

The next door opens into another bedroom, but unlike those on the other side of the house, this one is well furnished. Queen-size bed, a desk, dresser, art on the walls. I leave the lights off and check the window first, but all I can see are the vague shapes of trees, thick bushes below.

Inside the room are two doors. One leads to a well-appointed bathroom with a full walk-in shower. The other reveals a closet. Inside I find two pairs of shoes: leather dress shoes and a pair of Nike running shoes. These last I try. They're absolutely huge on my feet, but that's better than being too tight, I think. In a dresser drawer I find socks and pull three pairs on. Even with the extra padding I still have to pull hard to tie the laces tight enough. Walking in these feels ridiculous, though, like I'm wearing clown shoes. I take them off again, keeping one pair of socks. The shoes I put back where I found them, again hoping to keep my escape a secret as long as possible.

As I set the sneakers back down I spy a pair of boots pushed into the back of the closet. I've seen these boots before. Not mine, but familiar. Doc's, I realize. The brand-new green Wellingtons he wore when he came to look at the hiker's body. No wonder the sneakers were too big. Doc's feet are big enough to make a basketball player jealous.

*This is Doc's room.*

I glance around, looking at the space with fresh eyes. I check the desk first. It's empty, unused. Doc's treating this like a hotel room, I realize, and think back to his story about being at a conference. I bet he stood right here when he talked to me on the phone, the lying bastard.

The socks I'd found in the first dresser drawer I'd opened, so I move there next to search the rest. The second drawer is all undershirts. The third . . .

"Jackpot."

I smile at the Volvo logo staring up at me, its chrome circle set in a black plastic key fob. There's a silvery ring attached to it, to which three keys dangle, unlabeled. His own house? Maybe a PO box or a back fence? Doesn't matter. One must be for the car and that's all I care about right now. I set it atop the dresser and keep searching.

In the same drawer I find a small pad of paper, like a book for handwritten credit-card receipts where each page has a yellow carbon-copy backing. Roughly half of the pad has been used.

Across the top left are the letters RX, followed by "prescription." And just below, the name and address for Dr. Frank Ryan. I flip it open and see page after page of scribbled orders, but it's too dark to make out the details. I pocket this as well. Given what I've learned here, and what I've deduced about Doc's methods, this pad could be crucial evidence.

My search complete, I pick up the keys again. A Volvo station wagon is no Ferrari, but the sleek red speedster is of no use to me sitting dormant in a driveway. Besides, knowing Doc, his wagon is likely fueled and definitely well maintained.

I just need to get to the garage, and that means going downstairs. Unless . . .

I slip back into the hall after a quick look in each direction. I've heard nothing since crossing the living room walkway, and so far there's been no commotion from Captain Tweaker's absence. With any luck he was headed upstairs to get some sleep, and nobody will miss him for hours.

Instead of heading toward the stairs, I go right, deeper into the house, moving to the north side of the hallway. This will take me above the kitchen, I think, and I'm banking on there being another stairway, one for a housekeeper or live-in chef. Perhaps even a door leading out the side of the house instead of the back, and thus not perfectly framed by those massive living room windows.

A floorboard creaks beneath my foot and I freeze. It's impossible to listen with the blood pounding in my ears.

I try for calm. Slow my breaths.

A muffled sound, ahead and below. Footsteps coming up what must be a back stairwell.

I duck inside a pitch-black room and ease the door closed behind me, holding the handle so there's no click of the latch. Only seconds later the footsteps are in the hall just outside, growing louder.

My hand starts to shake from nerves. Only through sheer luck the door does not rattle in its frame.

The footsteps are at the door. They pass, continuing toward the front of the house, crossing the elevated walkway.

I breathe a sigh of relief, until I remember what awaits them. The room I was imprisoned in, where Captain Tweaker now lies. My time is running out.

I paw at the wall beside me until I find a light switch, and flip it on, half expecting to find myself in a room full of sleeping mercenaries on bunk beds. But it's only a laundry room, long and narrow, with fancy metallic red appliances on the right and a shelf with baskets of clothing on the left.

At the far end, opposite me, is a window with its blinds drawn. I rush toward it, but stop before I get there. A familiar color has caught my eye.

The blue fabric is piled in a basket, and when I lift it I see the gold reflection of a badge. Silvertown Police. My name, WHITTAKER, on the other side. Digging through the basket I find my pants, socks, and when I see the leather of my boots I almost shout with glee.

No vest or belt, though. My sidearm, pepper spray, Taser, cuffs . . . none of it is here. Not even a flashlight.

I hesitate. Weigh options. I could dress in my uniform again, but that would just make me an obvious target, wouldn't it? The basket next to this has clothing piled in it, too, and I thumb through it quickly. Khakis, a flannel shirt, a man's socks and briefs. Greg's, maybe. They might fit. Disguised, I could take these people on just like I did Captain Tweaker. One at a time, until . . .

*You need help.*

There're those words again, forcing my brain to overcome this innate desire to go it alone.

I push the clothes aside, and add Captain Tweaker's too-skinny jeans to the pile as well. Leaning against the cold metal of the washing machine, chanting the words written on my hand under my breath, I hastily put my own uniform back on. I'm going to get away. Drive to Granston. Straight to the sheriff's office. In plainclothes they'd think I was absolutely insane, maybe even throw me in the drunk tank until Davies wakes the next morning. But uniformed? I just might have a chance.

Clothes on and boots laced, I continue to the window at the back. The blinds are actually rigid shutters disguised as blinds. I pull them open and look out. It takes me a second to realize what I'm looking at, and in that second a wide smile grows on my face.

Directly below the window is the roof of the garage.

I slide the window open and remove the screen, pulling it into the laundry room and slipping it in between the washer and dryer. Climbing out is easy, and within seconds I'm on the roof of the garage and pulling the shutters closed behind me. I can't latch them from this side, so I hold them in the closed position for a second before letting go. A light breeze pushes the shutters open an inch or so, but I think it's not enough to spot at a casual glance. With any luck, my exit from here will not be noticed. Quietly I slide the window closed.

Crouching down, I start along the apex of the garage's roof. There must be a door at the back, or at least a window I can force.

The driveway is to my left, the darkness of the side yard on my right. I have only moonlight to guide my way, and the shingle roof is new, slick from the damp air. After a near slip I ease my pace.

Then I stop altogether. Something's happening in the house behind me. A commotion. Someone running down the hall, audible even from here. An urgent word.

Tweaker's been found. Has to be. Which means my absence has been discovered, too.

I take another step before dropping flat onto my stomach as the front of the house is suddenly lit up by brilliant security lights. They flood the driveway, the fountain, and cast a yellow glow on the trees leading off into the distance. But they're below me, the lip of the roof keeping me in shadow.

Still, I decide the spine of the roof, though flat, is not safe. If anyone looks up I'll be silhouetted against the sky. So I slide on my belly, halfway down toward the back of the garage. I come to a crouching stand and start to creep along carefully, keeping one hand on the roof for balance.

After only a few steps a crackling sound fills the air around me. Familiar but also confusing as hell. Without thinking I flatten myself to the roof once again. There I wait, and listen.

The rough, erratic noise comes from a speaker. A whole array of them actually, inside and outside the house. An intercom system through which a voice now booms.

It's a familiar voice.

The Conaty woman.

"You will find and subdue Mary Whittaker! You will bring her to me, alive!"

"Oh, fuck," I whisper.

# CHAPTER TWENTY-ONE

The urge to run spikes in my gut. I could sprint along the roof, clamber down at the far end, and find Doc's car.

My brain, though, is frozen with fear. There are too many of them. Lying here I'm aware of at least five people moving through the house, going room to room. A door opens from the front of the property. Flashlight beams play across the trees.

It's not Greg or Tweaker or any of the Broken Nose Gang that scare me, though. No, it's those four men who were standing behind Conaty's VIP guests, hands clasped in front of them like Secret Service escorting the president. Which is, I realize, close enough to the truth. Those men were rigid, disciplined. Professional. And muscled beneath their designer suits that failed to hide the gun-shaped bulge at the left breast.

A door opens nearby. The laundry room. Despite all my effort to disguise my exit, like an idiot I left the light on. Steps come toward its window, just fifteen feet from me.

Still on my stomach, I do the only thing I can: roll. Roll down the back of the garage's roof and over the edge. The Smith & Wesson I let go of, hearing it crash into a shrub somewhere below.

My fingers find the lip of the rain gutter just as the shutters blocking that window open with a *clack-clack* sound. Light spills out, and looking up I can see its yellow glow bright on my fingertips. I strain to hold on, hoping against hope that whoever is there won't notice the row of knuckles marring the otherwise smooth length of gutter running along the roof's edge.

Staring up at my hands, trying to find the best grip on the thin sheet-metal guttering, I see the words written there and almost laugh. Yeah, I do need help. Holy hell do I need help. But what I really need is to go unnoticed just now.

"She's here!" a voice shouts.

So much for that.

I let go, drop six feet, gritting my teeth for a hard landing that doesn't come. Instead of concrete or paving stones, I hit a bed of mulch. A landscaped area buffering the house from the expansive lawn. Well-maintained shrubs and plants surround me, along with several large trees. It's mostly dark, but lights are beginning to come on throughout the house. Of the dropped pistol there's no sign at all. It could be right at my feet and I'd still miss it in this gloom.

I glance left, along the back wall of the massive garage. There are three windows, dark, but they're too high up to reach. No door on this side, but maybe around that corner? I creep two steps in that direction, one hand on the stucco wall, but stop when two things happen simultaneously.

The person above shouts again. "She's in the garden!"

And through the wall I can feel the six garage doors opening all at once. The three windows above me are suddenly glowing from light within, and I can hear at least one person moving swiftly through the garage. There is a door around the corner, I feel sure of that now, but they're going to get to it before I do.

Then comes the final catastrophe. All around me, in dozens of places throughout the garden, landscape lights begin to glow. They create pools of yellow light every dozen feet, or cast their spotlight beams up the trunks of the trees. It's as bad as a minefield, I think, because any direction I run now will create a silhouette easily spotted from the house.

I cast about for the pistol again, aware that I'm wasting precious seconds, but it's useless. Even with all these lights, most of the bushes remain in darkness, and the pools of glow make it even harder to see into them. I press my back to the wall, glancing everywhere, but beyond the trees is a hundred yards of lawn before a high wall separates the property from the forest.

Every choice seems a terrible one.

My gut says to run.

To flee, now. Get the hell away. Sprint across that wide lawn, scale the wall, and disappear down into the valley.

I take a step in that direction before deciding my instincts are the last thing I should be trusting right about now. Running is what they're expecting. I do sprint, then, but not across the lawn. Instead I'm barreling at full speed toward the end of the garage's back wall.

One step from the corner I see a foot, then the bare legs of Captain Tweaker, whose jeans I had stolen. Closing the distance before he can see me, I strike with an upward thrust of my palm, straight into his broken nose. He howls, stumbling backward. I plant a kick in his chest that helps him in that direction. The scrawny bastard probably weighs less than I do, which is saying something. He flies three feet before crumpling to the ground, one hand covering his nose while the other belatedly protects his ribs.

I turn the corner. Ahead the property's surrounding wall blocks my way, but there is a door on the side of the garage, and it's open. I step in.

As I thought, all the rolling doors are in their up position, giving a wide view of the front of the house, the fountain, and the red Ferrari. There's no one around, so I ignore it all and focus on the interior of the garage.

Six stalls, six vehicles. The nearest is a yellow minivan with the Granston Brewing Company logo on the door. Beyond that is a silver Audi, then Greg's old police cruiser, then a low-slung black supercar of some sort, angular and evil-looking. The last two are dark SUVs. Range Rovers I think, but it doesn't matter. What does matter is that Doc's fucking Volvo is not here.

And its absence might have crushed the last shred of hope in me. *Might* have, if not for the presence of Greg's cruiser.

I run to it, remembering how every time we got in it together he'd lower the visor to let the keys fall into his hand. As he caught them he'd turn to me and wink, that Cheshire grin just visible beneath his bushy gray mustache.

The vehicle is parked facing outward, unlike all the other vehicles. Another stamp of Greg's personality, and a cop's training: always be ready to go at a moment's notice.

I reach the door and pull the handle, hearing the satisfying sound of the latch giving way. I throw the door open hard, slamming it into the black exotic next to me with a crunching noise that fills me with a queer pleasure.

"Fuck was that?" a gruff voice says from outside.

I glance toward the fountain.

Seconds ago there'd been no one there, but now two men stand by it, one on either side. I saw them earlier, standing behind the couch, flanking the senator meeting with Mrs. Conaty.

These men are professional bodyguards. No, that's not right. If they're here, they're complicit in all this. I should call them what they are. Thugs. Gangsters. Trained killers.

They're also twins, I suddenly realize. Blond hair, clean-shaven faces with sharp features, and identical assault rifles in their hands.

In unison they grin at me.

Then their weapons come up. Conaty may have ordered me brought in alive, but these two apparently haven't been injected with Ang's invention.

Their rifles roar.

As the bullets fly, I dive across the bench seat of Greg's car. The front window splinters into a million shards, then the rear window shatters. Rounds pummel the metal bodywork, the engine, the wall of the garage, and the vehicles around me as the two killers indiscriminately hose down the area.

There's no shotgun in Greg's car, but there is a fire extinguisher in the passenger footwell. I release it, the plan forming in my head subconsciously. When the men outside pause to reload I chance a reach for the visor, swing it down, and catch the keys just like Greg always did.

Bullets flying all around me, I push the key into the ignition and twist. The engine starts despite all the rounds slamming into the radiator up front.

Grunting with effort, glass in my hair, I shove the fire extinguisher between the base of the driver's seat and the gas pedal. The engine roars. Ignoring the thuds as the car is turned into Swiss cheese, I back out of the vehicle and, once my knees are on the floor of the garage, I stretch for the gear lever and shift the car into drive.

It lurches forward, tires screeching. At the same instant I throw myself the rest of the way out. My body slams into the black sports car beside me at the same time Greg's cruiser rams straight into the fountain in the middle of the circular driveway.

There's a thunderous crash. The car heaves upward, front wheels off the ground and spinning, the hood crushed. Water pours from the smashed side of the fountain. The two killers lie on either side, having dived out of the way. One seems to be hurt, but I don't wait around to find out.

I crawl backward, and at the rear of the sports car I dart toward the small side door I'd entered through, keeping low, hoping no one sees me. With any luck they'll assume I was in the vehicle, and waste time searching it and then the driveway beyond.

At the door I almost crash into Captain Tweaker. He's managed to get to his feet and is stumbling into the garage. Without breaking stride I ram my fist into his nose for the third time that evening, and this time the blow makes his eyes roll back and all the life goes out of his legs. He drops like a puppet with its strings cut. With a single long step I'm over him and rounding the side of the house, darting across the lawn while, I hope, all attention is on the driveway. I pass the dormant shape of the sleek helicopter, ringed by still-flickering fake candles resting on paving stones. Grass crunches under my feet as the house falls away behind me. Ahead is that big garden shed, its doors open. Inside I can just make out the shape of the ATV, and next to it, a red Harley-Davidson that is most definitely familiar. I assume neither will have keys, so I keep my focus on the wall instead.

Too high to reach the top. I cast about, then spot a small trestle table beside the ATV's shed, with some empty planting pots atop it. I brush them aside and move the iron table a few feet until it's wedged in the corner between the wall and the shed. The thing may be old and disused, but it's sturdy as hell and holds my weight just fine. Reaching the top of the wall is easy, hauling myself up not so much.

Perched there, I ready to leap down to the other side. If this were an action film, I think, that mansion behind me would be exploding right now. I pause, there, unable to let go of the image of the mansion exploding as I remember Ang's lab in the basement, likely full of his research. Not to mention their equipment. The machine producing pills.

I should go back. Destroy it all. End this right here, right now.

But I only manage to turn toward the mansion before Conaty's voice erupts from the intercom again. Shrill words, yet loud and clear even from a hundred yards away.

Her orders to the Broken Nose Gang have changed in a rather critical way.

"You will kill Mary Whittaker!" she shouts.

Over and over and over again.

# CHAPTER TWENTY-TWO

By the time I reach the river my nose feels like it's on fire. Pain throbs through my head, pulsating behind my eyes.

At the edge of the water I allow myself a chance to rest. There's a boulder the size of a shopping cart, about the only cover here, so I put my back against it and fill my cupped hand with some of the cool babbling water. This I trickle down the back of my neck and across my forehead. Tentatively I probe my nose under the bandage, and my fingers come away red. That entire area of my face itches like a dozen mosquito bites, but the cool water helps so I drip more onto the bandage and let it soak in.

Once my breathing is under control, I take a tentative look behind me. The first glance back I've made since scaling the wall perhaps fifteen minutes ago.

The hillside leading up to Ang's mansion is quiet. But then it would be, I suppose. From just about anywhere up there one could see this entire river. Me crossing to the other side would be a sniper's dream. Easy pickings.

There's really no choice, though. I have to keep moving. Every second I sit here is a chance they'll think to look this way, and post someone with a rifle up there. Crashing Greg's car bought me precious time, and I'm wasting it by resting here.

But God the water feels good.

I gulp some from the stream, not caring if it's polluted from the old mine. The icy liquid makes me gasp, burning like whiskey, but I take three more swallows all the same.

Then I'm up and trudging through the water. With each step I expect the light inside my head to go out as a sniper round rips through my body, but no shots ring out. There's only the sound of my soaking wet boots smacking on the rocks as I pick my way up the opposite bank, back onto the mountain that is my home.

At the tree line I stop and look behind me one last time.

No one has followed. At least, not that I can see.

There's only the moonlit river, the dark trees. An owl glides silently from the branches of one. It vanishes into a patch of tall grass, then emerges a second later, wings flapping soundlessly. Though a few hundred feet away, and in darkness, I can see a rat or squirrel dangling from its beak.

"That's an omen I didn't need," I mutter.

Retracing my steps from earlier, I start up the rocky bank. The switchback trail is grueling going uphill. Several minutes later I find the dirt trail Tweaker rode on his ATV, the tracks still visible.

A low noise begins to grow, like a deep humming, briefly reminding me of the sound of Kyle's ringtone. I hit the dirt, unsure what I'm really hearing, my eyes scanning the darkness around me, ears pricked. It's distant, I realize. A car engine? Yes, but not one. It's a pair of big V-8s, and they're on this side of the river valley. Ahead, well up the slope, I can see their headlights catching the trees. The two vehicles making their way up the mountain toward Silvertown, driving fast.

I'd be tempted to race the last stretch of this trail and try to flag them down, but chances are good that I'll be greeted by a red Ferrari and a black sports car with a badly scratched door. So I wait. Five minutes for them to go on past, heading toward town. The glow of their headlights is lost to me before the sound of their engines is. Finally I can't hear them at all and decide it's safe to continue.

But then comes the sound of a third vehicle. Slower, less powerful, but going the same direction. Unsure who it might be, I decide to let it go by as well, if for no other reason than to fully catch my breath.

Finally I set off again. My wet boots feel like they weigh a hundred pounds. The water, so blissfully cool on my feet just minutes before, has made my toes numb and set my teeth chattering. Add to that the comedown off an adrenaline high like I've never known before, and exhaustion starts to get the better of me. I stumble, skinning my knee on a rock. Warm blood trickles down my leg from the scrape.

I've no idea how long it takes, or when I stopped following Tweaker's ATV trail, but suddenly there's asphalt under my feet, the road half-hidden by red and yellow leaves. No lights in either direction. I look for a mile marker, but there are none to be seen.

A choice needs to be made, even though all I really want to do is sleep. I shake my head vigorously and try to focus on the two choices. Head east, up the mountain toward Silvertown? Or west, toward Granston?

"Neither," I mutter. The real goal, I realize, should be to return to my cruiser, which I left in front of that gate on Meridian Lane. I might not have its keys, but at this point I'm okay with putting a rock through the window in order to get at all the gear stowed inside. So for the moment I choose neither direction, instead turning around to study the valley behind me. Partly to look for any sign I've been followed, but mostly to look for the senator's mansion. If I can spot that, I might get a better idea of where I am, and which way my car is from here.

There's a glow in the trees on the other side of the river valley, which I think is probably the house, but knowing this doesn't help. It's too far away to help me triangulate. I'm about to turn away when a new light catches my eye. A blinking red beacon in the trees. As I watch it begins to rise.

The helicopter.

Instinctively I move closer to the nearest tree, even though the chopper is a mile off. It's going to head right for me, I think, with a searchlight scanning the road and those gangster bodyguards leaning out the doors with high-power rifles.

This doesn't turn out to be the case. The helicopter instead makes a direct line for Silvertown. I know I should move, get up there, do my job, but I'm transfixed by the blinking light and the distant thumping pulse of the rotor blades.

The helicopter slows and starts to lower, and I know the place instantly. It's landing in the parking lot of the graveyard, where Greg and I attended Johnny Rogers's funeral. Just west of town, and a full two miles from me at least. Now that I have a landmark, I know my car is to the west, and not far. Worried about the town, and Kyle and Clara in particular, I set off again, urgent now. I'm limping a little, thanks to my throbbing knee, and gritting my teeth at the pain and the fresh feel of warm blood snaking down into my ice-cold boot.

I see the wavering yellow glow before the cruiser itself.

Fire engulfs its aluminum frame. Even a hundred feet away I can feel the heat on my face.

I sink to my knees, not caring about the flare of agony that erupts from my wound.

Only the skeleton of the Dodge Charger is recognizable. Fire roils over its innards. The gear and computers and radios inside have long since melted away. A plume of thick black smoke spouts upward from the carnage, shooting up toward the treetops, where it seems to simply merge with the sky. On this clear night there's no clouds to catch the orange flicker of fire. No way anyone would have seen this and called it in. No fire trucks will come to help. Not from our volunteer force, or the professionals from County.

There's a pop as some internal component fails and its fluids ignite, sending a spray of flaming shrapnel out from the vehicle. A tire goes next, making the car list for a second before the other three all fail nearly simultaneously. The smell of burning rubber makes me want to gag, and I force myself to get to my feet and move away, back to the main road.

Now I really have to choose. It's a four-mile walk from here up to Silvertown, and roughly the same distance downhill to the edge of Granston. East or west. East or west.

I turn east, and start the long hike to Silvertown.

It seems like days later when I finally reach the thin narrow lane that leads up to the little bluff where the graveyard offers its striking view of the valley. The lane is curvy, walled in by trees on each side, which means from the state route I cannot see the parking area or the cleared hill and all its gravestones. The helicopter is still there, of that I feel certain. The sound of its rotor ebbed and vanished earlier when it landed, and I've heard nothing of it since.

The temptation to go that way is strong, but in the end I decide to keep on toward town. If the chopper is still there, it's likely guarded, and I'm unarmed. Those fuckers have already tried to kill me, more than willing to hose down a garage full of expensive cars with automatic gunfire just for the off chance they might get a bullet into me. They also set my own car on fire. Something tells me if they spot me approaching their aircraft there won't be any warning. They'll just shoot me dead and then chuckle at the realization that I've delivered myself quite handily to the graveyard. Nothing left to do but the digging.

So I keep on.

But not all the way to town. Not yet. Because half a mile out I recognize another street, and this time I feel there is something worth stopping for.

It's another winding narrow lane, but instead of trees walling in each side, there's a mixture of lawns, hedges, and houses. Of Silvertown's few neighborhoods, this is considered the nicest one. Back in the day, Conaty Corporation executives would have lived here. Not mansions, per say, but large homes with big yards that buffered them from any chance of having to suffer through the sound of a passing car.

With the company long gone, regular folk moved in, snatching up the chance at a nicer place as property values here nosedived in the wake of the scandal that sent all the executives scurrying off to Houston.

And one of them in particular is known to me, because almost every time I drive by it I see Doc's Volvo parked at the end of the long driveway, just outside a detached garage. The home is just three driveways down on the left.

Locals call it the Smiley Mansion, and I haven't yet thought to ask why. It's an older place, perhaps as much as a hundred years old. From the look of it, though, it's been renovated several times, and while not nearly as well preserved as Barbara Rogers's home, the structure and the grounds are well kept.

"Damn it," I whisper, upon seeing that Doc's car is not in the driveway.

The windows of his house are all dark. In fact, the whole street is dark. It takes my exhausted brain a second to understand. The power's been cut.

I hesitate, unsure now what to do. I'd hoped to find Doc's car where it always is. There is a garage, though. Might as well try there. I still have the keys to the car. And, I realize, his house.

Despite the cover of darkness I still move up the lawn slowly, hunched over, every sense on high alert. There's a good fifty feet separating his place from the neighbors on either side, and no fences, so I scan their windows, too, just to be sure no one is watching.

It's only when I'm halfway up the drive that I realize I'm doing it again. Going it alone. Doing the opposite of what used to be my strongest instinct. The thought takes mental effort to complete, like pulling an old friend's phone number from memory. Once I manage to grasp the concept, though, there comes a second conscious effort to ignore it. I do need help. I know that, even if I can't keep the idea in my head when it matters. But right now, I think maybe the new go-it-alone Mary Whittaker is the better one, because after everything I saw in Ang's mansion, I don't know who I can trust. Certainly anyone with a broken nose is to be avoided, but Doc's neighbors? Who knows if he's drawn them into this mess, or used them as early guinea pigs.

No, right now I want to get into Doc's place. Confront him if he's there, or at least search his bathroom for a first aid kit so I can bandage up my goddamn skinned knee.

I try the garage first, though.

The actual door has no external manual release. There's a keypad on the frame, but without power it's useless to me. I go around back, happy to be concealed from view to anyone driving by. Not that anyone is.

There's a back door to the garage. I twist the handle and open it a crack. Already adjusted to darkness, my eyes pick up nothing but stacks of moving boxes and the usual assortment of tools and lawn care equipment. No car, though, which is a bummer. Yet no car also means he's not here, and that's a decent consolation prize.

Resting atop a shelf by the door is a flashlight. A rechargeable one, but it's plugged in. I grasp it and flick the power switch while pressing the business end against my hand. A glow of red instantly appears.

"Nice," I breathe, and turn the device off again. Time to check the house.

A covered patio runs the length of the rear of the building, looking out on a slightly overgrown lawn and meager garden. Double French doors look in on a dark interior. The door itself is locked, but a quick jab of my elbow to the pane by the handle is all it takes to gain access.

This is far from proper behavior for a cop, but given the circumstances I figure no one is going to mind, especially since my boss is one of the bad guys. The thought of Greg Gorman, with his bandaged nose obscuring that kind and wizened face and that ridiculously bushy gray mustache, twists my stomach into a knot. I wonder how they got to him, and when. Must have been when he left for the airport, I decide. His nose wasn't broken before that. And I can just see how they might go about it. Perhaps staging an accident on the mountain road, waiting for someone to stop to help, then abducting them and bringing them to Ang's mansion for the "treatment" and the test.

Maybe that's what was going on with Rhod Mitchell and his

motorcycle, I think. Doc's claim that no one was there, not even a bike, now seems an obvious lie. And the fact that Rhod later came to my house to try to drug me makes a weird kind of sense, too. A second try.

I shake this line of thinking away. It doesn't really matter right now, I decide. Rhod was one of the gang. They got to Greg, too, and tried to get to me. The details don't matter.

Stepping into Doc's darkened living room I pause for several seconds, listening to the silence of the empty home. A tap somewhere drips rhythmically. Otherwise, silence.

There's an end table by the couch, upon which sits an old-school landline telephone. I pick the beige handset up, but there's nothing. No dial tone, no hiss. Nothing.

"Shit," I whisper, setting the phone back on the cradle.

Silvertown is completely cut off.

They've cut the power, and they've cut the phone lines, too. The speed at which this was accomplished shouldn't surprise me, but still I can't help but marvel. You have to plan something like this, even if it probably only meant cutting two cables somewhere down by the bridge. And, of course, Kenny's big mouth apparently took care of the cell tower for them. Considerate of him.

*Get moving*, I tell myself.

I take the first hall I come to. Hardwood creaks under my feet like a Nightingale floor in some old Japanese castle.

My goal is to find a bathroom, ideally one with a first aid kit under the sink. But the first door I open reveals a bedroom that's been converted into a study. There's a big L-shaped desk in the far corner, with a computer underneath and a big monitor dominating the surface. Piles of folders and pads of paper are scattered across the surface to either side of the keyboard, along with a few dirty drinking glasses and a bowl of some no-doubt-stale crackers.

Intrigued, I cross to the desk and flick on my borrowed flashlight. It's a risk to use in here, the light no doubt visible should anyone pass by, but nevertheless I use it. The room seems to sway slightly as the beam plays across the surfaces. I focus on the desk. Beside the keyboard is a pad of legal paper, upon which two columns of text in neat handwriting run from top to bottom.

In the left column of the first page is a list of names. Forty or so, in alphabetical order. I thumb through a few more and quickly understand this is a list of Silvertown residents, including myself.

The column next to my name is empty, as is the case with most of the other entries. But some have writing in another column. I seek out Kyle Rollins next, finding his name alone on the lined page, too. His brother, Kenny, though, is one of those with words written in the second column:

> Survival (individual), no longer seeking sustenance (food, drink), method of delivery: allergy medication

I remember how thin Kenny looked at the Gas-n-Go the other day, and his cracked lips.

Just up the page from that entry is another with a second-column entry. This one makes my gut twist into a painful knot.

> Johnny Rogers—Survival (individual), eschewing safe shelter/ indoors, method of delivery unknown (possible abuse, father scrip for Donepezil)

There is a red line through the boy's entry that makes my blood boil. At the very end of his line, in red ink, is a single handwritten word: "Accidental."

Just above his entry is his mom, Barbara, with a note that she is no longer displaying emotions, categorized as "social" instead of "survival." Method of delivery? Blood pressure medication.

Heart thudding in my chest, I seek out Clara's entry and swallow my rage when I see the comment next to her name. "Social—no longer mistrusting strangers." Delivery by sleeping pill. I think back to her in that missile silo with the urban explorers, and shudder at the thought of what I could have found down there, were it someone else she'd fallen in with.

"Sleeping pill," I whisper. That's why they didn't know I'd already been dosed with the old version. Doc hadn't prescribed me anything.

I scan the rest of the entries, some of which I can guess even before reading them. Sally Jones, social, her instinct to prioritize her own children over needs of others turned on its head.

*Ah,* I think. *So that's why she didn't abandon them entirely. The poor woman still* cares, *she just can't differentiate between the twins' needs and anyone else's.* I find only a tiny amount of solace in the fact that Ang's and Doc's little experiment only resulted in a few hours' abandonment for those children, rather than death. There's always tomorrow, though. I'll need to address that, if I make it out of this. *One thing at a time, Mary.*

I read on.

"William Jupitas, defense, no longer recognizing mortal danger." Hence stepping in front of my cruiser. *Jesus.*

I start to skim the rest.

In all, roughly two dozen of the town's six-hundred-plus have Doc's scrawled observations next to them. Some have question marks, others have lines through the observation but not the name, apparently misdiagnosed. Many simply have what appears to be Doc's best guess as to their most prominent instinct. As if we're all just rats in a mountain-sized maze for him to study.

At the end of the list are several recent entries, not alphabetical. Not from Silvertown.

The hiker is first. "Jeff Hall. Survival, fear of wild animals." And for the first time a delivery method that isn't prescription medication. Instead it simply reads "Granston Brewery—compromised beverage." There's a red line through the entire entry, just like Johnny's. Another test subject dead.

Just below Jeff Hall is Katherine Pascoe, the hiker's companion who I sat with, commiserated with. Her category is simply "social—chatter / conversation," the note indicating she no longer tells stories. That's not something that I would have ever considered an instinct, but then I'm no expert. Doc obviously is. I think about her constant silence, and how getting anything out of her required constant prompting. She has the same Granston Brewery comment for delivery.

Of course. I'd wondered about Tweaker and the powder he was putting into the water supply, but a controlled delivery makes way more sense.

I spend a minute trying to wrap my brain around what all this means, but soon enough there's only one clear thought that I can latch on to: Johnny Rogers and Jeff Hall both died from this. That means I have Doc on murder. Second-degree manslaughter at a minimum. This could apply to Mr. Ang, too, assuming the link can be proven, which at this point I think is highly likely. They're thick as thieves, from what I saw. Maybe it's better that I didn't burn the mansion down. The place must be full of evidence.

"Shit!" I practically shout, remembering now the small prescription pad I took from Doc's room at the mansion. Removing it from my pocket, I flip through the pages once again, only this time with the list of townspeople on Doc's notepad beside it. Corroborating evidence.

"Got you, you son of a bitch."

Both items need to be preserved. Carrying them around with me isn't going to work, though. I'll have to hide them. I search about the room, but everything seems somehow too obvious. Besides, if they want to get rid of evidence they'll just burn the place like they did my car.

A better idea comes to me. I stuff the notebook and the pad of paper into a thick envelope, the kind with a bubble-wrap interior. This I seal with some tape and then cover with enough stamps to get it to the moon. Despite the abundance of postage, I write my own address on it, for both "from" and "to," and then leave the house and walk across the street. I shove the parcel into Doc's neighbor's mailbox, and put the little metal flag up for good measure.

Then I return to Doc's house and do what I'd come to do: bandage my knee. I dab some antibiotic cream on it, wincing as I realize the scrape is actually a gash that might need stitches. I press some gauze over the wound and wrap a bandage around my knee to keep it in place. It's tight, painfully so, but at least the bleeding will stop.

Before leaving the bathroom I catch a glimpse of myself in the mirror. The woman I see is almost unrecognizable. What a mess. My hair is matted and sports several leaves and twigs. My face is smeared with dirt, my upper lip is caked with blood from my nose. The bandage across the middle is clean, save for a big red spot at my left nostril. And to top off this picture of loveliness, there're the bags under my eyes.

In Doc's bedroom I steal a pair of clean, dry socks. They're big enough for me to wear like stockings, given my diminutive frame and his resemblance to a basketball player who has been on bed rest for roughly fifty years. But at least they're dry and not caked with blood.

The only thing I can find that serves as a decent weapon is a folding knife from the toolbox in his cramped garage.

So armed, I ease the back door to the garage closed again and round the corner, heading for the driveway.

Halfway there I freeze and press myself against the wall.

A black SUV is pulling into the driveway, headlights blazing right into my eyes, blinding.

I inch backward, trying to return to a pocket of darkness that grows smaller with each second as the car gets closer. Finally the car is too close, though, and the corner ahead of me blocks the light.

The vehicle comes to a stop just in front of the garage door, and the driver kills the engine. The lights wink off, plunging my world into total darkness once again. Did they see me?

The car door opens, then slams closed. Footsteps, moving away at a casual walk. I hear mumbling. Doc's mumbling, I'd know it anywhere. I let out a breath. It occurs to me I could arrest him now. Tie him up, maybe, and come back later with proper handcuffs and all that.

This, I think, is a great idea, so I move quickly toward the front of the garage.

But then another car door opens.

And another.

And a third. Three more people get out of the SUV, slamming their doors almost in unison.

"You've got five minutes," a man says in a southern drawl. "Then we go."

They're barely ten feet away from me. I hear some rustling of clothes. A Zippo flipping open, clapping shut. A plume of smoke soon curls around the side of the garage, half in shadow, half in light. They talk in low voices, too quiet to make out what they're saying. One of them chuckles. Another steps up to the corner. I can see the edge of his shoe and I pivot, ready to run. But he stops there and turns to put his back against the wall. I let out a slow breath, not daring to move.

The sleeve of his black jacket is visible. When he lifts his cigarette to his mouth, the motion swivels his weapon into view. The glint of moonlight on a steel barrel.

"She's been here!"

It's Doc, shouting from the front porch. The three men discard their cigarettes, one landing just three feet from me, red ember fading to black in the damp grass. Doc's footsteps are clumsy as he runs from his front door to the driveway.

"She took my notes!"

"Did you check the house?"

"I just said she took all my notes."

"I meant is she still in there, moron."

A hesitation. Doc clears his throat. "I, uh . . . I didn't think to check."

"Amateur," the bodyguard says. He snaps his fingers and all three men are moving, jogging off toward the front door, away from me. Though I can't see him, from the sound of things Doc has not moved.

With any luck I can subdue him and take the vehicle. I move in that direction. A single step.

But then there's a whistle, and the muffled voice of the lead bodyguard. Though I only have the sounds of their feet to go by, the shift in tactics is obvious. One of them is moving toward the back of the house, and the third is returning this way to search the garage.

I take a step back, then turn, tiptoeing several steps before I break into a run toward the rear of the property. There's a gap in the hedge, and I see no fence between Doc's yard and the neighbor's, so I dart through.

"Hey, look everyone, Granston Brewery in the house! Fuckin' finally!"

"Kyle Rollins? I'm so sorry for the delay. Had some problems with the van."

"I'd be mad, but you did say on the phone earlier that the beer would be free, didn't you?"

"Yep, there's no charge on account of the delay. Twenty kegs of the October Bavarian, on us, with my boss's apologies. It's all in the truck."

"Need help unloading? We can store it out back, but bring one in here so I can get all these freeloaders a pint or three. My so-called planning committee. They did wait all this time. Didn't you, you magnificent troupers?"

"Anything for free beer!"

"Settle down, Dent. C'mon, all of you, let's help unload the van, huh?"

"Actually, that's not necessary."

"Sure it is. You've had a rough day. Van trouble. And that broken nose . . . how'd that happen, anyway? You're the third person I've seen this week with a broken nose."

"I brought a few friends."

"*You did? Oh. Hey guys. Jesus. You look like a well-dressed rugby team. Whoa, whoa! Chill, put the guns away!*"

"*Shut the fuck up. Everyone in a chair, now. Hands clasped behind your heads.*"

"*Look man, take the money. Take our wallets. Just ——*"

"*Kyle, do what he says. This will only take a few minutes.*"

"*Doc?! Are you with these pricks? What the fuck is going on? Who are—*"

"*All will be explained. For now you need to do what he says.*"

"*Okay. Okay. Just . . . Doc, seriously. What are you . . . what's the gear for?*"

"*Kyle, I mean it. Be quiet. You don't want to mess with these guys. Ang, how would you like to proceed? Shall I start taking vitals from each of them?*"

"*There is no time, Dr. Ryan. We don't need test subjects anymore, we need an army. Give them the beer.*"

"*But the timing—*"

"*Play the message on repeat for ten minutes. That should be enough for anyone. It's time we move out of the testing phase and into applica-tion.*"

"*Doc, who is this prick? What's he talking about? What message? What are you—OW! FUCK! Try that again, you giant shithead mother—*"

"*I say we kill this one. An example to the others.*"

"*No, Deon. We might need him. He and Mary are . . . friendly.*"

"*Mary? Doc, what the hell? What does she—*"

"*All in due time, Kyle. Now, please, sit down and shut up. Who wants a drink?*"

# CHAPTER TWENTY-THREE

One block from the edge of downtown. That's how close I get before I'm forced to dive into a ditch by the side of the road and flatten myself in the mud.

Ahead, fifty yards away, a black Range Rover is parked across the road, blocking the only route into town. A man with an assault rifle stands at the front bumper, sweeping a flashlight from left to right, forcing me to bury my face in the mud every few seconds.

Worse, though, is what's behind him.

Silvertown is dead. With the power off the whole place looks like a *true* ghost town.

But the street and its buildings aren't entirely dark. There is a roving, shifting, almost amoebic light moving through the alleys and buildings.

The source of which is like something out of an old movie. I believe the correct term is "lynch mob."

They move from store to store, kicking doors in and shouting. Their words are garbled, too distant and numerous to make much sense of. But now and then there is one recognizable phrase: my name.

The mob is about two dozen strong. Even from here I recognize some of them. They're people I see every day. People I'm sworn to protect.

But even they are not the worst thing. Far from it, really.

The absolute worst thing is the constant, repetitive voice of Mrs. Conaty, booming from the speakers inside a second black SUV parked in the center of town.

Her recorded voice says the same thing, over and over. A short clip played on repeat.

"Kill the liar Mary Whittaker. Kill the liar Mary Whittaker. Kill the—"

I try to tune it out. After a time it's actually not that hard, so monotonous are the words. They're driving the mob, though, that much is obvious.

Kill me I get, but why "liar"? What's that about? The only reason that comes to me is as diabolic as it is genius. Trusting her words are the driving instinct for everyone in that mob, after all. Simultaneously she's not only telling them to execute me, but also short-circuiting any plea I might make to convince them not to.

Flashlight beams swing and bounce as the buildings are systematically searched. One structure at a time, windows alive with light and shadow as the group moves through, the glow only to die again when they depart and move on to the next.

"Just burn the whole fucking place!" one of the bodyguards shouts. The alpha of the pack who gave the orders in front of Doc's house.

"No!" comes the reply. From Doc, I think. This is immediately confirmed. "She has my notes! We need them!"

Okay, that's good to know. Thanks, Doc. I may have some leverage after all.

I try to spot him, peering over the edge of the ditch and scanning the shadowy buildings, but it's all too far away and there's so little light. My guess is he's right near the center of town, which I'm pretty sure means the police station.

Closest to me is the Gas-n-Go. The windows are dark, as are all the freezers inside, but the gas pumps are still on. Backup generator, maybe. Of Kenny there's no sign, and my mouth goes dry at the possibility of him running around with that mob. Then comes the nightmare thought of Kyle being with them, too, and my whole body goes cold with the idea. I lower my head to the dirt and whisper, "Please don't be part of this, Kyle. Please."

The urge to head straight to the pub is strong, but I have to get to the police station. The arms locker. Two shotguns are kept in there, along with several boxes of shells. That's the only way I'll have a fighting chance against these armed bodyguards. The townspeople I resolve to avoid at all costs, because I can't bear the idea of having to put one of them down.

A flashlight beam sweeps over me. The flare of light is almost blinding. I curse and press into the earth. The light remains fixed on my spot. It takes every ounce of will I have not to look. In my haste to duck I somehow lost my grip on the folding knife taken from Doc's garage. I don't dare search for it with the beam on me, though. All I can do is wait, listening, expecting to hear the man call to his companions any second, or to come walking this way for a closer look.

Somewhere in the distance a familiar sound returns, steady under the commotion. The *wump-wump-wump* of the helicopter's blades. "Shit," I mouth into the dirt. I'm completely exposed here. If they start searching from the air, it's over.

But the sound fades, and with its departure the voice of Mrs. Conaty returns. That order to kill me, blasting on repeat, like a constant forceful nudge to those searching the town.

A nightmare image flashes into my skull. Not a mob of ten or twenty, but an army of thousands. Millions. An army that never disobeys, or questions, or even flinches, no matter what task they've been set.

I begin to shiver uncontrollably, crippled with a dread unlike any I've felt in my life. This . . . this vision of a global catastrophe, germinating in this quaint little place. Like the birth of some super flu, on the cusp of exploding before anyone realizes what's happening.

And Silvertown—my town—is ground zero.

I feel as if I'm being pressed into the dirt, crushed under the weight of this waking nightmare. My whole body vibrates from fear. Not of what they'll do to me if they catch me, but what will happen if I fail.

*Get it together, Mary. Take a breath. Take another. Another.*

Lifting my head a little, I peer into the beam of light, almost daring the bastard to notice me and do something. The white flare bores into my skull. But I must be too far off to discern, because nothing happens.

Ten seconds pass. Then the flashlight beam moves away. Back to scanning.

I squeeze my eyes shut again, waiting for the afterglow to fade. As the blurry freeze-frame dissipates I grope through the muck and leaves around me for the folding knife. It's as if the ground has swallowed it up, though. Without light I'll never find the damn thing.

I give up. Glance back toward town. See the outline of the SUV, and his form beside it. In front of all this is the vague outline of my hand on the edge of the ditch. I can just make out the three words scrawled there. Once again I've managed to forget about them, like that part of my brain has been hidden away behind a heavy curtain.

*I need help. I need help.* Repeating this, forcing it to stay in my mind, seems the only possible way to bury the instinctual dead zone in my head.

I need help. The words become a chant, a song, constantly running just beneath my inner thoughts. I need help. With each syllable I crawl slowly backward, deeper into the darkness, farther from Silvertown.

When my foot strikes the trunk of a tree I shift to a crouch and then, eyes on the town in front of me, I slip into the woods and start to circle around.

The police station had been my plan. Way too obvious, in hindsight. They're expecting it, almost counting on it.

So I go somewhere else, instead. With any luck, the last thing they'll expect is me coming at them from the east. From the mountain.

Keeping well back from the road, I creep along through the greenbelt that serves as a buffer between downtown and its nearest homes. Getting my bearings in the blackout takes several minutes. No streetlights, no landscape lights, no motion sensors flooding driveways. In fact, at this hour I doubt most of the residents are even aware the power's off. Can none of them hear the commotion? Conaty's voice? A helicopter, for fuck's sake?

Perhaps they already did have a look. Walked into town and right into Conaty's hands. I think about the size of that mob, marveling at how quickly it was formed. How'd they pull that off? A memory hits me, then, of a banner draped across the mural inside O'Doh's.

SILVERTOWN OCTOBERFEST—OCT. 8–10

It starts tomorrow, though, doesn't it? Then I remember something Kyle had said before we'd fallen asleep. Something about a planning meeting, happening tonight. He'd wanted me to come by toward the end.

"No offense, dude, but I've got enough on my plate. Not going to get roped into joining some committee."

"I mean after the business part," Kyle had replied. "It's kind of a tradition to sample all the seasonal beers before the rest of the town. Honestly it's the only reason anyone shows up."

*Of course.* O'Doherty's! Where else could Doc find twenty-plus people in a confined space. All it would take is one of those gangster bodyguard assholes with a menacing assault rifle and they'd get into a line pretty damn quick. A blast of Ang's drug into their mouths and *voila*, instant army.

Still, it doesn't seem right to me. Doc had taken my blood pressure. Weighed me. The works. All to get the perfect timing for Conaty's message. The idea of them arranging all that for so many people in the time it took me to come up the road seems almost absurd.

Which means . . .

"Fuck," I rasp. "Fuck fuck fuck."

The lab in Ang's house. The Granston Brewery truck. The chemicals at the water tower. And Ang's words in the elevator, most of all. *One size fits all.*

These are pieces of the same puzzle.

Then bringing both Greg and— though it failed—me, into the Broken Nose Gang. Why? To own Silvertown's police force, obviously. All this right before Octoberfest, when the whole town would be gathered and . . . drinking.

"Compromised beverages," I whisper into the cold night breeze, recalling Doc's note next to Jeff Hall and Katherine Pascoe's names. This isn't some kind of sick experiment. It *was* an experiment, back when Doc was just giving people bogus meds. That phase is over. Now it's a goddamn distribution.

I start to run, no longer caring about the weeds and blackberry vines clawing at my legs, or the hired guns with assault rifles prowling the main road, or their gang of mindless converts. I have to get to O'Doh's, and when I get there, I'll need to spill a whole-fucking-lot of beer.

# CHAPTER
# TWENTY-FOUR

Two rows of old buildings make up the heart of Silvertown. Other than the original brick facades, most have been renovated at one time or another. Despite more than half being empty, the place looks pretty damn cute from Main Street.

Get around the back, though, and it's a different story. Everything's old, falling apart, or functional only thanks to decades of retrofitting modern utilities onto 150-year-old bones.

Then there's the back alleys, one behind each row. Each is really just a twenty-foot-wide stretch of broken pavement that buffers the buildings from the ever-encroaching forest.

Weeds push up through every crack. Broken glass and bits of rock crunch under my feet, impossible to avoid in the near-total darkness.

"I need help, I need help . . ." I whisper over and over, forcing myself not to forget.

Coming toward O'Doherty's from the rear, and from the east, I decide to stick close to the tree line rather than the backs of the buildings. If anyone spots me, it's three long strides to my left and I'm gone, vanished among the ferns and black gnarled trunks.

The pub is exactly at the midpoint of the row, taking up the first floor of a four-story building. Kyle uses the top floor as his apartment, while the two between are currently vacant. Behind the place is a small parking area for employees, a shed where supplies are likely stored, and a fenced-in area where the pub sometimes puts on barbecues in the summer.

"I need help . . . I need help." Repeat it enough and I figure it'll become impossible to get out of my head, like a song from a Disney film.

A fire escape runs zigzag along the back of the building, all the way to the roof. Kyle might be up in his apartment on the top floor even now, hiding out or simply asleep. There's no way to tell with the building dark. But even if he's not there, there is that antique Luger pistol in the gun safe. I saw him enter the combination when he showed me the weapon. If only I could remember what it was! I'd seen him enter the damn numbers but hadn't bothered to commit them to memory. It seemed . . . untrustworthy, I suppose, to do so. I have to try, though. Force my mind to see the wheel spin. Or find it written down somewhere. Better yet, find Kyle there, hiding out, waiting for all this to blow over.

The alternative—that he's with them now—is not something I'm prepared to consider. Greg was bad enough. Doc, too, really. But Kyle?

The base of the fire escape is about thirty feet from me, requiring a sprint across empty concrete and gravel to reach. Crouched between two ferns, I hesitate, listening and whispering my mantra. I'll try the back door to the pub first, I decide, then climb if it's either locked or the pub is occupied by any of Conaty's minions.

I look left, right, and left again, making sure the alley is clear. Then I'm off like a rabbit.

Two steps into my sprint the back door to the pub opens and a man in dark clothes emerges, shining a flashlight beam off to my left. I veer right, and it's only the creaking old door that keeps me from being heard as I flatten myself against the wall of a building two doors down from O'Doherty's. The man's light sweeps in quick jerks. From the barbecue patio to the storage shed to the bushes across the back-alley lane.

Inching backward along the wall, my fingers find a corner and I slink into a recessed doorway, only a split second before the cool white light plays over the ground and the walls. My world fills with brightly lit brickwork and pitch-black shadows. A second later, the beam swivels away, scanning the other direction.

I let out a breath and peer around the corner. The man has stepped out into the alley now. Silhouetted against the disc of his own flashlight beam as he scans in the opposite direction. AR-15 assault rifle held casually.

It's tempting. If I rushed him I think I could get a solid punch in before he could bring the rifle up. Maybe use his surprise to wrestle the weapon away, or at least the flashlight, and be gone before he even knew what hit him.

But then another man steps out into the alley. They converse in clipped conversation for a few seconds before one goes right and the other left, toward me. I duck back around the corner and consider my options.

It's in that instant I feel something cold and metal press against my cheek.

"Are you with them?" someone asks me.

"No," I manage, trying to look without turning my head. Impossible to see who it is. Just a shadow within a shadow. "I'm the one they're trying to kill."

"Why? Who are they?"

"Long story," I manage. "Please. They're coming."

A hand tugs at my sleeve, and we're moving inside. The door clicks shut behind us. The cold metal remains firmly pressed into my jaw.

There's a slight grinding sound and then a flame. A Bic lighter. Held up between myself and a pale man with stringy black hair. Damian Blackwood, owner of the crystal healing and occult gifts store.

I sigh, relieved.

He smiles, but it's only a half smile, one tinged with worry.

"What the hell is going on?" he asks, and takes the weapon away from my cheek.

It's not a gun he holds, but a small hammer or chisel, made of solid steel.

"Kill the flame," I whisper. "They'll see it."

He nods, and his thumb releases the switch, plunging us into absolute darkness.

I feel a hand against my own. He wraps his fingers around mine.

"This way," he says, barely audible.

I let him guide me, understanding we're in the back part of his shop of mystical bullshit. Then his motions become more abrupt and the tone of his footfalls changes. We're descending stairs. Passing through a door.

He flicks the lighter on again and uses it to light a row of candles along the wall.

I take in the room he's brought me to, and my mouth goes dry.

The walls and ceiling are painted black, matching the carpet. Along each wall are shelves that hold cups and chalices in every imaginable size and shape.

In the center of the room is an eight-foot-high statue of a demon seated on a throne. It has the head of a goat and holds up one hand in some kind of satanic gesture, a pentagram amulet dangling from its fingers. Symbols are carved into every last inch of the stone. But my eyes are fixated on the brass bowl in the statue's lap. It appears to be filled with blood. There's a long, serrated knife lying across the rim. It gleams in the dim light, ceremonial and wicked.

"Damian . . . what the fuck."

"It's just for show," he says quickly. "Don't worry."

"Dude," I say, shaking my head.

"I mean it. This is all . . . to impress certain customers, I guess. Remember the Latin phrase above my front door? Look, that's not blood, it's just chocolate syrup. Unsweetened. They can't tell the difference. Here, I'll prove it."

He moves.

"Whoa, whoa. Hang on there." I grip his arm, my eyes on the ornate knife.

"Oh," he says. "That's fake, too. Look." He picks it up and runs the blade over his palm, then holds it up for me to see. There's no cut. No blood. Only the faint indent.

"You fill it with water, a little gelatin, and food coloring," he says, showing me how the back of the knife's handle unscrews. "And there's foam here along the blade's edge. Looks convincing enough in low light. Bought it on eBay!"

I nod, a little disappointed the knife is fake. Could have been useful. "What's all this for, Damian? I mean, I get separating fools from their money, but you said something before about personal hobbies. I'm a little afraid to ask now."

"That's what I wanted to show you."

For a second I think he's going to grab a silver chalice and pour the fake blood down his throat. But instead he walks around the statue and pushes through the wall behind it. It's not a wall, I realize then, but a set of heavy curtains.

Tentatively I follow him, thinking this is a terrible idea but somehow unable to stop myself.

Pulling back the curtain with one hand, holding out the candle to see better, I take in the other half of the basement.

Damian Blackwood stands between two long tables, their surfaces covered with tools and . . .

"Rocks?" I ask.

"Rocks." He grins, sheepish. "My hobby."

He holds a hand out to me, offering up a half-sphere containing a crystal geode.

"All I really know about this mystical nonsense is what I learned hanging out with the goth kids back in high school. I figured why not open a store and—"

"Dude, I'm sure this is a great story, and I want to hear all about it, but right now I've got a bunch of assholes with assault rifles, not to mention a mob of brainwashed townspeople—*friends of mine*—trying to kill me."

"Why, though? What's all this about?"

"Seriously, there's no time to explain."

"We've got time now. That's why I brought you here, so we can hide."

"I'm our police force, dude. I'm not going to hide. But you should, okay? Until it's safe . . . Oh, God, I almost did it again. Damian, I do need your help. Do you have a gun in here? Or, you know, a real knife?"

He shakes his head. "Just rock hammers, that's about the best I can do. Don't really care for weapons."

I jerk my chin toward the small hammer he still holds in his hand, the one he'd pressed to my cheek. "That as big as they come?" I ask.

He glances down, almost surprised to see he still has it. "Oh, yeah. Pretty much. I borrow a pickax from Geezer when I go out rock hunting."

My exasperated sigh cuts off his words. He stands there, silent, as I glance around the workshop. "Nothing here actually works."

His only response is a guilty shrug.

A silence begins to stretch, one I don't have time for.

"Okay," I say, thinking fast. "New plan. I need you to get that fake knife ready."

"You do?"

"Yeah. But first, give me your shoes."


Five minutes later I'm in the back of Damian's shop, standing by the door, the soles of my boots dripping with his fake blood.

His sneakers hang around my neck, the laces tied together. In one hand I have a chisel about twelve inches long and made of stainless steel. In the other, the fake knife.

"Okay. Ready?"

"Are you sure this is a good—"

"Yes. Here goes," I say. Then I turn and burst through the back door, sprinting hard.

Behind me, Damian hesitates a second, then slams the door closed. It's perfect, I think. Just loud enough to draw attention from anyone in the alley, but not the rest of the town. I can only hope he follows my directions from there, sneaking upstairs and hiding out in one of the empty apartments above his shop.

Flashlight off, I race across the twenty feet of cement and gravel before crashing into the greenbelt, leaving a neat line of footprints in my wake. They make no sense, of course, but I don't need them to. I just need my pursuers to take the bait.

A thunderous crack tears down the alley, and at the same moment the tree next to me shudders as a bullet slams into it.

Adrenaline flooding my veins, I crouch, turn back, and surge into the forest.

Shouts from the alley, toward the pub. The gangster with the southern drawl. No sounds of running feet yet, though.

Ferns crowd my path. I push them away, sprinting until I'm surrounded by trees. A low branch smacks into my wrist, causing me to drop the flashlight, but using it would only give me away, so I leave it. I go about a hundred feet farther before I stop, sit, and pull my boots off.

Someone's running hard down the alley. Flashlight beams begin to play off the backs of the buildings, and then the trees around me. Shadows dance. More shouting. Barked orders.

Working fast, I pull Damian's running shoes on and tie the laces as tight as I can. They're a few sizes too big, but they'll work.

I come to a crouch and throw my own boots as far as I can into the forest, toward the east. They crash into a bush somewhere in the darkness.

Someone back by the buildings calls out. A light focuses in the direction of my boots, followed by a second gunshot that rips through the foliage.

Perfect. Turning ninety degrees to my right, I jog while bent at the waist. A twig snaps under my foot, but I don't stop. I can only hope no one heard it. The lights remain on that spot east of me, the footfalls still going that way.

After another hundred feet, I turn right again, working back toward the alley.

Several people are off in the forest now, searching the area where my boots landed. I have a minute, I think—maybe less—before the ruse is up.

The sound of gunshots and commotion has unleashed a flurry of activity from Main Street. Multiple people heading this way, rushing down the connecting alleys or through the buildings themselves. Flashlight beams swing erratically as they race toward their prey, egged on by the ever-present droning voice of Mrs. Conaty. "Kill the liar Mary Whittaker. Kill the liar Mary Whittaker!"

I expected a few of them to come.

From the sound of it, though, they're all headed this way.

Time to make my move.

"Kyle, it's me."

"Mary? What the f—"

"Quiet. I don't want to hurt you, so listen, and don't fucking move."

"Hold on, what—"

"Quiet. Did they inject you with something? Give you a pill?"

"No."

"Force you to drink something?"

"No! I—"

"Bullshit. They told you to lie."

"Just listen. They tied everyone up, forced us to drink some Granston Ale. But none of them knew how to tap a keg, so Doc had me do it while they were busy with the others. I poured my own from a different keg."

"Just yours? Why not everyone's?"

"That was my plan, but they were watching—at fucking gunpoint by the way—as I poured most of them."

"Then what happened?"

"They made us all sit on the floor, on our hands, and watch a video on repeat. Mrs. F'ing Conaty, telling us—"

"Okay. And then?"

"They thought I was under their control. I snuck away when—"

"Keep your voice down. I believe you."

"Mary, what the hell's going on?"

"I'll explain later. If there is a later. Right now I need you to get the hell out of here. Run and don't look—"

"Your nose."

"What?"

"What happened to your nose, Mary?"

"It's a long story."

"What happened to your fucking nose?"

"I tricked them! Like you did. I'm not with them. Okay? Okay?! I'll tell you everything later, I promise. Now get the hell out of here. Get off the mountain. Far as you can."

"Like hell I will. You need help."

"I . . . what?"

"Remember? You need help, Mary."

"Fuck. I forgot again."

"Is that related to all this?"

"Yeah . . . Yeah it is. I'll explain that later, too. You're right, though, I do need help."

"I'm not sure I like that look in your eye."

"Just had an idea. Maybe there is something you can do for me."

"Anything."

"First, your gun safe. The Luger still inside?"

"Yeah."

"I need the combination."

"I'll just open it for you. Come on, let's go up there. We can hide out—"

"No, Kyle. Hiding isn't going to work now. Give me the combination. There's something else I need you to do. Does your Jeep—"

"If you're going to tell me to run, to go get help in Granston, forget it. I'm staying with you."

"No, you're not."

"You need help."

"And you are going to get me that help. But not from Granston. Okay? Now tell me, your Jeep, does it have a standard power outlet?"

"It has two."

"I could kiss you right now."

# CHAPTER TWENTY-FIVE

The Luger is cold and heavy in my hand.

Before Kyle showed me this one, I'd only ever seen them in movies. World War Two films, usually. Some German officer wearing the pistol high on the hip, ready to draw and fire at the first sign of insolence from a captive. Kyle said the man who gave him this one found it in Vietnam, but that still means the damn thing is an antique.

I stare at it, wondering if it will even work. It could just as easily jam, or explode in my hand. It's awkwardly weighted compared to a modern pistol. Back heavy, I guess is the way to describe it. It beats a fake knife, though.

Kyle's got a flashlight in a kitchen drawer that I grab as well. I test the beam against my hand, cupping it over the bulb to block any illumination from giving me away.

His bedroom window overlooks Main Street. Even though the window is closed, the repetitive voice of Mrs. Conaty still manages to push in, blaring from the SUV's speakers in constant droning repetition. "Kill the liar . . . Kill the liar . . ." And my name. Over and over.

I glance at the clock. Kyle's task should take fifteen minutes, maybe twenty if he has to stop and hide from the gunmen. That's assuming he makes it at all.

I can't stand the idea that I might have put him in danger, but he was right, of course. I need help. If only I could keep that idea in my head for more than thirty seconds.

Maybe I can increase Kyle's chances. Cause a distraction.

I head for the door, open it. Dark stairs lead down. I creep into the hall and take the first step before I recognize the change.

Conaty's mantra about killing me has stopped.

I freeze on the darkened stairwell and listen.

Replacing the recorded order to kill me is her voice, talking normally. I turn and go back into the apartment, moving quickly through the living room to Kyle's bedroom, around the bed, and to the window. I pull the blinds back slightly and look out at the street below, listening to her words.

". . . all night chasing you, but there's another way. You can come to us. Give up. And perhaps you'll save some lives. These are, after all, the people you swore to protect."

I swallow. This is something I had not expected.

The SUV is parked in between O'Doherty's and the police station now, right in the middle of the street, all four of its doors open to let the sound of Conaty's voice out. Of the woman herself there's no sign. Two of the bodyguards, or whatever they are—mercenary seems more apt—stand beside the vehicle, assault rifles held at the ready. Their eyes scan the buildings. I have to duck back and let the blinds close as one of them glances this way. A second later, I peek through again. He's facing the other side of the street now, still looking for me. I let out a breath.

"Hugh Wilkinson," Conaty says, "step forward please. To the truck."

My mouth goes dry as the owner of the diner emerges from the police station, almost robotically. He comes up beside one of the mercs.

"That's perfect, stop there."

Hugh complies.

"Officer Whittaker? Last chance," Conaty's voice booms.

I'm frozen in place, knowing what's about to happen but not yet believing it, paralyzed by the ramifications.

"So be it, Mary. This is on you. Hugh Wilkinson, shoot yourself in the head."

There's no time to call out, to scream for her to stop this. Without even the slightest hesitation, Hugh Wilkinson, the mild-mannered longtime citizen of Silvertown, pillar of the community, owner of the diner, and Clara's boss, lifts a pistol to his temple and fires.

He crumples to the ground, lifeless; a spray of blood hits the road beside him a second later.

I close my eyes, shut them as tight as I can, trying to get that image to go away. The spray of blood and brain, the innocent man collapsing.

Worse, though, is knowing exactly what Conaty will say next. The bitch doesn't disappoint.

"Plenty more fodder where he came from, Mary. You can stop this whenever you like. All you have to do is come out of your hiding place and no one else need die."

The weight of what she's doing is like nothing I've felt since the day my partner was shot back in Oakland. I felt so helpless then, watching him bleed as the perp got away and the ambulance took way too long to arrive. I was helpless then, but I'm not helpless now.

Conaty's right. I can stop this. I must.

I reach for the window, grasping the latch to slide it open. Even in the darkness I can still see the words on my hand.

## YOU NEED <u>HELP</u>

*Too late*, I think. Help's not going to get here in time. Kyle won't be fast enough.

And for perhaps the only time in my goddamn life, going it alone is the right choice. It's going to save lives.

"Greg Gorman," Mrs. Conaty booms through the SUV's speakers. "Approach the vehicle."

And there he is. My chief. The man who's had to bear the burden of a town ripped apart by his actions. All because he did the right thing. And now it's all come back. Conaty has come back.

"More blood on your hands, Mary," she's saying. "Greg Gorman, shoot—"

I yank the window open. "Okay!" I shout. "Okay. Enough."

A dozen flashlights swing to the window, illuminating me from below. I hold up a hand to block the glare.

"Well, well," Conaty says. "Do not move. Someone will be up to fetch you."

Her voice still comes from the SUV's stereo, but it suddenly occurs to me that she's watching all this. She's nearby, or at least being fed a video of the situation. The former seems more likely, though.

"Are you alone up there, hon?" Conaty asks.

*Hon? Go fuck yourself.* I swallow, glancing behind me. "Kyle's here," I say, forcing as much tentative worry into my voice as I can.

"Get him to the window. Both of you place your hands on the glass."

"He's hurt," I say. "He can't stand."

"I don't believe you, dear."

"It's the truth."

"We'll see about that. Greg Gorman, show these two men the way to that apartment. Bring Mary and her companion down here. And no talking, please."

Greg had been ready to shoot, and there's a fraction of a second where I imagine him opening fire on the thugs instead, finally revealing that his condition, like mine, had all been a ruse. He lowers the weapon to his side, though, and immediately starts to jog across the street toward the stairwell next to O'Doherty's, disappearing from view. The two men from the helicopter follow him, eyes on me until they vanish from sight below.

Seconds later I can hear them coming up the stairwell, boots pounding. Six flights of steps between the entrance and Kyle's door.

I wait until they hit the halfway point, then I turn and run.

Conaty roars something, shrieking like a banshee, but I'm too focused on my path to hear the words. Some variation of "kill her," I assume.

The footsteps on the stairs go from a steady run to a stampede.

I race through Kyle's bedroom door, through the kitchenette, and across his living room, vaulting the coffee table. Magazines and a remote control scatter in my wake. There's a big window behind the couch. I throw it open and stare out at the greenbelt, the forest, and in the distance the peaks of Two-Shits, barely visible against the starry night sky.

I slither out onto the fire escape and start down. The steps clang so loudly I'm sure they can be heard for miles. But it doesn't matter now. The time for hiding is over.

Part of me expects the fire escape to lead me right into the clutches of the enemy. Either the stone-cold killers who arrived with Conaty, or the obedient slaves of the Broken Nose Gang and those who drank the tainted beer at the pub.

No one's there, though. My oversize shoes hit the ground, and I'm off. I tear past the back of Blackwood's shop, firing a glance that way, half expecting to see him waiting there in his long black duster, eager to help despite my insistence that he hide. But the door to his store is closed, the place quiet. Good. At least he might survive this.

A gunshot rips through the night. Behind and above me. The round cracks off the pavement to my right, only a few feet away. I swerve left, into deeper shadow, my shoulder scraping against the side of the building there. Ahead are two large Dumpsters, with black plastic bags piled up beside one. Instead of going around, I press myself against the wall and stop, catching my breath, listening.

There's activity all around. The footfalls of someone clanging down Kyle's fire escape. Others coming from both right and left, ground level. Pinching in from each side of the alley. They'll have me trapped here, soon.

A smell hits me, then, weirdly overpowering despite the imminent threat I face. It's the smell of flowers. Cloying and old, but not unpleasant.

This is the rear of the flower shop. All the leftover bouquets from the Rogers funeral. The event, I suppose, where this all started.

Or where it went wrong, I guess. For Doc and his friends. If Johnny Rogers hadn't died, perhaps the rest of the strange behavior around here might have passed unnoticed. For a while, anyway. Just the quirky behavior of a fucked-up little town. But Johnny's death made it real. Doc, Ang, and the rest of them had blood on their hands after that. The boy's untimely demise meant investigation, which is likely why Greg was one of their first targets for the newer version. And me as well, come to think of it, once Doc realized I was poking around in the Rogers' house and looking into the death of the hiker, too. That's why they sent Rhod when they did.

The footsteps close in.

I pull the Luger from my belt and slide its bizarre, hinged loading mechanism back, then forward, putting a round into the chamber. With my thumb I flick the safety off, aim, and crack off two rounds in rapid succession into the trees.

The footsteps around me skid to a stop, people scrambling for cover.

In the chaos of shouts and hasty retreat, I turn and shoulder into the back door of the flower shop. The door buckles but remains stubbornly closed. I step back and kick it in, then race inside as flashlights begin to sweep toward the now-open doorway. More shouts behind me, all coming at once.

"Follow her!"

"Go around!"

"Mary! I can't stop! I'm sorry!"

Conaty's chant blares from the SUV somewhere outside, but it's not a recording anymore. She's still live, improvising now, her voice tinged with desperation. *Kill Mary. Don't talk. Obey Doctor Ryan.*

I sprint through the store, able to see only from the mixture of flashlight beams that swing and sweep across the front and back of the flower shop. The smell in here is wonderful and dense. Despite myself I inhale deeply as I pump my fists and knees, powering straight ahead.

The front door is a wood frame with a big single pane of glass in between, the shop name and its hours printed on the other side, writ backward for me. All I can read is the sign hanging from a suction cup at eye level. OPEN, it says, the CLOSED side facing out.

I bring my arms up in front of my face and leap at the last second, crashing through the glass, the sign slapping against my forehead.

My feet land on the sidewalk beyond. Shards of glass tinkle against the concrete, spreading out before me like a spray of stars. I turn my landing into a roll, going over the curb and into the street. Pain erupts from my shoulder as it takes the brunt of the fall, but the roll is smooth, and I turn it into a stand and then, ultimately, a run. I'm on Main Street, the SUV bellowing Conaty's orders is off to my left, parked diagonally, blocking the road. The doors are all open to allow her voice to boom.

I rush directly across the street, aiming at the SUV's front grille as I squeeze off three more shots. One of the headlights explodes. The other two rounds clang into the metal bodywork.

The SUV's remaining light stays stubbornly on. Conaty's voice still drones from the sound system. "Kill Mary Whittaker! Kill Mary Whittaker!"

I stop now, near the center of the road. From here the parked SUV is almost side-on to me. I take more careful aim. One of the mercenary fuckers is beside the vehicle, and at the sight of my shooting posture he twists and spins around the rear, ducking down behind the bumper.

I don't fire at him, though. I squeeze two more rounds off, both at the driver's door and hopefully on into the dashboard beyond. No result. Conaty's voice still blares. Only one round left. I take three long steps to my right so I can see in through the open driver's side door, aim again at where the stereo is, squeeze, and feel the old pistol recoil.

There's a shower of sparks from the dash. Indicators flicker, then vanish.

With them goes Conaty's voice, too, as the vehicle shuts abruptly off. I start to grin, but the sudden bark of an assault rifle changes my mind and sends me sprinting again. The mercenary is firing from behind the vehicle. Even with the deafening series of cracks from the rifle I can still hear his bullets hiss through the air around me.

Somehow I reach the other side of the street unscathed, darting into a narrow alley between two boarded-up storefronts.

The alley is a straight run. Fifty feet of dank, shadowed nothing. Nowhere to hide, no cover to be found. I race down it, my lungs on fire from the effort. I don't need to look back to know they're only seconds behind me. I race on. Need to buy time.

Something punches me.

Pain erupts from my arm as a bullet tears through. A searing heat fills my mind with total agony. I stagger but somehow keep going, feeling the warm trickle of blood pouring down my left bicep and into the crease at my elbow. It feels like my arm is being sawn in half.

Another shot sparks off the brick wall beside me, just inches from my head, so close I can feel the shrapnel spray on my ear and cheek.

Consumed with pain, I almost don't realize I've reached the end of the alley. It simply ends, no wall, no nothing. Just the wider back alley separating the row of buildings from the greenbelt.

I turn a sharp left. The rear of Flour Child bakery is beside me, a blur. Raccoons suddenly scatter from the enclosed trash area, hissing as they go.

The first of my pursuers rounds the corner a few seconds later, and from the calamitous noise and wild yip that follows, I guess he or she tripped over one of the animals. Someone else cries out. Confusion ripples through the mob, maybe enhanced by the sudden lack of orders from Conaty. Conscious thought starting to override their instinct to do her bidding. Maybe. I can't stop to find out.

I force myself to slow down, though. Let them recover, let them close in. Let them focus on me instead of on Kyle. None of this will matter if they find him.

And *her*.

My left arm feels like it's on fire by the time I reach the back of the police station. I stumble, already dizzy from blood loss.

There's a small parking lot behind the building. Weeds poke up through cracks in the pavement. Faded lines delineate unused stalls. Once full of police cars when the town required a bigger force, these days the lot sits empty most of the time, as Greg prefers the visibility of parking out front, a habit he impressed upon me.

Right now only one vehicle is in the lot. Kyle's huge custom Jeep, empty and dark. It's in the first spot, right next to the back door.

"Thank you," I whisper, and deliberately ignore the vehicle. I stagger toward the rear of the station instead, wincing each time I accidentally move my arm. Even the slightest shift in position brings a fresh wave of searing agony, like someone taking scissors to the wound and opening it wider and wider.

I reach for the back door.

It opens before I can grab the handle. Someone's rushing out, and we almost collide. The look on his face is half surprise and half recognition. Perhaps my broken nose has bought a fraction of a second's confusion. It's all I need. One knee to the man's groin and he's doubled over and moaning. I kick him for good measure, then move into the dark building.

Behind me, those chasing are near enough to see the door close. One of them shouts, "She went in there! The police station!" Not for the benefit of the mob chasing me, but those around front, the ones with the rifles.

I make an immediate left, racing down the hall at the back of the station. If I can just make it to the weapons locker—

A figure rounds the corner ahead of me, blocking the way. An assault rifle coming up. I take the open doorway on my right and almost slip on the tile floor of the drunk tank. Somehow I have the presence of mind to kick away the wedge that holds the heavy door open. It swings shut behind me with a deep thud, plunging the room into darkness.

I flick Kyle's flashlight on. Sweep the beam across the foul, stained tiles of the room. A dense odor of bleach makes my already tear-filled eyes sting like mad. My arm's no longer on fire. It's gone ice cold.

I press myself into the corner by the door. The only hope now is to get the thug's assault rifle away from him. Have to fight my way out. Have to get back to O'Doherty's in time to meet Kyle. Have to find a first aid kit.

Have to live.

The building around me rumbles with the footsteps of dozens of people, and from the sound of it most are still hell-bent on killing me, even without the constant words of Mrs. Conaty.

I wish now that I had sent Kyle away. Sent him to Granston to get a SWAT team up here. Or the fucking National Guard. Anything but the plan we concocted, which now seems woefully inadequate. Leaning against this wall, bleeding out, nowhere to run or hide, I can't believe I didn't head down the mountain myself as soon as I saw my car burning. What an idiot. Old me would have done it. Would have realized the need for a team to tackle this problem. New me, though . . . thanks to that fucking sleeping pill, new me had to go all cowboy on the situation and rush up here to save the day.

I slide down the wall, leaving a smear of blood, no longer feeling the bullet hole on my upper arm.

I'm done. They're here, the handle is turning, and I don't have the strength to wrestle an AR-15 away from a trained killer.

I drop the flashlight, which lands standing on its lens, plunging the room into darkness. How fitting, I think.

It's over. I crumple to the floor.

Except my butt says otherwise.

I don't reach the floor. I hit something thin and metal instead. A bucket. A full bucket. Sloshing with the acrid stench of bleach. No wonder the smell is so strong.

I drop the Luger and grab the rim of the bucket, rolling to my left at the same time, flinging the container toward the door as light begins to spill in from outside.

There's a wet slap. A grunt of surprise, and then a heartbeat later the cry of pain follows. The man staggers backward, firing off his assault rifle blindly, each shot utterly deafening in the small, tiled room. He's fired straight ahead, an act of panic. I'm off to his left, though.

As he stumbles backward, arm over his burning eyes, I rush him.

Rounding the doorframe I slam my good shoulder into his midsection. He bounces off the wall opposite and goes down, his rifle trapped under his body. I reach for the weapon, then change my mind. People are starting to come in the back door of the station, just fifteen feet away. Flashlight beams swinging this way. None of them seem confused now. I silenced the SUV, so Conaty herself must be close. Close enough for them to hear her.

I run away from their lights, deeper into the station. The hall goes another fifteen feet, then rounds a corner, into the main room where the cells are, and beyond those, my desk. Greg's desk. Weapons locker. Everything.

That's when the lights come back on.

And the weirdest thought enters my delirious head. I expect them all to shout "Surprise!" and throw confetti.

Instead they hold in their hands the weapons from the very locker I've been working toward.

This is not going to plan at all.

# CHAPTER
# TWENTY-FUCKING-SIX

Instinct.

It's the root of this entire mess, and yet the thing that saves my ass, at least for now.

Without a conscious thought I fly into motion.

The bad guys are on the other side of the room, just entering from the front door. As surprised that the lights have come on as I am.

But there's one person who is in the center of the room, standing between us.

Doc.

Dr. Frank Ryan, town shrink, coconspirator to Mr. Ang and Mrs. Conaty. He's seated at my desk, a penlight between his lips, riffling through my files and drawers. Looking for his notes, I'll bet.

I race toward him, crouching low as I weave around the four empty jail cells and the watercooler. Someone fires at me, a single shot that shatters the bottle, splashing cold water across the carpeted floor.

From the small of my back I draw Damian Blackwood's ceremonial knife.

Doc comes to a stand, unsure what's going on. He's not looking at me, but at the people pouring into the front of the station. So many guns, aimed at me, but I'm behind Doc so he freezes at the sight of all those weapons pointed his way. Everyone's shouting at him. "Get down!" "Move, idiot!" "Out of the way!" Doc's too slow to understand. He thinks they're here for him, and starts to raise his hands.

I slip up behind him and clamp my left hand across his forehead, heaving it back to expose his neck. I thrust my knee against his, pushing his leg outward. Fresh pain flares in my left shoulder, but the adrenaline pounding through me tamps it down. For once I'm thankful for Doc's flabby six-foot-eight frame. At nearly a foot taller than me, and with his bulging midsection, he makes damn good cover.

My right hand holds the fake knife from Damian's staged satanic dungeon. I press it lightly against Doc's throat. He needs to feel it, but too much pressure and the chocolate syrup inside the false blade will start to flow and give away the ruse.

Eight people stand before me. Perhaps as many behind now, filing in from the back hall. They need new orders, or I'm a dead woman.

"Call them off," I say in Doc's ear, "or you die."

"Stop," Doc utters, terrified. "All of you, stop!"

The room goes instantly quiet, the mob obedient to his command.

I scan the faces of those in front of me, blocking the door. No sign of Sandra Conaty. Her two guests—Mr. Secretary and the wealthy sleazebag—aren't around, either. God forbid they get near the action.

Two of the professional badasses who arrived on Conaty's helicopter are front and center, though. The twins. It's a repeat of when they cornered me in the garage, standing in front of that fountain. They exchange an amused glance, perhaps recognizing the replay of that earlier encounter. As before, each have AR-15 rifles pointed at me. Well, at Doc, but I've no doubt a round fired at this range would pass right through Doc and into me. Everything depends on whether Doc matters to them as much as I've guessed he does.

From the looks on their faces, I might have misjudged that.

One of the men lifts a finger to his ear. Listens. His eyes narrow, fixed on me.

I press the knife a little harder into Doc's neck, hoping against hope the fake blood won't seep out.

"Get out of the way," I say to the gunmen. "We're leaving."

"You shut the hell up," the mercenary barks in his southern drawl. He tilts his head slightly down and to the left, replying to the voice in his ear. "She's got the doctor. Can we shoot?"

Captain Tweaker comes to stand beside him, licking his lips. Greg Gorman, my boss, appears next to the other thug.

Tweaker and Greg look almost calm. Both have their earpieces in, perhaps receiving a constant barrage from Conaty to keep their minds from overriding their instinct-driven behavior. Other members of the Broken Nose Gang file in behind them, and the new recruits from Kyle's bar all loom on the periphery, some behind me, blocking that exit. They're all waiting, Doc's command holding them back for the moment.

The two professional killers, though, simply watch me. Cool as cucumbers, but with postures that hint at their readiness to strike. These men haven't taken the drug, I realize. They're doing this because it's their job, fully aware of their actions. That makes them infinitely more dangerous. And right now, all they're waiting for is a voice in their ear to tell them if Doc is expendable or not.

Doc, perhaps finally sensing this, too, makes a low whimper sound.

"How the hell did you get caught up in this, Doc?" I ask him.

His body is trembling. He's leaning back on me, too, and getting hard to hold up. The gentle giant must weigh three hundred pounds. "A dumb mistake. Years ago. Then Ang . . . he showed me—"

"Shut up, moron," the thug says.

He dips his chin again, listening to his earpiece, nodding. He says, "Yup, just a knife. Can we shoot, or . . . ?" More waiting, listening. Finally, he glances up at me, and smiles.

I've miscalculated. They don't need Doc, and they certainly don't need me. It's over, I realize. I brace myself for the bullet.

Instead of shooting, he steps aside. The other thug moves, too, and behind them, sauntering into the police station, is Mrs. Conaty. Behind her are the two guests she was entertaining at the mansion. The one referred to as Mr. Secretary, and the flashy bastard who reeks of money. The senator, owner of that mansion, is with them as well.

"Officer Whittaker," Sandra Conaty says, "you've made this whole business quite complicated, haven't you?"

I hold her gaze, defiant but not sure what to say. Not sure where this is going yet.

Nowhere good, that much is obvious.

From outside, very faint, comes the sound of small squeaky wheels. The noise reminds me of a medical gurney. No one else seems to notice, or care.

"On the plus side," Mrs. Conaty adds, "you've given me a wonderful opportunity to demonstrate the product." She smiles, a glint of evil in her dark eyes.

"Why . . ." I start, then let it go. "Forget it."

"No, no. Go ahead. Ask your question."

"I was going to ask 'why here?' Why Silvertown? But the answer's obvious. Petty revenge. Still butt-hurt that your corrupt company was exposed for the failure it is."

I hate to admit it, but her smile catches me off guard. She shakes her head, just a little, as if amazed how stupid I am. It's infuriating. I guess that's the point.

"Mary, you should understand something: I don't give one shit about this awful little place, much less two."

"Then why?"

"Familiarity, mainly. I grew up here, after all. Then there's the isolation. One cell phone tower. One power line. One road in and out. Put some cones across the bridge, snip a few cables, and voilà; the mountain is ours." Then she takes a small step forward, and her voice lowers a little. "The absolute best part, though, is using Silvertown's own reputation against itself. You morons are so steeped in conspiracy nonsense that by the time anyone figures out something is actually happening, it's too late."

"*I* figured it out," I say.

"And you're too late. See what I mean?" Her self-satisfied smile conjures the most punchable face I think I've ever seen or ever will see.

Eyes never leaving me, Conaty addresses her VIP guests. "Gentlemen, this woman is Mary Whittaker, a police officer here in good old

Silvertown. And over there, under the control of our newly perfected product, is her boss. Chief of Police Gregory Gorman. Greg, say hello."

"Hello," he says without the slightest hesitation.

"Good, now be quiet again."

Greg nods, mouth clapping shut.

"Imagine this," Conaty says for the benefit of the two men standing beside her. "You have a budget committee, or a board of directors, who go about their work, their *lives*, without any hint of what's happened inside their heads. But one command from you, and they obey without question. Vote your way. Sign off on your next scheme. Whatever."

Mr. Secretary's only reaction is a single, impressed grunt. But the wealthy sleazebag shifts on his feet.

"The board already does what I tell them to," he says.

"Sure they do," Conaty replies. "Because you tell them to do things they'll agree with. You've already anticipated their objections and factored them into your proposals. You water it down. Imagine no longer needing to do that. Imagine a rubber stamp on your vision for the company. And anything else you like. Your wife. Your family. Your competitors. Or," she adds dramatically, "anyone . . . and I mean *anyone* . . . above you."

Some of the man's swagger drains away as he considers this. But the reaction my attention is drawn to is that of the one called Mr. Secretary. There's a sudden smile on his face as his imagination runs wild. Conaty has pressed all the right buttons with this asshole, clearly.

The sound of squeaky wheels outside grows, but no one's paying attention to it.

"You guys are idiots if you think that's her plan," I say to them. "I saw them putting that shit in the water supply. One of her companies is a pharmaceutical manufacturer, for fuck's sake. This isn't going to stop at a fucking board of directors or whatever."

The room goes stone quiet.

Save for Mrs. Conaty, who is *tsk*ing me.

"Bless your heart" she says. "See what I mean? Conspiracy theories, already. Hon, I can barely manage a rabble of this size. What would I need with an entire population? That would be tedious in the extreme, and entirely unnecessary."

Her words are not for me, I realize, but the two VIPs. Her customers.

"Control the head of the snake and the body will follow." This from Mr. Secretary, who is rubbing his chin, deep in thought, his smile still there. Then a dark look passes across his features. An evil look. He's practically salivating at what Conaty is proposing.

Sandra Conaty sees it, too, and gives the satisfied nod of a salesperson who knows when her client cannot say no. "What I'm offering you is not blind obedience, gentlemen. It's absolute confidence. A lever you can pull, whenever you need to make sure your orders are carried out to the letter."

"Prove it," Mr. Secretary says. "These people could be acting, for all I know."

"Of course. Why do you think I brought you along?" She turns to me. "Greg? Step forward and shoot Mary Whittaker in the head."

Greg turns to me again. The blank expression on his face leaves. Replaced with utter sadness. He steps out from the group, in front of them, between them and me.

His arm comes up. His pistol is in his hand. Standard police issue, black and shiny. His face contorts and tears begin to fall. "Mary, I can't stop. Mary, oh God, I'm sorry . . . "

"I hid Dr. Ryan's notes," I blurt out, playing for time. "Kill me and you'll never find them."

It's the second-to-last card I have, and it's a dud.

Conaty smiles at this, amused. "Stop there, Greg."

He stops. Relief washes over him, if only for a moment.

Before continuing, Conaty grins slyly at her power over Greg. Then she turns and speaks directly to me. "Yes, the notes. The thing is, dear, we don't need them now. That phase of the project has concluded. We just don't want anyone else to get their hands on them. They'd be evidence, which I assume is why you took them. Evidence is what Gregory here had when he nearly destroyed my company."

I swallow, waiting. She goes on.

"The notes are here in town somewhere, that much we can take for granted. I'm also sure a veteran sleuth like Greg Gorman can find them. And if not, well, by morning all of Silvertown will be under my control. A rabble, I know, but it's necessary now thanks to you, Mary. This commotion won't go unnoticed, so I'll need to ensure the town is on the same page when some actual law enforcement arrives to investigate. And in the meantime, the townsfolks' first task can be finding Dr. Ryan's notes."

I level my gaze on her, trying to force myself to look tough.

"*Nihil hic actu operatur,*" I say.

For a moment her cool facade falters. She blinks in confused annoyance. "Meaning?"

"'Nothing here actually works.'" This I say not to Conaty, but to the two men with her. A desperate ploy to buy myself more time. I point at my broken nose. "Her drug doesn't work. Didn't work on me. She's a fraud, and you two are being played."

Conaty's smile only widens, though. "How delightful! An attempt to turn the tables. The thing is, Officer, I've already explained to them the recent improvements in the product. It's regrettable that you somehow slipped under Doc's radar, but then so did the Rogers boy. Regrettable, but of course not an issue anywhere else other than this mountain."

Her smile vanishes.

"Continue, Greg. Shoot Mary Whittaker."

Greg's hand had been halfway aimed at me as if frozen in place. It rises the rest of the distance now.

From the sidewalk outside, the squeaking wheels abruptly stop, right in front of the station.

Time to play my last card.

"NOW!" I shout.

At the same instant I draw the fake knife over Doc's throat. He makes a mewling squeal as chocolate syrup erupts from the blade and runs down his neck.

There's a gasp of surprise from the onlookers. I release Doc's forehead and kick him, sending him into Greg just as Greg pulls the trigger.

His shot zips past my ear, clanging off one of the cell bars behind me. Doc falls against him, but Greg's too fast. He sidesteps and renews his aim before I've even had a chance to figure out where to run. Not that it matters. There's nowhere to run.

I breathe out through my broken nose, and hold my hands out, placating. The gesture makes no difference. Greg sights down the barrel and . . .

His face scrunches up. Everyone's does.

A sonic assault pulsates through the room, so loud and grating it makes my stomach heave.

The barrage of noise comes from two places. At the front door, blaring some death metal, is the massive speaker from Kyle's pub, which he's spent the last few minutes trying to wheel across the street without earning anyone's attention.

And from the rear of the building, booming from an inherited amplifier once used by Quiet Riot, plugged into Kyle's Jeep, is the horrid wailing bombardment of Clara and her electric guitar.

She was right. She's terrible at the guitar.

It's fucking perfect.

Everyone reacts in the same way. Hands over ears, doubled at the waist. It's so loud in the room I can't hear myself think. Greg staggers, the gun that had been aimed at me now beside his head as he tries to stop the wall of noise.

Comprehension dawns on Conaty's face almost instantly.

Panic washes over her features. She shouts something, veins in her neck straining with the force of her bellowed cry. An order, I'm sure. Kill me. Kill whoever's outside. Shut off that goddamn noise.

No one can hear her, though.

No one can hear the windows rattling, or the coffee mugs in the station's kitchenette falling and shattering. They can't hear their own bowels churning from the pounding noise.

There's only one difference between me and them, in that moment.

*I was expecting this.*

Greg's the closest. I know he's an unwilling participant in this madness, but he's armed and has orders to kill me. So I step into him, grab his collar, yanking him forward as I kick his legs out from under him in a move deliciously similar to the way I was subdued at the door of the mansion.

When he hits the carpet and breaks his nose again the sound is probably awful. Good thing I can't hear it. The gun in his hand falls to the floor and slides toward me. I dive for it. In that instant one of the bodyguards manages to regain his senses. He fires his AR-15 at me. At where I was, rather.

Then Greg's pistol is in my hands. From the floor I shoot, barely taking the time to aim. I squeeze the trigger.

The bodyguard drops.

Again I squeeze.

His twin staggers and falls.

And I squeeze a third time.

Conaty simply stares at me. Through her evil dark eyes. Eyes that suddenly flutter. She crumples to the floor, unable to stay upright because my third shot blew her right knee to smithereens.

She collapses into the dead body of the bodyguard beside her, a bloodstain growing all up and down her pant leg.

To her credit, I suppose, she doesn't pass out. Doesn't even scream. She just lies there, slack-jawed, staring at me.

Behind her, Mr. Secretary and his wealthy counterpart turn and flee, finally realizing it will be the end of their careers, maybe their lives, if Conaty's plan falls apart.

There's a crash outside as one of them runs into Kyle, or his speaker. The sound from it dies, leaving only Clara's guitar.

I keep my pistol aimed at Conaty.

"One fucking word and you're dead," I shout at her.

Whether she can hear me or not, she seems to get the message. Despite the pain contorting her face, she manages to nod.

"Clara, stop!" I shout.

I have to repeat the cry two more times before it manages to get through. The screeching guitar noise fades away.

"Kyle?" I call out.

"I'm here," he says from the front door. He steps into the room and wastes no time picking up an AR-15 from the floor and training it on, well, everyone but me.

"If she so much as makes a noise," I tell him, nodding toward Sandra Conaty, "you shoot."

"With pleasure." He checks the weapon, seems satisfied it at least has one round left, and levels it toward her again. "No brainwashing required to follow that fuckin' order, eh?"

The rest of the people in the room all wait. Addicts who can only get their fix from the words of Mrs. Conaty.

"Tell them all to put their weapons down and go home," I order her.

The woman hesitates, the calculus of crime and punishment, surrender and escape, all going on behind her steely eyes.

"Do it now," I say, with more calm than I knew I had in me.

I can see the moment she reaches the end of her deliberations. Her features slacken, the stress lines across her forehead fading away. She sighs and slumps in one motion. A recognition of defeat.

"You will put down your weapons and go home," she says.

"Louder," Kyle snaps. His aim is steady, his finger on the trigger.

The woman's mouth curls into a vicious snarl, but she relents and does as he asks. "You will put down your weapons . . . and go home!"

This time the voice carries. The reaction is immediate.

Greg comes to a stand, turns away from me, and begins to walk calmly from the station. The others file out, too, leaving Conaty, Ang, and Doc to their fate.

Doc's on his knees before me, hands at his neck, still mewling.

"You cut me," he rasps. "I can't believe you cut—"

"Shut the hell up, Doc," I say. "You're fine."

He pulls his hands away and stares at them, face contorted with confusion. Then he brings his fingers up to his face and sniffs. Even hazards a small taste of the syrupy liquid. "Chocolate," he says, incredulous.

"Yep."

"You . . . that . . . that is *interesting*."

I slap a cuff around his left wrist. Before he can understand what's happening, I wrestle his arms behind his back and cuff the right, too. He's too stunned to say anything more as I walk him to the holding cell and push him inside.

"Stay here," I tell him, slam the cell door, and walk back toward the others. The room seems to tilt, suddenly, and I have to grab the bar of the cell for support. I pause, letting the dizziness pass.

"Your arm," Kyle says.

"We'll deal with that in a minute. Something more important to do first."

He seems about to argue but thinks better of it, nodding at me to continue.

Conaty stands facing me but with her gaze cast sidelong at Kyle's rifle.

"Sandra Conaty," I say. "You have the right to remain silent. Anything you do say may be—"

She rears her head back and screams at the top of her lungs. "YOU WILL BELIEVE I HAD NOTHING TO DO WITH—"

The crunch when the butt of Kyle's rifle smacks the back of her head is—not gonna lie—*very* satisfying.

Sandra Conaty's proverbial lights go out. She falls to the floor, unconscious.

I glance at Kyle.

"No telling what she was going to say," he offers apologetically. "Had to put a stop to it."

"Better be careful, dude. I'm starting to like you."

He grins.

I return it.

But his grin fades as quickly as it came on. "That's still bleeding," he says, nodding at my arm.

He takes a step toward me, eyeing Mr. Ang, who has said nothing this entire time. The man just stands there, staring at Conaty's prone form, and I wonder if seeing her like that has released him from her spell somehow.

I wipe cold sweat from my brow, and in doing so notice the words on my hand once again. Yep, still need help.

"Clara, are you back there?"

She emerges from the hallway at the back of the station, Taser held in one hand. At the sight of the bodies and the fake blood on Doc's neck, she blanches.

"It worked?" she asks, bewildered by the scene.

"It worked."

"No one tried to run out the back," she says. "Kinda bummed about that. I was ready if they did."

"So I see."

Her hand comes to her mouth when she sees my blood-soaked shirtsleeve. "Holy crap, Mary."

"Doc," I say over my shoulder, "you want to examine Conaty's skull or something?"

"No." He sits on the bed, rocking back and forth.

"Maybe look at Mary's arm, then," Kyle suggests.

"Yeah, asshole," Clara adds.

But Doc doesn't move. Nor do I.

The room moves, though. Tilting to one side.

I somehow manage to smile as I collapse. I've lost too much blood, I know, and didn't get the wound bandaged in time.

But I still feel happy. And that's not entirely from the lack of blood.

We did it. Kyle with that speaker. And Clara . . . bless her lack of guitar skill, it just saved all our asses. I could kiss her.

Can't see her, though. There's just the floor, racing to meet me.

Me and my broken nose.

# CHAPTER TWENTY-SEVEN

I'm in the Mansion again, and my instinct is to flee.

The beige walls, the window, the bright light above me. And Doc, leaning over, injecting something into my arm.

All I can manage is a groan of protest.

"Welcome back," Doc says.

He has a woman's voice.

"Huh?" I say, my voice no more than a croak. I blink, lift my head up.

It's not Doc at all, but a nurse in scrubs. She's checking an IV drip running into my wrist. My whole left arm feels numb and, also, tingly somehow.

"Where . . ." I want to say, but my mouth feels as if it's stuffed with dry grass.

"Providence," the nurse replies.

The hospital. I lean my head back, exhausted.

Sometime later I wake once more, and though I'm groggy, this time there's no confusion as to where I am.

The nurse has gone but the room is not empty. Sheriff Davies sits next to me, reading his phone. When I stir he glances at me, smiles, and puts the device away.

"About time," he says, kindly.

"Where's Kyle?" I try. My mouth barely works. "Clara?"

"They're fine. Here, have a sip of water."

He holds a straw to my lips and I take a sip. It's ice cold. I take another, then six or seven long swallows, greedy.

"Don't hold back. The nurse said you can have as much as you want," the sheriff says.

I drink and drink, then slump back, tired again from the effort. I say the first thing that comes to my mind. "I can't even imagine how much paperwork I've created."

He chuckles at that, dryly. "Oh, you have absolutely no idea. Right now, Mary, I can't even remember all the three-letter government agencies involved in the cleanup of this. It's truly epic."

"Agencies?"

He arches an eyebrow at me. "Hell yeah. FBI. CDC. FDA. Seems like every one of them has someone here asking questions about Conaty's little project. And her . . . uh, *clients*."

I blink, absorbing this. "Wait, how long—"

He glances at his watch. "About three days," he says. "You lost a lot of blood."

"I guess I did."

We sit in companionable silence for a time. Sheriff Davies happy to wait for me to recover, and me waiting for the fog to clear from my brain.

"Sally Jones!" I suddenly blurt. "Her kids. I have to get back up there. She might—"

He pats my hand. "Clara told us. Don't worry. There's an army of people on the mountain helping out, including assisting Ms. Jones."

I hold his gaze for as long as I can, then lean back, eased by his words.

"So the feds, huh?"

"They're anxious to speak with you," he says, nodding. "They all are."

"I'm surprised you're the one sitting here, then."

He shrugs. "I'm supposed to let them know when you're awake and alert. Happy to keep that info between ourselves for the moment."

I nod. "Thank you."

"De nada."

I close my eyes, and when I open them again, it could have been a minute that passed, or an hour. I glance at Davies. "Sheriff," I start.

"Call me James."

"James, then. Look. I'm exhausted. I just want to listen. Can you tell me what you've figured out? What they were up to? Why they did it? I have theories, but . . ."

He shoots a slightly nervous glance toward the door. "I'm not really supposed to say. But, fuck it. You've earned some answers." He sighs, takes his hat off, and begins to spin it around with his fingers, slowly. "It's muddy, and I'm not being told much, but one of the FBI guys is a friend of a friend, and he shared a little." James eyes me, a silent oath of secrecy being requested and one I'm content to grant. At my nod he continues. "You're aware that the Conaty family has had a pharmaceutical division for decades?"

I nod again.

"Well, Sandra Conaty was in charge of it. Mr. Ang worked for her. A scientist, and a brilliant one at that. From what I understand, he was working on some new drug to combat anxiety and phobias, which had a side effect of screwing with people's instincts."

I hold up a hand, which takes more effort than I expect. "Wait. How'd you guys learn all this? I can't believe any of them are talking, not with the kinds of lawyers Conaty has."

"Oh," James says, and smiles brightly. "That's the best damn part of this. The irony is absolutely wonderful." He leans forward, eyes twinkling. "Most of it's coming from your chief."

"Greg?!"

"Yeah, I know. Crazy, right? He may have been under Conaty's little spell or whatever, but he was aware and listening. With all that going on the tenacious old son of a bitch was gathering evidence."

I smile. Can't help it.

Davies goes on. "Conaty, Ang, Dr. Ryan, even Senator Meecham . . . they all spoke as if Greg and the others weren't even there, so confident were they in their ability to control the gang. So yeah, Greg learned a lot in the week he was with them, and is sharing all of it with the investigators."

"Time-out. The first thing Conaty said after they dosed me, after telling me to obey her, I mean, was to speak to no one of the treatment."

"Yep. Greg was told the same thing, of course, and with that drug in him he could do nothing but obey Mrs. Conaty. But she made a simple mistake. A greedy mistake, really."

"Which was?"

Davies grins ear to ear.

"What?" I ask him.

"This is the best part. It was your friend Clara's idea, actually, inspired by how you guys foiled her plans up there."

"Well go on, dude, tell me!"

"*Trusting Conaty requires only her voice.* A visual helps, but it's mostly the voice. All we needed was a recording of her saying 'cooperate' with the investigation and, boom, they do. Greg rolled over like no witness ever before him. Told them everything he could. Is still talking, actually."

I close my eyes, picturing the wise old fart with his long mustache and squinty gray eyes. "I hope they don't go too hard on him. He's not responsible for his actions, Sheriff . . . err, James."

"I know, Mary. They know, too, I think, but this is all uncharted territory. Going to take a long time to untangle it, and figure out what to do. Especially with so many agencies involved."

It's the best I can hope for, I suppose. "Thanks," I say, even though I know the sheriff is not the one calling the shots in this matter. "What about Conaty herself?"

He shrugs. "Cooperating to a point. Well, she was until her lawyers arrived. But that was enough. We got her on tape, saying what was needed to help, uh, contain the situation. For now." He says this last very quietly. The implications don't take long to sink home.

"Her words are dangerous," I mutter, thinking it through. "For certain people. Greg. . ." I let the thought trail off with an involuntary shudder. "I should have aimed for her head."

"Don't say that, Mary. No one's blaming you for anything. You did good."

For a long time neither of us speak. He pours me more water, holds it for me as I sip through the straw. Then he settles back in his chair and waits, giving me time to process, I suppose.

"What about Mr. Ang? Doc?"

A shadow passes over James's face. The sheriff rubs at his chin, considering his words. Perhaps figuring out what he's allowed to tell me.

"Mr. Ang's in the wind," he says, simply. At my stare he grimaces and adds, "Slipped away while Kyle and Clara were getting you help. Seems he boarded the helicopter with Conaty's . . . clients."

"Any idea who they were, by the way? She called one Mr. Secretary . . . "

"That," he says weightily, "is a big ball of wax, and one I'm definitely not cleared to know about. Whoever they are, it appears Ang left with them. Or they took him. I guess it doesn't matter. The worry is that they see all this as a setback, not an end. As long as they have him . . ."

"They can try again," I finish.

"Bingo." He takes a deep breath. "They stopped long enough to burn the senator's mansion to the ground, then left. Swapped the chopper for a chartered jet just across the border in Canada, then flew on to who-knows-where. A reported destination of Anchorage was bullshit, obviously. They could be literally anywhere now and are officially the feds' problem. That is all I know."

"Well, whatever, as long as they're far from Silvertown."

The sheriff takes my hand and turns it toward me. The words are still written there, though they've faded a little. " 'You need help,' " he reads.

I stare at him.

James stares back, then pulls away his hand and returns to spinning the hat around with his fingers. "Did you know you were acting differently?"

"Only after the fact, when it no longer mattered."

He gives a slow nod. Thinks some more, then nods again. "There's a shrink here. Can't remember which agency he's with. The CDC, I think. Anyway, I heard him say something interesting. The human brain has something of a flaw. It trusts its own instincts, and so when those instincts change, our mind apparently just rolls with it. So the theory goes. This is all uncharted waters."

It makes a lot of sense, I think, and say as much. "So what about Doc? Is he cooperating? Unlike Greg and the others, Doc's like me. He didn't get the latest—"

"Dr. Ryan is dead, Mary."

My jaw clamps shut. For a long minute I say nothing at all.

"Shot himself," James adds, quietly. "In the police station, right after you collapsed."

"I cuffed him. I—"

"He couldn't aim for his head, so he shot himself in the leg, hit an artery. A trained doctor, so he knew where to aim, I guess. Bled out before a life flight could get there." The sheriff watches my face, conflicted. Probably thought Doc was no great loss, and my reaction isn't meshing with that.

I say, "I suspect he felt guilty for everything that had happened, but for Johnny Rogers in particular." A shudder passes through me. "Unlike Greg, Doc wasn't acting out of some programmed loyalty. He was a willing participant."

"Maybe."

I cast the sheriff a glance. "Meaning?"

He lifts his shoulders. "There're other ways to manipulate people. The old-fashioned ways, if you will."

It's a good point. Still, for some reason I can't help but feel a pang of remorse at Doc's fate. "I locked him up in the hope that he could help unravel all this. And maybe, just maybe, help figure out a way to undo the damage."

Sheriff Davies leans back, contemplative. "You know, I'm not sure if you're lucky or not."

"How do you mean?"

"You received the version before Ang perfected his creation. If they gave you the final product, a few words from Conaty and you'd be absolutely back to normal. As it is . . . well . . ."

The sheriff holds my gaze. Understanding takes me a while.

I squeeze my eyes shut. "It can't be undone. That's what you're telling me."

"There's talk of looking into it, but of course that's a minefield—"

"I'm stuck this way. Maybe for good."

"Yes," he says, barely audible.

"Fuck." I sigh. Somehow I knew, but to hear it from him all but crushes me. "Welcome to the new Mary." I breathe.

The sheriff pats my hand again. The words written there. "What's it like?" he asks.

I shrug. "Weird. Like . . . like your brain has a mirror in it. I don't know. That sounds dumb, but I can't think of how else to say it. You just . . . go the opposite way than you used to, without even realizing."

Davies lowers his chin to his chest, mulling that over.

"What about Silvertown itself?" I ask.

He eyes me.

"I mean," I add, "one of them was pouring that shit into the water supply. Is everyone . . . is the whole place . . ." I can't quite find the words to finish the question, but James is shaking his head already.

"From what I heard, the chemical was meant to neutralize the . . . drug, or whatever. Before people took it, not after. Sorry."

"Wait, did you say neutralize?"

"Yeah." He shrugs. "Doc had been slipping Ang's first version to people with their prescriptions, from what we understand."

I sit up a little. "I found proof of that," I tell him.

His eyebrows climb. "Oh?"

"In the Mansion."

"Which burned down."

I shake my head. "Check my mailbox, assuming mail's been delivered." The whole town is probably on lockdown, I realize. "Otherwise, check the mailbox of Dr. Ryan's neighbor."

"I'll be damned. Okay. Nice work."

I ease back into the pillows, exhausted. "Who's policing the place now, though? You? Your office?"

The sheriff shakes his head. "Feds are handling everything. In situations like this, we locals are lucky to get traffic duty."

"The mountain must be swarming with reporters, huh? News choppers?"

"Oh, no. No way."

It's my turn to eye him. I open my mouth to ask why, but the answer is so obvious it hurts. "They're going to cover it all up, aren't they."

"'Course they are, No way this gets out. I guess it's good it happened where it did. Even if there are rumors, it will just add to the pile of tall tales already rolling down that mountain."

"You're more right than you know. Sandra Conaty said something similar to me."

There's a soft knock at the door.

Davies stands and opens it. There's a part of me, quite a big part actually, that expects the real-world equivalent of Mulder and Scully to enter, badges flashing.

Instead, I see Clara. When our eyes meet the smile on her face is dazzling.

"You're awake," she says.

"Well, duh." I laugh.

There's a bouquet of flowers in her hands, and not from the hospital either, but Silvertown's own little shop.

Clara enters and, a heartbeat later, Kyle's in the doorway, too.

"I'll leave you guys to catch up," the sheriff says, and steps out without even giving me a chance to thank him.

Kyle waits for him to go, then turns to me. He, too, carries a gift, but it's not flowers.

"Kenny made it just how you like," he says, setting the pizza on the table beside me. Then he leans over and kisses my cheek, gently. "Hope you're hungry."

"Doesn't matter if I am," I say through a fresh wave of grateful tears.

"Why not?"

"Silvertown police policy," I say, gripping both their hands. "No slice left behind."

# ACKNOWLEDGMENTS

My thanks as always to the following wonderful people: Sara Megibow, Michael Braff, Jake "OddJob" Gillen, Shelly Perron, Kate Caudill, the Wheel of Awesome, everyone at Skybound and Simon & Schuster, booksellers, librarians, and last but definitely not least, you lovely readers.

This book would not have been possible without the support of my wife and our children, who as I write this are currently upstairs doing their best to give me some peace and quiet despite it being week four of the COVID-19 lockdown.